THE DRAGON QUEEN

THE DRAGON QUEEN

SECRETS OF SAEMAR

BOOK THREE

TUPPENCE VAN DE VAARST

To our mad god, Josh

1

ELLRIHEIM

A flash of light, so blinding it forced Niara to shut her eyes, even though she knew doing so was pointless. The light did not exist here, not in the dark reaches of the Ellriheim tunnels, not even in the physical world.

Niara curled into a ball as the vision overtook her. Her mind clutched for tree roots as it sped upward, until she paused, grasping at a fire-scarred yew in the middle of the ruined castle.

Ilhelm. Not again.

The once-proud castle lay in a heap of rubble, the outline of the walls still visible, as well as the skeleton of the keep. Destruction continued through the city. Niara hardened her heart to the sight, reminding herself that at least the people had survived. Houses had been ripped from their foundations, cobblestone streets torn up, and anything wood had long ago burned. She looked away from the destruction and turned her eyes skyward, for that could be the only reason the Lady had for guiding her vision to a place she'd seen so many times before.

Above the ruined castle, further up the hill, a new gleaming compound overshadowed the devastation of the city. Constructed from stone scavenged from the castle ruins and polished by dragonfire, it shone in the sunlight, acting as a beacon of authority and power for the surrounding region. Further up, a blue dragon swooped down from the sky, sunlight glinting off its scales. Niara's breath caught as it roared, a primal beast of power and glory. From the compound, a cheer rose from the soldiers dressed in burgundy and gold. In the ruins of the city, the few remaining civilians huddled in fear, flinging themselves on their faces as the dragon passed close overhead.

Faenor. The name burned in Niara's mind. She wished she could close her eyes to blot out the knowledge. With every vision, she learned more of the beings who now controlled the lands that should be hers. With that knowledge, however, came complications. There were individuals, different commanders with different motivations, who treated the remaining civilians with either cruelty or kindness, according to their personalities. And there were different dragons...

If only she could believe all the dragons were terrifying tyrants, as most of the people of Ellriheim believed. Her own brother remained defiant in his declaration to stand against any dragon until they were all bound again and other races were free to walk in Saemar once more. Niara tried to embrace the same belief but at moments like these...

Niara knew Faenor was one of the kinder dragons to rule in Ilhelm for the past two years. He led with more of an indifferent benevolence, rather than an iron claw. In many ways, he ruled better than Andreas had.

Well, Faenor's back from wherever Auriel sent him to. Thank you, Lady. Is that all you had to show me?

The vision held firm, and Niara fought the despair in her heart. None of her visions in the past two years had held any hope.

A gong started ringing from the gleaming compound, echoing like funeral bells through the ruined city and into the countryside. Instantly, soldiers poured out the door and organized themselves into ranks, ready for when their commander arrived.

Faenor landed on the edge of the compound and roared, loud and triumphant, like a challenge. From the distance came an answering roar, and a streak of fire illuminated the sky.

Not another one.

Green scales flashed in the sunlight as a different dragon flew over Ilhelm, roaring loudly. Faenor launched himself from the roof, flying over to greet the newcomer. They flew together, locking claws together and tumbling in circles through the sky in a strange greeting.

Niara shivered at the power on display. Even with the gift of the Swaying, that unpredictable gift of her blood, she could never hope to match the strength of one of the dragons. And how many did Auriel have now? They had come from all the corners of the world, and more were still arriving, even two years after Auriel had unbound them.

Flaven. Unbidden, the name sprang to her mind. She took a deep breath, allowing the knowledge to pass through her unhindered. She didn't know why her visions had started giving her information as well as sight since the destruction of Ellriheim. She could only be grateful and use what she acquired.

The knowledge sent icy fingers down her spine. Flaven saw mortals as playthings, as toys to be used and discarded. He would kill a human as easily as breathing, then summon another to do no more than amuse him.

The vision finally released her, and Niara gasped, blinking as her eyes adjusted to the darkness again. She crouched in the corridor in the inner sanctum, where she had been walking to a meeting with the leaders of Ellriheim. But she was no longer alone.

Serana knelt beside her, gentle concern on her face. Niara straightened with an effort, giving her sister-in-law a wordless nod of thanks.

Serana grimaced and shrugged. There was nothing anyone could do to help with Niara's visions, and everyone in Ellriheim knew it.

"Lady Sindarilae? Lady et-Alim? Is everything alright?" The concerned voice made both Niara and Serana look up.

Serana assured the human guard all was well. Niara forebode to answer, instead focusing on rising to her feet. She avoided meeting the guard's eyes. She had no idea when the humans of Ellriheim had started calling her Lady Sindarilae. She'd claimed the name for herself on her journey northward to establish her legitimacy to the nephelm, but the humans of Ninaeva prior had known her as Lady Rochelle, Vinet et-Alim's bastard daughter.

Serana gave Niara a sideways glance but said nothing, to Niara's relief. In some ways, it still hurt to hear Serana being addressed as Lady et-Alim, much as she deserved the title. That name, in Niara's mind, would always belong to her mother. *Mother, where are you?* she thought with a pang of longing. *We need you here. Now more than ever. I can't protect this place by Sight forever.*

"Do you have news for the council?" Serana asked.

Niara sighed. "Faenor is back. As well as another dragon. They're sending more resources to help with the search."

Serana nodded, her hand involuntarily straying to her stomach, where the bump of her pregnancy was just beginning to show. "Mazda pray they never find us," she whispered.

Niara swallowed her response. It was only a matter of time before the dragons and their slaves stumbled upon a hidden entrance to Ellriheim, one the residents had failed to discover and seal off. Auriel knew Vinet and her children were alive, and as long as they lived, he would continue to search.

We're one of the only ones who can threaten him, or so he believes. Mazda's light, I wish I believed that too!

Her visions had shown her that Auriel had offered a reward for any information which led to the discovery of the whereabouts of Vinet, Nazir, Thalion, Serana, or herself. So far, they had remained hidden, but they would be discovered one day. She knew it in her bones.

She shook off her thoughts and started walking toward the meeting room of the council again. *Council, indeed. If our motley collection of leaders can be considered a council.*

Evikan, the leader of the refugee nephelm, was already seated, the only one looking comfortable in the oversized room. Thalion sat at the head of the table, looking even shorter than normal under the ceiling built to accommodate eight-foot-tall giants. Behind him stood Mar, the young man rescued from Tigri who now acted as Thalion's page. Aevir, the leader of the Thorns from Alfheim, sat on his right. To Niara's surprise, a second dark-skinned figure sat at the table, the shadows of the flickering lamps almost obscuring him entirely. Her stepfather rarely attended the meetings of the council, preferring instead to devote his attention to the study of Ellriheim. At least, that was the excuse he gave. He spent more time writing, composing letters to Vinet, than he ever did studying. Niara didn't know what to do about it. Nazir missed her mother like he missed a part of his soul.

Serana took the seat to the left of Thalion. Niara sat further down the table, choosing to sit next to her stepfather. Nazir gave her a tired smile as she sat down.

Oh Mother, I wish you were here, Niara thought again. *Nazir needs you.*

Evikan cleared his throat, his voice rumbling through the chamber. "Zeria won't be here today, so we might as well get started."

Thalion nodded. He had become the de facto leader of Ellriheim. Niara had to swallow the lump in her throat every time she saw him at the head of the table. It should have been her there. If her visions didn't hold the constant, looming threat of the Exile, she would be the people's leader.

Thalion's initiative hadn't placed him in his current seat, either. If she asked, Thalion would immediately yield the place to her. Her own insistence kept her younger brother there, for he would never be called away on Exile to become an Eye of the Lady.

It's not Thalion's fault he doesn't have the Sight. Mazda's light, it's a blessing one of us doesn't have it. That way the whim of the Lady won't make both of us abandon our people.

"First order of business," Thalion said. "We discovered another potential route to the surface, but it leads back up right underneath the city. Men are working on sealing it as we speak. We'll need Zeria or another of the nephelm to inspect it when we're done."

Evikan, as the only nephelm present, nodded in acknowledgment.

Niara lowered her eyes to the table. Two years ago, the news of another route to the surface would have been greeted with speculation as to whether they could escape via the new route. Now, however, everyone knew if they found one, it would have to be one that exited Ellriheim far from the ruins of Ilhelm.

"Second, overcrowding," Thalion sighed. "As expected, the population is growing. We have an influx of new children, and while most family blocks are capable of supporting a new infant for a few years, soon we'll need to find another way to handle the issue." He exchanged a glance with Serana.

Niara grimaced. When they had first fled here, they had had no idea this would be any more than a temporary escape. Now, after two years...*families still exist. That should give me hope, I suppose, but it doesn't.*

She listened as the discussion swirled around her, barely paying attention. Whatever they decided would only be temporary, in any case. If they spent another two years down here, it would only happen again. They needed a permanent solution. They needed to get to the surface again.

We need to live in a world free of Auriel and the dragons, Niara thought bitterly. *We can't go to the surface until the threat of enslavement by the dragons is gone. How in Mazda's name are we supposed to manage that?*

"Niara? Any news?"

Niara looked up at Thalion's question. "Faenor's back," she said without preamble. "And another dragon, Flaven. They're going to intensify the search for us."

Silence greeted her pronouncement. She bit her own lip. There were no words, for no solution existed.

Thalion sighed. "Keep us informed if they come close," he said. "If there's any sign they're closing in..."

Niara nodded, though she knew the effort would ultimately be fruitless. By the time the dragons found an entrance to Ellriheim, it would be too late to flee again. There was simply nowhere to run.

"Anything else?" Thalion surveyed the room. No one answered. "Then meeting adjourned."

Niara. Niara.

Niara flinched, her head swiveling around to try to locate the source of the voice. Who was calling her?

No one else seemed to have heard the voice, and Nazir glanced at her curiously. She took a deep breath to steady herself.

You're just short on sleep, she told herself. She'd had another vision wake her out of her slumber last night, preventing her from going to sleep afterward.

She remained seated as everyone except her stepfather left the room. His eyes never left her, concern and curiosity mingling together.

"I had a dream about your mother last night." Nazir's voice broke the silence of the chamber.

Niara's head jerked up involuntarily to meet Nazir's eyes.

"She was searching for you." He continued to gaze steadily at her.

Niara swallowed and looked down at the table. "She can't see down here," she whispered. "There're no roots to ground her Sight." It was one thing to reach up and out, away from the darkness, but to try to see in… the danger would be great.

Her stepfather closed his eyes and bowed his head.

Niara felt a brief pang of guilt for her words. As much as she missed her mother, Nazir's grief was stronger. She reached out to place a hand on his shoulder. "She'll find us eventually," she said, although the words sounded hollow to her own ears. "When she's finished with the Exile. When she's a true Eye of the Lady." She had to fight around the lump in her throat that formed whenever she mentioned the Exile, for it reminded her that one day she too would have to disappear.

Nazir nodded, his eyes tired.

Niara. Niara.

She flinched again, the sound of her name seeming to echo through the room.

Nazir frowned in concern as he looked at her. "Is everything alright?"

"I'm fine." She shook her head. "Just short on sleep, is all."

Nazir didn't appear convinced, but he nodded anyway. "Get some rest, then," he said. "Of all our people, we cannot afford to lose you."

Niara managed not to wince. *I am not the person everyone should be relying on,* she thought. *I am not reliable, I can't control the visions, they come and go as they please. And is it really worth knowing what is going on up there?*

She didn't let any of those thoughts show on her face. Instead, she rose, giving Nazir a brief smile before she left the room and started down the corridor to the small chamber she'd claimed as her own.

Niara. Niara.

Niara gasped, bracing her hands against the stone wall. What in Mazda's name was happening? What was she hearing?

Am I going insane at last? Has the lack of sunlight damaged me this much?

She held her breath, waiting for the voice again but nothing came.

She let out a shaky breath. She needed sleep. She was imagining things, mixing visions with reality. A little sleep and everything would be normal again.

***

"There you are."

Niara looked up at the sound of her brother's voice. She managed a smile as Thalion sat down beside her. If he was sitting, then nothing urgent could be happening. "Good morning."

Thalion merely nodded in response as they sat together, gazing out across the open expanse of darkness of their fields. Darkness wasn't perhaps the best term. The giant cavern glinted with faint blue light, some nephelm enchantment that allowed special foods to grow deep underground. Tasteless foods, in Niara's opinion, but better than starving.

"I was wondering where you'd gone," Thalion finally said, after sitting in companionable silence for a time. "You usually don't wander far."

Niara shrugged. "I needed some time to myself," she said. "The inner city was too crowded."

Thalion grimaced in sympathy. "I hear you," he said. "People packed in so tight…"

Niara returned to gazing out across the fields. Whatever Thalion had to say, he would tell her in his own time.

They sat in silence again, watching the flickers of dim blue light, each lost in their own thoughts. Despite herself, Niara began to relax. Her brother had grown steady since his marriage, a rock she could lean on. Sometimes she could even forget he was eight years younger than she, that she should be the strong one he could lean on.

"We need a way out of here," Thalion spoke so softly, it was only thanks to Niara's pointed ears she could make out his words at all.

She turned her gaze to her brother, raising her eyebrows. "What makes you say that?" she asked.

"Humans can't live down here forever. We need the sunlight. People are getting sick, getting weaker, from lack of light. Even I…" Thalion's voice cracked.

Niara's eyes widened in alarm. "Thalion?" she asked anxiously.

He shook his head. "I can't live down here for much longer," he said, his voice a strained whisper. "I need…I want…" he looked up to meet her eyes. "Niara, I don't want my child to be born in this darkness."

That was the crux of it, then. And Thalion's child was not the only one. There were other women who were pregnant down here, other children who would be born. Would they be born to a fate of never seeing the sunlight?

Niara swallowed. "Where would we go?" she asked helplessly. "Even if we could get out without being detected?"

"We could go north," Thalion spoke determinedly. "Into the Gray Mountains. Somewhere up there has to be a place we could build a settlement without Auriel noticing. We could build defenses into the mountains so we could flee if there was ever an attack, raise sheep and goats on the hillsides. Even if the Manyu-cursed dragons ever found us, we'd be safe."

Niara closed her eyes. She didn't want the vision his voice conjured, the hope of someplace warm and green. That hope would be destroyed, as all their hopes had been dashed since fleeing here.

"It could be done," he said desperately. "It has to be done, Niara, can't you see?"

Niara. Niara.

Niara spun around, trying futilely to locate the source of the voice. "Will you stop calling me?" she demanded of the darkness, standing. She stared into the dimly lit cavern, every muscle in her body tightening in anticipation.

Thalion frowned. "Niara? What is it?"

Niara. Niara.

Niara ignored her brother and reached out with her Sight, searching for the source of the voice. She had managed to sleep the previous night, so exhaustion no longer sufficed as an excuse. And she was not going crazy.

For a moment, all she could only see darkness. Then something caught her vision, held her in an iron fist. She stumbled, heard Thalion's worried voice as he caught her, but her consciousness was whisked away, further than she'd ever cast her Sight before.

She flailed, trying to ground herself, trying to reach for a tree, any tree, that she could use to guide her path. The iron grip of whoever held her in their grasp, however, did not allow any time to stop and take a breath as she sped further and further away.

This is dangerous. The thought passed through Niara's mind, but she could do nothing about it. Her grandfather had warned about ungrounded visions. If she wasn't careful, she would get lost...

Light nearly blinded her, and she gasped as she took in the scene of the barren wasteland in front of her. It stretched out for miles in every direction, with nothing but boulders and brush to even give a sense of distance. The only distinguishing feature was a lone mountain at the edge of her vision, standing ominous against the clouds.

"Niara!"

Niara spun around, her heart pounding as she recognized the voice. She could barely believe her eyes as she took in the figure before her. A little thinner, and her clothes were certainly more ragged than when she'd last seen her, but the woman had the same red-brown hair, the same green eyes.

"Mother?" she gasped.

Vinet et-Alim took several steps forward and drew her daughter into a hard embrace. "Thank the Lady," she gasped. "Niara, there's not much time."

Before Niara could respond, Vinet placed her hands on either side of Niara's head. She stared into Niara's eyes, speaking rapidly as visions flashed between them.

A city, in the middle of the wastes. A library, with only the covers of books.

"Niara, you have to leave and leave now. Head south."

A statue carved of onyx, standing in the center of the city.

"The fate of the world will depend on it."

Dragons flying over the capital of Saemar.

"We must find a way to defeat Auriel."

The town of Hillsdale. Kishtar and Lyra huddling in a boat. A dragon swooping down upon them.

"You must make it there by Papsukkal! You must!"

Niara gasped as her vision cleared, and she found herself staring into her mother's eyes once more.

"Where are you?" she demanded, fear rising up inside her.

The world began to blur, and Niara gripped her mother's arm in a panic. She couldn't leave! Not now! Not yet!

"Shan Serin..." her mother's voice faded with the vision. One final vision appeared, that of the ruined city in the badlands, the lone mountain in the distance. "South...Remember...Papsukkal..."

"Mother! No!" Niara flailed, reaching out with all her might to maintain the contact. She fell into nothingness, the vision evaporating in a pillar of fire.

The roar of a dragon drowned out all sound. Niara screamed, but whatever sound she made was lost in the roar of flame and fire. A huge burgundy dragon swept down from the sky, wings spread wide to envelop the world. A volcano erupted below, two men, one light-skinned and one dark, locked in combat beneath the pillar of fire. An elven woman hurled a spear skyward. Three other dragons roared in triumph, the two gold dragons flanking a red, rising up to circle the burgundy dragon. A male elf stood quietly, his eyes dark with shadows.

"Niara! Niara!" Thalion's desperate voice brought her back to the present. She knelt on her hands and knees, gasping for air. Her arms shook with remaining adrenaline. Tears streamed down her cheeks.

She reached up to stop Thalion from shaking her shoulder. "I'm alright," she gasped. "I'm alright." Dimly, she knew that was a lie, but it was the only thing she could think to say.

Thalion withdrew his hand, only to crouch next to her, his intense gaze boring into her. "I didn't share it this time," he said.

Niara blinked. The last two years, if Thalion was nearby, he could usually manage to share a piece of her visions, to lessen the burden of the Sight.

That he hadn't seen this one…that he hadn't seen their mother…

As if her thoughts were plain on her face, Thalion spoke again. "You called for Mother," he said, his voice low. "Niara, are you sure everything's alright?"

Niara closed her eyes. The vision flashed before her eyes again, her mother's words, the intensity and fear in her voice.

She took a deep breath before opening her eyes again. "You're right, Thalion," she said. "We need to find a way out of Ellriheim. Not for everyone, however, just for me." She met Thalion's gaze with an intensity that matched his. "Thalion, I need to leave."

2

ESCAPE

I hope you know what you're doing."

Niara paused before answering her brother. The two of them huddled in the darkness with only a single torch for light, heading toward the entrance the workers of Ellriheim had unearthed earlier. She knew as well as he did this was the only option.

"If I'm to get south by Papsukkal, especially across a land occupied by dragons, then I need to leave now, as in today. If we present this to the council, there won't be a decision made for weeks. You know Evikan would never hear of me going, and I doubt Aevir or any of the Thorns would want me departing undefended. And I need to go alone."

Thalion shook his head, obviously not happy with her answer. "That's the part I don't like," he grumbled. "If I could at least come with you…"

Niara shook her head. They had been over this already. "You're needed here," she insisted. "If anything happens, you're the one they'll all turn to."

Thalion didn't appear happy or fully convinced. Niara winced as she played her trump card.

13

"Besides, Serana is going to need you soon. I doubt she'd thank you if you went haring off across Saemar right now."

Thalion grimaced. "I know, I know," he grumbled. "It's just…I don't like sending you out by yourself. Are you sure you won't take anyone with you? Not even one of the Thorns?"

Niara gave him a look, suppressing her exasperation. She couldn't say why, only that she had a distinct impression that whatever happened, she needed to do this herself.

Thalion sighed and turned his attention back to the cracks in the stone. "If we can even get you out of here," he grumbled under his breath.

Niara clenched her hands into fists. The unblocked entrance was one of the nephelm gates. Although they'd lived together for two years, the nephelm still guarded the secret to opening their doors. Privately, Niara speculated they simply didn't know why the doors didn't work for others. "We'll get it open," she said, projecting confidence into her voice.

Niara adjusted the pack on her shoulders as she stared at the carved runes in front of her. This door was smaller, less intricate than the main door had been, with none of the ornamentation. Only a single rune stood out against the stone, a stylized sun making her heart contract with longing.

"So how do we open it?" Thalion asked.

Niara remained silent. She didn't want to admit she didn't know. Hesitantly, she reached out to trace the sun glyph. Although the stone felt oddly warm underneath her fingers, nothing happened.

Thalion made a speculative sound, and Niara turned, eyebrows raised in a question.

"Do we need to open the door? You've moved earth before. Can you just move the earth around this door?"

Niara shuddered. *Use my magic to shift Mazda knows how many tons of solid rock?* The last time she had moved earth had been in Utgard. And then it had been dirt, not solid rock, and magically manipulated to only respond to the Swaying, as well. Nevertheless, she had been exhausted after moving a tiny fraction of the amount that held the door sealed. "Not that much, Thalion," she said. "That much would probably kill me."

"Well, it was worth a try," Thalion sighed. "Any other ideas besides tracing glyphs?"

Someone cleared their throat behind them, and Niara whirled around, holding her torch in front of her like a weapon. She had to blink against the light for a few seconds until she saw her stepfather.

"Father," Thalion said, his voice expressing both relief and apprehension.

Nazir just raised an eyebrow. "So, this is where you are," he said. "Serana was asking if I'd seen you."

Niara held her breath as she weighed how much to tell Nazir. She had had to tell Thalion; he was the only person in all of Ellriheim who wouldn't try to talk her out of this.

But Nazir...at one time, she would have placed him in the same category as Thalion. Her mother trusted him above anyone else, after all. But the past two years had changed him, made him more withdrawn, more inwardly focused.

Pot and kettle, Niara thought, grimacing. She was hardly in a position to complain about anyone else becoming withdrawn.

Thalion glanced hesitantly at Niara, obviously waiting for her to take the lead. A flash of gratitude, then annoyance, and then love sparked within her.

"We're trying to figure out how to open the door," she said, keeping her explanation as simple as possible.

Nazir tilted his head slightly. "Without a nephelm? And at the entrance that's under Ilhelm?"

Niara nodded slowly. Belatedly, she remembered the thing that made most people feel apprehensive about her stepfather. He noticed everything. He would soon realize...

"You're leaving, then," Nazir's voice seemed calm, untroubled.

Niara took a deep breath. "I have to," she said. "I had a vision of Mother."

Nazir's eyes widened, and Niara felt a flash of satisfaction that she'd managed to surprise her stepfather. "Of Vinet?" he gasped, his voice suddenly harsh.

Niara tried to ignore the rising guilt inside her. How could she have kept anything about her mother from Nazir, knowing how much he missed her? "She called me," she said. "I need to go to her."

For a moment, Nazir gazed into the rock, as if he believed if he could stare hard enough and long enough, he could pierce through solid stone and across the distance to see Vinet. Then his eyes dimmed, and his face became worn and tired again. "It's not time yet, then," he whispered, his voice almost inaudible.

Niara swallowed and took an involuntary step forward. "Father..." she whispered.

Nazir met her eyes and gave a small smile, which Niara found herself answering. It had been years since she'd called him Father. Since she'd been introduced at court, back before the dragons, she had known that if any noble heard her addressing Nazir as her father, they'd have an apoplexy, and she had thus fallen out of the habit.

"You need to get out then," Nazir straightened his shoulders. "Well, I guess that's why I've been studying the glyphs of the nephelm."

For the first time, Niara felt hope tighten her heart. Could she get out? Was it actually possible?

Nazir walked forward to stand beside Thalion and Niara. He turned his attention to the glyphs in the wall, his eyes tracing the pattern.

"The glyphs here aren't like the ones elsewhere," Nazir said slowly, his voice wondering. He held up a hand and placed it on the wall, then sighed and shook his head. "There's no magic in them, though. I could feel every other glyph I've touched, and these lack..." he shrugged. "I don't know how to activate them. Evikan or Zeria might."

"Too many people know already," she said flatly.

Nazir raised an eyebrow again as he turned toward her. "It won't take long for your disappearance to be noticed, Niara. You're not exactly inconspicuous, and everyone relies upon your visions."

Her shoulders dropped. She didn't want to be reminded of her duties here.

"Hey," Thalion interrupted. He placed a hand on her shoulder. "I told you, we'll manage. If this is something you have to do, then this is something you have to do."

Niara gave her brother a look of gratitude.

Nazir nodded. "Unfortunately, if we can't get these glyphs active, then your only option is to search elsewhere for a functioning exit."

Glyphs. Magic. Niara furrowed her brow. She couldn't move tons of stone, but perhaps the Swaying was the answer here, after all. She reached out to touch the sun glyph again and slowly began tracing it. After a moment, she closed her eyes, reaching within herself to summon the power that was at once a part of her, and yet separate. She swayed gently back and forth, breathing it into life. A glow illuminated the front of her eyelids, and she heard Thalion gasp. She opened her eyes, blinking to adjust to the now-glowing glyphs in front of her.

"Mazda's light," Thalion whispered.

Niara took a deep breath and removed her hand from the wall. The glow remained steady, but nothing else happened. Her initial elation at having activated the glyph faded. Something was still missing, something that would actually open the door.

"Now what?" Thalion asked, stealing the thought from her mind.

Niara frowned, raising a questioning eyebrow at her stepfather. Nazir shook his head and placed a hand on the glyphs again. He gently traced the glow.

"The main door could only be opened by a nephelm," he said softly. "I've speculated it might have something to do with their blood, perhaps a gift given to them by the mountain god. Mazda's light, I hope I'm wrong about that."

Niara shuddered. "Mother didn't have control of the Swaying when we found that door," she said. "Maybe I could force it? Make the door believe I'm nephelm?" How she would do that, she had no idea, but she had to try something.

Nazir didn't answer, his fingers continuing to trace the glyph, his eyes far away. "The sun," he whispered. "Mazda, how I miss it." His hand finished tracing the glyph, and a low rumble echoed through the passage. The door shifted with a *click,* sliding sideways to reveal a dark, narrow passageway.

"How did you do that?" Niara gasped.

Nazir expressed equal astonishment. "It shouldn't have been possible," he murmured.

Niara stared at her own hands. If all that had been required was to trace the glyph, then shouldn't it have opened as she'd activated it? Or was it something only Nazir could do? And if so, why?

"Does it matter?" Thalion's voice broke through both of their thoughts. "This is what you needed, isn't it?" Despite his brusque words, Niara could read the tension and fear in her brother's tone.

She stepped forward and embraced him hard, surprising both herself and him. "I'll come back, brother," she promised, far too aware that her words were an echo of their mother's.

She turned to her stepfather, words catching in her throat. How could she ever say…

Nazir understood, of course, without any need for words on her part. He embraced her, holding her tight to his chest. "Stay safe, daughter," he whispered. "Give your mother my greetings."

Tears stung her eyes as she pulled away, adjusting her pack on her shoulders.

"We'll make sure the door is closed and hidden behind you," Nazir said.

Niara shivered, hearing the unspoken words. She would not be able to find the door, either. Once she left, there was no coming back.

Niara nodded, still unable to form any words. She swallowed, finally forcing the words out of her throat. "Thank you," she whispered.

"Love you, sister," he said, his voice hoarse.

"Love you too, brother."

She couldn't take it anymore. Without another word, she turned, holding the torch in front of her to illuminate the passage. She took a step forward, and then another, and soon was walking quickly up the slanted slope, climbing higher and higher.

I will never come back to Ellriheim. The thought was strong and sudden, a knowledge that came from outside of herself. She nearly choked on a sob as she continued climbing toward the surface.

Behind her, she heard the click of the door swinging shut. She paused, her light the only illumination in the tunnel.

She was alone now.

Mazda's light. Of all the times to escape.

Niara huddled underneath the fallen pile of timbers, anxiously waiting for night to fall. Only in darkness did she have a chance of eluding notice, both from guards on the ground and the sweeping winged shadows high in the sky. She had already been waiting for nearly half the day, having escaped the tunnel in the early light of morning. The sun beat harshly against her eyes, and the light breeze chilled her to the bone. She had been underground too long.

I'll have to adjust again fast, she thought. Not that she thought that would be much of an issue. The sunlight already had her wide awake, despite having been awake for presumably most of the night.

As long as I can stay awake for tonight, as well, she thought. *I need to get as far from Ilhelm as quickly as I can.*

She shifted, trying to get comfortable and rest a few hours before darkness fell. The knowledge that there were two dragons out there, however, kept her on edge.

What if they find me? What if they were looking for me, specifically? What if they have a way they can track me? We know so little about them... they must have magic of their own. Or do they? Do they even need magic, with how much power they naturally have?

The thoughts roiled around in her head, jumbling together in a quagmire making sleep impossible. They also kept her distracted enough to jump in fear as a boy came crashing into the ruined pile of timbers to join her.

Her eyes widened, and her heart pounded with adrenaline. He stared back with equal shock, his mouth falling open in astonishment.

Before Niara could regain her wits and beg him to be silent, the boy was backing out of the pile of wood. "Ma!" he shouted. "Ma, there's a woman here!"

Niara cursed under her breath. She brought a hand up to her head, making sure she'd bound her headscarf securely over her hair, concealing all traces of her pointed ears. She hadn't expected to need it so soon.

"What?" The woman's voice came from close, far closer than Niara had hoped. She held her breath as footsteps approached, and a woman's face peered into her hiding spot.

The woman's face remained calm and serious as she took in Niara's appearance. She held Niara's gaze as if she was trying to communicate something.

"Ah, silly boy!" the woman said loudly. "Don't you recognize your cousin? I'd thought she was lost to us!"

Cousin? Niara blinked at the woman in bewilderment. The woman continued to hold her gaze, staring intently, willing Niara to follow along.

Niara took a deep, shaky breath. "Hello, Aunt?" she whispered.

The woman smiled with relief. "Come on out, my dear niece," she said. "We need to tell the captain you've arrived safely. Then we can set about settling you in."

Niara didn't see a choice except to follow the woman into the sunlight. The air bit crisp and cool, and Niara felt grateful for the wool cape she had draped around her shoulders.

The boy stood next to his mother, his sandy blonde hair tousled by the wind. He stared at her, uncomprehending. "Cousin?" he asked.

"Of course she's your cousin!" The woman's tone rang bright and cheerful, clashing with her serious blue eyes which focused on Niara. "If she wasn't your cousin, we'd have to take her directly to the dragon overlords, on suspicion of being a stranger, and who knows what'd happen to her then! But since she's your cousin, all we have to do is take her to the captain, and he'll assign a work schedule for her."

Niara listened, her heart pounding hard in her chest. Was this how things worked, then? If someone was a stranger...was that policy everywhere in Saemar now, or was it specific to Ilhelm, where they had reason to believe there were fugitives?

The boy still appeared to not fully understand, but he accepted his mother's words. "So, what's your name, then? If you're my cousin?"

Niara swallowed, her throat dry. "Niara," she managed.

The woman's eyes widened, and Niara's throat closed.

"Oh, it's Nia, of course! Jos, why don't you run ahead and tell your father your cousin *Nia* has arrived, alright?" The woman's voice sounded unnaturally high.

Jos eyed his mother warily, but ran ahead, seemingly to do her bidding. Niara's mouth dried again as the woman turned toward her, eyes dark with worry.

"That name is dangerous to say here," she whispered under her breath. "That, and the name of anyone who used to belong to that family."

Niara inclined her head, unable to say anything else. The woman nodded in satisfaction and started leading her through the ruined maze of streets. "I'm Carol, by the way," she said softly. "Your Aunt Carol, in fact. We'll meet your Uncle Jon here shortly, I'm sure."

Niara took a deep breath, trying to process the information. "I... thank you, but I can't stay here," she managed. "I need..."

Carol skidded to a halt, slapping a hand over Niara's mouth to silence her. Niara bit her lip, but she stopped talking. Carol hastily withdrew her hand as the sound of marching feet approached, and a group of burgundy and gold-clad soldiers appeared around the corner.

The leader of the soldiers held up his hand to halt the soldiers behind him. He raised an eyebrow at the two women.

"Well, what have we here?" he asked. "A stranger, Carol?"

Niara saw Carol's shoulders tensing, and she willed the other woman not to lose her nerve. Of all people, she could not afford to be sent to the dragons.

"Not a stranger, sergeant," Carol said courteously. "It's my niece, in fact. We've been wondering where she'd gotten to, but she just arrived today, thank the Sky-Lord!"

Niara managed to keep a neutral expression on her face, but a shock like a bolt of lightning jolted through her all the same. She hadn't thought Auriel would be openly worshipped, despite the fact that he had risen to godhood.

"Your niece?" The sergeant appeared skeptical. "And where's she been, then?"

Carol hesitated the barest instance, and Niara cleared her throat. "The east, sergeant," she said, keeping her answer as vague as possible.

"Where in the east?" The sergeant's lips quirked into a smile. "You'll have to be more specific than that, my girl."

The words came out unchecked, as if she'd planned it. The story her mother had used, the story she'd used to believe. "There used to be a convent, three days ride to the east. My mother was sent there after she became pregnant with me." She held her breath, hoping that mentioning a convent of Mazda wasn't about to get her marked as a blasphemer, hoping that the soldiers might still remember…

"A convent? To the false god Mazda?" The soldiers murmured together under their breath.

Carol winced, but Niara held the sergeant's gaze and gave him a small nod.

A moment of understanding seemed to pass between them, but it passed swiftly as the sergeant's expression hardened. "Make sure she's registered with the captain, Carol," the sergeant said, his voice sharp. "She'll be expected at the quarry tomorrow, same as everyone else."

"Yes, sergeant," Carol's voice trembled slightly with suppressed emotion.

The sergeant spun around on his heel and marched off, followed closely by the rest of the patrol. Niara let out a breath she hadn't realized she was holding as he disappeared around the corner.

Carol stared at her in disbelief. "Are you mad, girl?" she asked. "Mentioning a place of Mazda to a man like that?"

Niara shook her head, unable to explain her decision. *Aunt Nimue,* she thought. *Mazda, what's happened to you? Is the convent still there? Or was it destroyed? And were you able to flee, or were you killed in the destruction?*

Carol sighed. "Well, we'd best get you signed up," she said. "There's no exceptions to the duty roster."

Niara automatically began following Carol before sense reasserted itself. "Carol, I can't stay here," she said. "I need to leave, the sooner the better."

The look Carol gave her was pitying at best. "No one leaves Ilhelm, *Nia,*" she said, emphasizing the false name. "No one except the wandering traders, and those who serve the Sky-Lord and the Great Burner. The rest of us stay here."

It was as if someone had splashed cold water on her face. "The Great Burner?" she whispered. The legends of her childhood, coming to haunt her.

"I won't ask where you've been that you don't know that name," Carol said. "But you'd best be quick on your feet. The soldiers don't like those who don't fit in, and you're going to have a time of it as it is."

Niara pressed her lips together. "I won't fit in," she said. "I told you, I need to leave."

Carol rounded on her. "If you leave now, then I'm under suspicion for having vouched for you. They won't let up until they know where you've gone."

Niara felt a moment's purest gratitude that she hadn't yet revealed the direction she intended to travel. "What will they do?" she asked instead.

Carol shook her head and started walking again. "Who knows," she said. "Double hours at the quarry, half rations, and whatever else those bastards can think up."

Quarry? That was the second time that had been mentioned. Niara frowned. In all her visions, she'd never seen any sign of a quarry in Ilhelm. "What quarry?" she asked.

Carol sighed. "It's where we all get put to work," she said. "A little way to the west of the city. Don't know why the dragons decided to put us to work there, as there's no good rock, but they seem determined regardless. My theory is it's simply to keep us busy. Why else would they be digging deeper and deeper, rather than sideways? Keeps us too busy climbing and hauling to get up to any mischief."

Niara's eyes widened, and she turned to gaze toward the west. She stumbled over a stray stone as she did so, nearly falling on the ground. Carol caught her before she fell.

"Careful, girl!" Carol said. "Can't have you falling and injuring yourself your first day here. You won't be able to work or run, then."

Niara continued looking westward, still processing Carol's words. *A quarry that just goes down, that doesn't produce good stone, that no one knows why...it's west of the city. Ellriheim...Ellriheim runs west of Ilhelm. It's on the outskirts, certainly, it has to be, but the fact that they're digging so close...and that I never had a clue...*

"Nia?" Carol's voice was worried. "You're not one of those who gets lost in her own world now, are you?"

Niara shook herself, bringing her mind back to her present situation. She forced a smile. "I don't think so," she managed.

Carol seemed unconvinced. "Well, we'd best get you to the captain," she said. "Tell him the same story, but perhaps without the bit about the convent. The captain's a much stricter man than the sergeant."

Niara nodded in understanding, half her mind still on the issue of the quarry. *I have to warn Thalion,* she thought. She swallowed. *But Mazda's light, how?*

"Here's your home. Dinner at six at the mess hall, and best be prompt." The quartermaster vanished before Niara had a chance to ask him any questions. She stared after him, barely mastering the impulse to curse at him. *Stop it, Niara. It's not like you'll be here long enough for this treatment to bother you, anyway. No matter what you told Carol.*

Sighing, she turned her attention to what the quartermaster had called her 'home.' Despite the comforting word, the place in front of her was little more than a shack that looked ready to fall to pieces in the slightest breeze.

A very good thing you won't be staying here long, she thought. *It's already cold at night. I hate to think of what this place would be like later in Manyu's Time.*

She opened the door slowly, praying its decaying hinges wouldn't break. The wood creaked ominously, but it opened, and she stepped inside, wincing as she saw light coming through the cracks in the window.

Home indeed. This place is more like a tent. And lets in more cold air than one.

There was a bed, though the mattress was only burlap stuffed with straw. The table and single chair were made from rough wood. Niara grimaced, settling her pack down at the foot of the bed.

She had to work the quarry at least one day, in order to find out its location. *Why couldn't I see it from Ellriheim?*

She sat down on the untreated chair and swallowed, hesitating before closing her eyes. Her visions didn't obey her, had never obeyed her, but she had to try. Surely the Lady would let her see something as important as the quarry, wouldn't she? Slowly, she reached out, letting her senses expand. For a moment, it seemed to be working. She felt the trees of Ilhelm, those stubborn trees that hadn't died, no matter the fire that raged. She started to reach further west, toward the area Carol had described...Her control slipped, and she was grabbed, pulled farther west. She gasped, putting all her focus into making sure the trees that grabbed her were safe, that there were no elder or apple...

Small ships sailed on the water, casting their nets over the side. On the coast, a dragon rested on the cliff, overseeing the humans below with watchful eyes. Two figures stood together on one boat, hauling in a net full of fish. As Niara watched, the man glanced carefully around before leaning down to give the woman a kiss.

Kishtar! Niara's eyes flew open as the vision faded. She took a deep breath as her hands shook, and she grabbed the edge of the chair to steady herself. She hadn't dared seek anyone out with her Sight, for fear of what she might find. She felt her knees go weak with relief that Kishtar and Lyra were still alive.

That doesn't help my current situation, Niara reminded herself. *I didn't see the quarry. I don't know if it's over Ellriheim or not, if Thalion is in immediate danger, if they need to move.*

She cursed under her breath. She'd had the faint hope that if she could find the quarry with her Sight, then she'd be able to let Thalion know and flee tonight, getting as far south as she could.

Warn Thalion! She sat back on her heels as the enormity of that task struck her. How on earth was she going to do that? She couldn't just walk back up to the passage underground. Not only had Nazir closed it behind her, but by now it should have been blocked and barricaded.

*Not to mention the danger it would put Ellriheim in if someone followed me and realized there was an entrance they didn't have to dig for...*She cursed again, using language she'd learned from Gwyn. *What I need is the ability to speak in Thalion's thoughts, like Mother did to me...*her thoughts stuttered to a halt, and she stared at the unfinished wall without seeing it. Could she? Was it even possible?

She bit her lip. There were no roots in Ellriheim, nothing she could use to ground herself. She still remembered what it had felt like to be ripped along, flailing in the darkness, out of control. But once Vinet had found her, the vision had settled. As if their shared blood had been enough of a ground...

She had to try. She closed her eyes again, this time reaching down, trying to locate her brother.

Down, into the earth, past the roots of the trees. She hesitated when she reached the end of the roots, sensing nothing but darkness before her.

I have to. She flung herself into the darkness, reaching out, searching for Thalion. A moment's panic struck her as she drifted in darkness with nothing to ground her, nothing to guide her back. Then, like a red beacon, she sensed a presence that drew her like a magnet.

Thalion! she called. She reached forward, desperately reaching for him. *Thalion!*

He jerked with surprise and fear as she reached him. She tried to reassure him, but his fear was only marginally greater than her own.

"Thalion!" she exclaimed. Exerting her will and drawing strength from she knew not where, she steadied both of them. Then she was gazing at her brother's face, his expression wide-eyed with astonishment.

"Niara?" he asked.

Despite it only having been less than a day since she'd last seen him, Niara felt a surge of homesickness as she looked at her brother. When would she see any of her family next?

Her control of the vision slipped, causing Thalion's form to flicker in front of her. Hastily, she brought her attention back to her task.

"Thalion, there's a quarry to the west of Ilhelm," she said quickly. "I can't see it with my Sight; there don't seem to be any trees there. I'm going to go there tomorrow to narrow down a location for you, but I'm positive it's on the outskirts of Ellriheim, and that they're trying to break in."

Thalion cursed, the same curse Niara had used earlier.

"Thank you for the warning," Thalion said. "Niara, how?" he gestured at her.

Niara knew what he meant. She shrugged helplessly. "I don't know," she said. "I only know it's real. It's how Mother spoke to me."

Thalion took a deep breath, and Niara saw him squaring his shoulders. "I'd better get a defense party organized. We'll want to seal the area as soon as you determine its location." He eyed her warily. "Are you certain it's safe for you to do this?" he asked.

Despite the seriousness of the situation, Niara had to laugh. Dragons ruling the land, she was planning to travel across Saemar on foot through Manyu's Time, and he was worried about her going to a quarry?

"It will be safer for me to look at it than not," she said. Thalion's form flickered again, and she grimaced. "Thalion, I can't do this much longer. I'll contact you again tomorrow night."

Thalion nodded. "Take care of yourself."

With relief, Niara let the vision fade. Abruptly, she found herself back in her body and leaned back on the worn chair. Exhaustion hit her, and she buried her head in her hands. She shook, huddling in on herself as tight as possible.

Lady, Mazda, whoever might listen, please help me. I don't know if I can do this.

3

—————

A STRANGER

weat rolled down Niara's back despite the chill of Manyu's Time, making her grateful her headcloth kept the sweat out of her eyes as well as covering her ears. Her shawl lay on the ground, discarded several hours ago in the battle between the heat her body produced and the chill of the air. She paused to take a breath, the pickaxe heavy in her hand. Mazda's light, she had never done this much labor in her life. *No wonder Mother would send criminals and convicts to work in mines,* she thought. *By the end of the day, they'd be so tired they wouldn't have the energy to cause trouble.*

The thought hardly comforted her, considering her own task. If she wanted to escape Ilhelm, then she needed to do it tonight. The soldiers came to collect everyone from the ramshackle village at the crack of dawn and guarded them constantly until dusk.

The soldiers had already directed several curious glances toward the 'new girl,' making Niara shiver. Some of the looks reminded her of Niall.

A man walked by with a clay cup and bucket of water, and Niara took the cup from him, draining it gratefully. It was Jon, Carol's husband, her supposed uncle. He raised an eyebrow at her as she drank.

"Keep a watch out, Nia," he said. "I've already had five soldiers asking questions about you. I don't think you'll be in the quarry much longer."

"What do you mean?" Niara asked. "I thought everyone worked in the quarry?"

Jon frowned, and he handed her another cup of water. Niara took it, understanding that he wanted her to drink slowly so that the soldiers wouldn't be suspicious of them talking.

"There're other places to work," Jon said. "The mines, for one. The dragons love their gems. Those who go down there never see the sun again. Then there is the barracks, and those who get sent to the dragon hall themselves." He shuddered. "Only one has ever come back from there. Be grateful it is Faenor here right now, he doesn't send for 'toys' like some of the others do."

She shivered at his tone. "Toys?" she asked.

Jon shook his head. "I don't know." His expression was unreadable. "They called my daughter up there," he said, his voice flat. "I never saw her again. Don't let the same happen to you." He took the clay cup from her hand and walked over to the next worker without giving her another glance.

Niara shivered as she stared after him. The secrecy and ignorance about what happened to humans who entered a dragon's presence produced more terror than stories of gruesome torture. Surely someone had to know what happened to a dragon's 'toy,' didn't they?

She cursed under her breath as a soldier started toward her and hastily hefted her pickaxe again. She didn't want to be caught not working. There existed some kind of punishment for that, and Niara did not want to find out what it was. *Then again, there's some kind of punishment for everything.* She had heard a litany of rules already, which seemed to boil down to 'do everything the dragons and their soldiers tell you to.'

The soldier leaned against the side of the quarry and watched her with speculative eyes. Niara pretended to ignore him, but every hair on the back of her neck was standing on end. He could have been a handsome man, with dark hair and eyes which went well with his burgundy uniform. Niara shuddered. He looked like a man from the Gray Mountains. He reminded her of Niall.

"Nia, hmm?" the soldier finally said.

Niara pressed her lips together instead of answering to her assumed name. *I don't need this attention. Really, I don't.*

"Why'd you come here, Nia?" the soldier asked.

Niara ran her fingers down the haft of her pickaxe as she deliberated what to do. Should she continue ignoring the soldier, or would it deflect more attention if she answered him?

He grinned at her. "You're not 'not working' if you're talking to me," he said. "I'm sure that pickaxe is heavy."

Warily, Niara set the pickaxe on the ground, her shoulders sighing in relief at the loss of weight. She eyed the soldier, gauging his intentions. She didn't like the way his eyes examined her, how they roamed up her body, lingering on her chest.

The soldier nodded in satisfaction. "You're new here, so I figured I'd take pity and tell you some things you might not be aware of," he said. "Your aunt might have told you that working in the quarry is your only option, but then again, she's a troublemaker. It's the only option for *her,* but there are plenty of other options for you."

Niara swallowed the dryness in her throat. "Oh?" she asked, attempting to sound curious. *Don't raise suspicion.*

The soldier took a step toward her, and Niara had to restrain herself from taking an automatic step back. "The dragons are quite kind to those who decide to serve them, or their immediate servants," the soldier said. "There's plenty of positions up at the barracks. A woman like you would have everyone's protection. For just a little effort on your part, of course."

As she understood the implications of the soldier's words, Niara's heart leapt to her throat. *Protection. Mazda's light...Gwyn would murder every single one of them for just that.*

She stood there, frozen, as the soldier took another step toward her, close enough to whisper in her ear. "I'd love to give you my personal protection."

Niara's hands tightened around the pickaxe resting at her feet.

Memories surged within her, Niall's face close to hers, him grabbing her shoulders, pulling her into a kiss. She had lashed out, striking him across the face, but if her brother hadn't arrived...her throat closed. The soldier's face was just as close as Niall's had been, with the same presumptive leer. Her hand trembled and clenched into a fist.

A bell rang above them, and the soldier stepped back, the smile lingering on his face. "Think about my offer." He winked and retreated, stepping onto one of the lifts and shouting for someone to hoist him up the sides of the quarry.

Niara stood motionless for another long moment before taking a deep, shuddering breath and wrapping her arms around herself to keep from shivering. A familiar anger boiled up in her, an anger which wanted to reach for the fire she could call. She couldn't do that here. He was a soldier of the dragons, and if she called on magic...

*I can't fight him, I don't have the training. Mazda's light, I need to leave here tonight. If I stay here too long...*she shuddered again. Even though Niall lay dead, the ghost of his assault lingered.

A shout rang above her and she started, realizing she was one of the last people left at the bottom of the quarry. She moved to the first of the series of ladders that led out of the quarry, knowing from the morning's lecture that the lifts were only for soldiers and other servants of the dragons, not for the common quarry worker. The physical exertion distracted her a little, although the soldier's words still haunted her. His meaning spoke clearly, even though it hadn't been stated outright. A woman could 'service' the soldiers at the barracks with her feminine charms, and thus be safe from working in the quarry, and other equally unpleasant tasks. *Mazda's light, how many other women has he made that offer to? Is it even true, or is he just trying to get me into his bed? And do the women who do take him up on it actually enjoy protection, or are they just given to the dragons as a toy once the soldiers are done with them?*

"Look out!"

Niara looked up and froze at the sight. She had been working on the lower level of the quarry, helping cut the stone into large rocks which would be hauled to the surface. Higher up, other workers had been cutting stones out of the side of the quarry. One of the rocks was poised to fall right on top of the ladder Niara was standing on.

Niara didn't think, just shifted her weight as far to the right as she could, clinging to her ladder with all her strength. An involuntary scream left her throat as she fell sideways through the air. Above her, the boulder started to fall as if in slow motion. Niara's throat closed as she caught a glimpse of the bottom of the quarry. The stone was going to miss her, but not her ladder. Once it hit, she would tumble down the quarry wall onto hard rock.

Before she had a chance to truly panic, her ladder abruptly stopped flying through the air, flinging her into the stone wall and smashing her knuckles between the ladder and the rock. She glanced upward to see a young red-haired man perched on his own ladder, one hand reaching out to grip the top of her ladder.

"Get off!" he yelled.

Niara jerked her hands away from her ladder and reached across the gap between her ladder and his, her fingers just barely managing to brush the wood. A crash echoed below her, and her ladder disappeared beneath her feet. She screamed, gripping the new ladder with all her strength as she dangled against the rock, scrambling to find her footing. Below her, the rock crashed like thunder on the quarry floor far below her. She found a rung behind her feet and she clung to it, taking huge gasping breaths that quickened as the ladder wobbled to the side.

"Steady the ladder!" The man's voice was tight.

The ladder shifted precariously again before it steadied, evidence of someone grabbing both the base and top. Shakily, she looked down to see the boulder had cracked into four large pieces. Dimly, she heard screams and saw a man lying on the ground next to one of the pieces, his leg trapped underneath the remains of the boulder.

Her arms shook, and she wanted with all her might to stay there, clinging to the ladder that seemed like the only solid thing around.

"Climb up!" the man called from above.

She took another deep breath, reminding herself that the security she felt was only an illusion. Her hands and legs shook as she climbed to the top of the ladder, and it took the last of her strength to hoist herself over the edge and pull herself up to collapse on bare stone.

The red-haired man helped her to his feet, his strong fingers curling around her wrist. "Are you alright?" he asked.

Niara met his eyes. Instead of green, like most redheads, his eyes shone sky-blue. His hair stuck out in all directions as if he had a habit of running his hand through it, and freckles scattered across his face. He wore tattered work clothes as if he were no more extraordinary than any of the workers here, and yet he had something, a confidence, about the way he held himself.

He had asked her a question. "I...yes, I'm fine," she managed. She glanced down, shuddering as workers rushed to help the man whose foot had been crushed. "Thank you."

The man squeezed her arm gently. "Such accidents are not uncommon." His eyes never left her face, gentle and earnest. "But I am most definitely glad to have saved you from one. It would be a tragedy if you were to fall victim to an accident before we had the chance to be properly introduced." He stepped back and bowed extravagantly, holding her hand in his in an imitation of a courtly bow. She could just catch a glimpse of his eyes sparkling. "Enlil, at your service, my lady."

Niara felt a flush rise to her cheeks. She had been around her foster-brother, Kishtar, too long not to know when someone was flirting with her. And yet it had been years since anyone had spoken to her like this.

She gave him a curtsy, her muscles still remembering how to do it despite years of disuse. "I am Ni—Nia, my lord."

"Nia," Enlil smiled, his sincerity warming her. "Well, Nia, perhaps I can convince you to take a safer way up to the top of the quarry for the midday meal? While there are no falling objects above right now, I would venture you are not as steady as you seem?" He gestured toward the lift, but otherwise made no motion to guide her decision in one way or another.

The thought of climbing the next ladder made Niara's heart give way. Three more ladders awaited her, rickety things that appeared ready to fall to pieces at a moment's notice. She managed a small nod. The lift, though primitive, seemed far safer.

The smile on Enlil's face grew brighter, and he bowed, offering his arm to her in a courtly manner. "Then shall I escort you, my lady?"

Her cheeks flushed and a genuine smile stretched across her face. She accepted his arm, trying to appear as casual as possible, and let him guide her over to the lift.

"Hoist us up, lads! And be careful, there's a lady on board!" Enlil shouted up.

Niara noticed the other workers giving them odd looks as they were pulled up, and her breath caught, remembering the lecture. "Maz —" she stopped her curse before the incriminating words could lead her mouth. "The lifts are for soldiers!" she gasped. "We shouldn't be using them."

Enlil blinked, a bemused expression on his face. "Is that why no one else uses them? That would explain it."

Niara stared at Enlil in disbelief, but he appeared entirely serious. Carol and the other workers had been so frightened, so cowed by the soldiers. She wondered what they thought of this man, who disobeyed the soldier's edicts with little to no consequence. "Why has no one stopped you?" she asked.

Enlil shrugged. "Perhaps they thought I was allowed?"

Niara could see why no one would have stopped Enlil from doing anything he wanted. He was tall, far taller than most of the soldiers, with broad shoulders and rippling muscles that his tattered clothing did a poor job of concealing. More than that, however, he walked with an air of unshakable confidence that would make many men hesitant to challenge him.

The lift jerked to a halt a foot short of the top of the cliff. Without asking, Enlil placed one hand on either side of Niara's waist and hoisted her up, setting her gently down on the top of the cliff before jumping up himself.

Niara gaped in surprise, staring at him as she steadied herself. He had lifted her as if she weighed no more than a feather!

He smiled at her, eyes twinkling as if he knew what she was thinking. "Shall we find some food? It's not the best, but it's far better than starving." Niara nodded and let Enlil take her arm again, guiding her over to where two disgruntled men in Auriel's livery were standing by a table, dishing up bowls of pottage to the workers. Niara saw soldiers eyeing her speculatively, but to a one, a glance at Enlil decided them against approaching her. He seemed entirely unaware of the looks, and she took a step closer to him as a soldier handed her a bowl. She grimaced at the contents, the same pottage as for breakfast, this supplemented by a slice of brown bread.

Enlil raised an eyebrow at her. "Not a feast, definitely. Used to better fare?"

Niara felt the tension settle into her shoulders. She couldn't reveal anything about herself; nothing that would give him a clue to her identity. *Lady, did I already let my noble heritage slip when I curtsied?* Her words caught in her throat, and she gave him a noncommittal shrug as an answer.

Enlil made no comment on her silence, and instead led her to a misshapen boulder that rested on the edge of the quarry. Niara sat down, wincing as her aching muscles relaxed. She kept her eyes cast downward. She didn't want to see the devastation around her.

It was as if Enlil had read her mind. "It's a tragic sight, isn't it?" he asked, his voice low.

Niara glanced up and saw only sympathy in his expression. She risked a glance around. No one else was in earshot, but the devastation was still plain for everyone to see. All around the quarry, for miles in every direction, the forest had been burned to the ground. Nothing remained except empty fields of ash.

"What happened?" she whispered.

Enlil shrugged. "The dragons decided to burn the area," he said. "I can't tell you their reasons."

Niara shook her head and cast her eyes down again. She knew their reasons, but it sent a shiver down her spine. *They know how the Sight works, they must. Why else would they destroy what I use to ground around the one project that would lead to our discovery?*

She shivered, and Enlil frowned. "Are you cold?" he asked.

"No, I'm fine." Niara looked around and cursed under her breath. She had left her shawl at the bottom of the quarry.

Enlil nodded in acceptance. "So, dare I ask where you are from?" he asked. "Carol said you were her niece, but then again," his eyes twinkled, "she also said I was her nephew, so forgive me if I don't take that at face value."

Niara met his eyes warily, but she read nothing but truth in his expression. *Still...I can't tell him. I can't reveal anything.*

"I just arrived yesterday," she said. "I've wandered a bit around Saemar. I'm from here originally, however." She grimaced, biting her tongue before any more information spilled out. "What about you?" That would get him talking about himself instead of asking about her.

Enlil smiled. "A similar answer," he said. "Wandered here, wandered there. I'm originally from a bit further north, however. And I've been here a week."

North? Niara blinked, examining Enlil more closely. Was he from one of the hillman tribes? That would certainly account for his height and physique. *He must be. The only other people who live further north are the nephelm. And despite his height, he's definitely not one of them.*

She eyed him, realizing that despite his words, he had been just as vague about answering her question as she had been. "So where have you wandered?" she asked, poking a little at the secrecy.

Enlil grinned. "Oh, here and there, and everywhere," he said.

Niara narrowed her eyes at his evasiveness. "Are questions about the past a bad idea?" she asked, making no effort to soften her words.

Enlil laughed out loud, a genuine, surprised laugh that made people turn and look at them before returning to their meals. "You don't beat around the bush, do you?"

"Well, it's better than you being evasive and me stumbling onto things we can't talk about," Niara stammered as she flushed. "And it's not like not talking about the past is a bad thing, I just hate asking questions and them not being answered, and...I'm going to shut up now." She stared at the ground, aware her face was flaming red. *Mazda's light, what's wrong with you? You've dealt with evasive people before! Even if they weren't half as attractive as Enlil.*

To her relief, Enlil stopped laughing. Instead, he gave her an understanding smile and half-bowed from his sitting position. "Then we will avoid questions about the past, for both of us. What else is there, then? The future?"

Niara froze, every muscle in her body tensing. She opened her mouth to say something, but Enlil shook his head.

"No, I see that's a bad idea. So, not the past, not the future. I guess it's the present!" he grinned. "Well, what about the present shall we talk about?"

What, indeed? Questions for this strange, enigmatic man filled her, but most of them concerned who and what he was. And those were questions about the past, a subject both of them had made off limits.

She glanced down at her plate. "Is this always the standard fare?" she asked.

Enlil's eyes twinkled, and she got the sense he knew the questions she was dying to ask. "Oh, usually," he said. He winked. "Some of us find ways to supplement it, however." Seemingly out of nowhere, he produced an apple and tossed it to Niara. She caught it instinctively and gasped in delight. An apple! She hadn't had one of those since retreating into Ellriheim!

"Where..." she started.

Enlil shook his head. "A secret!" he whispered, a mischievous grin still on his face. "Some things are better left a mystery."

Niara hardly felt like challenging him as she bit into the apple. It was crisp and tart, and she closed her eyes, savoring the taste.

She opened her eyes to find Enlil watching her. She tensed again.

Enlil smiled reassuringly. "Sorry," he said. "You just...I've never seen anyone like you, Nia."

Niara looked down at the blackened ground again. "What do you mean, like me?" She bit her lip after she asked the question. Did she really want to know the answer?

Enlil considered before answering. "Well, I admit I'm not exactly familiar with the culture here," he said, "but there are some similarities I've noticed. You don't fit any of them."

This was venturing dangerously close to the past, a topic they had agreed to avoid. Niara frowned at him. "Well, I've never seen anyone like you, either, so that makes us even."

Despite her sharp tone, Enlil laughed, nodding his head in acknowledgment. "A point," he said. "My apologies, Nia."

Niara felt herself relax again, and she mentally kicked herself. She had to remain on alert. He could be a plant, sent by the dragons to interrogate strangers. If Carol had already claimed two newcomers as relatives, then surely the soldiers would start to get suspicious soon.

"Why did you come here?" She shook her head, realizing her mistake as soon as the words were out of her mouth. "No, forget I asked."

"We're both too curious for our own good," he said, keeping his voice low. "We can each tell the other has secrets, can't we." Despite his words, his tone was not a question.

Niara eyed him, feeling her muscles loosen even more as she read nothing but sincerity in his eyes.

Enlil straightened his shoulders. "Well, I suppose I can let a little slip," he grinned. "I haven't been here long, and I intend to stay here even less time, and curse any who think to stop me." His eyes twinkled. "They have told you no one leaves without permission, haven't they? And that anyone who does is caught by the dragons?"

Niara grimaced and nodded. She looked around, at the tired, ragged people who were trying to make their pottage last as long as it could, even out here in the chill wind. Anything to keep from going back into the quarry for as long as possible.

"Well, that might be true for most of the people here," Enlil sighed. "Poor souls, they've been beaten and exhausted for years. They don't have the strength to flee. But," he met her gaze, his eyes intense, "if I wanted to leave, then I would wait until midnight. Dragons can't see very well in the dark, you know. Rather like hawks in that way. So, leave during the darkest time of the night, and all you have to avoid are human soldiers, whose patrols are lighter on the north side of the city."

Niara felt her ears prickling underneath her headscarf. *Why is he telling me this? Is it a trap? Or is he being genuine?*

"Why don't they patrol the north as much?" she asked, keeping her voice as casual as possible.

Enlil shrugged. "They seem to think there's no threat from that direction, that the northern army has everything well in hand. They only watch for the odd wild beast, and to keep the people inside the city, of course."

Niara gazed northward, toward the rolling foothills of the Gray Mountains, and frowned thoughtfully. It was the opposite direction she had to travel, true, but would it be safer in the long run?

"Alright, break's up!" a soldier started moving through the crowd of people, chivvying everyone onto their feet again. "Back down the ladders with you!"

Niara groaned as she stood up, every muscle in her body complaining. Enlil grimaced in sympathy. "You get used to it," he said.

Niara winced, but she couldn't help glancing northward again. If Enlil was right, then she wouldn't have time to get used to it. She could warn Thalion and leave that very night.

The night was freezing cold, and Niara wrapped her cloak tight around her before tying her belt in place over it. Her pack nestled under her cloak, tight against her back to immobilize it against sound.

She pulled her hood up over her head and made her way to the door of the ramshackle hut she'd been given, leaning against it and listening. No sound threatened, only the quiet sigh of a cold breeze.

Taking a deep breath, she opened the door, slipping silently out into the night. She made certain the door closed behind her before she started walking. The last thing she needed was for her absence to be noted before dawn.

No moon shone, but the stars twinkled bright enough to illuminate the broken streets. Niara paused a moment, leaning against her hut to let her eyes adjust to the night. She breathed a prayer of thanks, to Mazda and the Lady, for her elven sight. If she had had to use a torch, she didn't think she would have made it.

Footsteps echoed in the dark, and she drew a quick intake of breath before scrambling around behind her small hut. She caught the flicker of torch-light and realized she had just narrowly missed one of the night patrols.

She leaned against the hut, taking another deep breath. She needed to be as soundless as possible. The north gate stood a fair distance away, and she could not afford to be caught.

As quietly as possible, she began making her way through the streets, blessing her mother for allowing her free run of Ilhelm. She knew the streets of Ilhelm like the back of her hand, even if half of them were destroyed, and the landmarks had all disappeared. She had to watch her footing, and more than once she nearly tripped in holes or over loose stones, but finally she caught sight of the wall.

The north wall had been left mostly untouched during the assault on Ilhelm, a fact that had once cheered Niara's heart, but now she found herself wishing that it lay in ruins like the south side. The gate was closed, the great iron portcullis down, and the top of the wall illuminated by torches, spaced out sporadically, but often enough to provide dim illumination for the handful of guards patrolling up and down.

She paused at one of the last tumbledown buildings before the wall, little more than a pile of stone at this point. Crouching in the shadows, she stared at the wall, at how high it stood, and took a deep breath.

Memory flashed, the last time she had faced a wall she'd needed to pass beyond. Up in Utgard, during the trial. She had flown herself and Thalion over a wall, using the elemental power of the wind. She'd never used that much energy before, and that, along with the rest of the trial, had left her so exhausted she'd passed out. Since then, she'd used the Swaying only rarely, frightened by the way it drained her strength, as if it were using the very energy of her spirit.

Looking at the wall in front of her, however, she wondered if she had another choice. Enlil had said fewer soldiers guarded the north wall, but she saw figures standing on the wall, patrolling. There were far fewer than there ought to have been, but they remained there, and

Niara didn't want anyone to catch even a glimpse of her. They had horses, and she didn't. Once she got out of the city, she'd have enough difficulty making her way west to Hillsdale.

I hope that's the right way to go. She bit her lip. Her vision had shown her Kishtar and Lyra were alive, so there would be at least one place in the city where she'd be safe. That was more than she knew about anywhere else in Saemar. Hopefully, she'd be able to get a boat somewhere in Hillsdale and make her way down the coast. Still, it felt wrong to be going west, when her entire purpose told her she needed to be heading southeast.

I head straight southeast, and I end up at the capital, Auriel's seat of power. No, thank you. She shuddered and turned her attention back to the north wall. She had to leave Ilhelm first before she worried about the rest of her journey.

Taking a deep breath, she sank into herself, calling for the magic in her blood, the magic that allowed her the Sight, that allowed her to speak to her brother earlier that night and tell him exactly how deep and where the pit was situated, even though he remained underground. The cold night breeze blew through the city and wrapped around her, and she shivered. Focusing her concentration, she lifted herself up, until she was rising higher and higher in the air and drifting steadily over the north wall.

She couldn't look down. If she did, she knew she would lose her concentration, and all would be lost. Instead, she focused on her goal, the other side of the wall, the path that led into the Gray Mountains and up the coast toward hillmen and nephelm territory. She would have to follow it a little before she turned west.

She began to tremble as she passed over the torchlight on the wall. She held her breath, praying the soldiers would not glance up, that they wouldn't notice a figure floating where no figure should be, that they would mistake her for a bird if they did see her, or perhaps even a dragon. But dragons didn't fly at night.

Her strength sapped, and she desperately held onto the wind, guiding herself down until she collapsed on the ground at the edge of the trees, resting on her hands and knees and shaking in exhaustion.

No shouts of alarm rang from behind her. When she risked a glimpse over her shoulder, she saw she was closer to the wall than she wanted to be, but the soldiers didn't even glance her way. Two figures stood together instead, heads together, and she caught the sound of low laughter in the night.

They're more focused on keeping people in than out, she thought.

She stumbled as she rose to her feet, and braced herself against the nearest tree, swaying as her vision went a little gray. She hadn't slept after the day of working at the quarry. She needed rest, needed to sleep, but first, she needed to get further away from Ilhelm.

She could see less clearly through the trees, and the cold gnawed at her fingers as she clutched her cloak tight around her and stumbled over roots and branches, cursing the dragons who had taken over Saemar, cursing the cold, the night, and the wind.

She was so tired, she didn't notice the flickering glow of a dying fire until she was almost within the circle of light. She hesitated at the edge of the circle, drawn to the radiating heat, but cautious. Who had lit a fire, here, in the middle of nowhere? One of Auriel's men?

"Nia? Oh good, I was beginning to worry."

She nearly jumped out of her skin. Heart in her throat, she whirled to face the apparition in front of her, barely able to see his red hair in the firelight. Blue eyes twinkled, and a smile quirked on his lips.

"Enlil?" she gasped. "How—why—?"

Enlil grinned at her. "I've been expecting you since sundown," he said. "Come on, I can get the fire going some more, and you can warm up."

Niara stared at him blankly, and he took her arm and drew her closer to the fire. The warmth woke her up, and she shook herself, staring at him.

"How in Mazda's name did you know I'd be here?" she demanded.

Enlil shrugged as he set another branch on the fire. "Couldn't see you staying another day there. This was the only way out I'd been able to find, so it was likely you would come this way."

Suspicion bloomed. The north wall had been less guarded, but she had still had to fly over it. How had he gotten out? And why was he being so friendly to her? Could he be a spy for Auriel? She eyed him, not sitting where he gestured, turning the idea over in her head. Try as she might, it didn't make sense. If Auriel, or any of his dragons, had been suspicious of her, she would have been surrounded by soldiers and marched up to the fort. No, Enlil was not a spy for Auriel. But that didn't mean she could trust him.

"So, where are you going?" he asked, smiling as if it were a perfectly casual question.

A vision of the badlands city passed before her eyes, and she blinked, nearly saying "Shan Serin." Instead, she coughed and cleared her throat. "Hillsdale," she managed, then cursed inwardly. She shouldn't have answered. She should have lied.

"Nice place? I haven't been there yet," Enlil seated himself next to the fire and looked up at her, eyes questioning, clearly wondering why she wasn't sitting down.

Niara caught her breath at his presumption. "You're not traveling with me," she said. The memory of her words to her brother rang in her mind. *This is something I need to do alone.*

For the first time, Enlil appeared less than confident. "I did this wrong," he said, more to himself than to Niara.

He appeared so dejected that Niara took a step forward, wanting to comfort him, while at the same time wanting to remain firm in her resolve. Enlil raised his eyes to hers as she moved, and she stopped, watching the thoughts flit across his face.

"I don't know who you are, Nia," he said slowly. "But I can tell you're not like the rest of the people I've seen in Saemar, the ones under the dragons' rule. You walk with your head high, and you seem to have a purpose. I want to help you if I can."

Niara took a deep breath, caught by the earnestness of Enlil's expression. *I walk like that because that's how I was raised as heir to Ninaeva, and I didn't have to live under the dragons' rule.*

"Just to Hillsdale," Enlil said, his eyes never leaving hers. "If you've had enough of me at that time, then you can continue without me. But with two of us, we'll be safer. The land is wild here, and I'm not bad with a staff." He gestured at a polished wooden staff leaning against a tree. "And we can stand watches, so that no patrol will sneak up on us in the middle of the night."

"How do you know I'm not stopping in Hillsdale?" she asked, narrowing her eyes.

Enlil smiled and spread his hands out. "Lucky guess?"

Niara gazed into the fire as she turned the idea over. A part of her wanted to say yes, to accept his offer. She was just as curious about him as he seemed to be about her.

"Well, Nia? I'll take first watch tonight, if you want."

Niara took a breath, making her decision. "Alright," she said. "But my name's Niara."

No recognition flickered across Enlil's face, and his smile only widened. "Niara," he said, and she got the impression he considered every syllable. He gestured again, and she finally took the offer and sank down next to the fire, feeling the exhaustion of the day catching up to her. Her muscles screamed in protest, and she bit back a groan.

Enlil stood up, and she saw he had a pack of his own, one he pulled a sleeping roll from and handed it to her. "Use mine as well as yours, if you have one. It is cold tonight and likely to get only colder," he said. "I'll wake you up when I can't stay awake anymore."

Niara nodded, her eyes already drooping. She barely managed to get the blankets spread out before her eyes shut.

"Sleep safe, Niara," Enlil whispered.

She shivered at the way her name rolled off his tongue. Mazda's light, she hoped she was making the right choice.

4

HILLSDALE

Niara hiked in silence, huddling herself tight in her cloak to protect her from the icy drizzle of Manyu's Time. The rain had beat steadily all day, freezing cold. *At least it isn't snow,* she thought.

They had been on the road three days, and she had learned no more about her mysterious companion than he had first told her. She had tried to ask him questions about where he was from, what he was doing wandering Saemar, but he was evasive, always changing the subject, or turning the questions toward her. Questions she didn't want to answer. She'd given up eventually, frustrated that she still knew nothing about him.

Not quite true. I know he's handsome, and he's insufferably warm. He hasn't shivered once since this rain began. Niara shot him a resentful glance as he strolled through the rain, head uncovered and held high. The rain and cold drenched him to the skin, but he didn't seem to mind. He wasn't even wearing a cloak!

Almost as if he'd read her thoughts, he turned to grin at her. "Lovely weather! Is it always like this during this time of the year?"

Niara stared at him incredulously, trying to determine whether he was being sarcastic.

"Unfortunately, this is quite normal," she said, her voice dry. "The sunny days of Manyu's Time are gorgeous, but few and far between, at least this far north. Further south I'm told the sun appears more regularly."

"Manyu's Time," Enlil rolled his tongue over the words as if tasting them for the first time. "So that's what you call the season? What about the others?"

Niara nearly stopped dead. "You don't know the names of the seasons?" she asked.

"Not by the names you give them, certainly," her mysterious companion said. "Who is this Mazda and Manyu?"

For a minute, Niara couldn't breathe. How could a human, even one of the northern barbarians, not know about Mazda and Manyu?

Think logically, Niara, she told herself. *Just because the high priest was certain knowledge of Mazda was spread all over the world, doesn't mean it's true. After all, the Faithful don't worship Mazda. It's perfectly reasonable the hill barbarians wouldn't worship him, especially if they associate his worship with Saemar.*

She took a deep breath to allow herself time to think. "Mazda is the god of light and the sun," she said. "Most of Saemar regarded him as the only deity, or at least the supreme deity. Before Aur—the sky-lord rose, of course," she couldn't help the bitterness in her voice.

Enlil nodded, ignoring her last comment. "So when it's hottest it's Mazda's Time. Makes sense. And Manyu?"

Despite herself, she felt a shiver run down her spine. "Mazda's dark twin," she said, keeping her answer as short as possible. "He is…" she shuddered. "You do not want to encounter him." She closed her eyes briefly, remembering her mother's warnings, the brief, clipped descriptions of nightmares and the mark of Manyu. Vinet had bound herself to the Sight and the Lady after that experience and had encouraged Niara to do the same.

Enlil eyed Niara but didn't comment on her fear. "God of day and god of night?" he asked.

Niara frowned. "God of the sun," she corrected. "Mazda is fire and light, everything that gives life. Manyu is…his opposite," she finished lamely. The words seemed so inadequate to describe them. She was no priest.

Enlil nodded his understanding. "And who do the folk of Saemar worship now, now that the sky-lord has risen?"

Sky-lord. Auriel. Niara grimaced. "How should I know?" she asked. "From the reactions I got, Mazda's worship is certainly discouraged, if not outright prohibited, but some people most certainly still believe." Why else had the sergeant let her go, after all? He still remembered Mazda, or he would have sent her to Faenor or Flaven for coming from the convent.

"I see," Enlil said noncommittally.

Niara frowned. "How have you not heard of them before?" she asked.

He shrugged. "I lived too far north, I guess," he said. "Gods never seemed that important up there."

For a moment, Niara stared at him, unable to comprehend such a life. Unexpectedly, she felt a surge of envy. She knew far too well the existence of gods and other powerful beings, and how unpredictable and fickle they could be. *Manyu, the Lady, Auriel...* To not have to worry about divinities interfering... "That must have been nice."

Enlil let out a short bark of laughter. "Well, I had other things to think about. Don't know if that made up for the lack of gods or not."

A lack of gods. Niara shook her head. Nazir would have been overjoyed to meet Enlil, to be able to learn in person what the hill barbarian tribes were like. None of them had ever shown any inclination to even speak to Southerners before.

"What else was it like—" The words had barely come out of her mouth before her vision went white. Instantly, her mind raced northward, and she grasped desperately for trees, avoiding the elder as best she could.

An army, dressed in burgundy and gold, marching through a mountain pass. Behind them, swathes of devastation, a path burned through the forest to clear the way. Two dragons flying overhead, one red, one gold. Ahead, the stone towers of the nephelm, standing dark and ominous even in the sun. No banners hung from the towers or walls, and no trace of movement came from the city. It was as if every living being had vanished into smoke.

Niara gasped, finding herself kneeling in the mud of the road. *Utgard.* She swallowed hard, remembering the empty ramparts. She hadn't seen a single nephelm. Then again…the nephelm had originally built Ellriheim. It would stand to reason that Utgard would have a similar sanctuary. *They must be hidden. The nephelm were dragon-slayers, and they knew Auriel planned on rising. They can't have been caught unawares.*

"Niara?" Enlil's voice was concerned, and Niara looked up to find him only a few inches away from her, also kneeling in the mud.

"I'm fine." She waved his offered hand away and rose to her feet, wincing at the mud on her tunic. "Let's keep going."

Enlil stood up as well, but the concern didn't leave his eyes. "Are you sure? I know hu- you Southerners aren't as accustomed to cold as I am. Should we rest a while?"

Niara shook her head, blinking the rain out of her eyes again. She made certain her headscarf was still firmly in place. *One benefit to this weather; I haven't had to justify wearing a headscarf to anyone yet.* "I'm fine," she said again. "Let's keep going."

Enlil opened his mouth as if to protest again, then his eyes widened. "Get down!" he whispered. Without waiting for her to react, he grabbed her arm and started dragging her toward the side of the road.

A heartbeat later, Niara heard the same sound, a sound that made her forget about demanding an explanation and follow Enlil to huddle in the roadside undergrowth. The ferns were soaking wet, but at least they provided cover as the rushing, rhythmic sound of wingbeats passed overhead.

Dragon, Niara shivered. Was it Faenor or Flaven? Were they searching for her and Enlil? Or was it another dragon, heading toward Hillsdale to oversee the operations there? She didn't dare look up and find out, afraid that any movement would attract the dragon's eye. Enlil had said they could see like a hawk during the day…

It seemed like an eternity before the wingbeats passed, far out of sight toward Hillsdale again. Niara and Enlil waited for another long moment, huddled next to each other in the undergrowth before Enlil finally dared poke his head out.

"I think we're clear," he said.

Niara nodded and followed him out of the undergrowth, her body immediately missing the warmth of him next to her. She felt herself flushing, remembering his comment about Southerners not being used to the cold. All her life, she had been the Northerner, the one used to heavy snows and cold. She had never thought herself unused to the cold before now.

Straightening her shoulders, she started walking again, keeping her back as tall as possible. *You are Lady Niara Sindarilae of Ninaeva,* she reminded herself. *No matter what, you have no reason to feel ashamed.* She ignored her stomach as it churned at the thought of her title. She had failed her people, failed to protect Ninaeva. There were plenty of reasons for her to feel ashamed.

"It's two days further to Hillsdale," she said, pushing those thoughts to the far corners of her mind. "We should press on and make certain we have a covered place to shelter tonight."

Enlil nodded, agreeing without speaking. Niara bit her lip, torn between wanting him to talk more and being grateful for his silence.

Just to Hillsdale. You can think of the next step of your journey then.

There.

The wooden palisade stood nowhere near as intimidating as a stone wall would have been, but the presence of a newly built stone fort on the hill outside the wall made up for that lack. Especially since the stone fort had a gate large enough for several dragons to enter at once.

The last time Niara had seen Hillsdale, they had just come back from a successful negotiation with the nephelm and were hurrying back to Ninaeva with the news that Auriel was the sky-lord and father of dragons, and that he planned to rise again. Niara had been hopeful they'd find some way to prevent Auriel from breaking his bonds, to reveal his identity to the world before he could do anything…but by the time they'd arrived back in Ninaeva and found Serana missing, it had been too late. She straightened her pack on her back as they walked toward the gates. She hoped wanderers were still allowed, that only Ilhelm, where there were fugitives, indefinitely retained their strangers.

"So, what's our story?" Niara asked. Even if strangers were allowed, questions would arise, and they needed to be prepared to answer them. And from the looks of it, Hillsdale was much larger than the remnants of Ilhelm, with more soldiers as well.

Enlil blinked. "We have to have a story?"

Once again, Niara stared at Enlil in incomprehension. "Yes," she said simply. "Didn't you need one when you arrived at Ilhelm?"

"Oh, that." Enlil shrugged. "Carol mostly took care of that. She had everyone believing I was her nephew from somewhere in the south, and everything I said after that was irrelevant."

Somehow, Niara could not bring herself to believe that. From what she'd seen, Enlil acted far too confident, and he would have just walked in and pretended he belonged there. She shook her head in resignation. "We'll say we're looking for my brother," she said. "At least that's part of the truth."

"Your brother?" Enlil's eyes widened. "You have a brother?"

Niara managed to stifle a laugh at Enlil's surprise. "Yes. But he's not the one we're going to see." She hesitated. How to describe Kishtar's relationship with her? "Kishtar was raised with us. He's as close to a brother as anyone can get."

"I see," Enlil gazed at the gates of Hillsdale. "What's it like, having siblings?"

Niara smiled. "It's wonderful, most of the time," she said. "Then again, they were both eight years younger than I, and so I was able to see them as adorable rather than little terrors, as those born closer in age sometimes experience."

Enlil nodded, but his expression still showed slight incomprehension. Niara tilted her head curiously. "Do you not have any siblings?" she asked.

"No, only child." He stared sightlessly toward the north. "Only one of anything, really."

His eyes seemed so lonely, a wave of sympathy rose in her, and an urge to place her hand on his shoulder in comfort. She resisted, and he turned back to her, his expression light again. "So, we're looking for your brother. That's your excuse, anyway, what's mine? Are we husband and wife, or lovers, or just friends?"

His eyes were so mischievous, Niara's breath caught in her throat. She tried to clear her mind and answer him coherently, but he continued.

"Friends would be the easiest for us to act, I suppose, but is it really the most believable?" He grinned. "A husband has far more reason to accompany a wife than a friend."

Fire rushed to Niara's cheeks, not helped by the fact that he was absolutely right. Couples did travel together far more frequently.

"We're friends," she said, making her voice as firm as possible. She eyed Enlil. "If you want, you can be hopelessly in love with me, and I'm oblivious, and that's why you're following me."

"Perfect!" Enlil exclaimed. "That's a role I can act!"

Niara flushed again, and a lump formed in her throat. *If only you didn't have to act,* she thought.

The beat of dragon wings above was like ice in her blood. *What are you thinking? She castigated herself. You've known him a few days. Just because you like him better than any of the nobles you ever met in Saemar, doesn't mean you have a right to go fancying him. You have a mission, a task.* Not for the first time, Niara cursed the vagueness of her mother's visions. Why couldn't the Lady ever say anything straight out? Why did she always have to speak in riddles?

If I had to guess, I'd say AeresThonEsia is slightly insane, she thought. Maybe that's why she can't speak straight. She doesn't see straight, so how can she give sensible directions or advice? Her grandfather and the elves of Alfheim would have considered such thoughts blasphemy, but they weren't there to disapprove or be shocked.

She looked up to see the dragon flying overhead, heading toward the city. It landed at the stone fort, folding its wings in for a graceful landing before walking through the enormous door. Niara bit her lip, controlling her instinctive fear. *Don't act suspicious. If you don't act like you're afraid, or have something to hide, then they won't suspect you. It's not like you haven't kept secrets your entire life.* She grimaced at the thought.

As they drew closer to the gate, she could see the burgundy and gold-clad soldiers standing watch. Two stood on the wooden palisade, lookouts for whoever might be approaching. Four others stood at the gate itself, ready to question any traveler who approached.

"At least the gates are open," Enlil said quietly. "Means they must get people coming and going."

Niara only nodded in answer as they drew close. She felt the soldiers' eyes on them long before one of them ordered, "Halt!"

She and Enlil obediently stopped and waited until two of the soldiers approached them. One of them gestured to their packs. "Weapons check."

Niara swallowed unwillingly before handing it over. She had nothing more threatening than a knife in her pack, but she didn't like the idea that it might be confiscated. Her actual weapon was a dagger tucked in her boot, but that was a last resort. She'd use magic first.

Enlil smiled easily at the soldier before handing him his pack. The soldier glared in response and then started opening the pouches.

"Name, origin, and purpose," the second soldier snapped.

Origin. Mazda's light. Niara carefully kept the dismay off her face. "We're looking for my brother," she said. "I think he's here. We've been on the road a while, looking."

The soldier raised an eyebrow. "What makes you think he's here?"

"It's where he was heading." Niara shrugged.

The soldier rolled his eyes. "Your names?" he asked.

"Nia," Niara answered before Enlil could respond. Although her true name was unlikely to be recognized here, she didn't want to take any chances.

"Enlil," Enlil said when the soldier turned to him.

"And where'd you start? Which dragon gave you leave for this search?"

Niara felt her heart pounding in her throat. They needed a dragon's permission to be on the road?

"Izila gave us leave," Enlil spoke calmly, but deathly silence followed his words. The soldiers stared at him, their eyes wide and frightened.

"Izila?" the one who had been going through the packs breathed. "She's your overlord?"

Niara studied the ground, trying not to betray her ignorance of what was happening. Who was Izila, that she inspired such fear in Auriel's soldiers?

Waiting, Enlil regarded the two soldiers for a long moment, his expression perfectly calm but implacable. Finally, the soldier swallowed. "Visitors are required to stay at the guest house in the center of town," he said. "Register with the sergeant there. He'll tell you how to make an appointment with the registrar, so you can see if your brother is here." He gestured at Niara.

Niara gave a brief nod of thanks, still not taking her eyes off the ground. She barely acknowledged the soldier who handed her back her pack and only dared look at Enlil when they were well clear of the gate.

"Who's Izila?" she whispered.

Enlil shook his head, not meeting her eyes. Instead, he glanced all around them, forward, backward, and to the side, as if he were searching for something, or someone. "Not here," he said. "Too dangerous."

Niara bit her lip, refraining from pointing out that if they courted danger to talk about this Izila, then it probably had been dangerous to drop her name to the soldiers. She instead moved her attention to the streets around them, watching for hints about how the ordinary people conducted their lives.

Immediately, she was struck with a sense of unreality. No one wandered the streets, loitering or simply enjoying the day. Instead, everyone scurried to their destinations, their heads down, never daring to raise their gaze from the ground. The few friends who were meeting spoke in hurried, hushed whispers, and everyone gave the two strangers a wide berth.

Niara couldn't stop herself from searching for a bright blonde man, or a red-haired woman with her hair cut in her bob. It wasn't likely she'd see them now, she knew. If her vision indicated anything, Kishtar and Lyra worked as one of the fisher crews, and would spend most of their time out on the water. They wouldn't be on land at this time of the day.

It took her a few minutes to realize Enlil had started leading them toward the center of town in a roundabout fashion, wandering down several of the side streets rather than taking the main street directly to the center. She furrowed her brow as he made another right turn.

"Where are you going?" she asked. "The center and docks are that way," she pointed, recalling the location of the docks district from her previous visits.

"And you can just walk straight there?" Enlil asked.

Niara frowned. "Yes?" she made it a question.

It was Enlil's turn to stare in incomprehension. "So anyone can just walk right through town to the center of the populace? There are no defensive barriers?"

"There's the gate?" Niara offered.

Enlil rolled his eyes. "That palisade wouldn't stop anyone determined," he stated.

Niara sniffed. "Before Auriel, they wouldn't have had to," she lowered her voice, just in case a soldier stood nearby. "Hillsdale had an alliance with Saemar, bordered on the east by Ninaeva and south by Venia. The only people who would have threatened them were hill barbarians from the north, and they weren't that keen on Hillsdale's primary resource."

"And what was that?" Enlil seemed genuinely interested.

"Timber," Niara said. A loud groan of wood and gears interrupted them, and they pressed to the side of the street to make way for a long wagon, piled high with logs heading for the gate. "Which, apparently, it still is," she whispered. She gazed after the cart, wondering what use the dragons had for timber. What would they be constructing?

Enlil shook his head. "It's still odd that an enemy could just come marching straight through."

Niara felt her forehead wrinkle as she tried to figure out where a hill barbarian would have learned about defensive fortifications. As far as she'd been aware, they had no permanent structures and were constantly on the move from one temporary dwelling to the next. Why would Enlil know about defensive fortifications if he'd never had to build one?

Maybe his tribe attacked a few, she thought. *I wouldn't be surprised if there are ruins up there, old nephelm and human ruins, as well. Maybe the tribes occasionally occupy one of those. That's probably how he knows.*

It was irrelevant, anyway. "This way," she told Enlil. With her leading, they were soon on a straight course toward the docks. Enlil stared at her incredulously when they first heard the sound of the waves crashing against the piers.

"How did you do that?" he asked.

Niara shrugged, but inwardly she smiled. "Hillsdale is like half a wheel," she said. "If a road is curved, it goes around the city. If it's straight, it leads right to the ocean." She closed her eyes, breathing in the smell of the salt air, wishing it were Mazda's Time. A tiny village lay about a day's ride to the south, and the sun would warm the wonderful sandy beach. Vinet had favored it as a retreat whenever she felt the need to escape from politics. Niara, Thalion, and Kishtar had adored it. She wished they could be there again, that everything was back to normal.

A flash of white passed before her closed eyelids, and she gasped as the vision overtook her. South, to a few sturdy pine trees, standing some distance away from the water.

Burned houses. Empty wreckage. Ships beached on the sand. Niara struggled to maintain her grip on the trees, but she was torn further away, further south, to where a stone-walled city remained. She gasped as she took in the sight. *Venia.*

The stone walls still stood but were blackened and charred. Soldiers patrolled every street, weapons at the ready. A dragon flew above, golden scales reflecting the few rays of light in the drizzling rain. She landed on top of the gate, causing it to shake under her weight. A group of commoners stood huddled in front of her, surrounded by guards. The dragon hissed, black eyes flaring. "Move away." The guards stepped back, and the dragon released a breath of fire.

Niara choked on a scream as she broke free of the vision and fled back to her body. She shuddered, struggling to stand upright, and clutched at the closest thing she could find. The screams of the humans echoed in her mind as she gripped the fabric in front of her, taking deep, shuddering breaths, trying to clear the memory of charred flesh.

Another massacre. Mazda's light, will I ever see the end of them?

"Niara?" Enlil's voice was quiet but concerned.

Niara's eyes widened. She had been clinging to Enlil for balance, keeping herself upright by seizing his cloak. She hastily released him and stumbled backward. Panic gripped her as her heel struck a piece of debris and she tripped. Enlil caught her arm and pulled her closer to him before she could fall, his arms warm reassurance.

"I'm alright," she said quickly before he could ask. "I'm alright."

Enlil's expression clearly stated that he didn't believe her. Niara grimaced and straightened, pulling away from Enlil's grasp on her arm. "Let's find the guest house," she said.

Enlil eyed her for a moment longer, then gave a sigh and began searching. Niara took another moment to steady herself, trying to process what she'd seen.

There was a rebellion in Venia. That has to be what I saw. She shivered. *Maybe getting a boat south isn't such a good idea.*

Enlil gestured, and she shoved the vision out of her mind as she followed him toward a large square building, what had obviously at one point been the town hall, or some other governmental building. Two soldiers stood at the entrance, swords at the ready.

"We're here to spend the night," Niara said uncertainly to one of the soldiers.

He jerked his head toward the inside. "Speak to the sergeant."

Niara nodded and took a deep breath before entering the building. Ill-repaired, it looked more like a prison than a hostel. She blinked as she entered, letting her eyes adjust to the dark interior. Her sharp ears picked up on the conversation happening inside before she could make out the faces.

"Sarge, if you just give me two more nets—" a man's voice pleaded.

"Absolutely not, Hollstein," the second man was sharp and authoritative. "You've had as many nets as you're allowed. If you can't keep them in good repair, that is hardly my issue."

"But Sarge, we need those nets to feed your men," the first voice said again. "Your men wouldn't like it if they had to go short, would they?"

The second voice remained quiet. Niara blinked, her eyes adjusting to see a man in one of Auriel's uniforms sitting at a desk, glaring at the man in front of him. The other man had his back to Niara, and he was wrapped in his hood, but Niara frowned. Something about him was familiar…

"I'll give you a bolt of Jyrian silk," the man said, his voice dropping low. "I know you have a pretty thing you had your eye on, Sarge. I'm sure she'd like something just as pretty."

The sergeant glared at the man for another long moment, then nodded shortly. "Get your nets. And you better not lose or break anymore this month."

The man straightened, giving the sergeant a salute. "Absolutely, Sarge!" He turned on his heel to leave, and Niara's mouth dropped open. How had she not recognized that smooth voice before?

Kishtar's eyes widened, and he stared at her, gawking like a fish. A smile crept over her face despite herself.

"What is it, Hollstein?" the sergeant snapped. "Won't you just get out of my sight?"

Kishtar glanced back at the sergeant, then back at Niara, his mouth opening, then closing. Niara smiled grew wider, then took pity on him.

"Hello, brother," she said. "It's taken me a while to find you."

"I still can't believe it!" Kishtar exclaimed.

Tears stung her eyes, but Niara brushed them away impatiently as Kishtar ushered her into a small house. She hadn't realized how much she'd missed her foster brother.

"Lyra! We have a visitor!" Kishtar's voice was exuberant and loud.

Niara blinked as a baby's wail echoed from the back wall of the room.

Shortly afterward, Lyra's red bob of hair appeared at the door, a squalling child in her arms. "Kishtar, how many times have I told you —Niara!" Lyra's eyes widened.

"Hello, Lyra." She paused awkwardly. Niara had only known Lyra only a few brief weeks before Auriel's rise.

Lyra felt no such awkwardness as she strode forward, handed the baby off to Kishtar, and threw her arms around Niara. "Thank Mazda you're safe," she whispered in Niara's ear. "Kishtar's been worried sick about all of you for the last two years." She pulled back. "You are safe, aren't you? All of you?"

"We're all as safe as we can be," Niara promised.

From behind them, Enlil cleared his throat. Niara turned hastily, her cheeks flushing red. "Lyra, this is Enlil. He's traveling with me." She turned her gaze from Lyra to Kishtar, raising what she hoped was an unobtrusive eyebrow, letting them know they couldn't speak that openly in front of him.

Kishtar frowned, but Lyra gave an understanding nod. "Well met, Enlil," she said. "I hope you two know you are welcome to stay here as long as necessary."

"Unfortunately, that had better be as short as possible." Niara sighed, glancing sideways at Enlil. If only she could speak freely!

Enlil still stood in the doorway, surveying the room. He raised an eyebrow as he caught her glance, and she gazed at the floor, her face flushing.

"Perhaps I can acquire some provisions for dinner? Let you catch up with your family?" he asked.

Niara felt her heart lighten, and she gave Enlil a grateful look. He smiled at her. "I'll be back in an hour or so?" Despite his expression, something sad seemed to shadow his eyes.

Impulsively, Niara strode across the room and gave Enlil a quick hug. "Thank you," she whispered.

Enlil stiffened in surprise, but the shadow left his face. He gave her a more genuine smile and then ducked out of the house, whistling an unfamiliar tune as he left.

Niara waited until the whistling faded, then turned to Kishtar and Lyra again. She opened her mouth, then closed it again. How to start after two years of separation?

The baby in Kishtar's arms cried out again in complaint, and Kishtar grinned, bouncing the child up and down. "Want to meet our little girl?" he asked.

Niara chuckled and walked over to Kishtar, bending her head to examine the wide-eyed child in his arms. The girl's face was still screwed up in complaint, but even so, Niara could see the bright intelligence and beauty in her face.

"She's beautiful." She glanced at Lyra. "What's her name?"

"Evalynna," Lyra answered. "Kishtar chose it."

The name struck Niara like a blow. She stared at Kishtar, trying to think how to form the words. "Kishtar…"

Kishtar's eyes widened, and he hoisted his daughter up on his shoulder before gesturing Niara toward a chair. The three of them sat down in a small circle as Niara tried to find the words to describe what had happened.

"What is it, Niara?" Kishtar whispered.

Niara swallowed. "Gwyn and Evalynna are dead, Kishtar," she managed. "They died when the dragons first arrived and drove us down into Ellriheim."

Lyra caught her breath, but Kishtar only closed his eyes tightly and nodded. "I didn't think they would survive that," he said, his voice tight. He opened his eyes again. "What about everyone else?"

"Thalion and Serana are acting as Lord and Lady," Niara said. "Nazir's still quiet, as if he expects Mother to turn up at any moment.

The rest are still there. We're…surviving." She shrugged. "The dragons know we're there. They're digging a quarry to try to find us, but so far, they're having no luck."

Kishtar's eyes widened into a worried expression. "What if they find you?" he asked.

"They won't," Niara said. "I was able to find where they were digging, and they won't break through into Ellriheim until after Papsukkal." She winced, thinking of the journey ahead of her.

"Papsukkal?" Kishtar handed Evalynna to Lyra, his eyes questioning. "What's so important about that?"

Niara felt herself relaxing as the whole of the story came pouring out of her, her visions, Vinet speaking to her, the call to go south to the ruined city of Shan Sherin, and to be there before Papsukkal. "It has something to do with Auriel," she said in conclusion, "but I don't know what. I hope it's about binding him again," her voice tightened. "We can't live under dragon rule like this. The way they treat the workers at the quarry, and what happened in Venia today…" She shook her head.

Kishtar and Lyra exchanged a look. "What happened in Venia today?" Kishtar asked warily.

"A rebellion," Niara said flatly. "Unfortunately, I don't think it was successful. The soldiers executed a number of people who were probably the ringleaders."

Kishtar closed his eyes and mouthed a prayer. Lyra was more vocal. "Manyu take it!" she cursed.

Niara's eyes widened. "What?"

Lyra only released another string of curses, causing Evalynna to make inquisitive sounds that sounded suspiciously like the curses Lyra had just been uttering.

"We all knew it was a risk, love." Kishtar cursed under his breath. "I only wish it had gone better."

Niara looked from one to the other. "You knew about the rebellion?"

Kishtar's lips twitched into a smile. "We planned it," he said. "If it was successful, we were supposed to lead one here."

"How did you manage that?" Niara asked.

Kishtar nodded at Lyra, who seemed to have finally calmed down. She stroked Evalynna's hair as she spoke. "It was my name, mostly," she said. "Most of the folks around here know the name Hollstein, knew us as a respectable family. So, when we started spreading whispers of discontent, others quickly started following." She shrugged "It was small things, at first. Kishtar wanted to keep us safe, and the last thing you had told him was to keep his head down and obey the dragons," she raised an eyebrow at Niara. "But we couldn't just let things stand."

Niara shook her head. She doubted she'd have been able to sit still, either. "What kind of small things?"

Lyra sighed. "Smuggling information, at first. Scouts would tell us where a dragon was sighted, how many soldiers were stationed at the gate, when the patrols were...that kind of thing. Then we began smuggling people, which the job Kishtar and I are assigned to is uniquely suited."

"Fishing," Niara said quietly.

Lyra started, then nodded. "Yes, fishing. Have to keep the town supplied somehow, and since the soldiers won't hunt, it's up to us. Do you know how many hidey-holes I have on my boat?" her lips twitched. "They should have never let me keep my own fishing boat. Wrap someone in a pile of fishing nets, cover them with the day's catch, and no soldier is ever going to look twice."

Fishing nets. Niara shot a glance at Kishtar, remembering his conversation with the sergeant. Had that been how he'd 'damaged' his fishing nets?

"What kind of people do you smuggle?" she asked. "And where to?" A wisp of a plan, more of a hope, tickled the back of her mind.

"Usually no more than a day's sail away," Lyra said. "The dragons do patrol over the sea, even though they don't seem to like to. We don't think they can swim. But there's a group of outlaws about a day's sail south, and we set our refugees overboard where they can swim to shore, and then," she shrugged. "Then Mazda help them. We don't know the next step of the network and we keep it that way."

South. Niara bit her lip. It wasn't as far south as she'd hoped, but it was a step in the right direction. "I think—" she began.

The door burst open, and a haggard young woman ran in, her face white. "Mistress Hollstein," she gasped. "Mistress Hollstein, you have to help! They've sent Ovil and Pascal to the dragon fort, and they're coming for me next!"

Instantly, Lyra and Kishtar were on their feet. Lyra thrust Evalynna at Niara, who took the baby hesitantly, afraid that she would drop her. Evalynna immediately started crying.

"In the back, Mirri," Lyra said firmly. "We'll get you in hiding. Did anyone follow you?"

"No…" Mirri gasped as the door opened again, and Enlil stepped inside, carrying a basket that smelled of fish, his eyes dark with worry.

"There are soldiers searching every house," he said. "I don't know if—" his eyes widened as he took in the frantic girl by the door. "Ah, are they looking for you?"

Mirri's eyes filled with tears, and Lyra cursed. "We need to move," she snapped. "Kishtar, you and Enlil stay here and delay them as long as possible. Niara, help me hide Mirri. Bring Evalynna."

Niara nodded and followed Lyra toward the back door, still holding Evalynna in her arms. She grimaced as she shifted her hold on the crying baby.

Lyra led them through the small back room and stopped by the door, pressing an ear against the wood. "I think we're clear," she whispered. "Manyu curse it! Why now, of all times?" She placed a hand on the handle. "Here goes nothing."

"Wait," Niara spoke without thinking. She swallowed as the two women turned to her, questioning looks on their faces. Trapped now, she took a deep breath and closed her eyes, reaching out with her senses, trying to keep her Sight contained to the street outside. Straggly bushes were the nearest things to grab onto, and she held fast to them, seeing the cobblestone and trampled dirt of the street. A soldier patrol marched down the road, then rounded the corner, out of sight.

Niara pulled herself back to her body, shaking and sweating with the effort. She had done it. She had controlled her vision. "Clear," she said.

Lyra stared at her with wide eyes for the briefest second before nodding. She opened the door and pulled Mirri out, Niara following a half-step behind them. Lyra hurried them across the street to one of the ramshackle sheds. Niara grimaced at the smell of fish guts and bait. Oddly enough, little Evalynna seemed to like the smell, for she at least grew quiet as they entered.

"Help me, Mirri," Lyra ordered. She gestured to a pile of fish nets and tackle. To Niara's surprise, instead of hiding Mirri underneath them, the two women pushed, causing the board they'd been piled on to move away, revealing a hatch leading down to a cellar.

"Quick!" Lyra hissed.

Mirri whimpered but moved as fast as she could down the hole. Lyra began to push the wooden cover back over, her face red with exertion. Niara heard her heart pounding in her chest as she heard the sound of soldiers patrolling the street again. She looked down at the baby in her arms, then to Lyra, still struggling to close the hatch. She cursed under her breath, then set Evalynna on top of the pile of nets and pushed with Lyra, getting the nets in place just as a fist pounded on the door.

"Sit down!" Lyra hissed at Niara.

Niara obeyed, her eyes widening as Lyra hastily unlaced the front of her bodice. "What is it?" Lyra called.

"Open up!" a harsh voice commanded.

Lyra jerked her head at Niara as she picked up Evalynna and held her to her now-bared chest. Niara stood up and walked to the door, opening it to allow the soldiers a perfect view of Lyra feeding her daughter.

Lyra glared at the soldiers. "What do you want?" she snapped.

Of the three soldiers in the doorway, one flushed bright red and turned away, another cast his eyes down, and only the leader seemed capable of meeting Lyra's eye. "Lyra Hollstein," the soldier said, his voice changing into a sigh. "Why is it every time we meet it's in this situation?"

"If you had a wife with a baby, you wouldn't ask me such a sense-less question," Lyra retorted. "What can I do for you, then?"

The soldier's eyes flickered to Niara. "Who's your friend?"

"I'm Kishtar's sister, Nia," Niara said. "I just arrived in town today."

"Check with the gate guard," the leader ordered one of the soldiers behind him. The one who had flushed reddest set off at a run.

The soldier turned back to Lyra. "Have you seen Miriam Nichols anywhere today?"

Lyra frowned. "Mirri? Can't say that I have."

Niara schooled her expression in her best courtly mask as the soldier switched his attention to her. "And you, Nia?"

Niara shook her head. "I haven't met anyone other than Kishtar, Lyra, and the sergeant at the guest house," she said truthfully. After all, she hadn't officially met Mirri.

The soldier nodded shortly. "Report it if you see her anywhere," he ordered. "Xana wants a word with her."

Xana. Niara shivered in spite of herself at the dragon's name.

"If she comes to visit me here, I'll definitely tell you," Lyra said. "Now can I please get back to feeding my baby?"

The soldier rolled his eyes but spun on his heel and stalked out of the shack. Niara closed the door behind him, then leaned against it as she looked at Lyra.

Lyra smiled wryly at Niara, and Niara returned the smile. Her heart still pounded in her chest, but the rush of adrenaline was fading.

"Does this happen often?" she managed.

Lyra shrugged noncommittally. "Off and on. The rules here are so strict, someone's bound to break them on a regular basis." She sighed. "But Mirri, Ovil, and Pascal were spying on the fort, trying to deter-mine if Xana has any weakness we can use. Well, let me finish feeding Evalynna, and then we'd better head back. Mirri'll need to be smug-gled out, and we'll need a plan to rescue Ovil and Pascal, and fast."

Niara shivered. "What will they do to them?" she asked.

Lyra winced. "Xana's bloodthirsty, and will probably execute them by tomorrow, even if she doesn't think they're guilty. There's no trial anymore, no evidence. And Xana…likes fire. We know it, her soldiers know it, and they'll probably use that to try to get Ovil and Pascal to reveal if they were working with anyone else. If they do, they'll lead Auriel's men straight to me and Kishtar." Her voice was calm, but Niara could see the tension in her shoulders.

Niara took a deep breath. "Enlil and I should be able to help with the rescue," she said.

Lyra raised an eyebrow. "I thought you didn't trust him?"

Niara grimaced. "I don't know enough about him," she said. "But…" she flushed. *I want to.* "He saved my life. And he's helped me get this far." *And seems to intend to travel further.* She felt curiously warm inside, comforted at the thought of Enlil's continuing presence.

To her relief, Lyra didn't press any further. "We'll need all the help we can get," she said. "With our luck, they're locked up in the dragon's fort already."

5

THE DRAGON'S FORT

Niara held her breath as she huddled in the shadow of the wooden palisade that surrounded Hillsdale. No light pierced the pitch-black, but at least rain no longer poured down. The crisp air heralded an early Manyu's Time. Niara shivered as she stared at the small group of men who were brushing dirt away from next to the wall, keeping her ears as sharp as possible for the sound of any unfamiliar footprints. They could not afford to be discovered.

"We're through." Kishtar's voice was steady despite the tenseness of the situation.

Niara moved closer to the wall. The opening the men had uncovered was small, just barely small enough to crawl through, but it led to the outside of the wall.

"How did you manage to dig this without the soldiers noticing?" Enlil's blue eyes were bright in the darkness as he handed one of the other men his shovel.

Kishtar flashed a bright grin. "A little at a time, of course," he said.

Niara rolled her eyes, but she was impressed. The entrance had been cleverly concealed, dirt piled on top of a wooden board to protect the tunnel. It was obvious this escape route had been in place for a while.

Two of the men crawled through the hole. Kishtar gestured to Enlil, who followed through the tunnel, his red hair disappearing into the shadow.

Kishtar turned to Niara with a raised eyebrow. "You sure you can sneak in and rescue them?" he asked.

Niara nodded. "It's the only way to get them out without drawing suspicion to you or Lyra. Just make sure you don't get caught during your distraction."

"I still don't like it," her foster brother commented, "with how little you know about Enlil."

Niara pressed her lips together. She had been wrestling with that issue herself. "I'll be with him the entire time," she insisted. "If anything goes wrong, I can handle it."

Kishtar sighed. "I hope so," he said. "If we had any other options…"

"But you don't," Niara snapped. She softened the harshness with a quick smile. "Trust me, Kishtar."

Kishtar took a deep breath and nodded. Niara reached out to briefly clasp his hand before bending down to crawl through the tunnel.

It was a tight squeeze, even for her thin frame. *Good thing our diet in Ellriheim doesn't allow anyone to gain weight,* she thought.

Enlil and the other two men were waiting for her on the other side, and Kishtar followed seconds after. "The others will conceal the exit," Kishtar whispered. "Everyone know what to do next?"

Everyone nodded without saying a word. Kishtar looked at Niara and then disappeared with the other two men toward the Hillsdale gate.

Niara turned to Enlil. "Ready?"

Enlil nodded, his eyes dancing.

Niara refrained from pointing out the seriousness of their task. Enlil had to know the danger they were putting themselves in.

They crept through the trees to the wall of the fort, her eyes picking out the trail unerringly even in the darkness. Several times she heard Enlil stumble over a stone or branch she easily avoided, and she tried to slow her pace and offer him a hand, but he waved away her assistance with a grin. They paused at the tree line, still a fair distance away from the fort itself. Two soldiers stood at the gate, crossbows slung on their backs and swords at their side. Torches were mounted on the wall behind them, providing flickering illumination.

But that means they can only see as far as the torchlight. Good. I can see further. As long as they kept to the shadows, they should be able to sneak in. Now they only had to wait.

This was the riskiest part of the plan. Kishtar and the other men had to cause a distraction, enough to get the guards at the fort to investigate, but not be spotted or caught. All of them wore hoods and masks, and thus the guards shouldn't be able to identify them, but... Niara shivered. That was why she and Enlil had the riskier part of the job, rescuing Ovil and Pascal. They were strangers here, and leaving, so it wouldn't matter if they were identified.

"Hey," Enlil's voice was no more than a whisper. Niara looked up into his comforting blue eyes as he placed a hand on her shoulder. "We can do this."

Niara nodded, forcing her muscles to relax. His hand was warm on her shoulder against the freezing chill of the night.

Shouts echoed from the forest, and the guards at the fort immediately straightened. One of them shouted, and more soldiers came running out of the fort, right into three arrows dropping three soldiers where they stood.

Niara watched, waiting tensely for the moment when the gate would be unguarded.

"Attack!" The soldiers drew their swords, ignoring the bodies of their dead comrades. A bell began to toll from the fort, and more soldiers arrived as another three arrows flew into the crowd.

Niara held her breath. *Come on, chase them...*

The soldiers appeared undecided about whether to chase into the dark night, however. Niara wrapped her arms around herself, whispering a prayer to anyone who would listen, Mazda, the Lady, crazy or not.

It seemed like an eternity, though it couldn't have been more than a minute, before a golden-haired woman walked out of the fort, dressed in only a silk dressing gown. Niara gaped at the woman. Who was she? She held herself with an air of authority, despite her state of undress, and surveyed the soldiers with anger.

"Well, follow them!" she commanded. "Or must I do everything myself?"

"Yes, Umgallu Xana! I mean no, Umgallu Xana!" The group of soldiers started for the tree line, obviously grateful to be given clear orders. They stopped as another group of arrows flew toward them, dropping another two of them.

Umgallu? What does that mean?

She heard Enlil's harsh intake of breath. "What?" she asked.

Enlil's eyes were wide. "That's Xana," he breathed. "Naytar's stone, what is she doing?"

Niara blinked as the information processed. "The dragon?" she asked in disbelief. "That's a human woman."

Enlil shook his head and grabbed Niara's arm. "We need to be ready. We'll have our chance soon." He stared intently at the fort, at the human woman he claimed was a dragon.

"Don't tell me you're afraid of elven shadows," the woman scoffed. She sighed, tossing her hair dramatically. "I suppose I'll just have to show you how it's done."

Niara gasped as the woman's skin began to ripple, as if the torch-light illuminating her had transformed into a river of light. Her hair seemed to grow to cover her entire body, and her form rapidly expanded, causing the soldiers who had been standing too close to rapidly retreat. Her hands elongated to wickedly sharp claws, and her eyes turned the red fire of the sun.

Niara covered her mouth to suppress a scream. Only Enlil's hand on her arm kept her in place, kept her grounded and reminded her of their plan. The dragons weren't supposed to be awake at night! Enlil had said they couldn't see…

"Run!" Xana shouted, her voice echoing in the night. "Run, my little men, and light the way for me!"

The soldiers started moving toward the trees, those with torches holding them high despite their fear. Niara hoped Kishtar and the others would run. They had no chance against a dragon.

Xana roared her satisfaction as the soldiers reached the trees and launched herself into the air, breathing a line of flame at the sky. Enlil's hand tightened on Niara's arm. "Now!" he whispered.

Niara followed him as they ran straight for the gate, heads down, running as quietly as they could. They needed to be fast, to take advantage of the distraction while it remained.

They can change into humans. Niara felt the knowledge repeating over and over in her mind. *They can change into humans. Mazda's light, they can change into humans.*

She took the lead as they burst through the gate. Kishtar and Lyra somehow knew the layout of the fort intimately, and Lyra had drilled the route to where Ovil and Pascal would be held into Niara's mind.

Into the fort. Third door left, then down the stairs. The prisons. They would be guarded still, but with far fewer soldiers now that the distraction was underway. And if they were fast enough…

They ran down the stairs, Niara quicker than Enlil, and Niara nearly ran headlong into a soldier standing at the bottom of the stairs. He stumbled, obviously listening for what was happening above.

Niara stared at him, heart hammering in her throat, as Enlil stumbled down the stairs after her. He took one look at the dumbstruck soldiers and struck him on the side of the head, and he crumbled to the ground like a stone. A glint of stone reflected in the light in Enlil's hand, tinted with the blood of the soldier.

Niara caught her breath, staring at the soldier for another heartbeat more before she saw the keys dangling from his belt. She knelt down and began unbuckling them, her hands shaking in relief as she realized the soldier was alive.

Thank Mazda, I didn't want to kill him, though I don't want him to stop us, either. She stood up, the ring of keys dangling in her hand, and started down the corridor of the dungeon, searching for where Ovil and Pascal were being held. At the opposite end of the corridor, an opening let in glints of starlight and cold air, a place where the dragons could come down to the dungeon and play with their prisoners. *Though now that I know they can take human form, I don't know why they bothered building that.* Niara shivered. *Any of these soldiers could be a dragon in disguise.*

They passed empty cells, those left with only charred bones, and those with blood still fresh on the floor. Niara shivered at the sight of iron shackles dangling from the walls in every cell, and other iron implements that she had no desire to know the actual use for. Most of the cells were empty, however, and only near the end did she find one with two men, their hands shackled well above their heads.

"Here!" she whispered to Enlil.

The two men looked up as the key turned in the lock, and their faces reflected confusion and hope when they saw Niara and Enlil instead of soldiers. Niara put a hand to her lips, and they nodded in understanding. She eyed the shackles warily, locked above her reach, but Enlil took the keys from her, dragged a short stool over, and unlocked the shackles. The two men stood, rubbing their wrists waiting for her direction.

"Hurry," she whispered. She ran back the way they had come, heart beating in her chest, hoping Kishtar had managed not to get caught, hoping the gate was still unguarded, hoping the dragon hadn't decided to burn everything to the ground in vengeance...

She saw no soldiers at the gate as they exited the fort. Hope lightening her step, she ran forward, and they were out of the gate before a shout sounded from behind them. Niara risked a glance behind her and saw five soldiers following them out the gate, weapons raised.

We're not armed! Niara felt a flare of panic. They had to try to outrun them.

Enlil shoved her forward. "Go! I'll distract them!"

Niara wanted to protest, but Ovil and Pascal ran ahead without needing encouragement, and Enlil grinned at her, his eyes sparkling. She swallowed her words and followed them. "This way!" she whispered.

Third tower on the right. Mazda's light, I hope Kishtar and the others move fast. She heard the pounding feet of the two men behind her, and she skidded to a halt as they reached the tower, looking over her shoulder, searching for Enlil.

"Here," she gasped, gesturing at the ground.

The two men obviously were familiar with the hidden escape routes, and they immediately started digging at the ground with their hands to uncover the hidden hatch. It was only hidden by a light layer of dirt, and they soon had it open. One jumped down instantly, and the second followed, then paused, gesturing at Niara.

"Come on!" he whispered.

Niara's chest tightened, and she held her breath. *Come on, Enlil.*

A stream of fire broke through the night, and the man cursed and ducked into the tunnel. Niara knew she should follow him, but her feet felt like lead as she stared into the forest, heart hammering. *Come on, Enlil, come on!*

Pounding feet echoed, and Niara jumped as Kishtar and the men who had accompanied him burst through the trees. Kishtar saw her standing there. "Mazda's light, you made it," he whispered. "Ovil and Pascal?"

"Through," Niara whispered. She peered out into the trees again. "Enlil is—"

As if her words summoned him, Enlil emerged from the trees, calm as if he were strolling in the sun during Mazda's Time. "We should go," he said, taking one glance at the people standing around the hatch. "Xana won't be pleased."

A curse escaped Niara's mouth at his understatement, and she followed Kishtar and his men through the tunnel, feeling Enlil's presence behind her. His hand grabbed her arm, and she placed her hand over his, guiding him through the darkness of the tunnel until they emerged into the silent streets of Hillsdale.

Kishtar led the way through the silent town, the men who had helped him with the distraction disappearing into the shadows, and Ovil and Pascal started to lag behind. Twice they had to duck out of the way of passing patrols.

Other than the patrols, the city was deathly quiet, almost eerily so. In most towns, there would always be a few late-night parties, especially in a port city like Hillsdale. Sailors would be celebrating as much time as they could spend on land, and innkeepers and the underclass would be taking full advantage of them.

Not in Hillsdale, however, not tonight. Not anywhere across Saemar. The dragons had a curfew in effect for anyone who wasn't a sworn member of their army. No one was allowed on the streets on pain of death.

Maybe it's because of their poor night vision, Niara thought. *If I had a weakness like that, I'd probably take steps to guard against it too.*

Finally, they were at the docks, and Kishtar ushered them across a gang plank to the boat. Niara recognized the boat from her trip north, but she was still surprised when he led them down into the hold and pressed a small button, revealing a hidden hatch which led even deeper.

"We're here, Mirri," he whispered.

Mirri's head poked up through the hatch, and she gasped in relief. "Thank Mazda," she whispered. "You're safe!"

"Everyone get down there," Kishtar whispered. "We'll be out fishing tomorrow, but you need to stay quiet until then."

Niara followed Ovil, Pascal, and Enlil down into the lower hold. Kishtar caught her arm and gave her a reassuring nod, and she smiled back at him.

Her smile faded as she viewed the darkness of the hold, illuminated only by a small lantern. It was cramped, but Kishtar and Lyra had obviously done their best to make it comfortable.

I should be elated. We succeeded in a rescue, against a dragon. A dragon. But Mazda's light, dragons can turn into humans. How are we supposed to defend against that?

6

———

EASTWARDS

Stay safe, Niara," Kishtar's expression was serious as he regarded her.

Niara's answer was solemn, but she doubted the truth of her promise. "I will."

Kishtar's eyes flickered toward the bow, where Enlil was talking with Ovil, Pascal, and Mirri. "I think you're in good company," he said. "I wish you knew more about him, but at least you aren't alone."

Niara managed a smile. "It's not like we know much about anyone these days," she said. The memory of the woman turning into a dragon passed before her eyes, and she concealed a wince. *It just isn't fair. How in Mazda's name are we supposed to fight against anything that can do that?*

How could they ever know, unless they had met the person beforehand, that they weren't talking to a dragon in disguise? Or even if they knew the person, could dragons shape-shift into whatever form they wanted, or did they have one set human form, and one set dragon form? How were they ever to find out?

Ah, Mother, I hope you have an answer for me. Niara drew her cloak tighter around herself, shivering in the chill sea wind. Although they

75

were now further south, near the border of Venia, Manyu's Time never let itself be forgotten, keeping the days short and the air cold.

Shan Serin. Niara closed her eyes, fixing a map of Saemar in her mind. Mazda's light, how long was it going to take her? To cross the entire country, and then an unfamiliar distance south into the badlands... Would she make it there by Papsukkal?

I have to, she thought. *I have no choice.*

"Well, are you ready?" Kishtar asked, breaking through her thoughts. "I'm afraid you'll have to swim from here."

Swim. Until now, Niara hadn't fully comprehended the challenge before her. She stared out at the shore. It seemed close, but distances could be deceptive, especially on the water.

Mazda's light, it'll be freezing, she thought. *And I daren't wear my cloak.*

With a sigh, she took off her cloak and bundled it in her small pack of belongings. On the bow, Enlil, Ovil, Pascal, and Mirri had already done the same. "You're a day's walk north of Venia," Kishtar said, "but I wouldn't go there right now if what you said is true. Just head inland a few hours and talk about birds. That's the sign for our contacts. Hopefully, nothing's happened to them."

Niara nodded. She settled her pack on her shoulders, making sure the straps were secure. "You sure you'll be safe?" she asked Kishtar.

Kishtar shrugged, smiling wryly. "Not the first time I've done this trip."

"It won't be the last," Niara predicted. "I—"

Her vision went white, and she sat down hard, just in time for the vision to overtake her.

A tall, intimidating woman was riding through the woods around Hillsdale, surrounded by soldiers. "You will do as I command," she instructed.

The Regular riding next to her bowed his head submissively. "Of course, milady. But the people—"

"The people will obey," the woman said carelessly. "I must go to the capital until it's warm again. You will manage on your own."

The Regular nodded, seeming unhappy. "Of course, milady."

Niara gasped as the vision faded, hope suffusing her chest. "Start the rebellion," she gasped.

"What?" Kishtar started, and Niara realized his hand was grasping her shoulder. "Niara, what do you mean? Are you alright?"

Niara gripped Kishtar's hand, the information beating hard within her chest, like a bird fighting to escape its cage. "You won't have a dragon with you the rest of Manyu's Time. Xana's going to the capital. Organize the rebellion now and try to spread knowledge of it as far as you can. Be ready on Papsukkal."

Kishtar stared at her in disbelief. "How?" he whispered.

Niara tightened her grip on his hand. "Just trust me, Kishtar," she said, surprising herself with her own intensity. "We'll need it." Where the knowledge was coming from, she didn't know, but she was willing to trust her own certainty.

Kishtar nodded slowly. "It'll be harder, now that the rebellion in Venia failed," he said, "but we should be able to manage something. Especially if you're right, and our dragon will be gone."

Niara squeezed his hand one more time before releasing it. "Ovil, Pascal, and Mirri can go to Venia," she stated. "They've been helping you with the rebellions here, right? Then they can continue there."

Kishtar blinked. "I'll let you tell them that," he said. "Somehow, I think it'll sound better coming from you."

"You know them," she pointed out. "I don't."

Kishtar shook his head, and Niara recognized the stubborn line of his jaw. "Trust me on this one, Niara."

Niara glanced back toward the bow, where Pascal, Ovil, and Mirri were waiting with Enlil, all ready to jump into the sea. She swallowed down her uncertainty before walking forward to join them.

She nodded to each of them, hesitating before broaching the subject. "Are you ready to swim?" she asked.

Enlil grinned at her like a lunatic. Pascal and Ovil shrugged, while Mirri shivered and hunched her shoulders.

Niara took a deep breath. "I need to ask a favor of you," she said. "And it could be a big one."

The three of them gazed at her curiously. Niara squared her shoulders, wondering briefly how much they knew about her. They knew she was related to Kishtar, and if they knew anything about where he was from...

"You were organizing the rebellion in Hillsdale, right?" she asked.

The three of them looked at each other before nodding. "Were," Pascal said bitterly.

Niara forced her words out past her fear, the crystalline certainty that this was necessary pushing her forward. "I need you to continue organizing it in Venia," she said.

Pascal and Ovil stared at her like she was mad. Mirri clapped a hand over her mouth in shock.

"You mind telling us why you think such a hare-brained scheme will work?" Pascal said slowly.

Well, at least he asked. Niara paused, formulating her words in her mind. "Because something is going to happen on Papsukkal," she said. "And the cities need to be ready. They're the places most heavily under dragon control right now. They need to be willing to shake them off."

Something is going to happen. Niara held her breath as the three exchanged looks. She could tell Pascal was more than willing to continue, but if Ovil or Mirri tried to talk him out of it...

Mirri. She's the key. Niara couldn't tell how she knew this, just transferred her gaze to Mirri. "Will you help?" she asked quietly. "We can do this. I promise."

Mirri met her gaze, fear warring with hope in her eyes. Niara met her eyes as steadily as she could.

After what seemed like an eternity, Mirri nodded, tears stinging her eyes. "I'll hold you to that," she whispered.

Niara breathed a sigh of relief, the feeling of driving need gone from her throat. She looked at Enlil, who had been watching the exchange with a curious expression. "Ready?" she asked.

He gestured to the water. "Ladies first?"

Niara rolled her eyes and moved to embrace Kishtar one final time, then turned to the edge of the boat. Before she could second-guess herself, she jumped into the water.

The icy sea closed over her head with a shock, and Niara flailed frantically with her arms, fighting her way back to the surface. Her head broke the water just in time to hear another splash behind her, and she saw Enlil's red hair bobbing in the water. Her heart lightened in relief.

She waved once more to Kishtar to let him know she was alright and then started swimming toward shore, conscious of the presence of the other four around her. Mirri, Pascal, and Ovil appeared to be fine swimmers, and Enlil swam like a fish. Niara seemed to be the weakest swimmer of the group.

Well, the others lived in Hillsdale, she told herself. *And Enlil...who knows where he's been.* She glanced over at her traveling companion, conscious again of how very little she knew about him. He caught her glance and grinned at her, apparently oblivious to her thoughts.

Niara couldn't help but smile in return, and she found new strength in her strokes as they paddled closer and closer to shore. She needed the strength. The sea was warmer than the air, at least, but the cold still chilled to the bone. Niara's strength started failing the longer they swam, the icy water sucking the warmth from her body. To her relief, the current helped them as they drew closer, and finally she knelt on the beach, breathing heavily in relief.

Beside her, Mirri, Pascal, and Ovil appeared tired, but by no means exhausted. Enlil, of course, looked like he had enough energy to complete the swim three more times before he grew tired. "What was our way to contact...who are we contacting?" he asked, tilting his head at Niara.

Niara had to laugh. "We walk inland and talk about birds," she said. "They're supposed to find us."

"If they're alive," Ovil muttered. Niara's sharp ears tilted toward Ovil, and she hastily brought her hands to her head, checking her headscarf remained in place. It had been soaked and knocked awry by their swim. She would have to straighten it before continuing. *I can't have them being captured by Auriel's men and telling them I'm an elf. No matter if I trust them or not, I can't trust what they might say.*

Mirri rose to her feet. "Well, the sooner we start, the sooner we can get this over with," she said. Despite her words, a desperate hope shone in her eyes as she gazed inland.

Niara stood up as well, adjusting her headscarf as best she could without taking it off her head. "You're right," she said. "Let's go."

"Who are you, and why are you here?" The man leveled a spear in Niara's direction, mistrustfulness in his gaze.

Niara met his eyes squarely, refusing to be intimidated by the spear. "We came from the north," she said. "Surely you know better than to inquire further?"

The man didn't back down. Nor did he have any reason to. Despite Niara's assumed boldness, they were surrounded by a group of at least ten, and there were twice as many hidden in the trees if the sounds her ears were picking up were accurate. Pascal, Ovil, and Mirri huddled close together behind Niara, unsure of what to make of the inhospitable welcome. Only Enlil appeared to be completely at ease, regarding the spokesman of the group with undisguised curiosity.

"No one's used the signal for weeks," the man snapped. "I have to know where you learned it from."

Niara suppressed herself from growling at him. It had been hours since they'd swum ashore, and she was tired, cold, and hungry. "From my brother," she said, fighting to keep her voice even. "Kishtar Hollstein."

"Your brother?" the man seemed startled, even shocked. "Kishtar has a sister?"

Niara pressed her lips together, unwilling to elaborate on the story. The lie had served her well in Hillsdale, so she was not about to change it.

The man's eyes narrowed. "How do we know you're telling the truth?" he demanded.

Niara nearly bit her tongue to keep harsh words from escaping. "How do we know you're the ones we're supposed to meet?" she demanded. "We left Kishtar a few hours ago, from his boat off the coast. Now we're tired, damp, and hungry, and not in the mood to justify ourselves."

The man opened his mouth to retort, but another man placed his hand on his arm, stopping whatever words before they were spoken. "I think she's telling the truth, Ren," he said.

The first man, Ren, cast an uncertain glance at the other. "What makes you say that?" he asked.

The second man regarded Niara. "Because while I don't remember Kishtar having a sister, I do remember who he lived with. And that includes someone he would have called sister."

Niara held her breath as Ren met her gaze, first confused, then his eyes widened in realization. She stared at him, willing him not to say anything, not to reveal her secret in front of strangers. And in front of Enlil...

"My name's Nia," she said quickly. "And I am Kishtar's sister." She met Ren's eyes squarely as she spoke, trying to acknowledge the lie with her eyes, pleading with him to accept it.

Ren looked at the second man again, then nodded slowly, lowering his spear. The rest of the men surrounding them followed suit, and Niara felt her shoulders relax. She hadn't realized how tense she'd been.

"You'd best come with us," Ren said. "It isn't fully safe here." He began striding into the forest. The other men followed, barely waiting for the five fugitives to overcome their shock and start following.

"Well, that was interesting," Enlil said. His voice seemed almost cheerful.

Niara rolled her eyes. "Interesting is not the word I'd use," she grumbled.

Ahead of her, Mirri slowed to walk by her side. "They have good reason to be mistrustful," she said. "If the rebellion in Venia failed, then their existence is in jeopardy, even more so than usual. It's not a safe world anymore."

Niara refrained from answering that she knew, and that was the reason she wasn't revealing her identity to anyone, why she had to travel as secretly as possible. She kept quiet, however. To answer would be to reveal more about her journey than she wanted to.

To her relief, it took only a short time before they were at the entrance to a cavern. Niara grimaced as she regarded the opening, reminded of the entrance to Ellriheim. As safe as that place had been, it had still felt more like a prison than a home.

Enlil gave her a curious look as she hesitated, letting the others precede her into the cave. She shook herself and started moving, ignoring the chill that went down her spine as they descended into blackness. At least it wasn't as deep as Ellriheim. On the other hand, it wasn't nearly as well-lit. Only two torches hung bracketed to the walls of the cavern, providing dim, flickering light. Furniture existed, some battered chairs and stools, and plenty of warm furs draped over everything.

"Well, *Nia*," Ren emphasized her name. "What can we do for you? Dare I hope you bring word of a plan?"

Niara let the sarcasm in his voice wash over her. "Yes," she said shortly. "We have a plan. These three need to go to Venia, and Enlil and I need to head east. Another rebellion is being planned, and word of it needs to spread as far as it can before Papsukkal."

The silence which greeted her pronouncement was profound. Ren sat down on a rickety chair, laughing silently. Niara pressed her lips together, anger growing inside her. She kept silent, however, waiting for someone, anyone to speak.

Finally, Ren shook his head. "We can bring the three to Venia," he said. "But a rebellion? That's impossible. You haven't heard of what happened there, have you?"

Niara closed her eyes, the memory of the vision flickering behind her eyelids. "All those suspected of being rebels were brought outside the city walls. It didn't matter if they had proof, and a good number were those the guards had grudges against. They were immolated by dragon fire." She tried to state her words as simple facts, but her voice trembled slightly. She opened her eyes and met Ren's gaze.

Ren stared at her before nodding. "Then you know we can't

convince anyone to rebel again," he said. "They've been frightened out of their wits. We can't ask more of them."

"We have to," Niara said, feeling familiar desperation. "Something is going to happen on Papsukkal, and if the people aren't ready for it, it will fail."

"Something?" Ren's eyes sharpened. "Mind sharing?"

Frustration made Niara's voice sharp. "I can't," she snapped. "All I can do is follow the plan."

"The plan?" When Niara didn't answer, Ren shook his head. "I can't help you, lady. The people of Venia are too cowed to fight against the dragons."

"Use them as martyrs," Enlil's quiet voice interrupted Niara's rising anger and frustration.

Ren appeared just as startled. "What?" he asked.

Enlil blinked. "The people who died. They're martyrs," he said. "They died in a noble cause so that others could live free. Don't let their sacrifice be in vain. The dragons don't understand martyrs; they don't understand the willingness to keep fighting when all seems lost. They won't be expecting another rebellion so soon after a failed one."

The confidence Enlil projected was unshakable. Niara held her breath, looking from Enlil to Ren in silent anticipation, waiting for his answer.

Mazda's light, he would convince me, she thought. *Though I barely need convincing. That information about the dragons, though... I wish I had his sources of information.*

Ren stared at Enlil for another long moment, then nodded slowly. "We could work with that," he said. He glanced around. "What do you think?" he asked another man, the same man who had said he knew who Niara was.

The man inclined his head. "We can't live like this forever," he said. "Might as well fight or die."

Niara winced at the grimness of his words, but the people in the cavern straightened and lost their darkened expressions.

"Right," confidence filled Ren's voice now that he had made his decision. "We'll take your friends down to Venia tonight. You and your friend will have to wait until tomorrow. There's a patrol coming through, and we want to make sure it passes before we head east."

Niara felt herself relax in sudden relief. "Thank you," she said.

Ren snorted. "Thank me at Papsukkal, if this 'something' of yours happens," he said.

Niara shook her head, unable to assuage his fears any more than she already had.

Enlil cleared his throat. "Now that that's settled, I don't suppose you have any extra rations, do you?" he asked. "You see, we're a bit hungry…"

Ren barked a laugh, and the tension in the room broke. Someone offered Niara a chair, and she sat down as others went to prepare food.

She gave Enlil a grateful look as he sat down beside her. "Thank you," she said. "I don't know if I could have—" she broke off, unable to continue.

Enlil shrugged easily. "It seemed like the right thing to do." His eyes twinkled. "But I'm sure you could have managed, oh lovely one. You do have a way with people."

A blush stained Niara's cheeks, and she impulsively leaned over to playfully slap Enlil's shoulder. He grinned at her.

Her heart jumped. *Careful, Niara,* she warned herself. *You still know nothing about him. And you've a long journey ahead.*

Niara wrapped her cloak around herself, trying to ignore the light snowflakes that drifted down through the trees. They were nearing the road that ran from Venia to the capital, and although it would be dangerous to stay on it, it was the best landmark for Enlil and Niara as they traveled east.

East toward the capital, and then we need to head southeast. Without crossing into Tigri. Niara suppressed a shudder. She remembered what the border of Tigri had been like before Auriel's rise. She hated to think what it would be like now.

Andreas had already raped and pillaged that land, in the hopes of conquering it. Mazda's light, how much of an idiot was he? He had to have realized killing commoners was not the way to endear himself to the local population.

Niara bit her lip, shoving those thoughts aside. If she wasn't careful, she would begin to think Auriel had done Saemar a favor by sacrificing the king for his ascension to godhood.

In front of her, Ren stopped, raising a hand for silence. Niara crept forward as silently as she could, wondering what had caught his attention.

Ren gestured ahead of them, and Niara strained her eyes to see through the light mist. She heard the sounds before she saw them. Footsteps, many of them. A large group of people.

Mazda's light. She cursed soundlessly and saw her feelings mirrored on Ren's face. Beside Ren, Enlil grimaced and shrugged.

A large group of people could only be Regulars or other servants of the dragons. They didn't dare go any closer to the road.

Enlil gestured, first toward Ren, then back in the direction they had come from. Ren gestured questioningly at Niara and Enlil. Enlil pointed eastward and mimed walking.

Ren scowled and shook his head. He looked to Niara, and gestured at all of them, signaling his desire to move together.

Niara furrowed her brow in thought. The original plan had been for Ren to lead them to the road, then head south to Venia, where he would help with the rebellion. That had been before the soldiers, however. Then again, where would the soldiers be except the road? They had to be close.

She nodded her agreement to Enlil, then pointed at Ren, then back the way they had come. Ren frowned again but made no further protest. Niara nodded her thanks at him, and he shrugged before disappearing into the trees.

Niara found herself sighing in relief. *One less innocent I'm responsible for. Though I could very well have just sent him to his death in Venia.* She pushed that cheerful thought to the side. She had other things to worry about.

Enlil smiled at her and reached out to grab her hand. Niara managed a smile in return as she took his hand, following him eastward into the forest. She could still hear the soldiers camped on the side of the road, so they made no sound as they crept as silently as they could through the undergrowth, avoiding twigs and roots to their best ability. Enlil moved through the underbrush with an ease that reminded Niara of a fox.

She felt strangely relaxed as they strolled hand in hand through the forest. Despite the tension of the soldiers nearby, despite the danger surrounding them, and despite the fate of the world apparently sitting on her shoulders, she almost felt safe.

That illusion was shattered the moment they entered a clearing. Enlil's hand tightened on hers, and she looked up, horrified as her eyes met those of a red-eyed, tall, black-scaled dragon. He seemed to have been resting, but he drew himself up as he spotted them.

"Well, what do we have here?" he asked, a low, powerful voice which rumbled across the clearing. "Lost lambs returning to the fold?"

Dragon. Panic rose to her throat. Why hadn't her Sight warned her? There were plenty of trees, she should have been able to see, she should have been keeping watch…

The dragon let out a roar, and his black wings spread above them in awesome majesty. Belatedly, Niara turned on her heel to run, Enlil's hand still clutched in her own.

She barely made it five steps before she was confronted by Regulars running through the forest. She skidded to a halt, heart pounding in her throat as the dragon breathed hot air down her back.

In her panic, she could only remember the trial with the nephelm three years earlier. There she had fought an illusion of a dragon with her brother, using the Swaying and Thalion fighting. This was different, however. The dragon stood much bigger, and he had Regulars on his side.

"Naytar's stone," Enlil said flatly.

Desperately, Niara tried to reach inside her, to reach the magic of her blood. She didn't know what she would be able to do, she didn't know if she could even begin to fight against this many…

Enlil squeezed her hand tight. "We'll get out of this," he whispered. "Let them think we're helpless. We'll escape."

Distracted, Niara lost her grip on the Swaying. It spun out of her grasp as the Regulars surrounded them, their burgundy uniforms standing out in the rainy mist.

"Hands on your head," the leader of the Regulars snapped.

It took every ounce of Niara's willpower to follow his directions, especially when the soldier tore her cloak from her shoulders and forced her to relinquish her pack. Beside her, Enlil was getting similar treatment.

We have no story, she thought in horror. *What are we going to say? What if they separate us? We'll have different stories…*

The elaborately dressed man strode from behind them, not a hair on his head seemingly touched by their brief flight through the woods. He regarded Niara briefly, dismissing her as unimportant before turning to Enlil. Enlil kept his eyes downcast, avoiding looking up into the dragon's eyes.

"So. What are two lost wanderers doing in my woods?" he asked.

Niara bit her lip as Enlil blinked, slowly raising his eyes to meet the dragon's. "Traveling, m'lord," he said simply.

The dragon rolled his eyes. "Traveling to where, sheep?"

"Home, m'lord," Enlil said simply.

It wasn't difficult for Niara to keep an expression of fright on her face. She had no idea what Enlil thought he was doing. She could so easily see how his answers would start to anger the dragon.

The dragon sighed. "Two lost strays," he said. "Sort them out, captain. We can deal with them properly in Venia."

Niara swallowed her protest in her throat. Venia was in the wrong direction! They needed to go east, not west!

Stop it, Niara! she scolded herself. *Be glad you're still alive! You can figure out how to escape, and then move east!*

She forced herself not to resist as three Regulars came toward her, ready to bind her hands. One of them seemed bored, but the other two seemed wide-eyed and excited.

Fresh soldiers, she mentally categorized them. *This must be their first posting. They're still excited, thinking it's all wonderful and new.*

"Hey, didn't your girl want a new scarf?" one of them asked as he took Niara's hands and held them behind her. "That's a nice one."

Panic flared as she saw one of the Regulars eyeing her headscarf speculatively. Her hair was bound back in a braid. If he removed it, there would be no concealing her ears.

"Yes, she was," he said. "I don't think she'll mind where it came from."

As he reached for her headscarf, Niara reacted instinctively, twisting away from him, elbowing the other in the stomach, and then running flat-out toward the woods. Her scarf slipped as she started running, and she held one hand on it, hastily keeping it in place as she escaped.

"Stop her!" she heard the dragon roar. She didn't look around as she heard more shouts and orders, heard pounding feet behind her. She jumped over logs and roots, blessing her split skirt, trying desperately to find a place she could slip out of sight, where she could hide while they exhausted themselves, where she could escape...

A body slammed into her, and she tumbled to the ground, her hand slipping from her scarf as she tried instinctively to save herself. Another body joined the first, and she felt her scarf fall from her head. She scrabbled wildly, trying to break the Regulars' hold, but another set of hands joined and hauled her to her feet. She still fought hard, until one of them elbowed her in the stomach, forcing the air out of her lungs and making her eyes water in pain. In her shock, the Regulars were able to manhandle her arms behind her and tie them together.

"Stop!" the dragon's voice rang out.

Niara's heart sank as the Regulars froze, their grips on her arms remaining tight. There was nowhere for her to turn as the dragon walked through the trees, his red eyes amused as he regarded Niara.

"Well, well," he said as he approached Niara. "This is certainly unexpected!"

Niara put all the force of her fear and disappointment into her glare. The dragon gave a dark chuckle, and she flinched back as he brought his face level to hers, giving her an excellent look at his numerous sharp teeth as the hot air of his breath passed over her.

"Unexpected indeed," he said. "An elf. Izila will want to hear about this personally."

It would do no good to protest she was only part-elf, so Niara kept silent, continuing her glare. The dragon laughed, a laugh that sounded more like a roar. It made Niara tremble, and the soldiers holding her seemed no less affected.

"Change of plans, men," the dragon said. "We're returning to the capital. We have a prize to present."

The dragon turned, knocking a tree sideways with his body, and Niara was dragged back toward the clearing, where several Regulars were pointing swords at Enlil's throat, despite him being tied and held by other Regulars. When he saw Niara's bared ears, his eyes widened, but other than that he betrayed no surprise.

"Tie her up and put her in the wagon," the dragon said. "Then tie him behind. He can walk to the capital."

"The capital?" one of the Regulars dared to speak up. "But my lord, weren't we heading to Venia to suppress—"

The dragon's head swung suddenly, and the Regular who had spoken went as pale as ice. "Are you questioning my orders?" the dragon's voice was as silky as a spiderweb.

The Regular swallowed and shook his head. "I—no, my lord," he said.

The dragon smiled a wicked smile that sent chills down Niara's spine. "Good," he said. "To the capital."

Niara felt herself pushed forward, and she moved unresistingly, still trying to process the reveal of her secret.

They know. Enlil knows, she thought. Her heart pounded in her chest as she tried to determine the consequences. *We're heading to the capital. Mazda's light, what will happen to us?*

7

MARKED

Niara curled into a ball on the bottom of the supply wagon, the only comfortable position her bound hands and feet afforded her. She took deep, measured breaths, forcing her body to remain calm, not to panic, to think. It had been days since their capture, and they were getting close to the capital.

Around her, the soldiers were oddly silent. They marched without talking to each other, without chatting. Part of that may have been because of the occasional rush of wingbeats as the dragon flew overhead. Niara refused to glance up. She didn't want to see her captor.

I need to get out of here, she thought. She grimaced. *Mazda's light, I can't go to the capital, especially not as a prisoner. That's where Auriel is. I can't let him discover me.*

She swallowed. *What if he already knows where I am? He is a god. The Lady would have no difficulty finding me, and she's always denied her godhood. Then again, I am pledged to her as an Eye...*

She shook her head. Those thoughts were pointless and unlikely to help her now. If Auriel had learned where she was, there was nothing she could do about it.

Enlil grunted, and Niara knew without looking he had stumbled in his forced march behind the cart. Since they'd been captured, he had remained utterly silent, not even to respond to the soldiers urging him to walk faster. They'd been kept apart at night, unable to talk, unable to form an escape plan.

What does he think of me? Not for the first time, the thought crossed Niara's mind. He had shown no reaction in front of the soldiers, but that meant nothing.

At least I didn't lie to him. I didn't tell him the truth, but at least I didn't lie. What did most people even think of the elves, anyway? They had been hardly seen in Saemar before Auriel's rise. Ninaeva had been the largest concentration of them, and there had barely been a few dozen who lived at Ilhelm Castle.

Do people even know about the massacre in Alfheim?

Niara forced her thoughts away from those memories and focused again on her current situation. If there hadn't been the dragon…

If there wasn't the dragon, I would use what I learned in Utgard and set the whole lot of soldiers on fire, she thought, her chest tightening. *I could do it now, I know I could. I didn't want to kill in Hillsdale, but I could do it now.* The thought made her slightly sick, but she ignored her nausea. *Enlil would be able to get me out when I collapsed with exhaustion. But there's the dragon.*

She suppressed a grunt of her own as the wagon rolled over a pothole and her hip banged against the side. *I'm going to end up with more bumps and bruises from this ride.* She swallowed. Hopefully, bumps and bruises were the worst she'd get from this.

The wagon stopped abruptly, and Niara winced as she banged into the side of the wagon again. The soldiers started talking in low voices, moving around. Niara blinked. It was beginning to get dark. *We must be stopping for the night.* She felt a flare of relief. Stopping for the night meant they weren't going to reach the capital that day. Though it did mean once again watching the soldiers eat their fill while only being given a crust of bread herself.

There was a huge rush of wings, and the black form of the dragon swept down. Niara could barely see the top of its back over the side of the wagon.

"Continue as planned," the dragon ordered. "I will see you at the gates in the morning. If you're not there..." he trailed off, his voice dangerous.

"Yes, Umgallu Sirax! I mean, no, Umgallu Sirax! We will be there." The soldier stammered his reply.

"Good," the dragon spoke in a pleased tone. Niara winced as a rush of air passed over her, and heard the thumping wingbeats grow more and more distant. She held her breath. Could it be? Was the dragon truly leaving them alone for the night?

"Get him in there and out of the way," a soldier snapped. A few seconds later, Enlil grunted, and Niara saw him being thrust into the wagon with her, his feet now bound the same as hers. He raised an eyebrow at her, obviously attempting to make light of the situation.

"How is your traveling accommodation? As satisfactory as mine?"

Niara managed a slightly hysterical laugh. "Oh, better, I'm sure," she said. Her stomach rumbled, and she grimaced. "Do you think the food will match the accommodation?"

"Shut up," a soldier hissed at them. Niara swallowed as she saw the glint of bared metal at the edge of the wagon, and realized the soldier was pointing his sword at them.

Enlil shook his head, and the two of them fell silent. Around them, the sounds of soldiers setting up camp continued. Eventually, one walked by the wagon, tossed a few scraps of bread in, and left a small bucket of water at the end of the wagon. Niara reached for it as best she could with her bound hands, Enlil doing the same. The bread was hard and stale, but it would keep hunger from overwhelming them, and the water was a welcome relief.

"Light a fire," one of the soldiers ordered. He continued, naming various soldiers and their watches for the night, but Niara's thoughts stumbled to a halt, caught by an idea.

Fire. One of the easiest of the elements. I can make their fire go out of control, and then it'll seem natural. And when everyone's in a panic, I can burn our bonds. It would hurt...but it would be worth if it they could escape.

She turned toward Enlil, who now lay facing the sky, eyes closed. "Enlil," she whispered.

Enlil's eyes opened, and he regarded her with a curious expression.

Niara felt her mouth dry. "Midnight," she whispered. "I have a plan."

To her relief, he did not ask her any questions, just nodded, although his expression made his curiosity plain.

Niara laid back, ignoring her rumbling stomach. A crust of bread a day could not sustain her. At least they didn't stint on the water, though it rankled to drink from the same buckets as the horses. She listened to the crackling of the fire as the world settled into sleep, darkness creeping over the camp and most of the soldiers bedding down. One remained at the foot of the wagon, eyes still alert, alternating between watching her and Enlil and monitoring the camp.

Wait, Niara told herself. *You're only going to have one chance at this.* She'd never tried to do magic while her hands were bound, and she wasn't fully convinced she could. But she had to try. She had no other choice. She couldn't afford to be taken to the capital. If Auriel got his hands on her, he would kill her. But not before he forced her to reveal everything she knew about those dearest to her, so he could kill them too.

She waited while the hours crept by, pretending to sleep so that the guard at the foot of the wagon would relax. Beside her, she couldn't tell if Enlil actually slept or not. His eyes were closed, and his breathing measured, but he could have been faking it, just like she was. His hair fell untidily around his face, and she felt an urge to run her hands through it, to see if it felt as soft as it appeared.

Concentrate, Niara, she told herself. Above, she saw the moon rise in the sky, a bare sliver of silver, starting to reach the highest point in its peak. Midnight.

Cautiously, she moved her bound feet over just enough to tap Enlil's leg. His eyes flew open at once, and he looked at her with a questioning expression.

She nodded, trying to reassure him, then took a deep breath and reached inside, feeling for the power she knew was there. The fire in the camp called to her, and she reached out easily, adding her power to its own.

An explosion rent the air, the fire exploded in a whoosh of flame. Bits of fire rained down, lighting the surrounding grass and trees, some of them hitting the sleeping soldiers, if her hearing was accurate. Shouts of alarm immediately began to ring out, and the soldier at the foot of the wagon disappeared, drawn to the crisis.

That's done. Now, much smaller. Niara focused on the rope binding her wrists, willing a small spark into existence. Tiny flames danced around her hands, and she shook off the charred remains of her bonds with a muffled gasp of pain.

"There's a knife in my boot," Enlil whispered.

Much easier. Niara reached for his boot, barely having to fumble in the dark. The illumination from the fire made it easy for her eyes to pick out small details, like the gleam of a bone-handled knife. In moments she drew it out and slashed the ropes around his ankles, then released the rest of their bonds.

Enlil took the knife back from her with a nod. "Let's go," he said. He lifted his head up, then swung over the side of the wagon, dropping out of sight. Niara followed him, landing unsteadily on her feet. Enlil's arm was there to hold her, and then he pulled her off, away from the camp.

Behind them, the shouts of the soldiers were still unorganized, but someone, presumably the leader, had awoken. "You idiots!" he roared. "What did you do?"

Niara suppressed her pang of fear as she followed Enlil deeper into the woods. She was barely paying attention to where he was leading her, and she stumbled into a branch as Enlil walked straight into a tree.

"Naytar's stone!" Enlil cursed under his breath. "Niara, you have to lead."

Niara reached out to grab Enlil's hand, carefully picking her way through the trees. The further they got away before the soldiers discovered their escape, the better chances they would have.

We need to keep going, but we need to hide before morning, she thought.

The Regulars are going to notice we're gone soon, and they're going to do their best to find us so they don't have to report to their dragon that they allowed an elf to escape. We need a cave, someplace concealed, where we can hide.

She stopped, and Enlil nearly ran into her. She squeezed his hand and shook her head, forbidding him from asking any questions. Before she could second guess her own impulse, she reached inward and out, her sight skipping along the trees ahead of them.

A cave, that's all we need. Just a cave...

A small opening, right by the banks of a stream, entrance half-covered by leaves and vines. Perfect. East.

Niara tried to draw her vision back, but was sucked further and she felt herself stumbling. *A volcano, in the middle of the desert. Fire spitting toward the sky. Two figures fighting each other, laughing and dancing.*

A lone elf hunter moving through the forest, bow in hand, stag's antlers rising from his head. He met her gaze with a wry smile.

Three dragons, flying in lazy circles around each other. A fourth, larger, swooping in and roaring in triumph. A fifth, smaller, streaking away, hiding from the others.

Niara gasped and blinked, finally wrenching her vision back to the present. Enlil's arms were around her, and he looked down in concern.

"Niara? Niara, we have to keep moving!" he whispered.

Niara could still hear the shouts of soldiers behind them. Whether their absence had been discovered yet, she couldn't tell. "Follow me," she breathed.

Hand in hand, they moved through the forest, Niara picking up the pace as the trees cleared, and slowing down when the density increased. Enlil stumbled and cursed, but the small moon provided all the light she needed, and she led them unerringly to where she knew her vision had been.

She nearly stumbled herself as she stepped into a small stream, and she drew back quickly, not wanting to let the water soak through her boots. She glanced upstream and let out a sigh of relief as she spotted a veil of leaves. *We found it.*

And they were just in time, for she could see the forest lightening, signaling the arrival of dawn. Enlil wasn't stumbling as much, but his expression remained confused as she headed toward what to him, had to seem to be just a group of plants.

Niara didn't pause to explain, just brushed aside the vines with her free hand and stepped inside, drawing him behind her. She heard him gasp as they entered a small cave, barely big enough for the two of them to stand up in, but perfect for hiding.

Niara collapsed to the ground, panting in exhaustion. All her adrenaline had run out, and the only thing she wanted to do now was sleep.

Enlil collapsed on the floor next to her, but he didn't appear sleepy in the least. He smiled wryly at her. "Well, now I know three of your secrets," he said.

Niara stared at him warily, trying to read his expression. Was he upset at her? What was he going to do?

Then she frowned. "Three?" she asked.

Enlil nodded. "One, you're an elf. Since there's a reward for elves brought to the capital, I completely understand why you hid that. Two, you're a sorceress. Also understandable. Three, you're completely amazing, beautiful, talented, and cool under pressure. Don't know why you kept that one from me."

Despite herself, Niara felt laughter bubbling up inside her. *Well, he can't be that upset if he's still flirting with me.*

"I'm only part-elf," she said. "My mother was half-elven."

Enlil raised his eyebrows. "If you don't mind my saying so, you look fairly full-blooded to me," he said.

Niara shrugged, suddenly uncomfortable. "I don't know who my father is," she said.

"Ah," Enlil's voice filled with understanding. He remained silent for a while, before saying, "I don't know who my father is, either."

Niara closed her eyes, somehow unbearably grateful that he understood, that he wasn't going to press... "Enlil, there's more," she said, the words tumbling out of her almost without thought. "I'm not just part-elf, I'm—"

Quicker than she could follow, Enlil rolled over and pressed a finger to her lips, silencing her. His blue eyes met hers, clear and intense. A ghost of a smile flitted behind them.

"Don't tell me," he said. "Not here, not now. Not until we're safe, or you decide I need to know."

Niara caught her breath, her eyes stinging. Somehow, his declaration only made her want to trust him even more.

Enlil shook his head, and she subsided.

He's probably right. What if we get captured again, and they ask him questions about me? What if someone tries to trick him into revealing information? What he doesn't know, he can't reveal... She shuddered. She knew there was more than one way to get someone to talk.

Enlil sat back, and for the first time, she saw something other than amusement in his eyes, something darker, rather like...fear? "Don't misunderstand," he said. "I want you to tell me. But before you do," he reached out and squeezed her hand, "I want to be able to tell you mine first. And right now, I just can't."

Niara swallowed her disappointment. "Why not?" She wanted to kick herself, for asking the question.

"Because I don't know how you'd take it," Enlil said, surprising her. "Not yet."

She stared at him, knowing her questions were written clear upon her face. Enlil smiled at her, a wry, sad smile that spoke volumes of understanding, but he made no attempt to explain any further.

"We should get some sleep while we can," he said. "We'll want to stay here all day, at least. Maybe for a few days, until they stop looking for us. At the very least, we'll want to start moving by night for a while."

Niara forced herself to respond casually, to ignore the rising mix of questions she had about Enlil. "You're right." Her stomach grumbled, and she suppressed a groan. "We also need to find some food. All our provisions are with the soldiers."

Enlil raised an eyebrow. "And our weapons as well, except for my dagger. Unless you can do something with your fire?"

She blinked, caught by surprise. "I don't know," she said. "I've never tried anything like that before." She thought. "I probably could kill something, provided I could see it. It might be a bit charred, however."

"Then we won't need to cook it," he grinned. "Can you survive until evening?"

Her stomach rumbled again, and she firmly told it to be silent. "I can," she said. "You're right, it'll be safer then."

Enlil nodded. "Then let's sleep." He lay down, and to all appearances drifted instantly into sleep.

Niara stared at him for a moment longer before curling up into a comfortable position. *Who are you, Enlil? And what do you want with me?*

Niara lay still and quiet, holding her breath as she watched the rabbit in front of her, poking his nose through the undergrowth. It looked so cute, but the rumbling of her stomach prevented any more thoughts of that kind.

She reached out, fighting a wave of dizziness, and fire sprung up around the rabbit. It tried to flee, but the fire followed it, singing its fur until it keeled over and died.

Niara quenched the flames with a thought and sat back, breathing heavily. She blinked, trying to steady her vision. Enlil grinned at her. "Well done," he said, and moved forward to retrieve her kill. As he walked back toward her, he examined it. "And by well done, I mean perfectly cooked. Smells wonderful." He withdrew his knife and started skinning and gutting it.

Niara waited, prickling with impatience. The dim rays of sunlight were fast disappearing, and she was acutely aware she hadn't eaten a true meal for days. When Enlil handed her a leg, she tore into it with an alacrity that would have been shameful for the heir of Ninaeva.

Another leg later, and she glanced up to find Enlil watching her. She paused, flushing. What was he doing?

"I don't know why I didn't see it before," Enlil said as if answering her unspoken thought. "Now that you aren't hiding your ears, it's perfectly obvious. The rest of your face is elven, especially your eyes."

Niara focused her attention on her food. "Most people don't know what they see," she said. "They aren't expecting to see an elf."

"Maybe they weren't," Enlil said. He sighed. "Now that they know there's an elf around, however, they'll be on the lookout."

Niara shrugged. "We'll stay off the road," she said. "Cut directly southeast." It would take longer, but if it eliminated their risk of capture, then it would be worth it.

"Hmm." Enlil appeared unconvinced. "We can try it."

Niara closed her eyes, trying to remember what was to the southeast. "We'll pass through old Duskryn territory," she said. "Then we'll have to cross the river, somehow. If we're not on the road, there won't be a bridge, but we'll have to manage." They'd swum to shore from the sea, after all.

"After the river, there's Lokrian." Niara felt her throat close. Rian Lokris-Phythia, Lady of Lokrian, had been her friend. Was there any possibility she was still alive?

She shoved the hope down, unwilling to face the possibility of it being crushed.

"Lokrian?" Enlil's voice grew thoughtful. "I might know some people there who can help us."

Niara blinked. "How?" she asked. "You're from the north."

Enlil smiled crookedly. "So are you," he said.

Niara felt her chest tightening. *Part of his secrets. Part of what he's not telling you.* She turned aside, trying not to let him see the pain in her expression.

"We should get some more sleep," she said. "We haven't heard any sign of soldiers. Tomorrow should be safe to move."

Enlil nodded, his expression unreadable. Niara rolled to lie on her side and evened her breathing.

She tried to tell herself that Enlil wasn't lying to her, but it was hard. He had admitted he had a secret, one that Niara might have difficulties with. *What kind of secret could that be?* She thought. *It can't be that he's a hill barbarian, I already guessed that. Or that he's working for the nephelm; he swears by the mountain-god often enough that that can't be a secret, either.* She rolled onto her back and stared up at the roof of the cave, gazing blankly at the sharp, jagged edges of rock.

I haven't told him all my secrets, either. I'm not just part-elf, I'm descended from Queen Olvae, a user of the Sight, training to be an Eye. I'm also the heir of Ninaeva, the bastard daughter of Lady Vinet et-Alim of Ninaeva. Auriel wants me dead specifically, for my ancestor's role in binding him, and for fear I'll help bind him again. My Mother is an Eye of the Lady, and she's calling me to Shan Serin for some unknown reason, except that it involves the fate of the world. She sighed, rolling to her other side, and blinked, taking in the scene. She was alone in the cave. Enlil was nowhere to be seen.

Slowly, she got to her feet and looked around. "Enlil?" she said, her voice sounding loud in the silence.

No one answered. Using the dim light of the moon outside as guidance, Niara parted the veil of vines and stepped outside.

The chill night air cut into her bones, and she wrapped her cloak tight around her. A light flurry of snow fell outside the cave. They could only be grateful it hadn't snowed any more than a flurry.

There was no sign of Enlil outside. She stared out into the darkness, attempting to rationalize the situation.

He can't see very well in the darkness, at least, not as well as I can. So where would he be going? What would he be doing?

She swallowed. *What if he's returning to the soldiers? What if he's going to tell them my location in exchange for his own freedom?*

She tried to shake the thought from her mind, but it lodged there, insistent, whispering doubt. *He said he had a secret. And just because he reacted favorably to your secret, doesn't mean he's to be trusted.*

The mix of emotions rising up in her threatened to overwhelm her, and she sat down on a rock, trying to sort them out; strongest of all was an imminent sense of betrayal.

I wanted to trust him! I wanted to...Mazda's light, I wanted to like him. Her heart beat faster, and she clenched her hands into fists. *Be sensible, Niara. You don't know where he is. He could have a perfectly good reason for disappearing.*

What would that reason be? The insidious voice demanded answers, answers she couldn't give.

She glanced back over her shoulder, at the entrance of the cave, and her eyes widened. *It was reliable enough to let me seek this place out,* she thought. *Maybe it will let me seek Enlil out as well.*

She settled back on the rock, breathing deeply to calm herself. The Sight had been behaving much more reliably since she had left Ellriheim. Perhaps she was finally getting control of it.

She reached out for the nearest tree. Pine, from what she could see. Not the safest tree, but not dangerous, either.

For a moment, she could only see leaves, trees, trees, and more trees. She stretched out further, fixing the image of Enlil in her mind. *He can't have gone far.*

She felt a tug on her vision, and she followed it, skipping east across the forest, through fields and woodlands. When she saw a river, she tried to stop, realizing she had gone further than Enlil could possibly have walked. Her vision didn't obey her, however, and she was drawn further and further away.

She fought to ground herself, to reach back toward the trees where she had begun. Whatever drew her had a firm grasp, however, and with a start, she found her vision turning black until she was completely disoriented, with no indication of where she was.

Darkness, so dark that for a moment she couldn't see. She stood, shivering, for a long moment. Gradually, her eyes adjusted, and she saw a lake stretched out before her, small sparks of light reflecting in its water. She was in a giant cave, with no exit readily visible. Small streaks of fire visible on the ceiling provided the light and reflected in the water below.

"Come, child," the voice echoed through the cave. "Come to me."

She took an involuntary step back, trying to see the source of the voice. The cave trembled, and the water rippled, the reflection of fire dancing on the surface.

"Come," the voice said again.

Niara tried to swallow the fear rising inside her. "Who are you?" she demanded.

"I am your lord," the voice said. "Come, child."

"No," Niara whispered. Whoever this lord was, she had no interest in serving anything.

"You will come," the voice sounded amused. "By choice or not, you will."

Her heart beat faster and faster, and she backed up against the wall. Heat scorched the back of her hand as she touched the wall, and she flinched away, clutching her hand to her chest.

"By fire and darkness, you will come," the voice didn't seem angry, didn't seem impatient, just implacable.

"No," Niara whispered again. Her hand stung, but she ignored the pain as her eyes shifted around the cavern, searching for a way out.

The voice laughed. "You will come here," it said. "You have no choice."

The walls began to shake, and Niara stifled a yelp as a boulder fell from the ceiling, splashing into the pool of water. Water flew everywhere, soaking her dress instantly.

Dress? Why was she in a dress, and not her long split tunic and breeches?

Another rumble made her look up again, to see another rock about to fall right above her. She dove to the side, running toward the pool of water. She could see the lines of fire getting bigger, and she splashed into the water, hoping against hope it would keep her safe from the fire.

She gasped as the ice-cold water hit her skin. Above her, she could see the tiniest sliver of light. Sunlight, not firelight.

Hope rose in her chest, only to be dashed. How could she get there? It shone far above her head, far out of reach.

A memory, of herself lifting Thalion into the air with magic, of her floating upward herself. She closed her eyes and twisted, feeling her strength drain away as she drifted upward, out of the water and toward the light.

"Come!" the voice echoed again. Niara felt another flare of panic as she reached the ceiling of the cave, only to find the crack that let the sunlight in was barely wide enough for her hand.

"Come!" the cave trembled again, and Niara thrust her hands forward, gripping the rock in both hands. Magic poured out of her, and a piece of rock dropped, splashing in the water below. With a last burst of strength, she floated upward, squinting in the bright sunlight.

"Good," the voice purred in satisfaction. "Good."

Niara landed heavily on the ground, falling to her knees as her body went *limp. Earth magic was draining, the most draining of all the elemental magics.*

Heat warmed her chilled body, and she looked around, swallowing as she realized she was surrounded by molten rocks, all of them glowing ominously. She still saw no sign of the source of the voice.

She struggled to her feet, holding out a hand to help her balance. It stung, and she winced, remembering the burn. "Let me go," she demanded. "By the Lady of Lake and Leaf, let me go!"

The voice laughed, and the stones trembled remorselessly. "Come to me," it repeated.

"No!" Niara shouted. "No, I will not!"

She flinched as the earth she stood on shook, and molten rock started flowing toward her, threatening with its heat and fire. The voice remained silent, but Niara could sense its presence, an implacable will which forced obedience.

"No, I won't!" Niara whispered. Serving the Lady was one thing, serving an unnamed being who threatened her was something else. "I will not serve you."

"Good," this was a different male voice, calmer, quieter. Niara spun around, to be confronted with an elven man with a hunter's bow and quiver, antlers sprouting from his forehead. "Give me your hand," he said.

Niara stared at the man for a brief moment. She had seen him before, in another vision. That didn't mean he could be trusted.

The man said nothing, only held out his hand to her. The ground rumbled again, and Niara reached out with her right hand, the hand which still burned with fire.

The elf gripped her hand hard, like an iron vice, and she winced in pain. A knife appeared in his other hand, and she barely had time to feel shock and fear before he slashed at her arm, ripping through her sleeve and cutting into flesh. She cried out, more in shock than pain, as blood ran down her arm and dripped onto the ground. She tried to wrench her hand away, but the elf's grip remained firm.

"You have strength and courage," the elf said. He gave her a grim smile. "Keep those." His grip tightened even more on her hand. "Remember me."

Niara didn't think she would ever forget the way his green eyes bored into hers, intent and serious. His eyes flashed, and Niara caught her breath.

"Time for you to return," he said. He reached out to touch her forehead, and the world went black. She spun around, flailing, trying desperately to grab something, anything, but she was falling, flying...

"Niara?"

Her eyes flew open, and she stared into Enlil's concerned eyes, bright blue even in the dark of the night. "Niara, are you alright?" He reached out, touching her arm lightly, and she flinched, a small sound of pain escaping her.

Enlil's eyes widened, but Niara drew her arm back before he could examine it. Pain radiated, not just from her arm, but from the back of her hand.

"Let me." Enlil reached out again, this time taking her arm. Niara took a deep breath as he rolled the torn sleeve back, wincing as she saw the jagged red lines cut into her flesh.

"What is this?" Enlil asked, his voice confused.

Niara looked down. On her arm, right above her wrist, a symbol had been carved, jagged lines shaped vaguely like a stag. A stylized sun had been branded onto the back of her hand.

She shuddered, the entire vision hitting her like a wave. She clutched Enlil's arm with her uninjured hand. "Where were you?" she whispered, hating how desperate her voice sounded.

"I was getting more supplies," he said. "I couldn't sleep, but I didn't want to disturb you." He gestured with his free hand, and Niara saw a small bundle lying on the ground as if it had been thrown there. He shrugged. "It's not much, but it was better than what we had."

Niara felt herself begin to shake, hating herself for her earlier suspicion, that her suspicion had led to her seeking a vision, which had led to...another stab of pain from her hand made her gasp.

"Niara," Enlil's voice was intent. "What's happening? Are you alright?"

She shook her head. "I don't know," she said. "I don't know what these are, or who," she swallowed, "who put them there."

Enlil raised his eyebrows. "If there's anything I can do, just tell me. I will protect you in any way I can."

Niara nodded, the intensity of his words flowing over her like warm water. She tried to stand up and stumbled as her legs rebelled. Enlil caught her, and she leaned forward, drawing comfort from his warm body. He was real, he was an anchor. He wasn't working for Auriel. He would not betray her.

Enlil wrapped his arms around her, saying nothing, only supporting. They stood there for a long moment, Niara taking long, deep breaths, trying to draw the strength to stand on her own.

"Please don't disappear like that again," she managed to whisper.

"Anything you want, Niara," Enlil breathed.

I want you to tell me who you are. Niara bit her lip, unwilling to let the thought escape. She pulled back, taking one last steadying breath. The darkness blanketed the forest, dawn's arrival still hours away.

"We should get some more sleep," she said.

Enlil nodded, his eyes never leaving hers. Niara felt obscurely comforted by his regard as they entered the cave again and she curled up, wrapping her cloak tightly around herself again.

He won't betray me, was her last waking thought before drifting off into sleep at last.

8

LOKRIS-PYTHIA

Red and gold leaves illuminated the forest, streaks of golden sunlight turning the fallen brown leaves into golden rivers on the forest floor. Niara and Enlil walked as quietly as they could, but their silence was comfortable. There had been no sign of the dragon, or pursuing soldiers, for nearly a week. Niara had allowed herself to relax in Enlil's presence, certain now he hadn't betrayed her. His lack of questions about the marks on her hand and arm made her even more comfortable around him.

Not that she didn't want him to ask questions. She did, she also wanted to tell him the answers, wanted to trust him with her secrets, with her life. At least three times a day, she felt words bubbling up to her lips, but she kept them firmly contained, knowing whatever she confided in him, he wouldn't reciprocate. And he wanted to reciprocate, she could see it in his expression when he looked at her, when he thought she wasn't watching him. Whatever it was, it had to be serious, for those were the only times she ever saw his smile dim.

They had been heading steadily southeast, passing through mostly forest, but the forest was starting to thin out. Niara knew they had to be well inside what had been Duskryn territory. Every once in a while, she would swear she remembered some of the forest from one of the several Great Hunts she had participated in.

"Be on the lookout for wolves," she said, keeping her voice low. "They used to live here, if the dragons haven't scared them all away."

Enlil glanced sideways at her but didn't ask where her knowledge came from. "The dragons wouldn't have bothered about the wolves," he said instead. "They probably run even wilder now the human population has been contained."

She didn't ask where his source of information came from, either. She wanted to; the question rested on the tip of her tongue, but she kept her mouth shut. She feared he wouldn't answer her, and the fear of the pain that would cause was more than enough to keep her silent.

They crossed a small stream and followed it as it meandered southeast, through trees which rapidly thinned. Niara paused, memory tingling the back of her mind. She recognized this place.

"I think—" she began.

A twig snapped, and she broke off. She and Enlil exchanged glances, then they rapidly backtracked, heading for a group of bushes that would hopefully conceal their presence.

That wasn't an animal. Certainty filled Niara. Someone else moved in the forest.

She and Enlil huddled together, as quiet as they could in the midst of the bushes. Niara cursed the fact it was Manyu's Time. If it had been Manyu's Rise, Enlil's hair would have blended in with the changing leaves. He could only pull the hood of his cloak over his head and hope the fabric blended in with the bare bushes.

She froze, all thoughts flying away, as a man stepped into view in front of them. He stood tall, with black hair that hung shaggily around his ears. He wore rough peasant's clothing, but carried himself with an unconscious air of superiority, even alone in the forest. A bow rested lightly in his hand, a quiver of arrows slung over his back, and a sword hung comfortably at his side.

Not alone. Another man stepped into view, this one slightly shorter, with sandy-blond hair and bright eyes which spoke of mischief. He was similarly attired but wore the look of a hunter—poacher—much more comfortably.

Niara's eyes remained fixed on the first man. He had changed in the past three years, grown more muscular and more serious, but Arrex Lokris-Phythia stood there, the brother of Rian, Niara's best friend and the Lady of Lokrian.

She hadn't realized her hand had tightened on Enlil's arm until he glanced sideways at her, a question in his eyes. She shook her head, unable to explain. What was Arrex doing here? "I think all the game's been scared off," Arrex said. "Manyu-cursed dragons flying overhead."

The second man snorted. "More like the wolves and bears," he said. "Since the Great Hunts stopped, the dangerous creatures have been getting out of hand around here."

Arrex shrugged. "I'd be fine with that if we could find them," his voice was frustrated. "I'll hunt wolves and bear just as easily as deer."

"Oh, Arrex," the second man looked at Arrex in amusement. "We're fine. We have plenty of provisions. We'll make it until Mazda's Rise with no difficulty."

Arrex sighed, a vexed sound of frustration Niara knew all too well. She had felt the same frustration herself almost constantly over the last three years.

"There has to be something more we could do," he said.

The second man stepped closer to Arrex, a small smile on his face. "I know something we could do," he said.

Arrex returned the smile, and Niara blinked as he brought the shorter man to him for a long kiss. *Well. Looks like Arrex found some happiness, at least,* she thought. She had suspected his flirting with her had been half-hearted at best, but she hadn't suspected its cause. *Was this before or after Auriel's rise, I wonder?*

They broke the kiss. "We really should wait until we get back home, Petro," Arrex said.

"Why?" Petro asked slyly. "There's no one here."

A small sound escape Niara, and the two men instantly sprang apart, grabbing their bows and reaching for arrows. Enlil grabbed her arm, and she knew he was preparing to run.

She took a deep breath and straightened, sparing a thought of gratitude for the new headscarf Enlil had acquired during his night-time raid. She looked straight at Arrex as she stood, her heart beating frantically in her chest. "Hello, Arrex," she said.

"Niara?" he exclaimed; his voice incredulous. Arrex's hands went limp, and the bow he held dropped to the ground.

Niara managed a smile. "Yes, it's me."

Arrex stared at her for another long moment, then rushed forward and crushed her in a hard embrace. Niara stumbled, taken aback by the fierce display of emotion. She returned the embrace hesitantly. She and Arrex had never been especially close, but after three years of fearing everyone dead, seeing a familiar face brought an over-whelming sense of relief.

"We heard everyone in Ninaeva was dead," Arrex said, pulling back. "Mazda's light, you're alive! How is this possible? What about the rest of your family? Thalion, Kishtar?"

Niara had never remembered Arrex being this exuberant. "They're all alive," she assured him. "And yours? Rian, Ianna?"

Arrex's grinned. "We're safe, all three of us."

A bubble of anxiety popped, and she laughed in relief, throwing her arms around Arrex again. *Rian's alive!* She could barely contain her joy.

Petro cleared his throat, bringing her back to her senses.

She looked back to find Enlil standing up, an amused expression on his face. "Old friends?" he asked.

Niara nodded. "Enlil, this is Arrex," she said. She glanced sideways, but Arrex did not seem at all offended by him leaving off his surname.

"And this is Petro," Arrex beckoned Petro forward, putting his arm around Petro's shoulders in an easy, relaxed manner. Petro's eyes held quiet suspicion. "Petro, this is Niara, an old friend of the family."

Understanding cleared the suspicion from Petro's eyes. "Welcome," he said.

Niara shook her head, still trying to fully comprehend the reality of finding an old friend. "What are you doing here?" she managed. "Lokrian's over the river."

Arrex's expression darkened. "We couldn't make it," he said. "We fled the capital, but the roads were impassable, and so," he shrugged. "We ended up here. It's fine, as places go." He eyed Niara. "Dare I ask about you?"

Before Niara could figure out an answer, a howl split the air, and the four of them spun around, searching for the source of the sound. Another howl answered, this one closer. Niara shivered.

Arrex looked at Enlil, at one glance taking in his unarmored appearance. "Sword or bow?" he asked.

Enlil blinked. "Bow?"

Arrex picked his bow off the ground and threw it at Enlil, followed shortly by his quiver. Enlil caught them with ease and slung the quiver over his shoulder. Arrex drew his sword. "Niara, back against a tree," Arrex said, his voice firm. "We'll fight them off if they come."

Wolves. Niara followed Arrex's instructions, remembering her first encounter with a wolf in this very forest. She had been a child then, and the experience had terrified her, though it had been immediately overshadowed by her joy at meeting an elf. *My grandfather.*

There would be no rescue from a group of elves today. Kinaevan was long dead, and they were four adults, not a lone child. *Wolves don't tend to attack adults, especially not more than one.* She tried to calm herself with that knowledge, but another howl made it difficult for her pounding heart to listen.

"There!" Arrex's shout rang through the clearing, and Enlil and Petro both fired an arrow, hitting the wolf with two direct shots. It fell, and for a moment Niara allowed herself a moment to hope that that would be all of them.

A growl directly to the left disabused her of that notion. She let out an involuntary cry as the jaws of the wolf snapped right in front of her, and she saw its muscles preparing to pounce. Instinctively, she thrust her hands out, reaching for her fire.

Flame engulfed the wolf, causing it to howl in pain. At the same time, fire burned from Niara's right hand, as if she had dipped her entire hand into boiling oil. She screamed against the pain, clutching it to her chest. Her eyes blurred with tears, and she could just barely see another arrow hit the burned wolf, dropping it to the ground.

Howls echoed around them, but with two of their pack members dead, the rest of the wolves appeared disinclined to attack. After a long few minutes, which seemed like an eternity, the howls stopped, and Niara could hear rustling through the undergrowth as the wolves disappeared.

She leaned against the tree, the pain on her hand slowly dissipating. When she risked a glance, she saw the sun brand burned bright red.

"Niara?" Enlil was right next to her, worry plain in his face. "Are you alright?"

She released a shaky breath. "I'm fine," she managed, the best she could say without lying. *I'm uninjured, certainly, but whether I'm alright, I don't know.*

"What was that?" Arrex spoke in an awed tone.

Niara saw Arrex regarding her with amazement, and the suspicion returned to Petro's face. She felt her shoulders tensing, wondering how to explain, when not even Enlil knew what was happening.

When I don't even fully understand.

"Not here," Enlil said, his voice firm. "Her hand needs treating. I think she got scratched."

Arrex's expression changed to concern. "Right," he said. "Petro, grab a wolf. We'll count this hunt successful. I'll get the other, Enlil, you help Niara."

Niara opened her mouth to protest that she didn't need help, but Enlil silenced her with a look. "Do you have something I can use as a bandage?" he asked Arrex.

Arrex began searching, but it was Petro who took a strip of cloth from the inside of his vest and handed it to Enlil. Niara kept silent as Enlil wrapped the bandage around her hand, his fingers gentle and feather-light on her skin. She took a deep breath, trying to steady herself, as his touch threatened to unbalance her.

Enlil helped her to her feet, and Niara let him. Arrex nodded, and he and Petro each hoisted a wolf over their shoulders and started off, heading east out of the forest.

Niara and Enlil followed, Niara half-leaning on Enlil. As they trailed behind Arrex and Petro, Enlil whispered in her ear. "Are you certain you're alright?"

Niara glanced down at her hand. Heat still radiated from beneath the bandage. "I don't know," she said. "That's never happened before."

"Magic," Enlil sighed. "Always unpredictable."

Niara eyed him. Most Saemarians wouldn't have had the knowledge to say that. Magic had been rare, and most people barely thought of its existence. Those who had been harmed by it regarded it with suspicion, while others regarded it with awe. His reaction had been more everyday practical exasperation.

Enlil seemed to realize he'd given something away, for he shrugged sheepishly. He didn't elaborate.

Niara decided to ask anyway. "Is magic common where you're from?" she asked.

"You could say that," was all Enlil said.

Niara pressed her lips together. "One day I want to learn what you're not telling me," she whispered.

Enlil uttered a short laugh. "I don't think you do."

Before Niara had a chance to reply, Arrex waved a hand, and Niara blinked. The trees had almost disappeared, and right at the edge of the tree line was a small shack, what looked like an old woodcutter's hut. In front of the hut, a tall, striking woman with auburn hair was bent over, working in a small garden. She waved a hand as she saw Arrex approach, and straightened, brushing her hands on her dress.

Niara broke free from Enlil's hold and ran forward. "Rian!" she exclaimed.

"Niara?" Rian gasped.

Tears stung Niara's eyes as she wrapped her arms around her childhood friend. Rian returned the embrace fervently, her arms squeezing Niara tight. "Mazda's light, I can't believe it!" she exclaimed. "We heard everyone in Ninaeva had been killed!"

Niara managed a shaky laugh. "Not all of us," she assured Rian.

Arrex grinned. "Ianna! Look who we found!"

From out of the shack, a short woman emerged, her long black hair tied up in a peasant's bun. Niara's eyes widened as she saw the small toddler held in Ianna's arms, a boy of no more than two or three.

Ianna gasped. "Niara?" she managed.

"Ianna." Niara withdrew from Rian's embrace and moved to stand in front of Ianna. "It is so good to see you all."

The boy in Ianna's arms made a small, inquisitive sound. "Who dat, Mama?"

Ianna smiled at her son. "This is Niara," she told the boy. "Niara, meet Alex."

Unlike his mother, the boy had bright blond hair which curled into ringlets. He stared at Niara with warm brown eyes.

"Nice to meet you, Alex," Niara said. She glanced behind her, to see Enlil standing off to the side. She beckoned him forward. "This is Enlil. Enlil, my friends, Rian and Ianna."

Enlil gave them a gallant bow. Rian laughed in surprised delight and returned a curtsy.

"A pleasure to meet any friends of Niara's," Enlil said.

A distant sound of wingbeats made Niara's ears perk up, and she froze, staring at the sky. Arrex noticed her gaze and immediately looked at Petro, and both of them dropped the wolves they were carrying.

"Get inside," he said. "Petro, distraction time."

Niara blinked, but Ianna was already in the door, and Rian grabbed Niara's arm to draw her inside.

Enlil cleared his throat. "Could you use some help?" He spoke to Arrex, but his gaze was fastened on Niara.

Arrex beckoned impatiently. "Come on, then."

Niara hesitated, then gave Enlil a brief nod. She would tell him this secret. *He doesn't want me to be forced to reveal any secrets to him, things Rian and Ianna might want to talk about. Only Rian and Ianna don't know half of my secrets...*

She allowed Rian to draw her inside, even as her breath caught as she realized Enlil knew more about her than anyone aside from her immediate family. Even Rian, her closest childhood friend, was ignorant of the secrets that had bound the Ninaevan noble family.

The inside of the shack was just as small and ramshackle as the outside at first glance. That was, until Niara saw that the beds were lined with sheepskin, and a small trapdoor led to what must be a provision cellar.

Ianna set Alex on the ground, and together she and Rian opened the trapdoor. "Down we go!" Ianna told Alex cheerfully. She picked Alex up again, settling him in a one-armed hold against her chest, and started down the ladder into the cellar, followed by Rian. Niara swallowed a moment's fear at the darkness, then followed, closing the trapdoor behind her.

Rian reached up to the cracks of the ceiling and pulled a string, and the room darkened abruptly as a cloth covered the trapdoor. Niara heard the sound of flint and steel, and after a few seconds, Ianna held up a small candle.

The three of them looked at each other for a long moment, then Rian let out another breath. "Mazda's light, Niara, I still can't believe it," she said. "Tell me everything. When the army marched north, I thought for sure you were done for."

Niara took a deep breath. "The army arrived," she said. "But we had advance warning. We were able to hide."

Rian smiled wryly. "A story that I'm sure hides many details you can't tell us," she said. "Especially if the rest of your family is still in hiding?" she raised an eyebrow.

Niara laughed helplessly. "You are correct," she managed. "But they're alive."

"All of them?" Ianna asked. "Even..." she paused, swallowed, and held Alex closer, "Even Kishtar? He wasn't exactly your family, I know..."

Niara blinked. The last time she had seen Rian and Ianna, Kishtar had still been flirting with every eligible young lady, including Ianna.

"Kishtar's alive too, though he's not in hiding." She hesitated, uncertain if she should continue.

"Is he...is he still unattached?" Ianna whispered.

"Ianna." Rian leaned forward, trying to place a comforting hand on her sister's shoulder, but Ianna brushed it off.

Oh dear. There's a story here, and a broken heart. Niara looked helplessly at Rian, who simply shrugged. "He's married," she said. "He has a baby daughter."

Ianna cast her eyes down.

Niara swore she could see tears on her cheeks, even in the dim candlelight. "I'm sorry," she said.

Ianna shook her head. "It's me who's sorry," she whispered. She reached down to ruffle Alex's blond curls, and Niara's eyes widened as her gaze shifted from mother to son.

Arrex and Petro, Rian and Ianna, Ianna's child...and no sign of a father. Mazda's light, Kishtar, what did you do?

"Did Kishtar," she began to demand.

Ianna shook her head. "It's fine, Niara." Her lips pressed together. "It's an old wound by now."

Niara leaned back against the wall of the cellar. "I am sorry," she said.

"Thank you," Ianna said before sighing. "After all, I'm not sure I would have ended up any differently." She managed a smile.

Niara glanced around. "How did you end up here?"

"It was just luck I wasn't in the palace when..." Rian shuddered. "Auriel, the dragons..."

"I know," Niara interrupted.

Rian didn't ask how she knew, only nodded and continued. "Anyway, the city was in confusion, and then Arrex came running to tell us the king was dead, and we needed to get out."

Rian's expression was pained. "We managed to get out, but soon the countryside was crawling with soldiers and dragons," she said. "In the midst, we heard Duskryn lands were being spared the main wrath, so we headed here. No one was living in this shack, and so we took it over." She looked around, grimacing. "It's not what we were used to, but at least we're alive."

What you were used to...when last we were together, you were set on becoming queen. You had a suite in the palace and everything. Niara didn't voice those thoughts. Like her own story, there had to be more that Rian wasn't telling her.

"But enough about the tragic past!" Rian's voice lightened. "It hasn't been all bad. I made Arrex teach me sword combat. I can beat him three out of five times, now," she grinned.

Niara blinked. "Then why aren't you out doing whatever distraction they're doing?"

Rian grimaced. "Because I'm still terrible with a bow, and their distraction relies on that," she said. "Besides, someone needs to defend Ianna and Alex." She patted the ground at her side, and for the first time Niara saw the sword lying sheathed on the ground.

"How did you make it down here?" Ianna asked in her low, quiet voice. "Are you running?"

Niara's throat closed. How much could she reveal? "I'm traveling southeast," she said.

Rian nodded. "On your initiative, or that of your handsome companion's?"

Niara's face flushed red, and Ianna elbowed her sister in the side. "Rian!" Ianna whispered.

Rian grinned. "What? Niara's always been impervious to hints like that—" her eyes widened, and Niara's face heated even more. Rian's expression turned gleeful. "You like him?"

Niara tried to look away, but there was nowhere to hide in the tiny cellar. "I...I..." she stuttered.

"Does he know?" Rian demanded. "Does he like you back? He's quite handsome, and he does seem devoted to you." She smiled. "I assume he's not a noble, but that doesn't really matter anymore, does it?"

"Rian," Niara held up her hands in defense. "Rian, it's not that simple."

"Why not?" Rian demanded. "Just tell him you like him and let the rest work itself out."

Niara closed her eyes. She had forgotten this trait of Rian's; her uncompromising bluntness and directness. Usually a thing to be valued, but when it was directed toward her…

"He doesn't know who I am," Niara managed. "He doesn't know I'm the heir of Ninaeva, and that Auriel and his dragons would dearly love to kill me."

"So, tell him," Rian said in a matter-of-fact voice. "That's hardly the worst thing you could be. At this point, you're hardly in more danger than the rest of us."

Niara stared at her friend, trying to find the words to explain. "He also hasn't told me who he is," she finally said.

Rian's eyes widened. "Ooh, mystery!" she exclaimed. "I like him better and better! On your behalf, of course." Her eyes darkened for a brief second, and Niara had a sense of a past that was better left unspoken.

Niara groaned. "He doesn't trust me not to react poorly to his secret," she said. "How am I supposed to tell a man who doesn't trust me that I like him?"

Rian grinned. "So, you do like him!"

Niara groaned again, realizing that she'd been tricked into admitting it. "Mazda's light, Rian, you're horrible."

"You've missed me," Rian smirked.

"I have," Niara smiled back. She shifted her gaze to Ianna. "Both of you."

She heard a distant shout, and her ears perked up. Rian gave her a curious look, then tilted her own head, hearing the distant echoes of people.

"It's all right," Rian said. "Just the distraction."

Niara frowned. "What does this distraction entail?"

Rian glanced at Ianna, and Niara saw the same hesitancy to reveal secrets that she felt whenever anyone asked her questions.

"Only if you can tell me," she hastened to say.

Rian smiled wryly. "Your Enlil's already out there." Niara flushed at the mention of 'her' Enlil, but Rian continued without commenting. "There's more of us, scattered through the forest. Whenever we hear a dragon, the fighters go out and congregate, sending smoke and fire arrows as far away from our homes as possible. The soldiers all go on a wild goose chase, and we get left in peace."

"Clever," Niara said.

Rian shrugged. "It's what we have to be."

Ianna leaned forward. "But what are you really doing here, Niara?" she asked. "Traveling southeast, yes, but why? Where?"

Niara opened her mouth to answer, but her vision grayed, and she gasped, clutching at nothingness, trying to remain grounded.

No, Lady! she thought. *Not now! I can't explain...*

Duskryn, the old manor house. Not destroyed, but neglected, vines climbing the walls, the lake surrounding it grown over with plants and algae. No dragons, but a group of soldiers stationed outside, bivouacked in a small group of tents.

"Why are we here?" Two soldiers spoke together, behind one of the tents. Niara blinked. They were not common soldiers. Their collars held the decoration of officers.

"She ordered us to secure the area," one of them said, his voice tired. "We are obeying."

The second soldier looked down. "I don't like it," he said. "There's been no trouble from there, not ever. Lady Lokrian is dead, so there was no resistance when the sky-lord took over."

The first soldier sighed. "We've been given our orders. What choice do we have?"

"We're from Lokrian, Miken," the second soldier said. "That's our home, our people. What in Mazda's name are we going to do to them?"

"Shh!" Miken frantically shushed his friend. "Don't swear by Mazda, for the sake of your life, Jak! It's a death sentence if the dragons hear!"

"And it's a death sentence for any of our friends who survived in Lokrian," Jak's tone was bitter. "My parents might still be alive, Miken. Yours too. Are we going to round them up with the rest?"

Miken closed his eyes. "What choice do we have?"

A flash of pain on her arm drew her gaze down, where the lines of her scar flared red. "Tell them they have a choice," a voice whispered.

Niara gasped as the pain intensified. The voice was that of the stag-crowned elf, the one who had scarred her.

"Tell them," he insisted.

"We have no leader," Miken said. "No hope against the dragons. They'll burn all of us out if any of us dare rebel. The best we can do is to save the few who come under our control."

"They have hope," the elf whispered. "But you must give it to them."

Pain flared down Niara's arm, and she lurched forward with a gasp, clutching it to her chest.

"Niara?" Rian's voice was worried.

Mazda's light. Niara stared at Rian, her eyes wide. *I'm going to have to tell them.*

———

Niara managed to delay explaining what had happened until Arrex, Petro, and Enlil returned. When they arrived, they squeezed into the tiny shack and Rian demanded to know what was going on.

"Seriously, Niara, you were as pale as if you had seen a ghost. You weren't responding to anything!"

Enlil glanced at Niara in concern. Niara tried to give him a reassuring smile.

"This is going to take a little explaining," she told the other four, keeping her voice as steady as she could. "Please bear with me." She took a deep breath and reached up, removing the headscarf which concealed her ears.

All four of them stared at her in shock. "What?" Arrex said, his voice blank.

Niara closed her eyes, fighting her rising panic. She was breaking every rule her mother had ever constructed for her, every order she had ever been given. *There are no consequences anymore. Not the ones Mother was concerned about, anyway. Ninaeva is lost, the king is dead, and*

Auriel is a god. The remaining nobility knowing I'm part elf and can use magic is not going to change that.

"You all know I never knew my father," Niara said. She tried to meet Rian's eyes, but her courage failed her, and she looked down instead. "We hid it because it was safer. I still hide it because it's still safer. The dragons have standing orders from Auriel to bring any elves they find to him."

Arrex nodded. "It's true," he said. "We're heard whispers of a group to the east of us, but nothing certain, and the dragons do seem to patrol the area more frequently."

Elves to the east? Refugees from Alfheim? Maybe we can find them. Niara put aside the flare of hope at Arrex's words and continued. "Because of my blood, I have certain abilities." *My blood, indeed. Only it's Mother's blood, not my father's.* "I can do magic, like you saw earlier," she gestured at Arrex and Petro. Arrex's eyes widened, and Petro looked thoughtful. "I also have visions. Sometimes I can see what's happening in other places."

None of them responded. Niara forced herself to raise her eyes, to see Rian's expression. It was unreadable, Rian just stared at her as she tried to process the information.

"So you had a vision?" Ianna asked. "While we were below?"

"I did. Of a group of soldiers, camped around the Duskryn manor. They're heading to Lokrian to put the countryside to order."

Arrex gasped, and Ianna made a small sound of pain. Rian's gaze remained steady, staring at Niara. "We know what that means," she whispered. "We've seen it happening."

Niara nodded jerkily. "That's not the important part, however," she said.

"Not important!" Arrex burst out. "How is that not important? That's our home, our lands!"

"We haven't been there for three years," Rian snapped. "They're hardly our lands anymore."

Arrex turned an anguished gaze on his sister. "You're supposed to be the Lady there," he said. "Shouldn't we do something?"

"What?" Rian demanded. Niara sensed that if there had been room, she would have stood up and started pacing. "Go over there and get myself killed by soldiers?"

"They wouldn't kill you." Niara made her voice as firm as she could. "The soldiers I heard, they were the leaders, the officers. They're from Lokrian, two men called Miken and Jak. They want to rebel, they want to fight, but they have nothing to fight for. They have no Lady, no king, no hope anything will ever change."

She saw Enlil's eyebrows rise as he realized what she was saying. *Another rebellion.* She nodded at him, then stood up and walked over to Rian. Gently, she took Rian's hand and clasped it between her own. "Rian, you asked why I'm going southeast. I can't tell you the details, but it's to overthrow Auriel and the dragons' rule. Will you help me?"

Unshed tears glistened in Rian's eyes. Niara held her breath as she regarded her friend. Something had happened to her when the dragons had taken over. Niara only hoped it was enough to urge her to fight back now.

Rian stood up to face Niara. Even in her peasant's garb, she stood like a lady, her eyes shining brightly against the tears. "I will help, my lady, just tell me how," she said fiercely.

Niara reached out to embrace Rian, her arms trembling. She could feel Rian shuddering with emotion, and she held her close, the two of them steadying themselves against each other.

"Yes, how?" Petro's voice cut through. His eyes were no longer suspicious, but he did not appear convinced. "Forgive me, Niara, but you've told us nothing of how this plan is to happen."

"You'll start by subverting the soldiers," Enlil said calmly. "They're just looking for a cause. Would they recognize you, Rian, do you think?"

Rian nodded. "And Arrex, and Ianna. Arrex is actually the most likely."

"Once you do that, you'll have an entire group of Auriel's soldiers that you can use against him," Enlil said. "My suggestion would be to keep them mostly acting under Auriel's orders, but secretly use them to spread information of rebellion across Lokrian. They can warn people when they're supposed to round them up, miss watches and let prisoners escape, do everything to subvert the dragons' authority. Then, on Papsukkal, the rebellion can begin in earnest."

"Papsukkal?" Rian looked at Niara.

"It has to happen then," she answered.

"Then it will," Rian's voice was firm. "By my word as Lady of Lokrian."

Niara let out a sigh of relief. "Thank you."

In the corner, Alex woke up from where he had been napping and began demanding food. Ianna glanced up, a guilty expression on her face. "Mazda's light," she whispered. "If we're doing this, what about Alex?"

"Ianna," Rian raised an eyebrow. "Would you rather see Alex grow up free, or in a world where he fears for his life every waking hour?"

Ianna swallowed hard. "Rian…"

"We'll protect him," Arrex said. "Petro and I. But we're not leaving you here. You're both coming with us."

Niara watched as Ianna's expression cleared. "Home," she whispered, staring eastward at the wall of the shack. "We're going home."

9

FAMILY

Niara crouched behind a low stone wall, not daring to breathe. She was in a ruined garden, just outside the Duskryn manor. The tents of the soldiers were directly in front of them, just as she'd seen in her vision.

Niara watched as Rian and Arrex, both dressed in cloaks with hoods pulled down low, approached the camp. The soldiers came on alert as soon as they were spotted, and swords were drawn, steel glistening in the fading light.

Rian and Arrex stopped. Niara saw Rian straighten. "I'm here to speak to your commanders," she said. "Where are Miken and Jak?"

A murmur traveled through the gathered soldiers, and many of them exchanged glances. Two seconds later, the officers emerged from one of the tents.

"Who are you?" Miken demanded.

"I have a message for you, to be delivered in private, Lieutenant Miken and Lieutenant Jak," Rian said. Miken and Jak exchanged looks. "Who from?" Miken asked.

"I will tell you in private," Rian repeated. "I am unarmed, I give you my word. My companion will remain here as surety until you have received my message."

More murmurings ran through the soldiers, but no one voiced any objection. Miken and Jak looked at each other again, and then Miken nodded. "Keep an eye on him, sergeant," Miken said to one of the soldiers.

Niara could see Arrex making every attempt to remain as nonthreatening as possible as the soldiers watched him warily.

Ianna shifted beside her, trying not to wake the sleeping Alex. "What's going on?" she whispered.

Niara blessed her superior hearing. "Rian's in the tent with the officers," she said. "It's all going according to plan."

"This had better work," Petro grumbled from where he crouched, almost completely covered by a bush. "If anything happens to Arrex because of this, I'll…" his voice trailed off as if he couldn't think of a strong enough threat.

Niara didn't bother responding. Her own heart was pounding, even though she had seen what Miken and Jak thought of the dragons, what they thought of subduing Lokrian.

Enlil put a quiet, comforting hand on her arm. Niara gave him a grateful glance, and he smiled, sending warmth flooding through her, tingling down to her toes. She felt her cheeks heat up, and she turned her gaze away.

Ianna shifted. "What's happening?" she whispered again.

Niara shook her head. She was the only one who dared peek over the wall. She was the only one who had any hope of truly seeing what was going on, as well. *Before this trip, I had no idea my eyes and ears were that much better than humans.* "Rian's still inside," she said. "There's no one shouting, however, so I assume everything's going well."

Ianna sighed. "I wish this were over," she said.

So do I. The rest of Niara's journey spread before her in her mind's eye. *Cross the river, then cross Lokrian, to the Tigri border. Then directly south, through the badlands. Shan Serin.*

Niara looked up sharply at movement from the soldiers. A moment later, Rian, Miken, and Jak emerged from the tent. Miken appeared bewildered, while Jak had an expression of dawning hope and triumph.

Rian raised a hand, and Niara allowed herself a sigh of relief. "She's done it," she said. "She's signaling for you to join her."

Petro immediately scrambled to his feet and started forward, his eyes fixed on Arrex. Ianna got to her feet slower and turned to regard Niara before she left.

"Good luck, Niara," she said.

Niara nodded. "You too."

"I think you'll need it more." Ianna smiled wryly and shifted Alex in her arms. Without a further word, she turned and headed toward the soldiers, her head held high.

Niara watched until the four of them were ushered inside the soldiers' tent with Miken, Jak, and several other soldiers. She collapsed against the crumbling stone wall, a sigh of relief escaping her.

"Well, you're certainly spreading rebellion wherever you go," Enlil said. "Was this part of your plan?"

Niara glanced down at her arm, where her scar still glowed, red and angry. "Not mine," she said. *Somebody's, though.*

Enlil only grinned. "Well, it's working, anyway." He tilted his head. "Shall we? Still a ways to the river."

"Don't remind me." Niara groaned and got to her feet, careful to remain behind the crumbling wall until they were out of sight of the soldiers.

Enlil reached for her hand, grabbing her left, not her right. "It's been fun so far," he said. "And I'm sure it will only get even better."

Fun? Niara turned an incredulous gaze on Enlil, and he laughed. After a moment, she joined in, slightly helpless in the face of his amusement. Hand in hand they walked east, heading for the river.

Niara stared at the ravine in front of her and cursed. She had never been this far south on the river. Her entire experience had been in the central plains, where the water flowed level with the land in wide, gentle curves. Here, the water roared far below her, and the gorge, while narrower than the river up north, was still far too far to jump.

Enlil sat down on a fallen log. "Well, this is interesting."

Niara sat down next to him, every muscle screaming a protest. They had marched steadily since Duskryn manor to get here, and her legs cried for a break.

"We have to get across," she said. "We don't have time to go searching north for a crossing."

Enlil nodded. "I think the days are getting longer."

Niara pulled her cloak tight around herself. She had lost track of the days, but she knew the shortest day of the year had come and gone while they traveled. Papsukkal was only a few weeks away, but Manyu's Time lingered upon them. More than once, she and Enlil had woken in the night huddled next to each other, trying desperately to stay warm.

Niara pulled her thoughts away from the memory. Ever since Rian had teased her about liking Enlil, she had become more and more aware of her attraction to him. He made her laugh, as no one had been able to do since she'd been a child. He always approached everything with a sense of optimism and enthusiasm which was infectious as well as occasionally exasperating.

She found herself smiling at him, and he looked at her curiously. Her cheeks flushed red, and she sternly turned her attention back to the problem at hand.

"Well, we could build a bridge," Enlil suggested. "There are trees, if only we had a way to cut them down." He frowned. "I don't have an axe."

Niara shook her head. She swallowed, trying to ignore the only possibility that seemed feasible.

"Niara?" Enlil asked.

Niara sighed. There was no avoiding it. "Fire isn't the only magic I can wield," she said. "I can use all four elements if I have to. Air and fire are just easier."

"Air," Enlil tilted his head. "Are you saying you could fly us across?"

Niara felt herself shiver. "I think so," she said. "I've done it before for my brother and I, but not for so great a distance."

Enlil's face was still. "A brother?" he asked. "Not Kishtar?"

With a start, Niara realized she'd never mentioned Thalion's name. Even when they had met the Lokrians, Thalion hadn't ever been identified as her brother.

She forced a smile. "Half-brother, if you must know," she said. "The blood of elves is not as strong in him."

"Ah," Enlil blinked a few more times, then nodded. "Well, what are we waiting for?" he asked. He rose to his feet and held out his hand. "Shall we, my lady?"

"Enlil," Niara protested as he drew her to her feet. "Enlil, I don't know…my magic's been strange. The last time I tried to call fire…" she shuddered, remembering the pain that had surrounded her hand. Enlil tightened his grip on her left hand. "Then try to fly me first," he said.

Niara's eyes widened. "Enlil," she said again. Her heart began pounding. What if her strength failed? What if the magic refused to answer her? He would fall, to be dashed on the rocks in the raging water below.

"Trust me, Niara," he said. His expression warmed her to her bones. "I won't fall. I trust you."

One way or another, we have to get across, Niara reminded herself. *And this does seem to be the only way.*

She took a deep breath and released his hand, calling for the magic inside herself. She reached out, wrapping Enlil in a blanket of air, lifting him off the ground and sending him speeding toward the eastern shore.

She heard him laugh in delight, but she didn't dare lose her concentration. Only when he stood safe on the ground on the other shore did she relax, trembling from the effort.

"That was amazing!" Enlil called.

Niara shook like a leaf, but her job wasn't finished, not yet. Once again, she reached and called the air, this time wrapping it around herself. Her feet left the ground, and she fought the strange sense of disorientation as she moved to the shore without moving a muscle.

Enlil waited for her, arms outstretched. With a cry of relief, Niara fell into his arms, the magic flowing out of her, leaving her weak and shivering. "It worked," she whispered. Unexpectedly, a fierce joy flooded through her. "The mark didn't interfere. It worked."

Enlil grinned. "I had perfect faith in you."

Niara allowed herself to relax in Enlil's arms for another long moment. The crashing of the water below was enough to drown out almost all other sounds, but Niara could still hear her heart pounding. She pushed away, aware that her face flushed red again.

"We should move," she said. "We're standing in the open."

Enlil opened his mouth to reply, but anything he might have said was cut off as the thunderous flapping of a dragon's wings sounded above them. Niara looked up just in time to see the dark shadow pass above them.

Mazda's light. The area near the ravine was rough and rocky, but the rocks were all exposed, with no place to hide. A short distance away, a small grove of trees marked the edge of Lokrian's woodlands, but it was too far to run if the dragon had already spotted them.

Enlil gripped Niara's hand tightly. Without discussion, they started running for the trees as fast as their feet could take them. Niara felt her headscarf fly from her head, but she kept running, keeping her eyes fixed on the relative safety of the trees.

A roar echoed overhead, but Niara refused to look up, refused to acknowledge the possibility that they might be caught again. Her arm tingled as she ran, like sparks of fire running up and down her scar.

They didn't slow as they burst underneath the cover of the first trees. Another roar echoed, and Niara lengthened her stride, left hand still clutched tightly around Enlil's. She wanted to be as far into the trees as they could make it.

A hand grabbed her right arm, and fire ran through her scar, causing her to stumble, though she managed to muffle her cry of pain. Enlil's exclamation of surprise was just as quiet. The sharp voice ordering silence spoke louder than both of them.

Niara's eyes widened as she saw the figure who had stopped their headlong flight. She couldn't see much, only that the figure stood tall, cloaked and hooded, and probably male. A quiver and bow were slung over his back, and he beckoned with his hand that didn't hold Niara, urging them to follow him.

Niara hesitated only a split second before obeying, trusting that someone who was avoiding a dragon's notice would be unlikely to lead them into a trap. She and Enlil followed the figure a little way into the woods before the figure stopped at a rope ladder that dangled from a high tree.

Niara stared up the ladder in disbelief. The end of the ladder disappeared in the branches, far out of view.

"Climb!" the figure's voice was impatient. With a swallow, Niara put her hands on the ladder and started climbing.

The rope gave slightly under her weight but otherwise remained fairly steady. Niara held her breath as every step she took made the rope bend. She refused to look down. Above the trees, she could hear the steady beat of the dragon's wings as it swooped low enough to make the treetops rustle.

It seemed like an eternity before she reached a wooden platform, built high above the ground. Another figure reached down to help pull her onto the platform, and Niara moved over to lean against the trunk of the tree, away from the ledge. She had no idea how high up she was. She didn't want to know.

Enlil pulled himself up next, gazing around himself with wide eyes. The cloaked figure was last, swinging himself onto the platform with easy grace. He beckoned harshly for silence.

Niara didn't need to be told twice as the roar of the dragon sounded again. She sat motionless against the tree and listened, ears pricking up, as the wingbeats got further and further away until she could no longer hear them at all.

Only then did the figure relax. "Well," he said, turning toward Niara. "It seems you had a narrow escape."

Niara let out a shaky breath. "That's not uncommon these days." Belatedly, she realized her headscarf was missing, somewhere on the ground between the ravine and the forest. There was no concealing her elven heritage.

She could hear the smile in the figure's voice. "I am hardly surprised."

Niara took a deep breath. "Thank you for your timely intervention," she managed. "Might I have the pleasure of knowing your name?"

"You might," the figure said. He shook the hood off his face. His bright green eyes pierced into Niara, his angular cheekbones a match for her own. His ears were longer than her own, sweeping into sharp points. On his forehead, however...a tattoo, of a teardrop surrounded by thorns.

If Niara could have backed away any farther, she would have. As it was, she scrambled to her feet, still pressed against the tree. *Unfaithful.* The word echoed in her mind. She had been warned about them, by both her mother and her grandfather. Her mother had been nearly assassinated by one of them.

The elf laughed. "Now, daughter, is that an appropriate way to greet the appearance of your rescuer? I thought Vinet taught you better manners."

Niara felt as if he had struck her with a blow. She stared at him, eyes wide. "How do you know who I am?" she demanded.

The elf smiled. "I like to keep an eye on my flesh and blood," he said. "I've been watching you for years. Of course, I know who you are."

*Flesh and blood...daughter...*Niara's breath grew shorter. Surely not... surely he wasn't claiming to be...

Enlil came to her rescue. "In that case, you have the advantage over us, good sir," he said. "Won't you please enlighten us?"

The elf cast an amused glance in Enlil's direction before returning his attention to Niara. "Haven't you figured it out yet?" he asked.

Niara couldn't catch her breath. *He's Unfaithful. Mazda's light, he's an elf, as we suspected, but he's Unfaithful. Oh, Mother, how?*

"Tell me," she demanded, surprised at how strong her voice was.

She clutched at the tree for support, the bark crumbling underneath her hands.

"My name is Jaimalaeran Anderan, leader of the Steadfast, Hunter in the service of the Lord," the elf's voice took on a formal, ringing sound as he announced his titles. He gave Niara a wry smile. "But you probably know me as Jaim, minstrel visitor to Ilhelm Castle."

No. Niara brought a hand to her mouth, unable to believe what she was hearing. But there was too much, too much evidence that he was precisely who he claimed to be. "You can't be," she whispered.

Jaim's smile widened. "Who can't I be, daughter?" he asked.

Niara shook her head, still unable to put it into words. "You…you can't…"

Jaim's expression didn't waver. "What, because of this?" he gestured to the tattoo on his forehead. "Do you think it impossible that an *Unfaithful*," he spat the word, "could sire Niara Andaren, heir to the human lands of Ninaeva, and descendant of both Queen Olvae and King Lyaen?"

Niara heard Enlil's quick intake of breath, and she closed her eyes, feeling the last of her secrets from him being stripped away. *How does he know the legends of elves?* She would have to return to that thought another time. She opened her eyes again and glared at Jaim. "And how do I know you're telling the truth?" she asked.

Jaim laughed. "Do you really think I am not?" he asked. He held out his hand. "Give me your hand."

Niara hesitated, then stretched out her left hand, unwilling to let him see the brand on her right. Jaim clasped her hand in his and looked into her eyes.

Fire seemed to burn in her veins, and she gasped, staring wide-eyed at Jaim. The fire was singing, a harmony so intense she was dizzy, describing a deep and impossible-to-deny connection.

Jaim nodded in satisfaction. "You feel it," he said. "You are my daughter, Niara Andaren."

Niara slowly withdrew her hand, willing the fire in her blood to calm, to force her pounding heart to slow, to allow herself to think instead of reacting. "My name is Niara Sindarilae," she managed.

Jaim's smile didn't diminish. "That may be what you called yourself while you were ignorant of your heritage," he said. "But once that is remedied, I am certain you will change your mind."

Niara felt the flare of rebellion in her at his words, but she tightened her lips to avoid spilling any hasty words herself. *This man is your father,* she thought. As unbelievable and unlikely, as unwelcome it might be, she couldn't deny it. His blood was her blood. How she knew that she couldn't tell, but the ringing in her bones spoke the truth.

The second figure cleared their throat, and Niara jumped, having completely forgotten about their presence on the platform. The elf shrugged her hood off, revealing a young female, black hair braided tightly into a crown on her head. Emblazoned on her forehead was the same tattoo of a tear and thorns. She stared at Jaim for a long moment, seeming to speak to him without words.

Jaim nodded as if she had spoken aloud. "We should be moving." He turned back to Niara. "You've had a shock, I realize. Nevertheless, might I escort you and your companion back to our encampment? I am certain it is more secure than anywhere else you planned to spend the night."

Niara couldn't answer, couldn't think. She looked at Enlil, attempting to communicate her uncertainty to him with only her eyes. He shrugged and gave a small smile. *Go for it,* he mouthed.

She took a deep breath and returned her attention back to Jaim. "We would be honored to accept your hospitality, Jaim Andaren," she said formally. "Lead the way."

Jaim's smile widened. "Excellent." He nodded at the elven woman. "Ralanni will lead you there. I will see you in a short while." He swung himself around, and then was climbing another rope ladder, this one leading even higher into the trees.

Niara stared after him for a long moment, still trying to fully comprehend what had just happened. *I just met my father. My father is an Unfaithful elf. Mazda's light, how is this happening?*

Ralanni cleared her throat. When Niara faced her, she raised an eyebrow and gestured. "This way," she said, the first words Niara had heard her speak.

Niara blinked as she saw more ropes strung from the platform, these ones leading further into the forest, as if they were meant to be a bridge. Ralanni swung herself onto the rope bridge in an easy motion and glanced over her shoulder, as if impatient for Niara and Enlil to follow.

Niara looked at Enlil, her heart still pounding loud in her chest. What in Mazda's name was happening?

1 0

THE STEADFAST

Niara avoided Enlil's gaze as she climbed another rope ladder toward a wooden platform higher in the trees. She didn't want to know what he was thinking. After his urging for her to keep her secrets, to have them revealed by someone she didn't even know... She felt a surge of anger at the man who claimed to be her father, for the fact he had assumed her secret was safe to reveal.

She tried to tell herself to be reasonable, but it was difficult. Occasionally, she caught flickers of movement in the trees, too large to be birds. They were being watched.

Ahead, Ralanni abruptly stopped, and Niara saw they had reached another wooden platform, this one far larger than any of the others, stretching around several large oak trees. Ralanni gave a brief nod, and another elf appeared. "Prepare the guest quarters for these two," Ralanni said. "Our lord has welcomed them."

She didn't name me as Jaim's daughter, Niara noticed. *Then again, perhaps she wants to let Jaim make that announcement.*

The other elf bowed and disappeared into the trees. Ralanni turned to Enlil and Niara. "Follow me," she said.

The room she led them to had been carved out of the tree and wood built around it, so that it appeared to be part of a living, breathing thing. Niara blinked. One of the walls was covered in various outfits, all of different levels of ornamentation.

Ralanni picked two of the garments off the wall and thrust them at Niara and Enlil. "There is to be a feast," she said. "My lord believes you would feel more comfortable in these."

Niara looked down at the garment in her hands. She held a long, russet brown dress, trimmed with red and gold stylized designs. She didn't recognize the material, but it rustled in her hands like leaves and felt as soft as fur.

She glanced at Enlil. He shrugged, his eyes clearly communicating that he was at a loss.

Niara closed her eyes and concentrated. *Jaim's acting like a noble,* she thought. *This is a message, a message he wants me to send by wearing what he's chosen. The question is, do I want to comply with it?*

Ralanni cleared her throat and raised an eyebrow, obviously waiting. Niara opened her eyes and squared her shoulders.

Best not to offend anyone here until I know more of what's going on. And I could use a change of clothes. She was painfully aware, now the dress rested in her hands, that she'd been wearing her split tunic and breeches for nearly a month, and the last bath she'd had was a quick wash in a freezing stream.

She nodded to Ralanni. "We are honored by Jaim's thoughtfulness."

Ralanni gestured toward a divider near one of the walls. "There are two places for you to change, if you feel the need for privacy."

Niara flushed. Without looking at Enlil, she ducked behind the divider. A surge of gratefulness flooded through her as she did so. Aside from having a private place to change, someone had left a washbasin and cloth.

As fast as thought, Niara stripped herself of her old, worn clothing and washed herself down. The dress, when she put it on, caressed her skin like an embrace. She only wished she could see how she appeared in a mirror.

I haven't worn a dress like this in...how long? Not since before Ellriheim, certainly. Down in the caverns, she had worn the most practical dresses. All her noble garb had been destroyed in the siege of Ilhelm.

She hadn't thought she'd missed it, but she couldn't deny that she enjoyed dressing up.

She stepped out from the divider and came face to face with Enlil. Her eyes widened. Enlil's garb was more subdued than her own, but no less stunning to Niara. He wore a long, dark brown tunic with matching breeches, trimmed with dark red and orange, like the leaves of Manyu's Rise. His flame-colored hair matched perfectly with the trim, and his bright blue eyes pierced more than usual as he raised an eyebrow.

"Do I look ridiculous?" he asked.

Niara had to fight to keep a smile from her face. Enlil was acting confident, but she could see the tension in his shoulders. *He can't be used to wearing clothes like this.* "You look wonderful," she said, cursing herself as her voice caught.

Enlil bowed low. "And you are magnificent, my lady," he said. He straightened. "I knew when I first met you that you were as noble as a queen."

"Not quite that noble," Niara protested, blushing at the flattery. "Enlil, I—"

Enlil shook his head, and she saw the warning in his eyes. He tilted his head to where Ralanni waited at the entrance to the room, her back toward them. Despite her appearance of disinterest, Niara had no doubt she was listening to every word.

She nodded at Enlil and cleared her throat. "We're ready," she told Ralanni.

Ralanni turned, but showed no reaction to their changed states. "Follow me," she said.

Niara refrained from answering that they'd been following her for quite some time. She blinked, however, as instead of crossing another rope bridge when they exited, Ralanni swung herself off the platform, heading down to the forest floor.

Niara peeked over the edge. It was a long way down. She glanced at Enlil, who merely gave her a shrug.

Mazda's light. Trying not to think about how high up they stood, she swung herself over the side, grabbing onto the rope ladder as if it were the only thing standing between her and death.

It is the only thing between me and death, Niara thought. *Unless I use the swaying to float all the way down. Mazda's light, that might be safer than trusting this ladder!*

Nevertheless, she kept a firm hold on the rope, staring directly at the trunk of the oak tree. One step at a time, she climbed down, until her foot hit the forest floor.

"Well done," Jaim's voice sounded from behind her.

Niara forced herself to turn slowly, not to whirl in startlement. She gave Jaim a small smile as she regarded him. He had changed as well, into an outfit that matched her own. *So that's the message he wants to send.* "Thank you," she said.

Jaim smirked. "You are beautiful, my daughter." He offered his arm. "Allow me to escort you to our feast."

Niara glanced behind her to make certain Enlil followed, then accepted Jaim's arm. "Gladly," she said.

She almost felt as if she were back in court, where everyone was smiles and politeness, but everyone had a motive you didn't know. Certainly, she didn't know Jaim's motive. The only difference was her secrets were now on display for everyone to see. *Half-elf. Sight-user. Noble of Ninaeva, descendant of Queen Olvae of the Goldwood Realm. And King Lyaen? Who is he?*

She blinked as Jaim led her into a large clearing beneath the trees. Circular tables made from carved logs had been placed around the clearing, with wooden stools around them. Other elves already milled about, some seated, others walking to claim their seats. All were dressed in elaborate clothing which would blend in well with the trees.

Jaim led Niara to the center table and gestured to one of the seats. Niara felt eyes on her as she sat down, Enlil taking the seat on her right, and Jaim sitting on her left. This was unlike any noble meal she had ever been to. In most of the Saemarian noble houses, members of the nobility were placed at a high table, so that they could view and be viewed by all of their vassals. This place was set up so the lord, Jaim, had the illusion of privacy with those he considered important, but in reality, everyone in attendance watched him.

I'm sitting at his right hand. The place of honor. Mazda's light.

The murmur of conversation continued as the elves who remained standing took their seats. Once everyone took their seats, Jaim stood up, raising his hands for silence. The murmurs died until the only sound was the quiet rustling leaves in the breeze. "Fellow Steadfast," Jaim's voice rang through the clearing. "We offer our thanks for all the blessings of the day. For the food on the table, for the deer which roam, for the water in the stream. For our freedom, for our lives, for all we hold dear."

Niara saw the rest of the elves bow their heads, and she shivered slightly, seeing the tattoo of the Unfaithful emblazoned on every forehead. Despite her uneasiness, she bowed her head as well, unwilling to show disrespect when surrounded by dozens of strangers.

Jaim let them sit in silence for a moment, then continued. "I have a special reason to be thankful today," he said. "Today is the day my daughter and heir, Niara Andaren, is returned to us. The future of our people is now secure, and we can all rejoice!" He grabbed Niara's arm and tugged, obviously intending her to rise to her feet. Niara hesitated a moment, then obeyed, realizing that to do otherwise would cause a scene she was uncertain she could deal with.

Niara stared at Jaim amidst the applause that followed his words. *He didn't even bother asking me. He didn't even bother warning me! What in Mazda's name does he think he's doing?*

Jaim didn't appear to read anything to give him alarm in her expression for he smiled equally at her and all of the elves around them. *Unfaithful elves,* Niara reminded herself. *Although...they don't seem to call themselves Unfaithful. Not that that should be surprising. What was it again? Steadfast? A bit different from Unfaithful.*

The applause died down when Jaim raised his hands again. "We will have plenty of time to become acquainted over the course of the next few days," he said. "For now, let us eat, and celebrate our lives while we have them."

The final note of Jaim's speech sounded somber to Niara, but the rest of the elves evidently expected it as their signal. Jaim sat down, and Niara did as well, controlling a mounting sense of anger.

The least he could have done was warn me, she thought again. *Mother wouldn't have done anything like that to me. Nor would Nazir.*

At her left, Enlil raised an eyebrow, obviously attempting to ascertain what she was thinking. Niara gave him a slight shake of her head. She couldn't discuss it. Not here, not now.

"My apologies for that, daughter," Jaim said smoothly, as elves carrying laden trays of food began walking into the clearing. "But this feast was already planned, and it was the perfect opportunity to introduce you. I simply couldn't pass up the opportunity."

Niara waited until a platter was set down in front of her, laden high with steaming meat, before she gave her answer. *Where are they cooking all of this? There's no sign of a kitchen nearby.* "Is this a celebration of some special day?" she asked, waiting until Jaim took a slice of meat from the platter before copying him to take her own.

Jaim nodded. "Indeed," he said. "This is the day when the Lord reminds us life can just as easily be lost," he said. "We celebrate what we have, and enjoy it while we can, for every moment could be our last."

Niara shivered a little at Jaim's words.

Enlil leaned forward. "Forgive an ignorant human, Lord Jaimalaeran, but to what lord do you refer?"

Jaim's smile was polite. "Our god," he said. "The Lord of Life and Loss."

Fire blazed on Niara's arm, underneath her sleeve. She clenched her hand into a fist, willing herself to stay motionless. Before her eyes emerged the image of an elven man, tall, carrying a bow and quiver, with stag's antlers rising from his forehead. He seemed to hover before her, almost like a ghost. He met her eyes briefly and laid one silent figure over his lips. The vision flickered out.

"Of course," Jaim still spoke to Enlil. "Such curiosity is only natural, after all. I would not do anything to discourage it."

Niara forced her fist to relax before speaking. "How did you know where I was?" she asked.

She saw a shadow flash before Jaim's eyes. "The gift of the Lord," he said. "I have known where you are from the moment you first drew breath."

Niara's breath caught, and another shiver ran down her spine. "What do you mean?" Fear rose inside her, and she throttled it down as best she could. "Can you tell where anyone is? How exact is it?"

Jaim shook his head. "No, no," he said. "The Lord of Life and Loss, his gifts are those of blood and bone." He sat back in his chair. "Do you really know nothing of him or his gifts, daughter?"

Through an effort of will, Niara avoided looking at her arm. She was certain now the horned figure she had met was the Lord, and he had granted her some kind of gift. What it was, however, she had no idea. "Tell me," she said.

Jaim sighed. "This will take some explaining," he said. "The simplest version is this: I can sense anyone who is of my blood and track them over a long distance. Sometimes, if truly necessary, I can speak to them. I do not know exactly where they are, only a general sense." He gave her a ghost of a smile. "Does that reassure you? I have not been spying on you in your sleep, daughter."

Speak to them over a far distance. She had done that. She had spoken to Vinet and Thalion and used the gift of the Lord all unknowingly to communicate with her mother and brother, her blood. *Mazda's light, he's telling the truth. I am his daughter.*

She said her next words slowly, trying to avoid them sounding like an accusation. "If you knew of my existence from the moment I was born," she said, "then why have you not revealed yourself until now?"

Jaim remained silent for a long time, and Niara looked up, fearing she had offended him somehow. He stared off into the distance, an unreadable expression in his eyes. Niara caught Enlil's gaze, but he appeared just as uncertain as she.

"We should speak of this privately," Jaim said. "What I have to tell you is not for everyone to hear."

Niara blinked, a warning tingle running down her spine. Whatever her father had to say to her, she was certain she wasn't going to like it.

Jaim smiled again, all pleasantries. "Let us eat," he said. "It would be ungrateful of us not to enjoy what the Lord has given."

That was an obvious signal to change the subject. Niara turned her attention to the food, her mind still puzzling over Jaim's words. *If he knew where I was, then he was never the common minstrel Mother thought him. What does that mean?*

Niara examined the chambers Ralanni had led her to. Similar to the room she had changed in, it was halfway up a huge oak tree and both hollowed out of the trunk and built around it. It was larger than the tiny room she had changed in, but not by much. The only furniture was a small bed, a closet, and a chair, but they were tastefully carved, looking like living wood instead of dead.

"Thank you," she said politely to Ralanni. "Where is Enlil staying?"

She could have sworn she saw Ralanni's eyes darken. "He is in the chamber directly above yours," Ralanni said.

Niara decided not to ask any further questions and only nodded her thanks. Ralanni watched her for a long minute. "Jaim will likely be by later to speak with you," she said. "If I were you, I would suggest a proper bath first. There is a bathing chamber on this level. Just turn right and follow the circle."

Niara felt her heart jump. A proper bath! The washcloth and basin had been nice, but to be submerged in hot water... "Thank you," she said, letting true gratitude into her voice. "I appreciate it."

Ralanni made a small sound, but her expression lightened. "Till later, then," she said before disappearing.

Niara didn't waste any time. All thoughts of Jaim and Enlil could wait until she was fully clean.

She followed Ralanni's directions to another chamber, almost identical to her own. Someone had anticipated her desire, for there was a tub of water waiting. Steam rose from it, inviting Niara to strip and immediately enter.

Niara didn't hesitate. Her dress scattered on the floor, and she stepped into the tub, sighing in relief as the heat sank into her bones. Of all the luxuries she had had to leave behind, she had missed this the most.

Someone had left a bar of soap by the tub, and Niara gratefully scrubbed as much of the grime of travel off herself as she could. She even managed to wash her hair and spent a glorious few minutes relaxing nearly fully underwater, massaging all the soap out of her red-brown locks. Finally, she reluctantly got out of the bath, ready to face the world again. She caught a glimpse of herself in a tall mirror, and moved slowly toward it, drawn by some invisible power.

She stared at herself as if she were seeing a stranger. There were no mirrors in Ellriheim. She hadn't seen her reflection in three years.

She was taller than she remembered, and her body thinner, leaner. Her eyes were darker, but just as green and striking. Her face was thinner as well, which made her appear even more like an elf. Aside from missing the tattoo, she could have been one of the elves who lived here.

She shied away from that thought. *Aside from being Unfaithful,* she reminded herself. *Whatever else Jaim says, he has to explain that to me. Why did Grandfather call them Unfaithful, and why did one of them try to kill Mother? Especially if he already knew of my existence?*

She got dressed carefully, feeling an unexplained urge to appear her best for her meeting with Jaim. Just because he was her father didn't mean she trusted him.

Her room seemed the same as when she had left it, but she glanced around uneasily as she entered. There was an odd sense in the air, as if someone had entered to rifle through her things.

But that doesn't make sense, she told herself. *I have no possessions to search.*

She didn't have any more time to contemplate that. A brief knock on her door made her turn, and Jaim entered the chamber, a smile on his face. He stood still for a moment, his eyes taking in her appearance in a single glance. "Daughter," he said.

Niara remained silent, unwilling to answer, unwilling, for some reason, to call him Father. *I don't know him.*

Jaim's smile didn't diminish. "Would you care to walk with me?" he asked. "We can find a place with privacy."

Niara nodded, although her ears prickled at the implication. *My chamber is not private. Why would that be?*

She followed Jaim, expecting him to lead her to another chamber in the trees, but to her surprise, he instead led her to the forest floor. She followed him in silence until they reached a small, secluded clearing. Two boulders were set at the edge, and Jaim gestured for her to take a seat.

Niara sat, feeling the tension that had been swept away by her bath returning in full force. What was Jaim going to tell her? And would she like it?

Jaim remained silent for a period of time, staring out into the forest. Finally, he sighed. "You have many questions, I suppose."

Niara didn't dignify that with a spoken answer, merely nodded. He was a fool if he thought she would just tamely submit to whatever he told her.

"Where would you like me to begin?" he asked.

The words were out of her mouth before Niara could fully process them. "Why did you come to Ninaeva?"

Jaim blinked, as if he hadn't been expecting that particular question. "I went to Ninaeva because I was searching for allies," he said. "I knew your Mother was there, and I wanted to meet her."

Tension rose in Niara's body. "You knew my mother was there?" she asked. "Did you also know what she was?"

Jaim avoided looking at her eyes. "What she was?"

Her chest tightened in anger. "Half-elven," she said. "And of the Faithful, of the line of Queen Olvae."

For a moment, Niara was scared Jaim wasn't going to answer her, or worse, that he would lie. "Yes," he said. "I knew."

"Then why didn't you tell her who you were?" she asked.

Jaim spread his hands. "You have seen the hate the Faithful spread toward my kind, and you would ask me that?" Despite the disbelief in his voice, it didn't seem fully real to Niara.

"Mother didn't know about the Faithful or Unfaithful at that time," Niara pointed out. "You could have told her whatever you wished."

Jaim's eyes narrowed. "Then perhaps you will think better of me for not," he said. "Regardless, I enjoyed meeting your mother, but she was not the ally I was seeking, and so I left."

"And when I was born?" Niara knew there was more to the story, there had to be, but she didn't know the questions necessary to get the answers.

Jaim smiled in satisfaction. "When you were born, it was the answer to all my prayers," he said. "The lines of Olvae and Lyaen, combined into one? One blessed by both the Lord and the Lady? You could unite our warring people and lead them to peace under your rule. With me to guide you, you could do what the rest of us only dreamed." His eyes darkened. "If only I had been able to speak to you sooner."

"Why didn't you?" she asked, frowning.

Jaim shook his head. "Who could have predicted your mother?" he asked. "I expected her to do as most of your noblewomen did, and to give you up. I would have taken you, and you would have been raised as one of us, knowing full well your heritage. But no," his eyes darkened. "Your mother did the unexpected. She kept you at Ninaeva, in the security of the castle. I could not reach you there."

"And when I grew older?" Niara asked. "I can't believe you wouldn't have tried to contact me." *Contact me, or control me?* She felt as if she were sitting on a bed of nails. Just one question could tip the balance into painful territory.

Jaim grimaced. "You being your mother's niece was the only thing that gave me a chance," he said. "When you started traveling to the capital of Saemar, I thought I could contact you then. But Kinaevan," he spat the name, "got there first."

Niara blinked at the venom in Jaim's voice. She remembered clearly the first time she had met her grandfather. It had been at the Great Hunt, her very first. She had been excited and enthralled by the southern forest and had wandered off, seeking flowers or butterflies, when a wolf had attacked, threatening to kill her. It had done no more than threaten, however, when an arrow had struck it dead, and her grandfather had appeared to make sure of her safety.

Tears stung her eyes, and she looked away from Jaim, unwilling to let him see her pain. Kinaevan had spent Manyu's Time at Ninaeva, had taught her of her ancestry, had guided her first steps of exploring her heritage and abilities. She had loved him.

"Kinaevan died when I was eight," she said, fighting to keep her voice level. "What stopped you then?"

"I knew Kinaevan would have poisoned your mind against me and my people," Jaim said, "and by then, you were acknowledged as your mother's daughter and heir. My chance was gone."

You still could have tried, Niara couldn't stop the thought. *You could have told me, somehow. A note, a hint, that's all it would have taken.* She stood up from the boulder and stared into the trees, her arms crossed over her chest. Twilight rested well upon them, and the leaves of the trees were glistening in the evening light.

"And why now?" The words were dragged out of her almost unwillingly. She wasn't certain she wanted to know the answer. But she had to.

"I knew you were still alive," Jaim said. "I would have known if you had died. But I couldn't fathom where. And travel is dangerous these days, especially for our people."

Niara couldn't disagree with that. Her own capture by the dragons had made that clear enough.

"But I could tell when you started traveling, and you were coming closer and closer to me. All I could do was hope and wait and prepare for you to arrive. And welcome you home."

Home. Niara suppressed a shudder. Home lay in a mountain of rubble, the ruined castle of Ilhelm. This place, these rooms in the trees, was not her home and never would be.

"Daughter..." She heard Jaim stand up, and she turned before he could place a hand on her shoulder. His expression was solemn, unlike the easy smile he had worn most of the day.

I don't trust him. Niara didn't know where the thought came from, but she couldn't deny it. Jaim's story had plausibility, and in all likelihood he spoke the truth, but there had to be more. So much he hadn't told her. Despite that knowledge, however, she couldn't help but feel kinship with him. He was her father, after all, she could not deny that. And he did seem willing to welcome her as his own.

She forced a smile. "Give me some time," she said. "You've known for years. I've just found out today."

Jaim nodded, but he didn't seem satisfied. Niara bit her lip to prevent anything untoward from slipping out.

"Tell me about King Lyaen," she said instead, hoping to change the subject to something less painful.

Jaim's expression lightened. "To tell you of King Lyaen, I must tell you of the fall of Queen Olvae," he said. "Are you certain you are prepared to hear it?" His eyebrow quirked inquisitively.

The fall of Queen Olvae... Niara shivered. Vinet's favorite theory was that something had happened to Queen Olvae, something the Faithful never spoke of. After Kinaevan's death, her mother had never been able to determine the truth of that theory.

She managed to nod.

"Then I shall tell you the tale, as it is taught to all our children." Jaim stood back and closed his eyes, his voice taking on a tone of recitation. "After the Age of Great Fire, the children of the Goldwood lived in peace for many years, ruled by Queen Olvae Oakenspear, hero and savior. But all was not well. The Lady of Leaf and Lake grew proud of her victory over the Great Burner, and taunted her Lord, forgetting it was his gifts which allowed hers to blossom. She grew spiteful, and whispered in the ears of her people, turning them against her Lord." He paused to take a breath.

Niara blinked. This did not match anything she'd been taught by her grandfather.

Her father opened his eyes to regard her as he continued. "The hero, Olvae Oakenspear, did not listen to the Lady. She knew of the gifts the Lord had given and regarded him as equal. The Lady cast her out of her grace, stripping the gifts she had given her. Olvae did not go quietly, however. She met with others who worshipped the Lord, including her breast-companion, Lyaen. They fled, but she was forced to leave her son behind, causing the great rift of elvenkind. Her heart was broken by the rift, and she died in grief and sorrow. Lyaen, in his grief, vowed to reject the Lady as she had rejected Olvae. And so we follow the Lord until the day the Lady seeks repentance for her crimes." Jaim's voice lost the tone of recitation. "Olvae's son became the leader of the Faithful," he said. "Your mother draws her descent through him. He loved his mother, and so did not erase her name, but instead expunged any mention of her disagreement with the Lady. That is why we mark ourselves thus," Jaim gestured at his forehead. "In memory of Olvae's grief at losing her son."

That had the ring of truth around it, but Niara could not say why. "And Lyaen?" she asked.

Jaim sighed. "Olvae did not long survive her rejection by her son," he said. "She died broken-hearted. Her followers were grief-stricken and undefended. They turned to Lyaen, Olvae's closest friend, and asked him to be their leader and King."

"And you are descended from him," Niara murmured.

Jaim nodded. "And you from them both." He took a step closer to her. "Don't you see, daughter?" he asked. "The Faithful will listen to you. Granddaughter of Kinaevan, they follow you already, I do not doubt. The Steadfast will follow you. You have the blessing of the Lady. All that remains is to acquaint you with the Lord."

I've seen the Lord. He has marked me. Niara opened her mouth, then blinked as her vision blurred. Two figures stood before her, one a maiden, young and beautiful, and the other the stag-horned elf hunter. Niara stopped herself from falling to her knees. She had seen the maiden before, though rarely in this form. The mother was her far more common guide.

AeresThonEsia, Lady of Leaf and Lake. And the Lord of Life and Loss.

"Taledon," the Lord said. "You know my Lady's name, you should know mine."

The maiden laughed. "You have claimed her already, have you not, my lord?" she said. She smiled, and Niara shivered.

The Lord, Taledon, eyed the maiden coolly. "And you have not?"

"Not as you have, my lord," she said. "Certainly not as you have."

"But your mark is no less permanent," Taledon said, his voice prodding.

"But should it be as visible?" the maiden took a step closer to Niara, and Niara held her breath. The maiden's form was the most dangerous, and she didn't dare offend.

"Give me your hand," the maiden spoke sweetly, but with an underlying steel Niara couldn't disobey. She offered the maiden her right hand, but the maiden shook her head.

Niara swallowed and held out her unmarked hand. She knew what was coming.

The maiden took Niara's left hand, and Niara felt a cool sensation tingle her arm. She gasped and glanced down, and when she looked up, it was into the face of the mother.

"Travel well, elf-daughter," the mother said. Her eyes bored into Niara's. "Sky-lord has risen, dragon-lord comes. But you must travel your own path and create bonds forged in fire."

What does that mean? Niara wanted to ask, to beg the answer, but the Lady would never clarify her statements.

The mother turned away, back toward Taledon, and she became the maiden again. Taledon bowed to her, a smile playing on his lips. "Shall we hunt, my lady?" he asked.

The maiden laughed. "Can you catch me?" She glanced back at Niara, her eyes glinting in the light. "Till the labyrinth, elf-daughter."

"The labyrinth?" Niara asked, her voice barely a whisper.

"Mind what monster you bring with you," Taledon said.

Then her vision flickered again, and the two disappeared.

"Niara? Are you listening?" Jaim's voice penetrated her thoughts.

Niara shook her head, centering herself again. She was in the forest, talking to her father. He had been telling her about the Lord...

She knew without knowing why she could not tell him what she had just witnessed, what she had just seen. Taledon and AeresThon-Esia would not approve if she did.

"My apologies," she said. "It's been a long day, and it's a lot to think about."

Jaim nodded. "I apologize as well," he said. "I should not have burdened you with so much at once." He offered his arm in a courtly manner to escort her back, and habit bade Niara accept it.

They walked in silence through the trees until they reached the base of the ladder which led to Niara's guest chamber. Jaim paused and released Niara's arm, giving her a shallow bow.

"I will leave you now, daughter," he said. "Until the morning." He turned to leave.

"Wait," Niara said, the word leaving her mouth before her conscious mind had a chance to process it.

Jaim turned back, eyebrows raised. "Yes?"

Niara hesitated, trying to formulate the thought which hovered in her mind. "At the feast, you named me your heir," she said. "Why, when you know so little about me? How do you know you can trust me?" *How do I know I can trust you?*

Jaim smiled slightly. "I know because you are my blood."

"But Olvae's son betrayed her blood," Niara pointed out.

Jaim nodded in acknowledgment. "You speak the truth," he said. "But I have faith in my daughter. Tomorrow you will meet the Lord and receive his full blessing. My faith will be rewarded then." He bowed. "Goodnight, daughter."

Niara gazed after him, still uncertain. *If I've already met the Lord, how will that affect whatever his plans are for tomorrow? Is Taledon just as unpredictable as AeresThonEsia? Mazda's light, I wish I knew more about him.*

She glanced down at her arms, feeling as if the stag's mark was clearly visible through her sleeve. It was a miracle Jaim had not seen the sun brand on her hand, otherwise, she was certain he would have commented on it.

She clenched her left arm, trying to summon the courage to look. Finally, she drew back her sleeve, dreading what she would see beneath it.

A tattoo of a rose surrounded by thorns stared back at her.

11

____

LORD AND LADY

Niara woke slowly, for the first time in years. She had grown so used to waking instantly that she gazed at the ceiling for a long moment, blinking as she tried to recall where she was.

The Steadfast. Jaim, my father. The Lord and Lady telling me...something. Mazda's light. Can't they find someone else to play with?

She suppressed a groan and swung herself out of bed. A set of clothing had been laid out for her, simpler than what she had been wearing the night before. She stared at the clothes, worry tingling in her mind. They had not been there when she'd gone to sleep, and she had heard no one in the middle of the night.

They're elves, she reminded herself. *They can move as silently as a breeze.*

That did not comfort her. *I should be able to hear them,* Niara thought. *Even if I have human blood, I should have been able to hear it.* She shivered. There existed no privacy in her chamber. Jaim had implied as much last night, but now that was certain.

I should find Enlil. The thought came crystal clear. She hadn't seen him since the feast. After so many days of travel in his company, it felt odd not to be waking up beside him.

With that thought, she got to her feet and changed into the waiting clothing. She slipped outside her chamber, trying to be as quiet as possible. For some reason, she didn't want any of the elves to see her speaking to Enlil. She had a feeling they would try to interrupt.

Ralanni said his chamber was directly above mine. She located the ladder that led up, only to start at the sound of footsteps. Jaim came into view around the tree trunk.

"Ah, you are awake, daughter!" Jaim's voice was light. "Up with the sun, I see? That is well." He stepped forward and placed a hand on her arm. "Please, follow me. What we must do is best done early, before we break our fast."

Niara hesitated, staring upward. "I'd like to speak to Enlil first," she managed.

Jaim shook his head. "You may speak to him all you wish after we are finished. Please, daughter. This may not wait."

Niara hesitated a moment longer, but Jaim did not yield in his insistence. She cast one more look upward, then followed Jaim, back down to the forest floor.

Jaim said nothing as he strode through the forest, and Niara had to struggle to keep up. *Where are we going?*

Jaim stopped in a small clearing, one which appeared unremarkable to Niara's eyes. Only when he brushed aside a covering of leaves and moss did she see the entrance to a cave.

Not another cave. She swallowed, trying to restrain her nervousness. She didn't want to go inside.

Jaim seemed unaware of her fear. "This is where you will meet the Lord," he said. "Please, the best time is almost here."

"What time is that?" Niara asked, but Jaim had already disappeared into the cave. With a sigh, Niara followed, ignoring the jolt of fear that struck her when she entered the cave.

Darkness shrouded the cavern, not unlike the cave that sheltered Ren and his group of outlaws. Unlike that cave, however, this one was a passage, spiraling deeper and deeper underground. The dim light from the entrance faded the further she walked, and Niara felt her breath shortening the deeper and darker it became.

The darkness had grown to almost pitch-black when she saw a faint light ahead of her. She quickened her pace, and the passage widened into a room. The stone walls had been carved and painted, with symbols and pictures which meant nothing to Niara. Jaim stood at the far end of the cavern, and he beckoned impatiently when Niara entered.

Niara took a deep breath and crossed the cavern. Next to Jaim was a small painting of a labyrinth. It emitted a soft, glowing light, the source of the uncanny light in the cavern.

"Here," Jaim held a knife to her. "Prick your finger."

Niara hesitated, then took the knife and obeyed, drawing a small drop of blood from her index finger.

Jaim nodded in satisfaction and gestured. "Trace the labyrinth."

Niara stared at the labyrinth, trying to tease out the memory that hovered just beyond her mind. Her mother had spoken of something like this. And the Lord, Taledon, had said something…

Beware the monster you bring. Manyu's curse. Mother was marked by Manyu in a situation like this.

One glance at Jaim convinced Niara she would have no choice but to follow his instructions. If she wavered, he would grab her hand and trace the labyrinth with it himself.

I can do this, she told herself. *I just have to be careful about what I think about.* Thinking about nothing was out of the question, she knew full well that in this situation something would leak through, something terrifying and dangerous, in all likelihood.

What do I want to know? she thought.

"Now, daughter. Before the time is too late."

I want to know the truth. She fixed the desire in her mind and raised a hand, beginning to trace the labyrinth. *The truth about my father, the truth about Olvae and Lyaen, the truth about the Lord and Lady…The truth about Auriel, and what I'm supposed to do to stop him.*

Her finger reached the center of the labyrinth, and Niara held her breath. The light seemed to flare, and then everything went dark.

A scream filled her ears, and Niara clapped her hand over her ears, falling to her knees as the terror of the scream overwhelmed her. She felt her heart pounding in her throat, and her breath came in short, ragged gasps. The scream faded, but she still knelt on the ground, breathing quickly, waiting, wanting the light to return.

I can't see. Panic threatened to engulf her, and she thrust out a hand, to steady herself on something, anything. She touched nothing, and she heard herself cry out, a soft cry that sounded loud in the absolute stillness.

Don't panic, she told herself. *Don't panic, don't panic, don't panic. You can create light, you know you can, you just have to*—the thought was mother to the action. She reached for her power, and a soft, glowing light appeared around her. She centered it on herself as she knelt, shivering, trying to get her bearings.

She was in a passageway, two tunnels stretching out to either side of her. The walls didn't seem like stone, but she could not tell what they were. Instinctively, she drew her hands back to herself, unwilling to touch them.

The Labyrinth, she told herself. She caught her breath. *Mazda's light, what do I do? Which way do I go?*

There was no hint in the passages. Each stretched out as far as she could see, each looking exactly the same.

She stood up slowly, as quietly as possible. *The monster in the labyrinth. I brought it with me. Whatever monster the truth is, I'm going to find out.* She hesitated a moment longer, then chose the right-hand passage. It was as good a direction as any.

She lost track of time as she walked, and her worry faded into a distant memory. When she came up against a crossroads, a mirror standing in front of her, she blinked, trying to make sense of the figure in the mirror.

Her reflection stared back at her, or almost, she thought. A full-blooded elf, however, without any of the subtle hints that marked part of her heritage as human. The differences were small, but Niara knew the lines of her face. This was not her reflection. She turned away, following the passage to the right.

After several steps, she glanced over her shoulder. The passage behind her had disappeared, and the mirror as well. She shivered. She could not backtrack.

She continued on again, watching the walls of the labyrinth for some clue, some hint, anything that would give her a sign of what she was supposed to do. Although her worry had faded, she could still sense it, as if it hadn't faded, merely been blocked.

The second mirror caught her by surprise. Her reflection looked more like Vinet, more able to pass for human than Niara. Niara stared at it a long while. *This is what I would have been if Jaim hadn't been my father.*

For a moment, the temptation to reach out and touch the mirror overwhelmed her, to see if that reality would take hold. What would her life be like, if Jaim hadn't infiltrated Ilhelm and been her father? Who would have been her father?

She kept her hands at her side. Like it or not, Jaim was her father. This was her life. If she had wished for the truth, those were truths she needed to face.

She turned to the right again, ready, waiting for the third mirror. For there would be one. Things always came in sets of three.

She was so confident in that assumption she nearly ran into the blank wall. She blinked at it, dumbfounded. No passages stretched out, no curves, no choices. Only a dead end.

She glanced over her shoulder, unable to process what she saw. The passage still stretched out behind her, a temptation back to the second mirror.

No. She resolutely turned back to the wall. There had to be a trick, somehow. Was the mirror hidden? Did she have to do something to trigger it?

Hesitantly, she reached out to touch the wall. It felt like polished stone, but warm. She ran her hands down it, then tried to pull away. Her hand couldn't leave the wall.

Niara tried to jerk her hand back again, but it remained stuck fast to the wall. The sun brand on the back of her hand stared back at her like an accusation.

She heard footsteps behind her, and she tried to pull back again, unwilling to let any more of herself touch the wall, but knowing she needed to be able to face what was coming. *The Monster in the Labyrinth,* she thought, fear rising up inside her. *The monster. The truth...*

"The truth, she wishes," the voice came from behind her, a gravelly whisper. "Does she not know the truth hurts?"

Frantically, Niara tried to jerk her hand free. She felt the presence behind her, mere feet away. She squeezed her eyes tight, unwilling to look. *I can't face it. I can't, I can't...*

The voice came again. "Does she not know the truth blinds?"

Niara screamed as the figure touched her shoulder. Pain seared through her body like fire. Her hand fell away from the wall, but she could do nothing but fall to the ground. She clutched her head, trying desperately to control the pain.

Visions started flashing in front of her closed eyes. *A war. Four dragons. A spear. Two female elves kissing. A terrible storm. Wrathful anger.* More and more visions flew across her eyes, each one more confusing than the last. *An elf man lying dead in his bed, another raising a bloodied dagger. A puppet, dangling by strings. A dragon turning into a human with red hair, blue eyes staring at her, smiling.*

The fire inside her grew, almost as if it were growing wings and stretching out to fly. Niara screamed again and dropped her hands to claw at the ground. Her eyes were open now, but nothing would stop the visions.

"The truth!" the gravelly voice penetrated through the pain. "Here is the truth!"

An elven queen defeating the Great Burner's Consort. The dragon flew off with the Oakenspear still buried in its heart. Olvae Oakenspear being cheered, celebrated by her people. Standing side by side with two elven men, who could only be her husband and son. The Mother behind them, smiling in approval.

Another elven woman, this one with golden hair like a crown. She gazed longingly at Olvae. Taledon stood behind her, hand extended. Offering power.

Olvae and the golden-haired woman running through the forest side by side, looking over their shoulders in fear. Olvae's son angrily petitioning the Lady, fury on his face. The Lady demanding a blood sacrifice. The son stood over his father, raising a dagger. Blood dripped onto the ground.

Olvae and the gold-haired woman kissing each other. Olvae falling to the ground, screaming in pain. Thorns sprang from her forehead, carving a scar. An Eye. The woman cried tears of shock and pain.

The woman railing at Olvae's son. The son threatening her. People rallying around either one of them, shouting accusations at each other. A giant wall of fire separating the groups.

Pain seared through her, and Niara huddled in further on herself. What was she seeing? Who was the elven woman? The queen could only be Olvae, no other would have thrown the Oakenspear, but who was the woman?

Lyaen. The whisper came, but all thoughts about what it might mean were flung aside by the next vision.

Ilhelm castle. A minstrel arriving. Vinet flirting, Gwyn looking on with disapproval. A bedchamber, Vinet fast asleep. Jaim next to her, his hands hovering just an inch over her stomach, a mask of concentration on his face. "Lord, I call to thee. Grant unto me the Gift of Life, and let the Loss come where it may."

Niara gasped, struggling to catch her breath. Jaim had made certain Vinet had become pregnant. Even as she realized she could now replicate it, could control if she herself ever became pregnant, she was filled with anger and betrayal. *He lied to me. He lied.*

The capital of Saemar. The palace. A King, hunched over a bed, clasping the hand of a woman. She drew one, unsteady breath, then lay still.

A dark-haired man, with one dark eye and one of citron, stepped forward. "She was killed by magic, your majesty."

Niara's eyes blurred as the pain intensified. *He killed someone to create me.* The fire burned through her, and she clutched the wall in front of her, frantic for something, anything, that would stop the torment.

The ground disappeared beneath her, and she screamed as she started falling, falling through darkness. She reached out desperately, flailing to catch something. She screamed again as air rushed by her ears, and she fell through a bottomless pit. She closed her eyes, blocking out the darkness.

"Fight, child!" the voice echoed through the darkness, deep and commanding. "Daughter of two bloods, born to heal! Fight!"

Why? A small part of Niara couldn't help but question. The rest of her refused to surrender, however. She gritted her teeth and reached out her arms, forcing her eyes open. She reached inside, reaching for the only thing she knew how to fight with.

Air rushed up from the depths, billowing and encasing her, slowing her fall. Niara gritted her teeth in concentration.

No longer falling. Now I need a light. She twisted her power again, and the air around her glowed. For a moment, her heart sank. All she could see beyond the glow of the light was darkness. Then her breath caught. In the distance, she could see a thin speck of light.

She urged the air to wrap around her and carry her away. The wind needed little urging, wrapping itself around her like a blanket and sending her headlong toward the light. Niara felt her breath taken away in the rush of adrenaline. The light grew larger and larger. Niara desperately called for the wind to stop, to slow down.

She had waited too long. She burst through the light, tumbling head over heels to the ground. She clutched the dirt beneath her fingers and gasped for breath, panting with exertion.

Slowly, she looked up and took in the scene around her. She had landed in what seemed to have once been a garden. It had long since been overgrown, however. Vines grew along the fences, and trees and plants grew whichever way they chose. In the trees, birds sang sweetly to each other. In the distance, she could hear the trickle of running water.

"Welcome, child."

Niara whirled around, taken aback by the sound of the voice. Her eyes widened as she took in the sight of the woman sitting on an old stone bench. She scrambled to her feet, her heart racing. "Lady," she said.

AeresThonEsia, Lady of Leaf and Lake, simply raised an eyebrow at her. "You have come a long way, elf-daughter, royal one."

Niara took a deep breath. She had passed through the labyrinth. She had faced her monster.

The Lady chuckled, and Niara realized she had spoken her last words aloud. "So, she remembers the tales of her elders." The lady stroked a cat who had appeared on the bench next to her.

Niara shuddered. "There were two," she said, remembering. "The one that spoke of truth, and the one…the one who urged me to fight."

The Lady nodded. "Yes…" she whispered. "Two beings, two trials, two tests. The creature in the labyrinth is different for everyone. Your desire, your wish, for *truth*," her voice rasped. "Truth *burns*, burns like fire."

Niara flinched at the memory of the pain and the visions. "Then they were the truth?" she asked.

The Lady chuckled. "What is truth?" she rolled her eyes at the sky.

Niara's shoulders stiffened. She was in no mood for the Lady's cryptic words. The visions flashed through her memory. Her father and mother. Olvae and Lyaen. She shied away from the pain of her parents and asked about the second instead. "Were the visions accurate representations of events?" she rephrased. "Did you accept Olvae's son's sacrifice to strip his mother of her gifts?"

The Lady fastened her eyes on Niara, and a shiver ran down her spine. The sorrow in the Lady's eyes chilled her very soul.

"He came to me, so young and proud," she whispered. "Olvae had betrayed his father, fled her duty, fled her people. He wove such a lovely tale, one of the future, of trust, of honor." The Lady shook her head. "It all comes with a price, of course. There is always a price!" her voice rose. "Your mother knew that, the elfsdaughter. She paid the price, to save the sun-child, the dark one. I granted the choice. They paid the price."

Niara shuddered. Her mother had told her, eventually, about the death of her grandfather. Kinaevan had been dying anyway, according to her mother. And as far as her mother had been able to determine, then or since, it had been the only way to remove the curse of Manyu.

"Choices, choices," the Lady whispered. "So many choices. I cannot guide them all."

Niara squared her shoulders. A part of her wanted to pity the Lady, for the sorrow in her voice was certainly genuine. The greater part of her, however, wanted to press for the rest of the story. "And the Lord?" she asked. "What was his part in this?"

The Lady threw her head back and laughed, startling Niara. "Oh, the Lord, she asks!" The Lady continued to laugh until she wheezed. "My Lord, my lover, the giver of life and bringer of death. She asks what part he played!"

Niara stood warily. The very air around her trembled.

The Lady stood up and spread her arms. "The Lord!" she exclaimed.

Niara tensed as a rumble filled the air in the garden. The light dimmed, and the Lady laughed again, wild and carefree. Then the Lady was gone, and in her place stood an elven man. He stood perfectly still, regarding Niara with eyes that stared into her very soul. Power radiated out from him, flowing through the garden, until everything around them was part of his presence. Stag antlers rose from his forehead, and he smiled at her. "We meet again, Niara Sindarilae Andaren."

Her full name on his tongue made Niara tremble, the ring of truth in his voice undeniable. That was her identity, truly. Sindarilae was only part of it. The Andaren line was the rest.

"Lord Taledon," she managed.

Taledon's smile widened. "You asked for the truth in the labyrinth," he said. "The most dangerous wish of all, some would say."

"Olvae and Lyaen," Niara whispered. "They were…"

"They were lovers, yes," Taledon interrupted. "Lyaen was my servant, as Olvae was my Lady's. Lyaen was a true warrior, devoted to her people. And she loved Olvae dearly."

Her. Niara nodded. "The Steadfast call Lyaen King," she said.

Taledon snorted. "They remember wrongly," he said. "Lyaen was a woman, as female as any. After the divide, however," he shook his head. "Lyaen did not long survive Olvae's death. Memory faded."

If that part isn't true, then what else have the Steadfast misremembered?

Unwillingly, Niara's thoughts turned to her second vision, that of her parents. "Jaim knew when he slept with my mother there would be a child," she said. "He called on you, and you granted his wish." She looked at Taledon, her eyes accusing. "You killed the Queen of Saemar because of his wish to create life."

Taledon shrugged. "There is always a price," he said, echoing the Lady's words. "I do not control where the price falls; those who beg the boon take that risk upon themselves. But it is usually a blood relative. Blood calls to blood."

Niara frowned. "The Queen of Saemar wasn't my relative," she protested. "No one knows where she was from."

"Trace your grandmother's bloodline back, and you will find the connection," Taledon said. His voice remained impassive, as if a death in exchange for a life was of no matter to him.

He's the Lord of Life and Loss, Niara thought. Death would hardly be tragic to him.

She took a deep breath, steadying herself, steadying her emotions. *That's in the past,* she thought. *What matters is now. And now...my father lied to me, about my birth, and perhaps about other things. And I need to know what my task is.*

Taledon smiled as if he had read her thoughts. "You are strong," he said. "You will need that strength."

"Why?" Niara heard the desperation creeping into her voice. "Why will I need strength?"

Taledon's smile grew. "For the trials you will face."

Niara swallowed and barely prevented herself from taking a step backward. "The Exile." She clenched her fists to keep them from trembling.

"You have already begun that," Taledon said, his voice calm, as if unaware of her reaction. "Yours is of a different kind than any other shall face, however. The presence of our enemy leaves us no choice."

"Auriel," Niara said flatly. "The sky-lord."

Taledon nodded. "He will hunt down all of the world's first creation," he said. "Our people. And although I am Lord of Loss, I am also Lord of Life. One cannot have death without birth, and he brings too much death to this world."

Niara frowned. "So why don't you do anything about it?" she demanded. "You're the one with the same level of power as he has, not us mere mortals." She felt the frustration mounting within her.

"Mere mortals," Taledon shook his head, chuckling. "You are hardly a mere anything, Niara Sindarilae Andaren. That is why it is your duty to bring down the sky-lord."

Niara stared at the Lord. He had to be joking. Her frustration mounted even higher. This should not be her responsibility! "You want me to kill a god?" she asked. "The one who created humans and dragons?"

"No!" Taledon's voice rang sharply through the entire garden. The vibrations of his shout jolted into Niara. "No," he said, in a calmer tone. "To kill the sky-lord would be disastrous. He made half the world; you cannot destroy him and hope to live."

"Then what?" Niara asked, baffled.

"Bind him," Taledon said. "Bind him again, and you bind the dragons with him. The world will return to what it once was."

As if it were that easy! "How?" Niara demanded.

"You know how," Taledon said. "Follow your path. South, to Shan Serin. You will find your answers there." His expression darkened. "Beware the other who has marked you, though. Let not his desires cloud your vision."

Niara glanced at the sun-brand on her hand. "Who marked me?" she asked.

Taledon shook his head. "You have my blessing, as well as my mark, Niara Sindarilae Andaren," he said. "Now you must return."

"Wait!" Niara exclaimed. The world began to shift around her, the garden fading from existence. "You didn't answer my questions!"

"Follow the path." She could no longer see the Lord, but his voice echoed through the darkness. "Follow the path."

1 2

——————

LIES

Darkness consumed her. She floated, drifting in a sea of darkness. She was so relaxed, so comfortable…

"Niara! Niara!"

She tried to ignore the voice, unwilling to wake, unwilling to move. Couldn't they just leave her at peace?

"Niara!"

She groaned. Stones dug into her back, and the cold seeped through her body from the ground. She was uncomfortable. She wasn't lying in a bed but on cold, rocky ground. Where was she? What had she been doing?

"Niara, please!"

Her eyes flicked open, and she squinted. Even the dim light seemed bright to her. Blue eyes looked down at her, set in a shock of red hair. Enlil was shaking her shoulders, his expression frantic.

"Enlil?" she managed.

"Naytar's stone!" Enlil exclaimed, then leaned down and kissed her.

For a moment, Niara remained paralyzed. Then her body responded, and her lips opened to his, warm and welcoming. She relaxed, enjoying the sensation of his lips on hers, of his arms wrapped around her, of his body so close and warm against her own. She brought her arms up, placing a hand on his shoulder, pulling him closer to her.

Enlil's eyes flew open, and he pulled back abruptly. Niara blinked, staring at him, processing what had just happened.

"I'm sorry, I'm sorry!" Enlil looked like he wanted to pull away from her, but Niara's head lay on his lap.

The utter panic in Enlil's expression made Niara stop, taking a few deep breaths. Her thoughts felt muddled, and she raised a hand to her head, instinctively taking another breath to steady herself.

Enlil still appeared panicked, and Niara tried to sit up, to allow him space. To allow her the space to think about what had just happened. *He kissed me. Mazda's light, I kissed him back.*

The fear on Enlil's face receded a little as Niara sat up. "I snuck in here when I couldn't find you this morning," he said. "Jaimalaeren's outside, but he wasn't paying any attention to the side entrance. I was able to follow you here, but you were just lying there..." he shook his head. "I was scared you were injured, and you weren't moving," he took a breath. "You've had similar reactions before, but this seemed different."

Niara felt a brief flare of disappointment that he was doing his best to ignore the kiss, but she suppressed it, trying to keep any of her emotions from showing on her face. *He still hasn't told me any of his secrets. Just because you enjoyed the kiss...*

She shook herself. "I'm fine," she said. She grimaced, bringing her left arm up to her head. "I think." Her sleeve fell down her arm, and she saw Enlil stiffen. She glanced down, seeing her rose and thorn tattoo.

"That's new," Enlil said, his voice carefully casual.

Niara winced. *There are still things he doesn't know about you, as well.* She shuddered. *Not the best person to be kissing. Though it was nice, and he was certainly handsome...stop it.*

"Last night." She sighed. "Enlil, I—"

"Don't," he cut her off, his voice barely a whisper.

You don't even know what I was going to say. Niara looked up to meet his eyes. Enlil met her gaze with such intensity she shivered at the emotion revealed.

Her sharp ears twitched at the sound of footsteps coming closer, walking down into the cavern. She looked at Enlil in alarm.

"You need to hide!" she hissed. She didn't question her impulse that Jaim should not know Enlil knew about this cavern.

Enlil didn't ask for clarification, just sprang to his feet and raced around the side of the cavern. Niara gasped in astonishment as he didn't head for an exit on the ground, but instead vaulted up the wall, to a small opening near the ceiling of the cavern. He turned and glanced at her one more time before disappearing into the tunnel.

Niara forced her gaze away from where he had disappeared just in time to see Jaim entering the cavern. He smiled when he saw her sitting on the ground.

"Ah, you awake, my daughter," he said. "Then your quest was successful."

Niara suppressed a shudder. *Successful might be a strong word.*

She managed to climb to her feet before Jaim reached her. He startled her by drawing her into a hard embrace.

"I knew you were the answer to my prayers," he said. "Come. There is much to discuss."

Niara let herself be drawn out of the cavern, blinking as they emerged into the sunlight. From the brightness, she had probably been down in the cavern for half the day.

I need to get moving again. The thought came hard and clear. She winced as she stared up. A thick blanket of white clouds covered the sky, so white it reflected the sun. The air bit into her skin, cold and crisp. In Ninaeva, she would have said it looked like snow.

Jaim noticed her shiver and held up a hand. After a moment, a young elven man appeared from within the trees, two heavy cloaks draped over his arm. He bowed as he handed them to Jaim, then disappeared without a word.

Niara gratefully accepted the cloak Jaim offered her. She felt the fur lining warm her as she draped it over her shoulders, and she wrapped it tighter around herself.

Jaim didn't say a word, only strode forward, obviously expecting Niara to follow him. Niara wanted to stop, to ask where they were going, what they had to discuss, but she swallowed her tongue. *He lied to me once already. What else is he planning to lie about?*

Jaim led her up into the trees again, past the platform where her chambers were, until they were in the canopy. He paused before an entrance shaped directly into the tree itself and bowed slightly, gesturing for Niara to precede him.

Niara had to duck to enter the door. When she straightened, she was in another small chamber, this one clearly set up to be a study of some kind. Cushions were laid on the floor, and shelves had been carved into the walls, small cubbyholes filled with books. Niara stared at the books, wanting nothing more at that moment than to reach up and take one. What secrets about her father's people would she discover there?

"Sit, please." Jaim's voice interrupted her thoughts. Since there were no chairs, Niara sank down onto one of the cushions. Jaim lowered himself gracefully to another one. From a small table, he offered her a plate of foods too light to quell the growling in her stomach, but she accepted it anyway.

They ate in silence for a moment. Finally, Jaim spoke. "We will have to mark your forehead," he said. "But despite your human heritage, you look as if you belong here."

Niara kept her face blank with an effort. *I've been marked enough against my will.* "As long as I kept my ears covered, there was nothing to mark me as different from the nobles of Saemar," she said.

Jaim's eyes flashed, but his expression quickly smoothed. Niara made a mental note. *He doesn't like it when I talk about humans.*

"You did not belong with them," Jaim said. "I am sorry I did not bring you here long before this."

It was as much of an opportunity as she would ever have. "Have you always been here?" She couldn't quite believe it. Surely here, in Lokrian, even in the forests, someone would have noticed a group of elves.

Jaim shook his head. "We have only been here the last three years," he said. "When the dragons rose, things were chaotic, and we moved northward in an attempt to hide."

Northward? Niara looked up sharply. "Were you living in the badlands, then?"

Jaim narrowed his eyes. "Why do you wish to know?"

Niara shrugged, attempting to appear casual. "I wish to know about my father's people," She raised an eyebrow. "If I am to be your heir, should I not know about your history?"

"Our recent history is not important," Jaim said, his voice sharp. "What matters is the future. Combining the Faithful and Steadfast into one people again, and overthrowing the sky-lord called Auriel."

Niara straightened. "Is that your goal?" She couldn't keep the excitement from her voice. *If it is, maybe it wouldn't be a bad thing to tell him where the Faithful remnant is. If they could band together and fight, help spread the rebellion throughout Saemar, I can continue south.*

"Well, of course," Jaim said. His eyes darkened. "It is past time the sky-lord's children learned their place. The first-born children will guide the rest of divinity's creations to an age of peace and prosperity, and you shall be Queen overall."

Niara drew back, her eyes wide with shock. "What?" she demanded.

"The elves are the only ones with the wisdom to guide the rest of creation." Jaim smiled. "What has happened in the human lands? War, conflict, murder, kin fighting kin. The nephelm are no better, tucked up in their mountain kingdoms, and the dwarves are too scattered to ever unite. And the dragons, well, you've seen how that has gone." He raised an eyebrow. "The authority must pass to the elves. And you, my daughter, are the only one who can bring two divided people together."

Niara took a deep breath, hardly understanding what Jaim was saying. *He wants me to be Queen? Not just a leader of the elves, but Queen of all?* She couldn't fathom the idea. "Of course, you will need guidance," Jaim said. "You are still young, barely a child. I will be beside you, and I will choose someone from the Faithful as well."

"Like my mother?" Niara's mind reeled, but she managed to ask the question. If Jaim said he was going to choose an advisor, surely he would accept...

"No." Jaim's eyes darkened. "Your mother has too much of the human in her."

Niara frowned. "Too much human?"

"While I am certain you love your mother, her judgment is not to be relied upon," he said. "She followed Kinaevan unquestioningly and was part of the council that allowed the sky-lord to rise. Better that she retire into seclusion and allow you to spread your wings."

Niara bit her lip, keeping her angry words in check. "My mother is one of the wisest people I know," she managed. "My stepfather as well."

If anything, Jaim's eyes grew even darker. "Your stepfather is a man who never should have existed," he said. "Lord knows where he received his abilities."

Niara blinked. "Abilities?"

Jaim shook his head. "Surely you've been away from his influence long enough to tell. He has an aura, to make people trust him, to believe in him. It is how he survived as long as he has, how he seduced your mother."

Niara couldn't help it, she rose to her feet. "You've never met my stepfather," she snapped. "You know nothing about him. He is a good man, and you will not speak these lies about him."

Jaim only sighed. "More time is needed." He waved a hand. "I apologize, daughter. Please, sit down."

Niara hesitated, then reluctantly sat, though her hands still trembled with anger. She held them against her sides, surprised at herself. In all her time at court, listening to people whisper about Nazir, she had never reacted like that. She had always managed to reign in her temper, to politely correct or ignore. *I'm out of practice.*

"We have gone off-topic," Jaim said. "We should return to the most important part of the plan, the unification of the elves and the over-throw of Auriel."

"Do you have a plan?" she asked. If he did, it might be worth going along with, even if just for a short time.

"We must head north," Jaim said. "You will lead us to where the Faithful are hidden. I know you have the Lady's gift, as well as the Lord's. Use that to discover their hiding place. Once the elves are together, we will march on the capital, and lead an assassination of Auriel, the Great Burner, and her two consorts."

Niara felt her eyes widen. In her memory, she could see Taledon, exclaiming in horror after she suggested killing a god. And here was her father, blithely suggesting they assassinate not just a god, but his primary servants as well.

Has he ever spoken to Taledon? she wondered. *Surely the Lord would have told him how bad an idea this was...*

Jaim continued speaking, oblivious to her reaction. "Once the sky-lord is dead, the dragons will be in chaos. That will make it easy to establish our rule, our superior strength. With the Swaying you and some of the Steadfast and Faithful possess, we will secure our position in the capital, then spread our wisdom to the rest of Saemar."

"It won't work," Niara murmured. Her mind was still on Jaim's suggestion of killing Auriel.

"If they resist us, then we will cast them out of our grace," Jaim said, his voice flat. "The dragons who resist us can have them."

It took Niara a moment to realize what he was talking about. "No!" she protested. She stood up. "This is a terrible idea. I spoke to the Lord. Killing Auriel would destabilize everything. It would throw the world into worse chaos than it is in now! And I will not be part of an attempt to dominate humanity." She felt herself breathing heavily. "If you do that, you will be no better than the Great Burner and the rest of the dragons."

For the first time, she saw true anger in Jaim's face as he rose to his feet to face her. "The Lord told you this?" he demanded, his voice low.

Niara refused to back down. "He did," she said. She reached for her sleeve, intending to draw it back to show him the stag scar. Jaim's gaze flickered down, widening as they rested on her hand. Before Niara could react, he reached out and clenched her wrist in an iron grip.

"What is this?" he demanded, gesturing at the sun-shaped brand.

Niara tried to jerk her hand away. "None of your business."

Jaim's eyes remained dark. "You are my daughter. Everything of yours is my business." His grip tightened even more, and Niara winced involuntarily at the pain. "You must be protected until we march. Who knows what else is influencing your mind." He whistled, loud and clear. Before Niara could react, two elves ducked into the chamber, bows slung over their backs and swords at their side.

"Please escort my daughter to her chamber," Jaim said. "She is overwrought from her trial this morning and needs plenty of rest. Allow no one to see her."

Niara stared at her father in disbelief. "At least allow me to talk to Enlil," she said. "He'll be worried."

"I will inform Enlil of your situation myself," Jaim said. "Do not trouble yourself with thoughts of him any longer." He released her wrist, and the two elves stepped to either side of Niara. Niara shuddered as she glanced at their implacable faces.

"Follow us, Lady Niara," one of them said, his voice like stone.

Niara had the feeling they would not hesitate to manhandle her if they thought it necessary. She stood as straight as she could and glared at her father. "I will not be your puppet Queen," she said, surprised at how steady her voice was.

"Of course not," Jaim's voice was soothing now, a small smile in place. *For the benefit of the witnesses,* Niara thought. "You will be Queen in your own right, by virtue of your blood and birth. I will just be there to guide you." He nodded at the elves. "You may leave."

One of the elves touched Niara's arm, and she jerked away. "I am quite capable of walking by myself," she snapped.

The elf said nothing, merely gestured. Niara swallowed her rebellion and left the chamber, one elf walking ahead and the other close behind her.

Mazda's light, she thought, as they climbed down the ladder and guided her to the entrance to her guest chamber. *What am I supposed to do now?*

Niara paced the length of her chamber, back and forth, waiting. She had been in here for hours now. An elf had brought her a tray of food but had left without saying a word. *Surely someone will come at some point,* Niara thought. *If Jaim wants to use me as his figurehead, he can't ignore me forever.*

She swallowed down the bile in her throat. The last thing she wanted to do was be a puppet queen for her father.

He lied to me, she thought. *He intended for me to be born, and he's been planning to use me since then. If Mother hadn't been so protective...* She shuddered, unwilling to think of what might have happened. If Vinet hadn't acknowledged her as her daughter and heir, if she had died before doing so, Niara would have been easy prey. All Jaim would have had to do was treat her with a bit of kindness, and she would have been grateful just to have a father.

He has to have tried, she thought. *To put that kind of effort into seducing Mother, and then to just leave me... I don't know if I can tell Mother about this. She still believes Jaim was just a minstrel, that my birth was an accident. I don't know if I could tell her otherwise.*

Outside, the clear sound of a chime echoed through the woods. Niara's sharp ears picked up the sounds of gentle footsteps, of elves walking and climbing the platforms. Although there were no windows in her chamber, she knew nightfall approached.

Maybe Jaim isn't going to visit me, she thought. *If so, he's an idiot. If this is his end plan, he really should have tried to contact me sooner. Make me sympathetic to the cause. He knew what Grandfather was teaching Mother about the Unfaithful...*

The Unfaithful. Niara stopped, staring blankly at the wall in front of her. She had been trying too hard to understand where Jaim was coming from that she had ignored the fact that he was the leader of the Unfaithful, instead thinking of them as the Steadfast.

She felt her brow furrow. *Years ago, in the Mount Halon war,* she remembered. *The Unfaithful fought on the side of Mount Halon. I know they did. Could that have been part of an attempt to get closer to me? Why wouldn't he just send someone to...*her eyes widened. A memory. Vinet and Gwyn had been closed-lipped about it, but there had been an assassination attempt. And the assassin had been an Unfaithful elf.

Niara began pacing again, staring at the floor as she thought. *If I ask Jaim about it, he'll lie. He'll say it was a rogue agent, or Mount Halon influenced some kind of corruption. But he's their leader, with the Lord's gift. It has to work for more than relatives. If he didn't know one of them was trying to assassinate Mother, I'll...*she shivered. She could so easily imagine it happening. She hadn't even known Vinet was her mother at that point. She'd been calling her Aunt Vinet. All Jaim would have had to do was show up, introduce himself as father to the grief-stricken little girl, and she would have been lost.

She shook herself. *Well, it didn't happen,* she told herself. *Mother is alive, and somewhere in the south. Where you need to go, and soon!* Taledon had made that clear. She needed to get to Shan Serin, before Papsukkal.

Time is running short. She shivered. The chill of the night air penetrated even through the tree trunk. At least she still had the cloak Jaim had given her.

I need to get out of here. Niara glared at the door. She had heard guards moving around outside. *I need to get Enlil, and we both need to leave.*

*Enlil...*Niara's heart turned over in her chest. If she closed her eyes, she could feel his lips on hers, taste the warmth of his kiss. It was enough to make her want to run to him, to ignore his warnings about secrets and trust, and kiss him again. She could imagine his eyes, warm and gentle, and his hands running through her hair, down her body...

"Mazda's light!" she breathed, realizing where her mind was going. *Mazda's light, what am I going to do?* She had no time for thoughts like this! Even if she did, Enlil had made it clear he didn't have time for them, either! He didn't think she would trust him if she found out his secrets, and he didn't know all of hers. *He knows more of mine than I do of his,* she thought. She looked down at her arms. *The only one he doesn't know is why I've been marked by three gods, and I barely understand that myself.* She sighed. She wished she could tell him, tell him the entire truth, that she was chasing a vision sent by her mother, that she had no idea what she would find at the end, whether or not it was a wild goose chase. He would understand, she felt it in her bones. He would comfort her, give her strength, put a hand on her shoulder, hold her close...

She cursed again. She could not allow her thoughts to keep drifting like that. *Regardless, I need to get out of here,* she thought. *And I do need to find Enlil in order to do so. I can't just abandon him here. Who knows what Jaim would do to him if I disappeared.*

If only her father had allowed the two of them to speak! Even if they had been watched, they would have been able to pass some sort of message, some sort of signal. If only she could talk to him now...

She stared up at the ceiling. *Ralanni said Enlil's chamber was directly over mine,* she thought. *I wonder if that's completely accurate.*

Niara hesitated for a moment, then narrowed her eyes to slits. Earth and wood were the hardest to manipulate, but she had done it before. And she didn't need a large opening, just enough for her to squeeze through...

The oak wood above her head shifted and warped, resisting her gentle push of magic. She pushed a little harder, urging it to separate, to create an opening to let her through. Finally, an opening settled into place above her head, and she leaned back, panting. She strained her ears, but no sound came from above her.

*Well, hopefully I'm right...*Niara gathered up her strength again, this time calling on the air in the chamber to lift her up, as she had called on the wing to carry her over the chasm. She needed to be slower here, more precise, and she felt her muscles straining, as if she were climbing mid-air instead of just allowing the wind to carry her up.

Her head passed through the hole in the ceiling, and she glanced around sharply, watchful for anyone who might see her. If she wasn't in Enlil's chambers...

A startled gasp sent her eyes searching, and she nearly lost control of her magic in her relief. Enlil's blue eyes stared at her.

She struggled the last few feet up, landing heavily on the floor. She panted as Enlil made his way toward her.

"What are you doing here?" he breathed, so quietly she could barely hear him. He crouched down beside her. "The elves told me you were with your father."

Her throat tightened. "They lied," she said. "They've all been lying. I've been confined for not immediately agreeing to his plans."

"Then," Enlil blinked. "Then he's not your father?"

Niara sighed. "Unfortunately, that part is still the truth," she winced. "Enlil, we need to get out of here. We need to leave. I need to continue south, and time is running short."

To her relief, Enlil didn't waste time questioning or asking for details. "I've been looking for how we might manage that," he said. "The elves have mostly been ignoring me. Seem to think I'm insignificant or something." His eyes twinkled.

Her breath caught. "You could never be insignificant," she whispered.

Enlil's expression froze, and for a moment Niara's heart tightened with hope. Then his expression smoothed, and he continued, leaving Niara oddly disappointed. *What are you disappointed about?* she chided herself. *Just two minutes ago you were grateful he wasn't wasting time.*

"They have horses," Enlil said. "They're well hidden, but I saw two elves coming back from patrol on horseback. If we can steal two of them, we'd be able to cover a lot more distance."

"If we can escape undetected," Niara shook her head. "I don't think Jaim will just let us take horses and leave."

"My door is being watched," Enlil said, confirming her fears. "I don't think I'd be stopped, but I'd be highly encouraged to return here."

Niara glanced at the hole she'd created in Enlil's floor. "My chamber is not only watched but guarded," she said. "I'm certain they would turn me back."

Enlil frowned, then his expression changed into a smile. "Then we don't go through either door," he said.

Niara stared at him in confusion for a second, and he gestured at the hole in the floor. Her eyes widened in comprehension. "Further down?" she asked.

Enlil nodded.

Niara could think of a dozen ways that could go wrong. "What if there's someone in the chamber below us?" she asked. "Or if there's nothing but tree trunk? I can't hollow out the entire tree."

Enlil grinned. "I did a little poking around," he said. "Below your chamber is a storage room. After that, we can go out the side, where no one will be watching because no door exists, and we're only a short distance from the ground."

Niara sat back on her heels. Enlil made it sound so simple. "And the horses?" she asked. "You know where they are?"

"On the southern edge of camp."

"Guarded?" she asked.

Enlil's grin faded. "Yes."

Niara cursed under her breath. They needed to be as quiet as possible, to leave without violence.

Enlil frowned. "Do you think your father would have told everyone you didn't agree to his plans?" he asked.

Niara felt her own brow furrow as she considered the question. "Probably not," she answered. "If he wants me to seem to be queen, the more people who believe I'm the one in charge the better."

Enlil nodded in satisfaction. "Then you tell the guard you've been sent on an errand by your father," he said. "By the time anyone can check, we'll be long gone."

It was a thin plan, but it was better than anything else she could think of. The urgent sense that they needed to go south, and fast, did not allow for any more careful planning. "Let's do it," Niara said. "Let's go now."

Enlil stood up, walked over to his bed, and slung a bundle over his shoulder before concealing it with his cloak. When Niara raised an eyebrow in question, he merely shrugged. "I had a feeling," he said.

He had a feeling we would be leaving here in a hurry. Well, he was right. Niara didn't bother asking anything else, just moved to the hole in the floor. With an effort, she conjured the wind again and gently let herself be carried to the floor. She turned, ready to concentrate on Enlil. His feet dangled through the hole, and he suddenly moved, dropping toward the floor.

Niara reached out quickly, fearful of the sound his thumping feet might make. Her wind barely managed to slow him in time, but he landed on his feet light as a cat.

"Wait for me next time!" she hissed. "We need to be quiet."

Enlil looked contrite. "I wanted you to conserve your strength."

Niara wanted to protest, but she knew he'd seen her exhausted too many times by now. She felt her lips narrow, and she turned her attention to the floor, focusing her attention on coaxing it into two.

The old and sturdy oak wood warped and protested, but finally, another hole appeared, this time leading down into darkness. Niara breathed a sigh of relief. Even if it wasn't a storage room, there would be no one present.

"Want me to go first?" Enlil whispered.

Niara gestured, waving him forward. Enlil walked over to the hole and jumped down. Niara tensed, waiting for a thump, but even to her ears she only heard a light footstep, something that would, hopefully, go unnoticed by anyone outside.

I wish I could be as graceful as that. She couldn't afford to risk it. She stared at the hole, hating that once again she had to descend into darkness, but she had no choice. With a sigh she gathered up the wind again, whispering a brief prayer of thanks that wind remained easy to summon and control, and drifted gently down into the darkness, stumbling briefly when her feet touched the floor. Before she released the wind, she grabbed Enlil's arm.

"You have to lead now," Enlil said in a rueful tone. "I can't see a thing."

Niara bit back her exclamation that she could barely see anything, either. The only light source was a faint glow from where a lantern had been burning in her chamber.

She oriented herself by memory, from the location of the chamber door above her. Carefully, she made her way toward the wall, picking her way around boxes of supplies.

A glint of reflected light caught her eye, and she glanced at one of the crates, frowning as she spotted the emblem carved on the side. She crouched down to examine it, ignoring Enlil's curious look. It was familiar…

A sleeping dragon was stamped on the side of the crate, silver and red in its slumber. A glint of gold underneath it suggested a hoard.

Niara stared at her, the image clear in her memory. *Auriel, regent of Saemar, standing behind Prince Andreas. On his left chest, a brooch, a sleeping dragon that seemed to move in the light.*

She couldn't remember exactly what color the brooch had been, but there was no doubt of the posture. The sleeping dragons were exactly the same.

She looked around, straining her eyes to examine the other crates. Almost all of them that she could see were emblazoned with the same symbol.

"Niara? What's wrong?" Enlil whispered.

Niara shook her head, unable to speak. *What are crates marked with Auriel's stamp doing here?*

She turned blindly away, facing the wall once more. Her hands touched the rough wood, and she focused all her strength, all her will on making it separate. *I need to leave here. There're too many lies, too many secrets. I can't think.*

The wood parted before her, and she stood, trembling, staring out into the night. It was dark, well past twilight, but not a star shone in the sky. The clouds hung low, obscuring the trees in a veiled mist.

She reached back and grabbed Enlil's hand, wanting to steady herself, wanting to let him know to be ready. "Can you find the stable from here?" she whispered.

Enlil nodded. "As long as you don't let me run into any trees."

Niara suppressed a smile and squeezed his hand before releasing it. She closed her eyes and called upon the wind again, feeling it wrap her in a gentle bubble before drifting down to the forest floor.

She landed with a light step and released the wind, swaying as her energy left her. She leaned against the tree, panting slightly to get her breath back. *I think I'm getting better at this,* she thought. *I thought I'd be more exhausted.*

A dark form fell from above, and Enlil landed in front of her, dropping to one knee as he landed. Niara stepped forward to touch his shoulder, and he was instantly on his feet. "This way," he whispered, gesturing to the right.

Niara followed his directions, only intervening once, when, true to his prediction, Enlil almost ran right into a small tree. Finally, he stopped, nodding straight ahead. "If those are vines, through there."

Niara squared her shoulders. This next part would be up to her. She wrapped her cloak tighter around herself, trying to appear as confident as possible.

She strode forward quickly and brushed the vines aside, blinking a little as her eyes adjusted to a dim lantern glow. Two elves met her gaze, their eyes wide with startlement. Behind them, she could see the dim shapes of horses, tethered in an enclosure.

"Saddle two horses, please," Niara said before either of them could react. "I need it done quickly."

The elves stared at her, obviously uncertain. "Lady Niara, I—" one of them said.

The other elf cut him off. "Why do you need horses so late, Lady Niara?" he asked. "Surely your father—"

"My father knows of this." Niara held the elf's gaze as steadily as she could through the lie. "I had a vision, and I need to act on it now. By the will of the Lord and the Lady."

Her invocation of the deities had the desired effect. The two elves exchanged looks still clearly uncertain, but now awed. "The Lord *and* the Lady?" the first asked.

Niara fought to keep her hands from trembling. "Of course." She managed to raise an eyebrow. "I have to know about both to unite the Faithful and Steadfast, don't I?"

The second elf swallowed. "But Lady Niara, to ride out this late—"

"Let me be concerned about that," Niara said firmly. "This is of the utmost importance, and we are wasting time."

The two elves exchanged one last glance, then one of them walked back toward the horses. The horses nickered, upset about being disturbed so late, but none of them protested any more than that.

"Can I at least get someone to accompany you, Lady Niara?" the second elf asked. "A guard, or something? These forests are not always safe."

"That is why Enlil is accompanying me," Niara said. "His skills will be more than adequate."

The elf glanced dubiously at Enlil, who only smiled back easily.

"Although," Niara said as a thought struck her. "If you could lend us a sword and bow, that would be advisable. I'm afraid my vision happened so quickly we didn't stop by the armory."

To her relief, the elf didn't question her statement. He stepped back into the shadows of the stable and emerged with a sheathed sword, a bow, and a quiver of arrows. He handed the sword to Enlil with a dubious expression and appeared relieved when Niara claimed the bow and quiver for herself. Niara concealed her uneasiness as she slung the bow over her shoulder as best she could. *It's been years since I even fooled around with archery.*

The first elf finally emerged, leading two dark brown horses. Both seemed calm and sedate, and Niara concealed a sigh of relief. She mounted easily, noting out of the corner of her eye Enlil doing the same.

"Thank you," she told the guards. "Lord and Lady guide you." She barely heard the guards' response as she urged her horse through the vines, keeping it at a sedate walk, straining against her own impatience.

The horse did not like being out in the dark, she could tell. She patted its neck, murmuring calming words under her breath. Enlil urged his horse beside her. "Here," he whispered. He reached over and handed her a thin rope, tethered at one end to his saddle. Niara nodded, taking her hands off the reins for a brief instant to fasten it to her own saddle.

I have to be eyes for everyone, she thought. She bit her lip, feeling the tension creeping into her bones. At every moment, she expected the sound of shouts of alarm behind them. Surely someone would notice her absence, someone would question the guards, there would be some pursuit…

A speck of white in front of her eyes made her blink. It was quickly followed by another, then another, and she cursed.

Mazda's light, she thought. *Now it's snowing.*

13

THE BADLANDS

The horses plodded their way through the fast-falling snow. Niara drew her cloak around her as tight as she could, shivering in the cold air. The snow already blanketed the ground in a thick layer, and it showed no signs of stopping.

They had left the forest some time ago and were heading south, or as south as Niara could tell in the snowstorm. Enlil's horse trudged beside her. Her traveling companion huddled in his own cloak, buried so deep Niara could barely see his face.

A pang of longing struck her, and she flinched. At that moment, she wanted nothing more than to dismount, pull Enlil from his horse, and kiss him like he had kissed her. *I need to get him to tell me his secret,* Niara thought. *Whatever it is. If I can't trust him, then I can't trust anyone. He knows more about me than anyone.* Whatever his secret, she could bear it. She would trust him. And then they could talk about the kiss.

She closed her eyes briefly, the memory of the kiss sending warm tingles through her body, a welcome relief against the cold. She wished desperately for gloves. Her left hand was freezing.

A shriek split the air, and it took Niara a moment to register it as nothing more than the wind. As she squinted, trying to see ahead, she realized the distance she could see rapidly failed, until the only thing visible was a sheet of white. She shivered. All her years in Ninaeva told her trouble awaited them.

"We need to find shelter." She had to shout to make herself heard above the roar of the storm.

"Where?" came the barely audible reply, as a rush of wind snatched his voice away.

Niara refrained from shouting that she had no idea. She didn't even know if they were still heading south, if they had crossed the border into the badlands yet, or what the surrounding landscape looked like.

I need to use the Sight. She swallowed. She didn't know if there were trees anywhere around them. If there weren't, the risk of being ungrounded was great.

It's that or become lost in a blizzard. The wind picked up again, blowing snow directly in her face. She could barely see the figure of Enlil hunched over his horse, buried in his cloak.

She closed her eyes and reached, trying not to go far.

"Free me."

A mountain, rising tall among its fellows. Fire spit from the top, running down the sides in rivers. Dull roars echoed from around the mountain, a repetitive cry.

"Free me! Free me!"

Niara's right hand burned, burned with a fire so hot she could hardly bear it. She clenched her hand into a fist, trying to control the pain.

A dark shape rolled down the mountain, and more shapes seemed to rise from its base. A tall figure rose, dark eyes staring at Niara.

"Come."

Niara felt her breath catch as panic began. She knew that voice. It was the one who had branded her hand, the one who had trapped her in a volcano until Taledon had appeared...

She wrenched herself back, flying through the air, lost in a whirlwind of ice and snow. Boulders and rocks scattered the landscape, nothing she could hold on to, nothing...

"Niara!"

Enlil. She gasped and opened her eyes. She remained on her horse, but Enlil's hand on her arm was the only reason she hadn't fallen off.

"I'm fine," she gasped, finding her balance and taking her reins again. Her right hand burned, the only warm part of her body.

"Did you find any?" Even through the storm, she could see his blue eyes, dark with worry.

She shook her head. Her eyes stung, and her shoulders knotted with tension. *It should have worked. It worked last time. Why didn't it work?*

Their horses kept trudging through the snow. Niara didn't stop them, knowing movement was likely the only thing keeping the horses alive. *So cold...*

A huge shadow rose up in front of them, and the horses stopped, whinnying in fright. Niara bit back a scream of her own. *Dragon.* Then she frowned, realizing the shadow stretched as far as she could see in either direction. A wall?

"Here!" Enlil urged his horse forward, and Niara's, still attached by the tether, followed. The shadow morphed into a cliff, and then they were standing under an overhang, protected from the wind-driven snow by a huge boulder, fallen from the cliff. It was no cave, no house, but it would do.

Niara slid off her horse in relief, leading it to the cliff, Enlil right beside her. She sank to the ground next to Enlil, only realizing at that moment he was shivering just as much as she.

Enlil never feels the cold. "Here," Niara raised the edge of her cloak and pulled him under it next to her before he could object. She felt his tension, but he didn't say anything. He didn't stop shivering, either.

"Well, at least the elves won't be able to track us," Enlil's voice was strained. "Any tracks we left are long gone."

Niara managed a smile in response. Her father could sense her location, but the elves would be just as hampered by the snowstorm as they were. "True," she said. "And the dragons won't be flying either, right? If they come this far south?"

"They do, but they won't," Enlil confirmed. "Creatures with wings don't like to get them wet. Not unless they're water birds, which dragons are not."

Niara caught her breath. For the first time, when asked about some knowledge of dragons, Enlil hadn't hesitated in giving a response.

She was scared to press further, to make him realize what he had done. She cast her mind about for another topic, something which would distract him. He was still shivering, and she was beginning to get worried. If only they could light a fire...but there was nothing to burn, and the idea of using the Swaying to call fire made her flinch.

"So, please tell me if this is none of my business," Enlil said, his voice unsteady. "But your father...why did he want to make you queen?"

Niara groaned at the memory. The more she thought about it, the more ridiculous it seemed. She closed her eyes again. Where to start?

"There are two groups of elves," she said, attempting to keep the explanation as simple as possible. "They've been enemies for millennia now. My mother is of the bloodline of one queen. My father is of the bloodline of the other."

"Ah," Niara could hear the realization in Enlil's voice. "So you would be the one both groups would follow. And the rest of Saemar?"

Niara shrugged. "I have no idea why," she said. "He said something about the elves being the only ones left wise enough to rule after the dragons were defeated. But..." she shook her head. "There are plenty of humans still, humans who have lived in Saemar for hundreds of years. Rian and her family, for one, or Kishtar and Lyra. They have as much of a right to be involved in whatever new government is created as the elves do."

Enlil nodded. After a short silence, he continued. "So, who would become the next leader of Saemar, if the dragons are defeated?"

Niara blinked. She hadn't even considered that question. "I don't know," she said. "The last king never had a chance to have any children, and neither he nor his father had siblings. Anyone who might be related is dead."

"Hmm," Enlil made a noncommittal sound. "Sounds like a recipe for chaos, or at least disorder."

Niara wanted to protest, but she couldn't. She had read enough histories to know that when no clear leader existed those who desired power would do everything they could to gain it.

"Recovery from the dragons' rule will keep them busy for a time," she said, despite her own uneasiness. "Besides, we still need to be certain if we can defeat the dragons, much less if we will."

"Oh, we will." Enlil's voice was confident, even as he wrapped his arms tight around himself and started swaying back and forth.

Niara hesitated. She wanted to ask him how he was so certain, but he was acting oddly. She was getting warmer, sheltered from the wind, but he…she reached out and put a hand on his shoulder. He was burning hot.

He flinched and pulled away, her cloak falling off of him. "Don't," he said, his voice strained.

"Enlil…" Niara stared at him, worry rising in her. "Enlil, what's wrong? Are you alright?"

"I'll be fine," Enlil's voice was strained. "I—" he broke off with a cry of pain.

Niara scrambled over to him, heedless of his previous command. "Enlil, something's wrong," she said. "What is it?"

"I can't—" Enlil gasped, then stood up, backing away from her, toward the storm. "Niara, I can't!"

Niara scrambled to her feet, and grabbed his arm, preventing him from running out into the blizzard. "Enlil, stop!" she cried, her heart pounding in fear.

Enlil's bright blue eyes pierced through her, his expression a mix of fear and sorrow. "Niara, I'm sorry," he gasped.

She barely had time to register his words before Enlil's body began to change before her eyes. His skin stretched, and she heard bones crack and pop into place. His skin changed, turning red, growing metallic scales. He grew larger and larger, blocking the entrance to the shelter. His head stretched and malformed, growing red and scaly horns. He roared as he changed, a sound of anguish and pain.

Niara scrambled backward, panic thudding in her chest. The horses whinnied in terror and bolted, and she wanted to join them as she pressed up against the cliff wall. *Dragon. Dragon. Enlil's a dragon...*

She clapped a hand over her mouth to keep a scream from escaping as the dragon's eyes opened, blue eyes staring mournfully at her. The eyes were the same as Enlil's.

"Niara..." the dragon's voice rolled through the shelter.

Niara bit back a cry and sank to the ground, her eyes never leaving Enlil's. *Enlil is a dragon. Enlil is a dragon...*the thought replayed in her head, over and over again. More thoughts jumbled together, his reticence in telling her anything, his lack of knowledge about human customs, his uncanny knowledge of dragon habits...*Enlil is a dragon.*

She felt a whimper escape her. She had trusted him. He knew most of her secrets. But how could she trust him now, when this was his secret? *This is why he didn't want to tell you. Mazda's light, how can he not be working for Auriel? The dragons are his creations, his children, they were released when he was released...Mazda's light, and here I am, trying to bind Auriel again, which will bind him back in human form...but he can't be working for Auriel. He had plenty of chances to betray me, and he didn't. But what if that was all a plot, all a ploy to get me to trust him...but why would he kiss me...*

"Niara, I'm sorry." It was Enlil who spoke, as well as the dragon. They were one and the same. "I didn't want to...I wanted to..." he broke off, staring at her helplessly. Even in his current form she could see the anguish in his expression.

She needed to say something. She cleared her throat, dry from fear, and swallowed. "You're a dragon," she whispered.

Enlil nodded, light bouncing off of the silver interlaced with red on his horns.

Dozens of questions swirled around in her mind. Terror receded as he made no move toward her, only regarded her mournfully. It helped that his eyes were still the same bright blue. She took a deep breath, then another. She opened her mouth to speak, and her heart sped up again. *Dragon. He's a dragon.* Finally, only one word escaped her. "Why?"

To her relief, Enlil didn't ask her to clarify. "I didn't mean to lie to you," he said. "I never wanted to. But once I had hints of who you were, and what your ultimate goal was, how could I tell you? I didn't mean to tell you now, I just..." he turned away, and Niara's breath caught as his red scales glimmered in the snow.

"You just?" she asked.

Enlil sighed, a breath of hot air that warmed the entire overhang. "We can't maintain human form indefinitely," he said. "We have to take our true shapes, otherwise...well, you saw."

A potential weakness. Niara tucked the thought away in her still-buzzing mind. "How long?" she asked.

His scales rippled as he moved, and Niara realized he had shrugged. "It varies. Three days is the most I've heard of, but I managed to five, just now."

"Five?" Niara asked.

Enlil nodded, a movement so large his head brushed the top of the overhang. "I would sneak out at night and change," he said. "But with the elves, there wasn't the opportunity, and before that...you asked me not to leave you."

Niara flushed as she looked down, remembering that night. Enlil had spent most nights after that by her side, keeping her warm against the cold. *He risked revealing himself for me?*

She shook her head, unable to contemplate that any further. "Why did you follow me?" she asked.

She shrank back as white teeth flashed. Enlil blinked, and the teeth disappeared, and Niara realized he had been smiling.

"Because I was curious." He sighed again, the hot air wafting over her, almost comforting against the cold. "I have no better reason."

Some part of Niara wanted to laugh in disbelief, to demand the real answer, but she could easily see Enlil doing exactly that. "What were you even doing in Ninaeva, then?" she asked.

Enlil opened his mouth, then closed it. "This is going to take a little bit," he closed his eyes. "Naytar's stone."

"Why do you say that?" The question left her lips without thought, one she'd thought so many times but knew he wouldn't answer.

Enlil opened his bright blue eyes. "Naytar's the mountain god," he said. "Rival of Auriel sky-lord. I picked the curse up from the nephelm." He stretched, red scales glistening. "Naytar's stone, how to start?"

She waited as Enlil thought. Shadows moved in the snow, and she realized it was his tail, a long, red tail with wicked spikes that moved back and forth as he thought. Finally, he curled the tail around himself as he began to speak.

"The elves aren't united," he said. "I don't know as much about that as you do, but there're two main groups, correct?"

Niara nodded, uncertain where this was leading.

"It's similar with the dragons," Enlil said. "Although the two groups are not comparable in size."

Niara took a deep breath. She had to ask, she had to be certain... "You mean you're not allied with Auriel?"

"No, and I never have been." A puff of hot air emphasized his words.

Niara frowned. "But didn't he create dragons, and call you all his children?"

Enlil snorted, and Niara's eyes widened as a tendril of smoke escaped his nostrils. "Auriel created humanity as well, and you don't all follow him."

That is...very true. Although it helps that most of us didn't know about his existence.

"As for being his children," Enlil sighed. "That was true for the first generation. That's the problem with being nearly immortal, it takes a very long time to change."

Niara thought of Jaim and the Steadfast. Their conflict with the Unfaithful spanned only a few elven generations, but thousands of years. She could understand what Enlil meant. "So the younger generations are rebels?" she asked.

The tip of Enli's tail twitched where it ended by his front feet. "It's not quite as simple as that," he said. "To find the roots, you have to go back to the binding of Auriel, and my mother."

"Your mother?" Niara looked up, startled.

Enlil's teeth became visible, and it took Niara a moment to realize he was smiling at her. "My mother gave the nephelm the secret to binding Auriel, and they shared it with the elves and humans," he said. "She betrayed Auriel, and he has never forgiven her. So, when Auriel rose again," his shoulders moved in a shrug. "She began seeking out those dragons we could convince to rise with us again."

"And you thought you'd find them in Ninaeva?" Niara couldn't believe it. After what she'd seen the dragons who ruled Ninaeva doing...

Enlil snorted. "Not most of them," he said. "Izila sent the most tyrannical dragons there, I'm certain. Not certain why, though." He raised an eyebrow at Niara.

She flushed. She knew exactly why. *Me. My family. Ellriheim.*

She didn't say anything about that, though. She wanted to hear the rest of Enlil's story first.

Enlil continued. "Faenor, though, he had potential. I was about to approach him when you showed up."

He was one of the nicer dragon overlords, I suppose... Niara put aside her doubts as Enlil continued.

"When you showed up..." he shifted, causing the top layer of snow to lift in puffs from the ground, "I was...well, curious. And so I decided to accompany you."

"Because you were curious," Niara couldn't decide whether to laugh or shake her head.

Enlil looked away, and Niara blinked. Near his neck, where the scales grew small and tiny on his face, she could swear they were a brighter red than usual. Could dragons blush?

"My mother is going to kill me," Enlil muttered. "She always told me curiosity killed the cat."

The phrase was so familiar to Niara she didn't have to think about her reply. "But satisfaction brought it back," she finished. Only once she had said the words did she realize other meanings of 'satisfaction,' and she felt heat rush to her face, and she fought the urge to clap a hand over her mouth again.

Enlil chuckled, a warm sound that shook his sides and caused the ground to vibrate. "I like the sound of that."

Niara couldn't tell what he was thinking, but she had more questions to ask. "If you followed me first out of curiosity," she asked. "Then why did you continue? Especially once you began to learn who I was?"

Enlil stilled. "I justified it," he said. "You were organizing a rebellion, so was I. If I could manage to get you to trust me, then the two rebellions could work in concert, and have a greater chance of success." He sighed again. "But I could never find the courage to tell you."

"Why?" Niara's voice trembled. Her entire body felt tense, and her hands shook, on edge.

"Niara…" Enlil's voice was soft, a pleading whisper.

Niara swallowed. "Why did you kiss me?" *Please don't lie. I couldn't bear it if you lied.*

"I couldn't help myself." Enlil turned to gaze at her, bright blue eyes meeting her own. "I've never met anyone like you."

Niara glanced down. "Nor I you," she managed, her voice barely a whisper.

"Niara," Enlil sounded forlorn. "Can you forgive me?"

She looked up, surprised at his request. Her breath caught as she stared into his blue eyes. *He's a dragon. But he's not working for Auriel. His goals are the same as mine.* "There's nothing to forgive," she whispered.

Part of her was scolding herself, telling her that Enlil was a dragon, that anything he was telling her could be a lie. She hushed the voice firmly, telling it that Enlil had never outright lied to her.

Enlil's eyes widened. "Really?" he asked, hope lighting up his voice.

"Enlil…" Niara forced the words out of a mouth suddenly gone dry. "You've done nothing I haven't, and you've saved my life more times than I can count. Being a dragon doesn't change that. If I were to use that judgment," she swallowed. "Then I would have to judge my grandfather and father the same, just for being elves."

She stood up and made herself walk over to him. Enlil remained perfectly still, only his eyes moving as he followed her until she stood next to him, hands shaking as she regarded his new form. He stood as tall as two or three houses in Ilhelm, with red scales that glinted brilliantly, even in the darkness of the still-falling snow. Spikes ran down the length of his back, culminating in a long, whip-like tail with more spikes at the end. Two horns rose from the back of his head, long and curved, red interlaced with silver. She reached out a trembling hand and touched his cheeks. Rough scales scraped the palm of her hand, and Enlil's whole body shivered, then relaxed into her touch. More confident, bolder, she stroked her hand down his scales, marveling at how hard and strong they were, at the warmth that radiated off of him, heating the overhang so much the snow melted behind her, running in little rivulets down the cliff wall. His blue eyes followed her every move, the same blue eyes that had comforted her this entire journey.

She closed her eyes and leaned forward, touching her cheek to his. "I forgive you, Enlil," she said again.

"But I kissed you," he rumbled, as if ashamed at the liberty he had taken.

Niara knew her face was flaming, and not from the heat of his scales. She was glad she was already looking away, so he couldn't see her face. "I kissed you back," she whispered.

Heat rushed from his exhale of breath, and she felt his scales start to shift next to her cheek. She took a step back, and the dragon form began to morph again, stretching and shrinking, until Enlil stood in front of her again, the same Enlil who had rescued her in Ilhelm and accompanied her through the entirety of Saemar. He stood a hand's breadth away from her, watching her closely, then reached out to gently caress her cheek. She closed her eyes, his warm hand a gentle touch that sent fire through her.

"Niara," Enlil sighed, his voice almost worshipful. Niara opened her eyes and saw him gazing at her, a question in his eyes. "I can't maintain this for long," his voice soft.

She took a deep breath and raised her own hand, marveling at its steadiness. Enlil shuddered as she touched his cheek, but he didn't close his eyes, only continued staring at her.

He's a dragon, Niara knew that was something she would still have to process, have to understand. But at the moment, she didn't care. A half-elf and a dragon...was it even possible?

*If we even survive this. If our rebellion is successful, if we're still alive at the end, if we still desire each other...*for she wanted him. Even the revelation that he was a dragon hadn't dimmed the fire burning through her body, fire which only burned hotter the closer he was.

Dragonfire, she thought.

Enlil reached up to clasp her hand against his cheek. "You're beautiful, Niara," he said. "I wish I were an elf, like you. Then..."

"Stop," Niara interrupted him with a whisper. She didn't want to hear regrets and recriminations. *This is Enlil. And I want him.*

She didn't allow any further thoughts to get in the way. She brought her other hand up, the one branded by the sun, and pulled his face to hers, pressing herself against him in a kiss.

14

SHAN SERIN

Niara woke, huddled in a nest of cloaks. She was warm, even though she could see the snow had piled up overnight just outside the shelter of the overhang. She straightened up, shifting the cloaks to remain on her shoulders, then froze as she saw the red scales of the sleeping dragon next to her.

It's Enlil. Niara took a deep breath and forced herself to relax. *He's a dragon. And he's on my side. And I...I care about him.* She closed her eyes, remembering the feeling of the kiss. It had sent fire through her, fire she wasn't certain would have abated if he hadn't pulled back and admitted in a hoarse voice he wasn't certain he could hold human shape for much longer.

They had gone to sleep in the shelter of the overhang, while the blizzard still raged around them. Niara didn't remember curling up next to him as they slept, but she had. It felt...oddly right.

A smile played over her lips as she observed his sleep. His red scales glinted in the sunlight reflecting from the snow, and warm breath puffed out his nostrils every time he took a breath. She reached out a hand and stroked his cheek, marveling anew at his scales. They were soft on his face, softer than on the rest of his body.

Enlil blinked, and she pulled back as he stretched, unwrapping his tail from around himself, drawing his head up. He blinked again as he saw her, and she saw his expression change from confusion to apprehension. He shifted and stretched, and Niara watched closely as his form morphed again, shifting until he was in human form, standing next to her, breathing heavily.

"Does that hurt?" she asked.

"No," he said. He hesitated, then spoke again. "A lot of dragons don't like to be in human form, considering they were bound for thousands of years, but I don't mind. Then again, I've always had the freedom to choose."

"You weren't bound?" Niara asked.

Enlil shrugged. "My mother was spared the binding, considering she was the one who knew the secrets. I was born after that."

I don't have to bind him. The thought blossomed through her mind, hope tight in her chest. She could bind Auriel, but spare Enlil, his mother, and any others like him. There could still be dragons out of legend.

Enlil walked over to where they had dropped their belongings. "Food?" he said, offering a roll of bread to Niara.

Niara took it, not bothering to ask how he had managed to steal provisions from the elves. It was fresh bread, however, and she would not complain.

Enlil was thinking as they ate, Niara could see it in the crease of his brow. She finished her roll and waited patiently for him to speak.

"So...I know you've said time is short," Enlil said. "How much further do we need to go, and in how short of time?"

Niara stared southward, trying to reckon. "There's a ruined city to the south called Shan Serin," she said. "We need to be there by Papsukkal. It's not that far away." She shivered. If she was right, Papsukkal was only days away, and Shan Serin a few days by horseback...she looked around and cursed. In the heat of the moment, she had forgotten the horses had bolted, leaving them once more reliant on their feet.

Enlil shifted. "I could... fly us farther, now that you know what I am. It would be easier for me to shift shapes, anyway."

Niara's heart caught in her throat. She knew it would be a while before she reconciled the human Enlil, the Enlil she had kissed, the Enlil she cared about, with the dragon Enlil, strong, fierce, and magnificent. *They're the same. I know they are. But I still can't fathom it.*

Enlil sensed her hesitation. "I can remain in this form if you're more comfortable," he said. "We have the horses. I shouldn't have suggested it, not so soon after telling you…"

A smile tinged her lips. *As if he chose to tell me and wasn't forced to.* She took a breath. "No," she said. "It makes more sense this way. You can get us to Shan Serin much faster than we can by walking."

Enlil eyed her a moment, then nodded. "Alright," he said. He hesitated. "You don't have to watch if you don't want to."

Niara swallowed but merely took a step back to give him room, shaking her head. *I need to get used to this. If we're to continue to be together, I need to know him in both forms.*

She saw something flash in Enlil's eyes, something that could have been admiration, or maybe relief, before his skin began stretching in the now-familiar shift into dragon form. When he finished, he lowered his head in front of Niara, making her gasp. His head stood as tall as she.

She shoved her instinctive fear down and stepped forward, hesitant at first, then bolder, examining the scales on his face, feeling how they sat together, layered on top of each other to provide protection. They were hard and smooth, but warm, like Enlil had absorbed the very sun into his body. Her hand crept upward, toward the horns that rose from his forehead, and Enlil closed his eyes and sighed. "That's nice," he whispered. Even his whisper was a low growl.

Niara managed a smile. *This is Enlil,* she reminded herself. *He may be a dragon, but he's still the same man.* "How am I going to get up?" she asked.

Enlil opened his eyes. "You can climb up my leg," he said. "There should be a good place for you to sit between the spines on my back."

Niara nodded and slung the bundle of their provisions over her back before walking around to his side. Enlil knelt slightly, allowing her to step onto his front leg before gripping one of the spines that grew from the back of his neck, pulling herself up to sit mostly centered on Enlil's back. He shifted beneath her as he straightened, and she hastily grabbed the spine in front of her.

"Ready?" Enlil called back.

Niara swallowed. *Ready? I don't think so. I'm about to fly!*

"Ready," she said, not trusting her voice to say anything else.

Enlil's muscles tensed underneath her, and then he was jumping, beating his wings hard as he lifted off, climbing toward the sky. A strangled cry escaped despite her best efforts, and she clutched Enlil's scales as the wind hit her, buffeting them back and forth as they climbed higher and higher. She glanced down, biting back another scream as she saw the ground, so far away, the boulders of the badlands so tiny from this far up. She shut her eyes tight and clutched at his spines, refusing to look, refusing to do anything but breathe.

Breathe. It's Enlil. You're flying.

Flying was anything but smooth. They rose and fell, and she felt her stomach had been left behind on the ground. She regretted the bread roll as they climbed higher and higher.

"Are you alright?" Enlil asked, his voice a roar.

Niara opened her mouth, and a squeak escaped her. She forced her eyes open. Enlil was still staring straight ahead, focusing on his flying, but she could feel his muscles tense beneath her.

I don't want him to think me a coward. "I'm fine," her voice was barely a whisper. "I'm fine!" she said again, louder.

One more drop, and she shut her eyes again, wincing as her stomach protested the sudden movement. Then the flight smoothed out and turned into a gentle pattern of dip and rise.

Niara opened her eyes again but refused to look at the ground. Just by the sky, she could tell they were much higher than they had been a few minutes ago.

"It'll be easier from here!" Enlil called.

Easier? "Why?" Niara managed to call back.

"Because we're high up now! The air currents no longer fight me!"

Niara blinked. "Air currents?" she asked.

She was grateful Enlil could talk while flying, as it kept her distracted from how up they were. Dragons might be meant to fly this high, but humans and elves were not.

She relaxed as they flew, the minutes drifting into hours, their conversation about flying drifting into comforting silence. The sun moved until it was high in the sky, and Niara's arms were getting tired from holding onto Enlil so tightly.

Enlil dove slightly, and she clutched the spine in front of her, her stomach feeling as if she had left it behind somewhere above them. Despite that, however, a smile spread over her face. *I'm riding a dragon,* she thought. *Like King Enlil and the Dragonriders, except this time it's me. I'm riding a dragon.* How many times had she visualized this very thing as she reread her favorite legend? Despite the circumstances, she couldn't help but smile.

"Niara! Is that what we're searching for?" Enlil's voice interrupted her thoughts.

Mazda's light, now I have to look down. She fought the brief feeling of vertigo as she peered over Enlil's shoulder. Below them, barely a speck in the distance, she could see shapes that didn't match the boulders scattered around. Instead, rough brown walls rose high, tumbling in places, but otherwise mostly upright.

Shan Serin.

The certainty of the knowledge rang in her bones. This was where her mother had sent her. She was here, and here before Papsukkal.

We did it. Niara felt weak-kneed with relief. "Yes!" she managed to shout to Enlil.

"Alright! Get ready!"

Niara didn't have to ask Enlil why she was supposed to get ready. Her stomach dropped as he dipped again, losing altitude as he drifted down to the ruined city. She tightened her grip, wondering if she should close her eyes, or whether that would be worse. The sight of land rushing up toward her was terrifying, but if something happened, she wouldn't be able to see to react...

She settled for staring at Enlil's back, only seeing his wings beat out of the corner of her eye. The wind changed as he reared up, beating his wings hard to slow their descent, and then he stopped, still and steady on the ground.

Niara let out a breath she hadn't realized she'd been holding. In front of them, in ruined glory, stood the gates of an elven city, carved out of red rock which had crumbled from its original pillars. The writing above the gate was familiar, elvish rules that her grandfather had taught her. What they said, however, was a mystery. Although Niara believed her elvish was good, the symbols jumbled together in unfamiliar words that she couldn't make sense of.

Enlil turned his head to look back at her. "This is it?" he asked.

Niara caught back a laugh. "We made it," she said. She slid from Enlil's back, nearly tumbling to the ground, knowing she ripped her dress on one of his scales. She paid it no heed as she ran around to Enlil's front, throwing her arms around the right of his neck in exuberant delight. Her arms only reached halfway around his neck, but she didn't care. "We made it!"

Enlil seemed startled, then lowered his head, making it easier for her to stand close to him. Niara rested her face against his skin, enjoying the warmth emanating from his scales. Enlil leaned his head toward her, and she reached out a hand, running it down the length of his cheek. Her own smile widened as she saw Enlil's lips curve. Whatever else his being a dragon would complicate, they would figure out. And there would be complications. They hadn't talked after their kiss, hadn't discussed the future, even in the immediate, and hadn't told each other their feelings. But Niara knew they would figure it out.

I love him. The thought blossomed from nowhere. She kept her face buried in Enlil's neck, hiding her expression against the sudden realization. *Mazda's light, I love him. What am I going to do about that?*

Enlil blew out a hot breath, and she felt the wind disarrange her hair. "What do we do now?" he asked.

Right, I don't do anything about it right now, she told herself. *Right now, I still have a mission. Mother sent me here for a reason, and I need to figure out what that reason is.*

Despite her thoughts, it took an effort of will to pull herself away from Enlil. She turned her attention to the gate. The walls to either side mostly remained, but the tops were crumbling, and she had a feeling she didn't want to stand directly underneath them. "Now we go in," she said.

Enlil nodded, and she blinked as he shifted, appearing once again as human. He grinned at her. "Think I'll fit better this way."

Niara felt too breathless to respond. Would she ever get used to seeing Enlil shift like that?

She began walking through the gate, using the pretense of examining it to collect her thoughts. "Can you shift to more than one human shape?" she asked.

Enlil shook his head. "Only the one," he said. "And I'm probably one of the few who still uses it. The rest of the dragons have been celebrating their freedom."

Niara remembered her visions of the dragons flying around Saemar. "You've been trapped in human form?" she asked, double-checking her memory.

Enlil shrugged, and for a moment Niara thought she saw guilt pass across his face. "The rest were. My mother and I weren't."

Of course. When I saw my first dragon, Auriel hadn't risen. Niara's head came up, and she turned to stare at Enlil. "You and your mother, did you live north, near Utgard?" she demanded.

Enlil stared back at her. "How do you know about Utgard?" he finally asked.

Niara managed a smile. "I visited there with my brother. And I saw a dragon." She closed her eyes briefly, trying to remember. It had been flying so high, she didn't know if she had seen the color, but it could have been... "was it you?"

A grin spread across Enlil's face. "In all likelihood," he said. "My mother doesn't get out much anymore."

A comforting warmth spread through her. Somehow, the thought that she had seen him long before their lives had drastically changed felt nice.

Focus. I need to focus. Niara tore her gaze away from Enlil's and turned to regard the city in front of them. The road stretched long and straight, houses lined up on either side. Unlike the houses Niara had seen in her visions of Alfheim, or the tree-dwellings of her father's camp, these houses were built out of stone. They appeared as if they were each made from a singular piece, their rounded roofs polished by the passage of time. They could have been new, except for the occasional house that had collapsed, littering the area with broken stones and dust.

"Anything in particular we're searching for?" Enlil asked.

Niara closed her eyes, recalling her vision. Vinet had said to be here, to be here before Papsukkal. There had been something else, though, an image of empty books...

"We need to find the library." She started forward, attempting to appear confident.

It seemed to work, because Enlil followed her willingly, and they both looked around, trying to determine which building would likely be a library. At first, Niara couldn't tell. The first street all seemed like residences, or perhaps shops. The uniformity was disconcerting. Once they reached an intersection, however, the streets and houses began to change, some larger, some smaller.

"Which way?" Enlil asked.

Niara hesitated, wishing for a brief moment that he didn't have quite as much faith in her knowledge of what they were supposed to do. She glanced both directions, but there was nothing to give her a clue of how to proceed.

"Right," she said. *It served me well enough in the labyrinth. Hopefully, it will do the same here.*

Enlil didn't question her, just followed as Niara walked forward. After a few blocks, she knew she had been correct to choose this direction. The buildings were getting bigger and bigger, although they still had the same architecture, the same domed roofs. Finally, they came to an open space. On the other side, a large square building dominated, unique in its shape, as well as the pure white walls instead of the yellow-brown of the rest of the city. A few statues were scattered around, the one closest to them a tall, male figure carved of polished black stone. Niara hesitated, wanting to examine it more closely. It seemed familiar somehow...

"Is that a library or a palace?" Enlil asked, gesturing at the building opposite them.

I don't know. Niara shrugged. "Only one way to find out," she said.

They began to pick their way across the open space. Niara frowned, noticing the patterns in the ground. There had been paths here, and square enclosures. In the center, a statue of an elven woman lay broken in the center of a circle. Niara glanced at it for a moment. "I think that was a fountain," she said.

Enlil blinked. "A fountain here? Where did they get the water?"

Niara shook her head. "This city was built thousands of years ago," she said. "The land could have been very different."

Enlil looked around, and Niara felt the sudden urge to ask him his age. If he was a dragon, and dragons were immortal, or nearly so, then he could be any age.

"Mother was probably here," Enlil murmured. "I would have liked to have seen it then."

Niara swallowed. "You weren't there during the first binding of Auriel, then?"

Enlil grinned at her as if he heard the underlying question. "I'm not that old," he said. "Only a century."

Niara's breath caught. "A century?" she managed.

Enlil nodded. "My mother's been alive for thousands of years," he said. "In her eyes, I'm barely more than a child."

Niara frowned. *He and his mother were the only ones spared the binding.* "How—" she began, then stopped. He had told her that he didn't know his father.

"Dragon eggs take a long time to hatch, apparently," Enlil sounded like he was reciting something, probably something his mother had told him.

Niara flushed. "Sorry," she managed.

Enlil shrugged, then grinned. "Had some time to get used to it."

Niara shook her head, still trying to believe it. He didn't appear any older than twenty-five.

Mother is over fifty, and she gets mistaken for twenty, Niara reminded herself. The thought brought her up short. If she survived the rebellion, she would likely live just as long as Enlil.

If I survive this rebellion. Niara waved the gloomy thought away and continued toward the library. Surely there had to be answers in there.

The giant doors hung open, and Niara hesitated at the entrance, waiting, wondering if there was someone already inside. She heard nothing, however, not even the slight shift of a breeze from the building's interior.

She stepped inside as quietly as she could. Her footsteps disturbed the dust on the floor, causing it to gently billow around her feet. Enlil followed close behind her, and she could hear his breath catch.

The building was one huge room, with shelves stretching up to the high, vaulted ceiling. The bookshelves themselves were masterful works of art, carved with curved geometric figures, vines, and other plants that twisted and turned their way up to the ceiling. On every shelf sat a row of books, all dusty and untouched, waiting for someone to read them.

Niara felt her eyes sting. *Mother would love this place,* she thought.

"Are you alright?" Enlil spoke in a soft and concerned tone.

Niara blinked and gave him a smile. "Just the dust," she whispered, unwilling to raise her voice. She had thought the library in Ilhelm had been impressive. It was nothing compared to this.

She approached the nearest bookshelf and reached for one of the books. The binding was hard leather, and her hand trembled as she stroked it. As she did, it fell into her hands, and she stared blankly. Where there should have been pages was nothing. The binding was all that remained of the book.

"No," she whispered. Despite the memory of the vision, the rows of empty books, she had been hoping, hoping that here would be the answer to whatever they had to do. If this was a library of an ancient elven civilization, then surely someone would have written down how Auriel had been bound, and that would give them the knowledge to do it again.

She looked around frantically, but each book cover held the same story. A hard leather binding, some decorated, some not, but again and again, no pages existed.

"No!" Frustration rose inside of her, and she cursed, restraining herself from lashing out at the shelves by a force of will. "There were supposed to be answers here!"

"Niara!" Enlil stepped forward, reaching toward her.

His hands touched her arms, and she turned toward him, shaking. "They're all empty," she said. "There's nothing here."

"What were you expecting to find?" Enlil's voice was soothing, but Niara was in no mood to be soothed.

"Answers," Niara tried to pull away, but Enlil held onto her arms. "I came all this way, following a vision, a vision which promised to save Saemar, and there's nothing here. I'm here before Papsukkal, which was the deadline, and there's still nothing here! There has to be an answer, an answer on how to bind Auriel again, but I don't know how to find it." Tears welled up in her eyes, and she buried her face in Enlil's shoulder, unwilling to let him see her cry.

"Are you sure binding Auriel's what you were meant to do?" Enlil stroked her hair absently.

Niara pulled back, startled. "What else would stop him?"

"I don't know," he said. "But it seemed to be only a temporary solution, and none of the dragons were particularly happy about being stuck in human form."

Niara frowned. "You weren't stuck."

Enlil gave her a smile. "My mother was the one who betrayed Auriel. They made an exception for her."

"Your mother..." Niara's breath caught. "Your mother knows how to bind Auriel! Where is she? Can we speak to her?"

To her disappointment, Enlil winced and looked away from her. "I don't know where she is," he said. "She was on her own reconnaissance mission, and we didn't exactly make arrangements to meet."

"Manyu curse it." Niara sagged, all the strength draining out of her. "I don't know what to do."

Enlil held her close to his chest, and they sank down to sit on the floor, ignoring the dust that rose around them. "Well, you mentioned a vision," Enlil said, his voice hesitant. "Can you...have another?"

Niara shivered. "My visions are unpredictable," she said. "I can try to call one, but...I don't know what I'll see." Her mind shifted to the voice, to the scars on her arms, and she instinctively raised a hand to touch her sun brand. "And I keep getting marked," she whispered in a low voice.

Enlil said nothing, only held her closer. "Why?"

Niara leaned into him. "I wish I knew." She pulled back so she could roll up her sleeves. "This one is the Lord," she whispered, tracing the stag scar gently. "This is the Lady," she showed him the rose and thorns tattoo. "And this," she hesitated, staring at her hand. "I would think it was Mazda," she whispered. "But I don't know."

Enlil raised her hand to kiss it. "But why do they mark you? Why choose you, out of all the mortals to play with?"

To play with. Niara grimaced. "The Lord and Lady, because of my blood. My descent from Olvae and Lyaen. The other..." she shook her head.

"Only you know how much risk a vision is," he said slowly. "But you've had them many times since we met. And if your next one strikes with you unprepared again," he shrugged.

He was right, Niara knew. She suppressed a sigh and closed her eyes, reaching out, stretching out her senses for any trees, any vegetation. Surely there had to be some hint, some way that she could find Enlil's mother, or even a hint of what she should do next...

The rush of wingbeats. A ruined castle. Ilhelm.

Two dragons faced each other, tension in every muscle. With a roar, they leapt for the sky, fire dancing around them.

Thalion knelt by a door, ear pressed against the wall. "They're out there," he whispered.

Serana leaned against the stone, heavily pregnant. "I wish we knew what was happening."

"We have to trust Niara." Thalion stood up and drew her close to him.

Serana buried her face in her shoulder. "They're going to find us, and what will we do then?"

Niara strained, trying to comfort them, trying to tell them that there was a plan, but she had no plan! The only clue she had was Papsukkal...the day out of time...

"Papsukkal," Thalion whispered. She was his eyes, as if they were staring directly at her, staring through her. "We need to be ready on Papsukkal."

Niara gasped, leaning forward into Enlil's arms. "Are you alright?" he asked.

Niara took a deep, shuddering breath before replying. "Nothing," she whispered. "Nothing useful, at least. Papsukkal."

"Day outside of time," Enlil shook his head. "I don't know what significance that could hold."

"Neither do I."

***

Niara woke in the middle of the night, her cloak wrapped tightly around her. Even this far south, the chill of late Manyu's Time sank into her bones, and the few bits of scattered sacks and cloths she'd been able to find for a bed did little to dispel that.

Enlil was nowhere to be seen, but then, she'd been expecting that. She knew he was outside in the courtyard, curled up in dragon form.

She stood up, her eyes adjusting to the darkness of the library. The tall rows of bookshelves seemed to stare back at her, stubborn and intimidating, unwilling to yield their secrets.

There were supposed to be answers here. She gazed at the bookshelves, feeling a familiar tightness within her chest. *I can't bind a god without answers. Nor the dragons.*

She blinked. *If I bind the dragons, unless I find what allowed them to not bind Enlil's mother, then I bind Enlil. Mazda's light, I don't want to do that.* She swallowed. *I can't do that. I love him.* Niara shook her head and pulled her cloak tighter around her shoulders. These thoughts were getting her nowhere. Until she figured out what the binding ritual entailed any hesitations she had were purely academic.

Besides, what other choice is there? Auriel is a tyrant, and the dragons who follow him more so. The people of Saemar will be crushed into hopelessness soon, and we'll never be free of the dragons' rule. Tears stung her eyes again. Niara had seen the start of the hopelessness. In Ilhelm, in Hillsdale, in Venia and Duskryn, humans might be living free as outlaws, but they would be immediately taken as slaves if a dragon, or one of the dragons' soldiers, saw them.

We need to stop him. It was the inescapable conclusion. Her mind flashed back to what she had seen of Thalion and Serana, underground in Ellriheim. *And soon. But how?*

The book covers offered no answers. With a curse, Niara spun on her heel and headed out into the cold night of the courtyard.

Enlil's form was large, a bulwark against any who might think of sneaking into the library. An odd sense of peace and safety drifted over Niara as she looked at him. He lay fast asleep, but even so, she could sense the heat radiating off of him, hear the rise and fall of his breathing.

She strode across the courtyard and sank to the ground next to him, leaning against his warm skin. She relaxed, closing her eyes as the heat sank into her bones.

She heard Enlil's breathing change before he spoke. "Niara?" There was no trace of grogginess in his voice.

"I can't sleep," Niara said, not moving from where she leaned against his side.

"Ah," Enlil seemed content with that. "Is it more comfortable here?"

A blush stained her cheeks. "Yes," she said.

Enlil remained silent for a time, so long that Niara thought he might have gone back to sleep. Just as she allowed herself to relax, he spoke again. "Niara," he rumbled. "Naytar's stone, you are beautiful."

Her breath quickened. She opened her eyes, trying to see the expression on Enlil's face. His head turned toward her, watching her, but his expression was unreadable to her.

She swallowed. "Enlil," she whispered. "Why did you kiss me?"

She saw his eyes widen. "Because...because I couldn't not," he stammered. "Oh, Niara, I meant what I said earlier, about being an elf."

Niara shook her head and stood up, bringing a hand up to touch the scales of Enlil's cheek. She saw his eyelids droop with pleasure. "I don't wish you were an elf," she said. "If you were, then you wouldn't be Enlil."

"But," Enlil's head moved slightly, as if he wanted to shake his head but was unwilling to remove her hand. "I'm a dragon. And—"

"Is that any reason we can't be together?"

Enlil stared at her as if all words had escaped his mind. For herself, Niara couldn't quite understand why she was saying these things. Moonlight, it had to be, starlight and moonlight…

It was too late to back out, however. "You can shift to human form whenever you choose," Niara said. "I can't shift to dragon, but we can still talk and be together when you're in that form, so there's no impediment there. Why can't we be together?"

"I…I," Enlil stuttered, "Because…"

"No reason at all," Niara murmured. She brought her face up to his and kissed his scales.

Enlil groaned, a sound that reverberated through the ground, and she felt him start to shift before she saw it. In moments, he stood before her as a human man, and his arms wrapped around her, pulling her into a deep kiss. Niara responded eagerly, tangling her fingers in his hair, pulling him closer and closer.

Deep inside, some part of her whispered that they ought to talk more, that there were actual reasons a dragon and a half-elf would have difficulties, but she didn't care. His lips tasted so good, and dragonfire stirred within her again, wanting him, needing him to quench it.

Enlil broke the kiss long enough to tug her hand toward the library. Niara followed as soon as she realized where he was going, and soon they were in her corner, hands on each other, stripping each other of clothing. Between the heat radiating off of Enlil and the dragonfire building within her, Niara barely felt the cold air on her skin.

She hesitated when they were both naked, uncertain of what to do next, but Enlil silenced any doubts she might have had with a kiss. She arched up into him as he entered her, and the dragonfire consumed her.

15

BETRAYAL

Dawn came softly and slowly. Nothing disturbed Niara as she woke to the soft sound of a quiet breeze outside the library. She felt warm, fully warm for the first time in months. A body lay next to hers, and she took a breath, remembering what had happened the night before.

All her upbringing told her that what she had just done, as a noblewoman, was unforgivable. After all, Vinet had hidden Niara's own identity for years until she had the power to claim Niara as her daughter. If Ianna had had her son before the dragons had come, she would have been ostracized.

On the other hand, her mother had told her over and over she had never been ashamed of what had happened, that she would have chosen to repeat every moment for the sake of Niara's existence. There was no shame, not even for a noblewoman. And now…the dragons had come. No one would judge whether she behaved according to social propriety.

She closed her eyes, savoring the warmth for just a little while longer. Enlil was still in human form, she could tell by the feeling of him pressed against her.

She blushed. *If we do this again. Mazda's light.* Heat coiled inside her again, and knew it was not a question of if, only when.

Enlil shifted behind her, and she turned to face him, smiling at him as he opened his eyes. "Good morning."

Enlil blinked, then pulled her into a kiss. She welcomed him, holding him tight until he finally broke the kiss.

"I love you," Enlil breathed.

Niara's heart stopped in her chest. Although she had thought it, she hadn't yet said it. "And I love you," she whispered.

A smile broke across Enlil's face, warm and radiant. He kissed her again, and she responded with all the passion she could muster.

"I didn't know," Enlil breathed. "I never dreamed this could be possible."

Niara didn't bother pointing out all the difficulties still in front of them. They didn't matter. She kissed him back, matching his smile with one of her own.

Enlil's expression grew more serious. "I know there will be challenges, Niara," he said. "But I will stand by you as long as you want me, and never abandon you, and always protect you. I swear this on my soul."

Her breath caught in her throat, and she pulled him to her for yet another kiss. "I love you, Enlil," she said again. "And I will stand by you as well."

Enlil deepened the kiss, and her own body responded, wanting more. A low rumble interrupted her, and Enlil broke the kiss, looking sheepish.

Niara blinked, confused, until her own stomach growled, answering the rumble that had been Enlil's stomach. She laughed, and they broke apart.

"Food," she said. "At least while our provisions last."

Enlil nodded. "Should last for at least a little bit yet." He pulled away, standing up, gloriously naked and unashamed. Niara caught herself staring at him, breath catching in her throat. *I am the luckiest woman in the world.*

She stood up herself, dragging one of the cloaks with her. Not that she was ashamed, but her body didn't produce as much heat as Enlil's.

The sight of blood staining one of the cloaks made her cheeks flame red. She started searching for her clothes, trying to ignore her blush.

I don't care about the blood, she told herself. *It's perfectly normal. It's the blood of life, blood that...*her thoughts stuttered to a halt. *Blood of life. Blood is life.*

Hastily, she dragged her clothes over her head and walked over to one of the bookcases, staring closely at it. Could it be?

This is an ancient elven city. There's nothing that would have made just the pages disappear, except magic. Not the elemental magic of the Swaying, however. Not the Lady's gift. But the Lord's?

She closed her eyes. *Lord of Life and Loss. Blood is life. It's what was used in the ritual Jaim used to create me. Maybe...*

"Niara? Breakfast?"

Niara blinked and turned toward Enlil, who was standing behind her, holding a roll of bread and cheese in his hand. He had also managed to find his clothes. He raised an eyebrow at her, clearly curious. "What are you thinking?"

Niara took a deep breath to steady her emotions. "I think I know how to reveal the books," She shook her head. "At least, what the key might be."

Enlil handed her some of the bread and cheese. "What's that?" he asked, beginning to eat his own food.

She barely tasted the bread as she chewed thoughtfully. "Blood," she said. "If they were concealed with the gifts of the Lord, the Lord of Life and Loss, then blood is what would bind the magic."

"And what could unbind it," Enlil's forehead creased, and she could tell he was thinking hard. "But it can't be just blood, otherwise anyone who cut themselves accidentally would reveal the books."

She stared down at the stag scar on her arm and whispered, "They have to have the Lord's gift." She finished her bread and retrieved a small knife from their bundle of belongings. Without consciously thinking, she walked to the center of the library, the place where the ritual must have first been performed.

The shelves ended, leaving a round circle surrounded by tall bookshelves. Niara smiled in satisfaction. She had been right.

Enlil trailed behind her, his expression still hesitant. "Niara, what are you—"

Too focused on resolving the problem, Niara didn't respond, instead steeling herself, then slashing the knife down on her right arm, near the stag scar. Keeping her expression composed as the pain stung, she held her arm out, letting the blood drip to the floor.

She closed her eyes, reaching inside of her, twisting as if she was reaching for the Swaying. "Lord of Life and Loss," she whispered. "I call on you. Release the binding, reveal your secrets. By the power of my blood."

She nearly faltered as mist began rising from the floor, first obscuring the dripped blood, then her feet, then rising toward the bookshelves. Enlil took a stumbling step backward, his eyes wide. The mist continued to rise until Niara couldn't see the bookshelves at all. The only things she could see were in the circle.

Enlil stumbled forward, reaching out to her. Niara gripped his hand tightly, but her gaze never strayed from the bookshelves. She watched, tense with anticipation, waiting.

There was no sudden burst of light, no dramatic change. Slowly, gently, the mist started to recede, drifting back to the floor, back to the center of the room. It grew smaller and smaller until it was only a small circle in front of their feet. Then it was gone.

She let out a breath she hadn't realized she'd been holding. The blood on the floor was gone, and her arm no longer hurt. When she looked down, she saw that she now bore another scar, this one faint and white.

"Did it work?" Enlil whispered.

Niara shook herself free of the wonder and walked toward the bookshelves. She chose one at random, pulling the book off the shelf and opening it.

Pages stared back at her, hundreds of pages intricately designed and scribed. She felt her knees go weak with relief. She had done it. The books were revealed.

Excitement faded to dismay as she gazed at the expanse of the library. There were thousands of books here, and only one of them would hold the binding ritual.

"How are we going to find it?" she asked aloud.

Enlil squeezed her hand and stepped in front of her, pulling her in for a kiss. She wrapped her arms around him, finding comfort in the strength of his embrace. *Mazda's light, Enlil, I love you.*

"We made it across the entire country," Enlil said. "I'm sure we can manage searching a library."

"I don't know what even half of these are." Niara stared at the pile of books next to her. She had looked through them, flipping through the pages, searching for any mention of sky-lord, Auriel, or binding, but after several hours, she had found absolutely nothing.

No one answered her. Enlil was off in his own section of the library. Niara groaned as she crouched over, holding her head in her hands.

I don't want to be here. Hardly the first time this thought had surfaced, and yet still as strong and insistent as ever. *Mazda's light, why does it have to be me?* The scars on her arms seemed to burn, a stark reminder that she had not chosen this. Her blood, her abilities, had destined her for this fate.

A fate that means nothing if we can't find the ritual. A half-laugh escaped her. Wouldn't it be funny if, after all this effort, the binding ritual was nowhere in the library? The thought sent a start of terror through her. *No. It has to be here. It can't all have been for nothing.*

She pulled another book off the shelf at random. She frowned. This one had a sun engraved on its cover, a sun that was intensely familiar. She compared it to the back of her left hand. She hadn't been mistaken. The brand shaped exactly the same.

Curious now, she opened the book, skimming the pages more

carefully than usual. It had been years since she'd actively practiced her elven, and she needed to slow down, to concentrate on the symbols in front of her eyes.

And so, to save the world, Manyu was bound in the fire mountain, where he shall ever reside. Only the blood of his children can release him, and those have been slain. May the Lord and Lady have mercy on us, but without the sky-lord to check his evil, we were given no choice. May the sun-lord live in peace without his dark brother.

Niara blinked as she looked up from the book, feeling as if she were waking from a daze. Manyu bound in the fire-mountain? And he had been bound there because the sky-lord, Auriel, had been bound?

"Did you find it?"

Niara shook her head, the book's revelations fleeing in the face of renewed disappointment. "No," she said. "We need to keep searching"

Enlil nodded, though Niara could see the beginnings of exhaustion in his eyes. How long had they been searching? How many books? How many journals, accounts, and genealogies? She had lost track. She turned back to the shelves as Enlil wandered around the corner of the shelf, to the next section he intended to search.

She was reaching for another book when the sound of something falling made her jump. A shiver ran across her skin, and she froze, straining her ears.

Silence greeted her. Ominous silence. There should have been something to hear, the sound of pages rustling, the sound of Enlil walking to the next shelf…

"Enlil?" her voice sounded high to her own ears.

There was no reply. Panic cut into her, and she put down the book she had picked up, barely noticing how much her hands were shaking. Something was about to happen, she could feel it.

She began moving through the library, moving quietly, frantically searching. Where had Enlil gone? What section had he been examining?

She peered down one of the aisles, and her heart skipped a beat. A figure was slumped on the floor, only the shock of red hair visible.

"Enlil!" she strode forward, no longer moving quietly. What had happened?

"Well, we meet again, elf-child."

The deep voice made Niara freeze for an instant before she spun around, hands rising instinctively to defend herself. She didn't recognize the man standing behind her, but the night-black hair and the aura of power made her blood run cold. Enlil had the same aura.

A hand clamped down on her shoulder, and before she could even draw breath to scream her arms were seized and brought behind her back, at least four sets of hands holding her in place. Her brain finally caught up with what was happening and she yelled and fought to break free, twisting her body to wriggle out of their grasp. She turned her head and met a pair of green eyes, set between a pair of pointed ears. She sucked in a quick intake of breath. *An elf? Why...how...*

In that moment of distraction her hands were bound with a thick, heavy rope, bound tight enough to make her wince, dragging over the burn on the back of her hand.

Anger tore through her. *No. Not again. I know how to deal with this.* She closed her eyes, bracing against the pain as she reached for the fire.

Searing heat tore through her, and a scream burst from her throat as her hands and arms burned. Fire, more powerful than she had ever felt before, built up inside her, burning her bonds away and attacking her captors. She heard cries of pain behind her, and she wrenched her arms free, flinging fire out as she did so.

A handful of fire struck the elf in the face, and he screamed, whirling away from her and covering his face with his hands as his hair caught fire. The smell of burnt flesh and hair filled the aisle, followed by the crackling of burning paper.

Oh no. Niara wrenched herself away from the other figures, stumbling backward as a shelf of books burst into flames.

"Grab her!" the man's voice rang through the aisle, and Niara spun on her heel, fleeing blindly through the aisles, smoke chasing her as fire leapt up to the ceiling.

What have I done? The heat of the fire grew stronger, and she looked about desperately, knowing she was going to need to find an exit. *Mazda's light, I left Enlil back there!*

Her heart panicked, but her feet kept running, knowing her only chance of survival was to get outside the burning library and hide, as fast as possible. With the elf out of commission, there shouldn't be anyone with the senses to detect her…

Was he the only elf? Niara couldn't remember if any of the other figures had had pointed ears. *Where did he come from? Why was he here, and with a…*a roar echoed behind her, and the roof let out a threatening groan. She flinched as dust dropped from the ceiling, warning of an impending collapse. She risked a glance behind her and saw fire tendrils reaching up to the top of the bookshelves just as black wings stretched open and another roar shook the building.

Dragon. She swallowed the lump in her throat. One of Enlil's kin, working with an elf, had come to capture her.

The answer hit like a slap in the face. Only one elf knew enough to track her, could find her at any time, regardless of her location. Her father had sent them after her.

The heat rising behind her mixed with the heat of betrayal as she reached the door. She ran out, unable to restrain herself from coughing. The smoke had finally caught up to her.

Hide! Don't stop, hide! She staggered toward the nearest building, a mostly fallen-down construction of rubble. She crept under a pile of stones just as another roar split the air and a rush of wings and crash of stone heralded the dragon's exit.

She peeked out through a crack in the rubble, holding her breath, but still unable to look away. The black dragon was as awe-inspiring as Enlil in his form, but instead of twinkling blue eyes staring at her, red eyes glowed angrily. The dragon roared again, releasing a stream of fire into the sky.

"Find her!" he roared. "I want her alive!"

Niara froze as she saw two figures staggering out of the exit to the library, dragging a figure between them. All of them were covered in soot, so much so that Niara could barely distinguish the third figure as Enlil.

He's alive. The hope she felt was immediately quenched. She didn't dare risk rescuing him. The dragon would simply capture her as well. She had no hope of fighting one on her own.

Instead of obeying the dragon, the two figures took the time to bind Enlil's hands before leaving him slumped against a stone. They were both humans, Niara was relieved to see. They stared at each other, then around the courtyard. Niara held her breath, willing them not to search every building, to assume she'd been burned in the library. A crash echoed from within the building, and the roof collapsed, causing dust and debris to rise as fire licked the stone walls.

"My lord, she's likely dead!" one of the humans dared to shout.

The dragon released another stream of fire into the sky. "Bring her companion!" he ordered. "Back to the capital."

The two figures moved quickly, obviously eager to escape the burning pyre. Niara watched helplessly as the soldiers carried Enlil out to the center of the courtyard. The dragon swooped down, gathering Enlil in its claws before lumbering into the air and flying north.

No! Niara's heart contracted. Although Enlil was a dragon, he was in at least as much danger as she if he went to the capital.

Bastards! Anger burned in her again, and she didn't bother to control it. She called upon the fire again, ignoring the searing pain in her hand as she pointed at the two soldiers, calling a ball of fire to strike them where they stood.

Screams rent the air, and the smell of burning flesh and charred hair drifted, carrying to Niara's hiding place. Mercifully, the screams soon stopped, and the bodies fell to the ground, charred husks all that remained.

She shook as she huddled in the collapsed house, emotions fighting with each other, helplessness and fear biting as sharp as frost. There would be another dragon. And another. Her father would know she was alive.

I need to leave here. The impetuous urge came so strong it threatened to overwhelm her. She crept out of her hiding place, only to be confronted by the charred husks of the men she had killed.

She stared at the husks, her hands shaking. Bile rose within her, and she retched, unable to control her reaction. She leaned against a stone and emptied the contents of her stomach until nothing but emptiness remained.

I killed them. She shuddered, remembering the screams. *Not only killed them, I immolated them. Mazda's light, what have I done?*

The burn shone red on her hand, and she winced, torn between gratefulness and hate. Whoever had placed the mark on her hand had both saved her and made her do...this.

The crackle of fire and groan of wood caused her to look up, realizing the library was still burning. She backed away instinctively, even though the roof had already collapsed, and there was little danger of it spreading.

All the books are gone. Her heart sank in her chest as she realized what that meant. If there ever had been an answer in there, a clue as to how to bind Auriel again, it was gone, consumed in fire.

It's useless. She found herself sinking to her knees, hot tears running down her cheeks. *I might as well have let the dragon take me. Papsukkal is nearly here, and I didn't find the answer.*

She didn't know how long she knelt there, listening to the fire crackling within the walls. The heat warmed her, the first she'd been truly warm for this long since leaving Ellriheim. Except for the night she'd lain with Enlil.

*Enlil...*tears threatened to overwhelm her again, but she pushed them aside, instead using the surge of emotion to drive her to her feet. *Whatever else, I can at least attempt to rescue him. Even if I die in the attempt. It's better than living in this world.*

She turned and made her way across the courtyard, the library still burning behind her. At the entrance, the black polished stone statue she'd noticed before stared at her, eyes implacable as ever. She gazed at it, once again noting the curious familiarity. Not exactly, but...she knew those features.

Something drew her closer to the statue, and she found herself standing directly at its base, looking into its eyes. The face was familiar, and yet she couldn't quite tell why. Her eyes trailed down its body, ignoring the bare chest, running down its arms, until her eyes rested on the back of its left hand. A brand glowed, a sun brand that was the image of the one on her own hand.

Niara eyed the symbol for a long moment, eyes flickering between the back of her own hand and the statue.

*Sun. Sun-lord. Mazda. Manyuanmazda, Mazdaanmanyu...*thoughts whirled in her head, too fast for her to make any sense out of them. The text from the book she had found rang in her head. *Manyu was bound in the fire mountain...*

"Mount Halon," she whispered. More memories called to her. Her visions, the volcano. The voice calling her to free him. The fact that it was a sun, not a skull, on her hand...

Who else has been influencing me? Who else has marked me? Aeres Thon-Esia, Taledon, and...Mazda.

"Manyu isn't the only one in the fire mountain," she whispered. "Mazda is bound there as well." Somehow, when the elves had bound Manyu, they had bound his brother as well, even though they obviously hadn't intended to.

She looked up into the statue's face. "Only your children can release you," she said, as if she were talking to Mazda himself. "But they killed all Manyu's children, and how would I find a child of Mazda? A child of the sun?"

The face stared back at her the eyes dark and familiar, as if the figure patiently waited for her to find the answer. Exactly like Nazir had done so many times. That was his favorite method of teaching. It used to drive Niara crazy, that when she asked him a question half the time she'd get a question in return.

Niara's eyes widened as a realization struck her. She blinked, unable to process the idea, then shook her head and blinked again.

It can't be. But it had to be. The Lady herself had called her stepfather 'child of the sun.' And Nazir had never known his father, had always had mysterious parentage. Was it possible his mysterious father could in fact be Mazda, and not the demon the nobles had whispered about for years?

And her father. Her father had called Nazir 'a man who should never have been born.' If she was right, if Mazda was indeed Nazir's father, and he was bound in the mountain with Manyu…her thoughts were confused.

She shook her head again. How could she be sure? And even if she was right, how could she risk releasing Mazda, when she might very well release Manyu as well?

Do I have a choice? It's nearly Papsukkal. If only she knew exactly what day it was, but the gradual warming of the weather did not only reflect her southerly location. The year turned, preparing to end and begin again. Her time was running short.

And I have no answer as to how to bind Auriel. She stared blankly in the direction of Mount Halon, the volcano she had seen spewing smoke on their way here. The courtyard in front of her was filled with smoke, a mirror of her memory.

I have to try. She couldn't get to the capital before Papsukkal, if that deadline even mattered now she had lost the ritual binding. If she could get to Mount Halon, then perhaps she could do something.

And then I'll come for you, Enlil. Once I release a god to deal with another god. She took a deep breath, surprised at her ragged breathing. She turned back to the statue, half expecting a look of approval or expectation, but it just continued to stare at her benevolently, solemn and patient.

"As patient as the voice that said 'come,'" Niara whispered. She took another deep breath. Mazda's light, was she truly about to do this? To release Mazda from the prison the elves had bound him in?

The eyes of the statue gave her no answers, but they suddenly started flickering before her eyes, and the whole world shifted, as if she had been transported, back to the chamber beneath the volcano.

The earth rumbled beneath her feet, and she could feel the walls shuddering, as if the entire mountain was a beast trying to escape. Fire illuminated cracks in the ceiling, and the air burned hot, so hot she feared she might suffocate.

In front of her stood a man, the image of the statue she had been looking at. Dark haired and dark-eyed, he smiled at her, a smile warm and benevolent.

"I told you you would come," he said.

Niara trembled and raised her right hand, showing him the symbol on the back. "Mazda," she stated.

Mazda nodded. "And you are Niara, blood-kin to my own."

She blinked, uncertain as to his meaning.

"You must come here to free me," Mazda said. "The time runs short. You must leave now."

Her tongue stuck to the roof of her mouth as she tried to deal with his assumption that she intended to free him, that she would free him. He's a god, she reminded herself. Like AeresThonEsia, like Taledon. His mind works differently. And it wasn't as if his assumption was incorrect. I do intend to free him.

"How do I free you?" she managed.

"Come to me," was the only answer Mazda gave her. "All shall become clear then. Now go, before your protector arrives again."

The vision started flickering, and Niara found herself once again in the smoke-filled courtyard, staring at the statue of Mazda. She inhaled a lungful of smoke and coughed, broke back to harsh reality.

She cursed as she attempted to catch her breath, Mazda's words spinning through her head. *My protector? Taledon. He showed up during my last vision with Mazda.* She shook her head, her skin prickling. Taledon had told her to bind Auriel, had dismissed the idea of any other possibility. He would not like her current idea.

I have no choice. She turned toward the edge of the city and started walking, quickly, before she could second-guess her decision. *Besides, Mazda is the protector of humanity. And I am part-human. He'll protect us from Auriel. I hope.*

16

MOUNT HALON

Her dress hung in tatters, her shoes worn ragged and full of holes, and the chill wind cut to the bone. Niara wrapped her arms around herself, cursing her luck. She had no supplies, nothing to help her reach Mount Halon. The fire had consumed all.

She cleared her parched throat, wincing as she remembered her biggest mistake; leaving Shan Serin without collecting enough water. She had been so focused, so set on reaching her goal, that nothing else had crossed her mind.

How far is it? The mountain loomed in the distance, but distances were deceptive in the badlands. It could have been an hour's march, it could have been a week. They had flown the last distance so fast, she had no way of telling, no way to measure how far she had to travel.

She tripped and barely restrained a cry as a rock slashed her knee. She hissed as she reached down to examine it and her hand came away bloody.

If I ever again think walking across the badlands is a good idea, I am going to kill myself. Or tell Enlil to knock some sense into me. Her eyes stung as she remembered her last sight of Enlil, trapped in a dragon's talons as he flew into the distance, but she stood up and kept going, her momentum the only thing she had left.

One step. Then another. The steps blurred together, blurred with the scenery as her eyes blinked. She staggered from exhaustion but didn't care. She had to keep going. She had to reach the mountain.

She only faintly heard the sound of horse's hooves in the distance, and the sound failed to incite any panic in her until she had been listening for a full minute. Then her head came up, and she looked around frantically, knowing she had only minutes to find a place to hide. Scattered boulders around her provided the only possible sources of cover. The sound was coming from the north, so she threw herself behind the south face of a large boulder, hoping against hope that the riders would continue on, that they wouldn't stop, they wouldn't glance back, they wouldn't see her...

The hoofbeats came closer and closer, echoing dully on the hard dirt and stone of the rocky terrain. They were moving slowly, not galloping, not trotting. A slow walk. Conserving the horses' strength.

To her dismay, the sound of the horses' hooves stopped as they reached the other side of the boulder she hid behind. She leaned against the boulder, making her breathing as soft as possible. She needed to keep going. She couldn't stay here.

"We'll camp here," the voice was faint, but clear nonetheless. Niara's heart dropped. If the group was camping here for the night, then she would be stuck until darkness fell. At least the sun hanging low on the horizon meant that would not be long.

She lowered herself to the ground as quietly as she could, leaning over to rest her head on her knees. Behind her, the sounds of people setting up camp was almost comforting, a familiar sound from so many trips with her mother to Hillsdale, Venia, Jyria, and Saemar. A wave of longing swept over her, and she felt dizzy with the desire to go back, to return to a time where everything seemed simpler, where she wasn't marked by three gods, all warring with different desires for her.

Her eyelids started to droop, and she forced them open, blinking as she realized the sun had just dipped below the horizon. It would be time to leave soon. She had to be ready. As soon as the people settled around their fire, she would be on her way.

"Garreth! Get down from there!" the woman's voice rang like a bell, an order from a mother used to her child disobeying her. A smile played on Niara's lips as she remembered Vinet and Gwyn using a similar tone with her. She had usually listened, though. At least, she liked to remember it that way.

A child's laugh rang above her, a sound that startled her so completely that she failed to react to the fact that it was, indeed, above her, not on the other side of the boulder. "I can see for miles!" a boy's voice cried. "Mama, it's so pretty!"

"Garreth, I will not tell you again!" the mother's voice was sharp, frayed with worry and impatience.

"I'm coming, I'm coming," the boy grumbled. Above Niara, a rock shifted, and she flinched as the rock came free from the boulder, landing right beside her on the dirt.

"Mama! There's someone here!" the boy's voice was loud, shocked, and surprised.

It took Niara a few moments to react to the boy's statement. When it finally penetrated, she scrambled to her feet, panic setting in. She couldn't be discovered. She couldn't! She was so close!

It took the same amount of time for the boy's statement to be processed by the people on the other side of the boulder. As Niara stood up, the sound of many people moving quickly filled the air.

"Garreth, get down, now!" a man's voice this time, filled with authority. The boy didn't question as he scrambled down the other side of the boulder, away from Niara. Niara felt her heart pounding in her chest. Did she have the strength to run?

She hesitated too long. Figures came from both sides of the boulder, brandishing swords and spears in her direction. Niara pressed herself against the boulder to appear as harmless as possible. Even as she did so, she took in her attackers' appearance. They were not dressed in the uniform of Auriel's soldiers. Instead, they were as ragged as she, the only difference being some of them had armor, and their weapons looked well-used.

"Stay where you are!" one of the men, the same one who had ordered the boy Garreth down, strode toward Niara, sword held threateningly. Niara instinctively raised her hands, pressing herself flat against the boulder.

"Who are you?" the man demanded. "Are you one of the cursed Auriel's spies?"

Niara felt her breath catch in her throat. "I'm not an enemy," she gasped. The world was hazy, and she blinked, trying to get it to steady.

"What's your name?" the man's voice remained harsh. "Tell me!"

She didn't have the strength to lie. "Niara," she managed. "Please, I'm not—" not an enemy, she was going to say, but the world shifted again, and the only reason she didn't fall was because she was already leaning against the boulder.

"Lord Markus, she's an elf," one of the other men said. "Doesn't Izila offer a reward for any elves brought to her?"

Fear rose up in her. They couldn't turn her in for a reward. "Please, no," Niara stammered. "Don't...I'm so close."

The man addressed as Lord Markus furrowed his brow. "An elf?" His gaze sharpened. "What is an elf doing out here in the middle of the badlands?"

Niara wanted to explain, but the words died in her mouth. She didn't know who these men were, didn't know what they were after, what they would do to her...

"Is everything alright?" the female voice broke through the stalemate, the voice of the mother. Niara swayed as the woman walked around the boulder, taking in the situation easily before moving to stand next to Markus.

"Cenna, get back to the other side," Markus ordered.

Cenna gave him a long-suffering look. "You seem to have the danger well in hand," she said. "One lone woman?"

Niara's vision blurred again, and she swallowed, coughing as her throat only encountered dust. Cenna's gaze flickered to her, then back to Markus.

"Markus, you cannot seriously tell me you're interrogating this woman rather than offering her refuge," she said. "Just look at her!"

"Cenna—" Markus's voice was helpless as he tried to protest. At another time, Niara would have laughed, but she could barely keep her thoughts straight.

Cenna ignored Markus as she walked toward Niara, gently taking her arm. "Come here, dear," she said. "You seem exhausted. Sit, drink some water, and then," she shot a glance at Markus, "you can tell us your story."

Markus sighed, but he sheathed his sword, the rest of his men following suit. Niara gratefully leaned against Cenna's shoulder as she staggered around the boulder, to where a small fire crackled and burned.

"I need to get to the mountain," she managed to whisper.

"Shh," Cenna shushed her, pushing her down to sit before handing her a cup of water. "Drink first. Then speak."

It was impossible to disobey the woman. Niara took a long sip, savoring the sensation of the cool water on her parched lips. She drained the cup, and her breathing steadied.

"Take your time," Cenna's voice was low and soothing. Niara nodded, closing her eyes and taking another few breaths.

"Cenna, we need to—" Markus spoke in a low voice.

"Markus, she's a slip of a girl," Cenna whispered back. "One who's clearly had a rough journey. Even if she wanted to betray us to Auriel and Izila, I doubt she could."

At the sound of Auriel's name, Niara opened her eyes. She still felt unsteady, but far better than she had a few minutes ago.

"I'm not one of Auriel's spies," she managed.

"So you said," Markus stepped in front of her. "Then who are you, and what in Mazda's name are you doing out here in the badlands?"

Mazda's name. Niara's knees went weak with relief. If the lord was swearing by Mazda, then he wouldn't turn her over to Auriel.

"My name is Niara," she said.

Cenna smiled reassuringly. "And I am Cenna," she said. "My husband, whose poor manners you will have to excuse, is Markus."

Niara knew they were concealing part of their identities, just as she was concealing hers. She had heard one of the men say Lord Markus, after all. But none of that mattered right now.

"I need to get to the mountain," she gestured toward the shape that now appeared only a mere shadow on the horizon. Unconsciously, she straightened. "I have to go there to defeat Auriel and his dragons."

"You what?" Markus asked, his voice flat.

Niara took a deep breath, suddenly aware of how unbelievable her words must sound. "It's true," she said. "I need to get there before Papsukkal."

Markus exchanged a glance with Cenna. "You're on a tight schedule, then," he said. "Papsukkal is tomorrow."

Niara looked up sharply in fear. *Oh no. Time passed quicker than I thought.* She pushed herself to her feet. "Then I need to get moving."

"Hold on," Markus stepped in front of her, his eyes hard. "You aren't going anywhere."

Niara felt anger rising in her, exasperated by her exhaustion. "Try to stop me," she snapped.

"Peace," Cenna stepped between the two of them, hands raised in a calming gesture. "Niara, surely you can wait until daybreak. You need the rest." She narrowed her eyes at her husband.

"She's not going anywhere until we're sure she's no threat," Markus growled. "I'll not risk our safety."

Niara took a deep breath and closed her eyes briefly, willing herself to remember her courtly manners. "I understand the duty you feel to your men, Lord Markus," she said, measuring her voice carefully, "but my duty is to the entirety of Saemar. I cannot fail in this." Her voice cracked toward the end of her speech, and she silently cursed. *I already failed once. I can't fail again.*

Markus stared at her a long moment; his face unreadable. "Saemar?" he finally asked.

Niara nodded, trying to gauge his reaction.

Markus narrowed his eyes. "Why would an elf care about Saemar?"

Niara steeled herself. "Because I am Lady Niara Sindarilae

Andaren, heir to the lands of Ninaeva," she said. "And the one person Auriel and Izila would most love to see brought to them."

Markus's expression darkened. "A lady of Saemar," he said.

Tension crackled in the air. Niara felt the hair on the back of her neck stand up, and she knew she had made an error. Whoever these people were, they were no friends to Saemar.

Cenna stepped forward, head held high, standing half between Niara and her husband. "Well met, Lady Niara," she said. She gave a courtly nod. "I am Lady Cenna Ashridge, and this is my husband, Markus Ashridge, Lord of Rainvere, heir to the Duchy of Tigri."

Tigri. Niara blinked. Of all the people, she hadn't expected a Tigrian lord. *Much less the heir to the dukedom! If Auriel wasn't in control, wouldn't he be Duke in fact?*

She swallowed the lump in her throat. "Lady Cenna, Lord Markus," she said. "A pleasure to make your acquaintance."

Markus stared at her, his expression still dark, but her courtesy left him unable to answer effectively. "Your king destroyed us," he said.

"Our king was controlled and manipulated by the sky-lord Auriel," Niara kept her voice as level as she could. "He destroyed Saemar as well as Tigri, as well as the Jyrian Confederacy and all of the free city-states."

Cenna set her hand lightly on her husband's arm. "Did you say you were of Ninaeva?" she asked.

Niara nodded, uncertain as to what Cenna was getting at.

Cenna looked at her husband. "Didn't your great-aunt marry a lord of Ninaeva?" she asked.

Markus's expression remained dark. "She abandoned our family," he said.

"So did the queen of Saemar," Cenna pointed out.

Niara couldn't control her quick intake of breath at the confirmation that the former queen had indeed been Tigrian. Her origin had been whispered about in the courtly circles, but never confirmed.

A memory flashed before her eyes, Taledon standing before her.

Trace your mother's mother line back, and you'll find the connection to Saemar's queen.

"We are kin," she managed. Her hand itched to reach out and take Markus's, to see if she could feel the same blood connection she had to her father, but she restrained herself.

Markus's eyes flashed. "Saemarians are no kin of mine," he said. "Not until they leave Tigri in peace."

Niara felt her right hand begin to tingle, and she clenched it into a fist behind her back, willing her voice to remain steady. "Saemar and Tigri should be allies and at peace," she said. "But that will never happen as long as Auriel and his dragons are in control, and to stop that I need to get to Mount Halon." She gestured again toward the shadow on the horizon.

"How do we know you're telling the truth?" Markus demanded. "That mountain is dangerous. I remember—" he clamped his mouth shut.

Niara took a breath to steady herself, looking at Markus more closely. He wasn't that much older than she, if she had to guess, his late twenties or early thirties. Older by years of stress and strain, though.

Which means he was alive during the war with Mount Halon. Niara didn't remember much of it herself, but she remembered Rian's grief when her grandfather had been killed.

"I know it's dangerous," she said, trying to make her voice soothing. "But Mazda is bound in that mountain and releasing him is the only way to stop Auriel."

If she had wanted to silence everyone, she had chosen no better way. Not a sound beyond their own breathing echoed through the still twilight.

"Mazda," Markus finally said. His voice was the same, but Niara thought she detected a trace of uncertainty in his eyes. "Mazda, Lord of the Sun, Protector of Humankind, is bound in Mount Halon?" His incredulity made his voice rise.

Niara nodded, her heart pounding hard in her chest. She squeezed her hand tighter as tendrils of pain started shooting up her arm. "Yes," she said. "He—" her vision darkened, and she staggered before the Sight claimed her.

A dragon filled her vision, scarlet and gold against the sky. Fire streaked through the air as she roared in triumph. Her two consorts flew circles around her, exalting in their service.

"Fly to Tigri, my love," she crooned to one of them. "The humans think to rebel, but we shall show them once and for all that we are their lords and masters, and they are nothing but pitiful slaves."

One of the dragons nodded, his eyes dark, and he flew off, streaking across the sky. The second consort flew closer to Izila, affection and worship in his every movement.

"And me, Great Lady?" he asked.

Izila didn't answer as more wingbeats heralded the arrival of another dragon, burgundy and gold, far larger than Izila and her consort. Auriel.

"My children," he said. "How goes the plan?"

"I will remain in the capital, to deal with the uprising here," Izila answered.

"And I will fly to Ninaeva," her consort continued, his voice a low growl. "They have escaped us long enough."

"Good," Auriel's voice was almost a purr. "Then all is as it should be."

"Niara?"

Niara gasped a huge lungful of air, panic filling her body as she was yanked from the vision. *Ninaeva. Ellriheim. Mazda's light, I need to warn Thalion!*

She looked up to see Markus shaking her arms. "Niara? What in Mazda's name—"

He was touching her. Something in her blood stirred, the beginnings of the same sensation as when her father had touched her. Instinctively, she copied what he had done, reaching out to Markus with her magic, and feeling his blood answer hers.

He dropped his hands from her arms and took a step back, staring blankly at her. "What was—" he managed.

She took another deep, shaky breath, her mind still reeling from the vision. "We are kin," she said again, only half of her mind on her words. "One of my gifts. Blood calls to blood. But Mazda's light,

Thalion…" she stared blindly to the north, then spun back to face Markus. "Whatever else happens, I need to get to Mount Halon. So many lives depend on it, please!"

Markus blinked, and Niara could see the confusion in his eyes, as he tried to process the sense of kinship she now felt toward him, and he to her. They were only cousins, distant cousins at best, but the blood tie remained, and the Lord's gift made it stronger.

"Alright," he finally said, his words slow and measured. "But tell me what else is going on."

Did he see something? Niara ignored the thought and simply nodded. "There are rebellions happening throughout Saemar," she said. "All timed for Papsukkal. But Izila and her consorts know. They're preparing to stop them." She turned her gaze north again. "They're going to Ninaeva and Tigri, and more dragons are flying to other areas while Izila stays in the capital. Mazda's light, if I don't get to the mountain…" she couldn't finish her sentence.

"Rebellion," Markus's voice came out a whisper. "It all makes sense."

Niara didn't have time to react to his words as he spun around and started shouting out orders. "Soldiers, arm yourselves, prepare to move. Pack the saddles as light as you can. Cenna, you take the noncombatants. Make your way toward the border, but don't cross it yet. Not till you hear word it's safe."

The camp instantly sprang to action, and Cenna obeyed her husband with nary a murmur, pausing only to gently kiss his cheek. Niara blinked at the speed with which everything was conducted.

"Niels, lead the men to Tigri City. There's a rebellion happening, and we must be there to support them. I'll join you as soon as I'm able."

The soldier Markus was addressing saluted and turned away, walking swiftly toward his horse. Niara stared after him. "You're not leading them?" she asked.

Markus raised an eyebrow at her. "I'll join them later. For now, I'm taking you to the mountain, cousin."

Niara blessed the years she had spent riding through Ninaeva's hills and mountains as her horse trotted through the badlands, trusting her to be its eyes as they rode through the moonlit night. Niara blessed the full moon and the thousands of stars in the sky. If they hadn't illuminated the badlands to be almost as bright as day, she never would have dared go faster than a walk on the rocky terrain.

Markus kept pace beside her, bent over the back of his horse, a grim look on his face. Niara wished she could guess what was going through his mind. His reaction to her being Saemarian had been bitter, and for a moment she had thought he would keep her prisoner just on principle, but when she had used the Lord's gift…

Blood calls to blood. Niara didn't know how she felt about that. All her life, Tigri had been the enemy, sending Cossack raiders who were formally disavowed by the Tigrian Dukes to attack the border villages. Some nobles, the former king prominent among them, proclaimed they should be part of Saemar, and invested their lives and fortunes into attempting to bring the rebellious former province under control. Technically, Andreas had managed it, but who knew if it would have lasted if Auriel hadn't risen.

He's your cousin. The idea made her own head spin. She had never imagined her grandmother could have been from Tigri. Vinet had never breathed a word, if she had ever known.

Didn't Grandmother die long before Mother became Lady of Ninaeva, though? Perhaps there was a reason she'd never known of the connection.

She was using Tigri to avoid thinking of her true purpose. The mountain loomed before her, an unfriendly reminder of the task ahead. A task she had no idea how to accomplish.

It's not just Mazda in the mountain. An involuntary shiver ran down her spine. *It's Manyu too. Mazda's light, what if I release him as well? What will happen then? Will it be worth it?*

She couldn't shut the thoughts out as they drew closer and closer. She was grateful Markus had loaned her the horse to ride on, and yet she couldn't help wish she had a little more time to think, to plan, to find out what exactly would happen.

In far too short a time, they were at the base of the mountain. Niara reined her horse to a stop as she gazed at the slope in front of her. Above them the mountain rumbled, a quiet, consistent rumble which sounded like the heralding of a storm.

"Now what?" Markus's voice was harsh.

Niara stared up the mountain and swallowed. "Now I climb it." Somehow her voice sounded far more confident than she felt.

"Then let's go," his voice was little more than a growl.

Niara shook her head. "You have other duties," she said. "Thank you for getting me this far."

Markus gave her a hard look. "I said I'd take you here."

"And you did." She couldn't tell why she was trying to keep Markus from following her up the mountain. She only knew that whatever awaited her, she didn't want to be responsible if anything happened to him.

"You're sure?" he asked.

Niara nodded. "Thank you, cousin." The word sounded strange on her tongue. She'd never had a cousin before.

Markus gave her a small smile, the first she'd seen on his face. "May we meet again in better circumstances," he said. "Mazda light your path." With that, he wheeled his horse around and galloped away, quickly becoming a dim figure moving across the moonlit plains.

She stared after him for a long moment, drawing the courage and strength for what she had to do next. The mountain rose steeply before her, and her horse would have difficulty climbing it.

She slid off the horse's back and patted its sides. "Thank you," she told it. "Stay here, and I'll try to come back for you." She looked around, but there was no place to effectively secure the horse, and she didn't feel like hobbling it. It whickered, and she sighed as she stepped away, hoping it would still be there when she descended. If she descended.

She turned toward the mountain and started climbing, taking her first steps up the rough black surface. The rock was hard, unwelcoming, and as black as the night itself. If she leaned down to touch it, her hand would be scraped and battered before she could cry out.

One step. Then another. She lost track of time as she climbed steadily higher and higher. To the east, she could see the faint glow of light on the horizon and knew dawn would not be far off.

Fitting, she thought. *Release the sun god on the morning of the day where anything can happen...*

She stumbled as the ground seemed to give way beneath her, scraping her knees painfully on the sharp stones. She scrambled to her feet, blinking at the sight of a passage before her. She could have sworn it hadn't existed a moment ago. It stood dark and ominous, with no hint of welcome, only the sense of destiny and doom waiting for her in the heart of the mountain.

This is the way. Niara swallowed as she regarded the tunnel. To enter it felt like a final step, a step which would seal her fate for eternity.

The memories of the burned library, of Enlil being carried away, of Izila sending her consort to Ninaeva, and Markus riding north to Tigri on her word made her spine stiffen. She remembered the others she had talked to, who she had promised that something would happen on Papsukkal, something which would change their lives forever. *Kishtar, Lyra, Rian, Ren, Carol, Miken and Jak...*so many promises, so many lives. As well as everyone in Hillsdale, Venia, Ellriheim, the capital, and now Tigri who would be murdered if the rebellion failed...

I have no choice. She took a deep breath and stepped into the tunnel, feeling as if the light growing outside had abandoned her the moment she took the first step.

Steady. This is no worse than the labyrinth. She tried to keep that thought in mind as she walked deeper and deeper into the mountain, but it was hard. The labyrinth had been on a different plane, not her own physical body, real as it had felt. This was real.

Come. The voice seemed to rumble through the mountain, and she shivered, a chill running down her spine despite the growing warmth. *Come.*

"I'm coming," she whispered under her breath. "Mazda, give me strength."

The voice subsided, but the mountain did not. Ahead, she could hear a sound like water rushing and the low, steady rumble like a heartbeat that vibrated through her entire body. The tunnel grew warmer and warmer as she continued, and eventually she could make out a soft, glowing red light.

Finally. Her pace quickened instinctively as she moved toward the light. Whatever happened, it was better to face it in the light.

The tunnel opened up abruptly, and she found herself standing in an enormous cavern. The floor she was standing on stretched out in both directions, but in front of her it dropped into a fiery pool of lava, one that spit and bubbled, throwing up streams of fire that cooled before falling into the boiling pit again.

She shuddered as she looked around, feeling the looming presence of someone, of something. She reached out her right hand, trying to take comfort from the sun brand, but it only felt like a binding, a burden.

"I'm here," she said, her voice shaking. "Now what?"

The entire cavern rumbled, and the lava spit with more intensity. She stepped backward, only to find her back pressing into a wall. She jerked forward, spinning around, but the passage behind her had somehow closed. She was trapped.

She faced the pool of lava, fear and anger rising up inside her simultaneously. "Don't trap me here." Her voice shook. "I came to help you."

The lava rose, steadily moving closer and closer to the floor she stood on. She took another step back, pressing herself against the cavern wall as the lava crept over the edge, pooling on the floor in front of her.

Mazda's light. She wanted to squeeze her eyes shut, to pretend none of this was happening, but her gaze remained fixed on the fire in front of her. Fire that would be her death.

The lava moved on its own, rising up, until it stood as tall as she. It began to take solid form, cooling and solidifying before her eyes, turning black as the stone of the mountain, except smoother, like skin…

Her breath caught in her throat as the figure of a man took shape before her. The same face as the statue in Shan Serin, the same eyes stared at her.

"Give me your hand," Mazdaanmanyu held out his hand, his eyes warm and understanding, yet implacable and firm.

Niara barely felt herself move, as if she were being entirely directed by his power. She held out her right hand, the one branded by the sun, and he took it in his own, a grip as unyielding as stone.

His eyes flickered down to her arm, where the stag scar was visible through her torn sleeves. "You cannot be fully mine," he said. "No matter. Call my grandson."

"What?" The word escaped her in a breath of air. She had speculated Nazir was the son of Mazda but hadn't pondered the implications further.

"My grandson," Mazda's voice held no trace of impatience. "Your brother. He has called on me before, I know of his existence."

Niara swallowed, but the command in his voice was impossible to disobey. She didn't question how he knew of her ability, how he knew she could reach Thalion. She closed her eyes and went inward, stretching out, far across the north and to the west, following the faint call of her blood.

"Thalion? Thalion!"

"Niara?" Thalion's panic was unmistakable. "Niara!"

Her own fear flared in response to Thalion's. "What's happening? What's wrong?" she demanded.

"I don't know what to do!" Thalion looked frantic. "Serana—"

A scream split the air, and the edges of Niara's vision blurred as for a moment she saw through Thalion's eyes. They were still underground, in the compound of Ellriheim, with the familiar magical lanterns illuminating the small room. Serana lay on the bed, her head thrown back, grimacing against the pain. A woman stood next to her, gently soothing.

The child. Niara caught her breath. She hadn't realized Serana was due so soon…

"Another. Good." Mazda stepped into her vision, and she felt her knees buckle under the strain.

Thalion eyes widened as he beheld the god. "Who...How..." his voice trailed off as he stared at Mazda, his mouth dropping open with awe.

"Grandson," Mazda smiled. "Take my hand."

"Thalion!" Serana's scream echoed through the room. Thalion's face contorted with fear, and Niara's vision wavered again as she saw Serana gripping her husband's hand hard.

"Not now," Niara whispered. Her knees were losing all strength, and she didn't know how much longer she could maintain the connection. She couldn't do this to Serana, though. Not right now...

"Now," Mazda extended his hand. "Thalion, now."

Thalion hesitated, looking from Serana to Mazda. With the hand that wasn't in Serana's, he reached out toward the god.

Niara screamed as searing energy coursed through her, sending her to her knees. She still saw the vision of Thalion, but she was also aware of the god's implacable grip on her hand, holding tight even as she slumped to the floor. Strength drained out of her, replaced with pain and heat as the fire grew brighter and brighter until all she could see was light.

With one more scream, Serana pushed, and a baby's cry split the air. Niara felt Thalion's concentration falter, as he tried to pull his hand from Mazda's to go to his wife and daughter.

"Another one. It is enough." Mazda tightened his grip, and Thalion cried out in surprise. Blood dripped from their joined hands.

A scream escaped Niara's throat as fire burned through her. Mazda released her hand, and she curled up into a ball, tears streaming down her face at the intense pain.

"Yes," Mazda's voice filled with exultation. "At last!"

The whole mountain rumbled, and lava rose in fountains until it reached the ceiling of the cavern. Stones began to fall, splashing into the lava below them.

Mazda gazed down at her, a smile on his face. "You have released us," he said. "You have my thanks." He waved his hand. "There. The path is clear."

Niara managed to turn her head to see the passage she had come through open behind her. She stumbled to her feet, her entire body shaking. Unable to speak, she backed away from the god, never taking her eyes off him as she moved toward the exit.

Mazda was ignoring her, staring instead at the ceiling as the light of day shone into the cavern. "At last," he whispered. "We are free."

The mountain rumbled again, this time louder than before. Mazda looked at Niara once more. "You should run."

Niara couldn't help the small sound of terror that escaped her as she fled down the tunnel, back into the darkness, away from the fire behind her. She heard a laugh, a laugh which blended in with the rumbling of the mountain, and she sped up, running like a frightened deer.

She burst out of the tunnel and tripped, almost sprawling face-first on the hard rock. She risked a glance over her shoulder in time to see a spurt of lava erupt from the top of the mountain. In the smoke that escaped, she thought she could see the shadow of a man, one whose image flickered between light and dark, sun and moon.

Mazda and Manyu. Niara stared up at the mountain in dismay, even as more lava erupted and smoke burst forth, a threatening herald of things to come. *Mazda's light, what have I done?*

17

THE CAPITAL

She didn't remember scrambling down the side of Mount Halon, didn't remember finding her horse, which somehow had remained at the base, waiting for her. She didn't remember riding away from the explosion of ash and fire behind her, only remembered slumping out of the saddle and to the ground in a haze of exhaustion.

She leaned against a rock as her horse looked around for anything to graze on. She had released Mazda. And Manyu. *Mazdaanmanyu...*

Mazda's light, I hope Thalion is alright. The thought made her straighten, eyes widening. If the pain she had felt had been excruciating, then what had it been like for him? *And Serana? And...my niece?* Had she truly seen that? Had Serana had a daughter at the moment the gods had been released?

The urgency to find answers overwhelmed her, and she closed her eyes, reaching out again toward the north. Attempting to, at least. Her vision fizzled and died, leaving her panting, staring at the empty badlands before her.

I'm exhausted. Niara knew she should stop, should rest, but the uncertainty of what had happened made her try again. *Mazda's light, Thalion, if I hurt you or Serana I will never forgive myself...*

She reached out again, and this time, her vision caught and held. "Thalion?" she called, trying to find her brother.

Her vision blurred. Ninaeva. Ilhelm. The rocks were cleared away, and soldiers were pouring out into the open, brandishing swords and bows. Thalion lead them, his eyes burning with fire. The people of Ilhelm Village, Carol among them, greeted the soldiers with shouts of joy, while the dragon above them roared a challenge.

Lokrian. The burnt apple orchards. Rian sat upon a horse, raising a sword in a triumphant battle cry, Arrex next to her. The soldiers around them were dressed in Auriel's colors, but they aimed their fury at the dragon they used to serve.

Venia. Blood and battle, but Ren made his way through to stand above the gates, a flag of Saemar brandished as victory.

Hillsdale. Kishtar and Lyra lay in ambush, waiting for the gold dragon to reveal herself. She appeared behind them, her hands raised. "Let us talk."

More visions from all over the country overwhelmed her, and she shook her head, trying to break free. Part of her could not help noting she saw no sign of Enlil.

Enlil. She called his name, helpless, knowing the Lord's gift would not help her speak to him.

"Elf-daughter, what have you done?"

The figure of the Lord of Life and Loss rose before her, a stern visage. He was armed with a quiver and bow, and his antlers seemed to rise higher than before. His eyes narrowed as he regarded her.

She tried to catch her breath. There was no point pretending she didn't know what he meant. "I had no choice," she said.

"No choice?" Taledon clenched his fist. "Your mandate was clear. Bind the sky-lord."

"How?" Niara felt her voice cracking. "You gave me no answers!"

"Your path was clear," his voice remained unmoved. "All that was required of you was to follow it. And you failed."

White-hot anger rose within her. "I failed? What about you?" A niggling corner of her mind warned it was a bad idea to confront a god like this, but she couldn't bring herself to care. "Why didn't you bind Auriel, if it was so important? Why leave it to a mere mortal?"

Taledon's eyes flashed, and he raised his right hand sharply. Pain shot through Niara's arm, and she grabbed it with her other hand, barely stifling a cry.

"You are mine," Taledon said. "Beware your words."

Tears stung her eyes. "Yours?" she demanded. "Then what are these?" She raised both her arms, showing the mark of Mazda and the mark of the Lady to Taledon. "Am I no more than a plaything to you, that three of you mark me like this?"

Taledon's gaze rested on the burn. "My Lady's is acceptable. But that mark should have been gone by now. I thought you would have gone to my Lady to remove it."

Niara bit back another angry retort, that neither the Lord nor Lady had ever told her such a thing was an option. She was still forming an answer when Taledon spoke again, his voice echoing in the darkness. She couldn't understand his words, but she felt his intent. He was summoning.

The laugh took her by surprise, the female voice echoing through the gloom. "Let's return to my garden, shall we, my lord?"

The scene around Niara shifted, and she blinked, trying to find her balance. She no longer seemed to be in a vision. Instead, she was in a garden, an old garden, long overgrown. In the center was a bench, on which sat an old crone.

The Crone. Niara took a deep breath before dropping her head. "Lady," she said.

"Hmm. Courtesy to me, you show at least, elf-daughter, sun-marked." The crone shifted to Taledon. "What do you wish of me?"

Taledon stared at the Lady, an odd desire in his eyes. "Will you not show your form to me, Hiliakae?"

The crone bowed her head, and her vision flickered until it was the maiden sitting before them, smiling winsomely at the Lord. "Is this what you desire, my lord?"

Taledon released a sigh. "You are a bright light, my lady." He stepped forward, reaching out to take the Lady's hand.

The Lady, AeresThonEsia, or Hiliakae, raised her hand before Taledon could take it. "Speak, my lord," she said. "What do you desire of me?"

Taledon's expression hardened. "Remove the mark of the sun from our chosen," he said, gesturing toward Niara. "It is not fitting for one who would lead the elves."

Niara felt as if she had been struck by a blow. "Then you support my father's plan?" she demanded. "To have the elves rule over all?"

Taledon snorted. "The elves have ever been their own people," he said. "Your father knew that once. It should return so."

"But the mix is so…delightful." The Lady smiled. "Would you not wish to see more like Vinet Elfsdaughter?"

"Lady." The Lord's voice was impatient. "Our plan has failed, and you removing this mark is our only chance to have it succeed again. The sky-lord is still free, but we may yet be able to bind him, with Niara free from the sun-lord's mark."

Niara clenched her right hand into a fist. She could almost feel its fire, the intensity it loaned her Swaying. Although it was painful, perhaps that was not always a bad thing…the memory of the charred corpses in Shan Serin swam before her eyes, and she bit her lip.

"My lord, you know you cannot make such a request of me," the Lady said with chiding eyes. "Niara must make that request herself, of her own free will. And she will not."

Niara glanced up sharply to meet the Lady's eyes. She read a calculation there which sent a shiver down her spine.

Taledon frowned. "Why will she not—"

"Because it is the wheel." The Lady leaned back, her posture seductive. "Come, my lord. Surely you have realized it is the changing of an age?"

"No," Taledon's voice was flat. "There will not be a return to Great Fire."

"I did not say that." The Lady stood up, hips swaying as she moved to stand next to Taledon. "The ages change, and we all change with them. Nothing shall stop it, least of all Niara. She is an instrument of that change."

Niara didn't like the two talking about her as if she wasn't there, but she kept her mouth shut.

The Lord and Lady gazed at each other for a long moment, an

endless conversation passing between them with only their eyes. The Lady inclined her head. "A bargain, then," she said.

Niara couldn't help it. "What bargain?" she asked.

Taledon turned toward her. "The dragons may live," he said. "They are the problem of mortals. But the one known as Izila, the Great Burner, must die for any elf or human to know peace."

Niara swallowed as she remembered her visions of the gold and red dragon. She had no trouble believing the dragon would do everything in her power to see that she remained in control of Saemar, any other races her slaves. She nodded.

"Go to the capital," the Lady said. "My Eye awaits you there. May your aim be true, elfsdaughter."

Niara opened her mouth to ask another question, but her voice died as her vision shifted again, and she was left staring at the empty wastes of the badlands.

Cursed visions. She slumped forward, covering her face with her hands. Why couldn't they just leave her alone?

Her horse nickered and pushed at her shoulder. She straightened, looking to the north, trying to gauge the distance back to Saemar. *How long did the journey here take me? Mazda's light...* the rebellion would be over by the time she got back, if Izila didn't crush everyone.

I have no water, no food...only a horse. Mazda's light. I hate gods. They never think of anything practical. With a sigh, she got to her feet. She couldn't stay in the badlands. She might as well start moving.

Days later. She wiped the haze of dust out of her eyes, blinking in the harsh sunlight. The sun was her only indication she was still moving in the right direction.

She had found some water, at least, but her stomach growled as she slumped over the saddle. Not for the first time, she blessed Markus and the fact he had given her the horse. She never would have made it this far without it.

Wingbeats overhead drew her eyes up, straining them against the harsh glare of the sun. She could barely see a black silhouette against the sky, wings beating, coming steadily closer and closer to her.

Dragon. Niara searched for worry, for panic, for any sense of emotion, and found nothing. She was simply too hungry and exhausted. Whatever the dragon had in store for her, it couldn't be worse than this.

She kept riding, keeping her horse at a steady walk as the dragon flew closer and closer. She tried to ignore it, to force herself to keep moving. Perhaps it wouldn't see her, perhaps it would keep going. Maybe it wasn't searching for her, maybe it had another goal entirely. Anything was possible...

The dragon dipped low and started flying straight at her, aiming for a landing. Niara blinked as she saw red flashing in the sunlight, light glinting off scarlet scales. She blinked again. The silhouette... familiar. But it couldn't be...

Her heart rose in her mouth. She urged her horse faster, riding toward the area the dragon had marked as his landing spot. "Enlil!" she shouted, her voice hoarse. "Enlil!"

The dragon landed with an explosion of dust, and Niara could tell it was indeed Enlil. She knew those bright blue eyes, the ones that looked at her with every indication of happiness and relief. She slid off her horse and ran to Enlil as his shape shifted and shrank. She collided with him, and he wrapped his arms around her, warm, familiar, and comforting.

"Niara," Enlil held her tight to his chest. "Naytar's stone, you're alright. You're alright."

Niara's eyes stung with tears of happiness, and she pulled back just enough to lift her face and reach up and kiss him. He responded eagerly, and their kiss deepened, as if all the time in the world had slowed to a halt.

Enlil pulled back to stare at her, and Niara found herself truly smiling for the first time since he'd been taken away. He was back. Whatever else happened, all was right with the world.

"I was so scared you were dead," Enlil whispered. "That's what Sirax said. I didn't believe him; I had to check..." he shook his head.

Part of her noted that Enlil knew the name of the dragon who had carried him off, the other part didn't care. "I was terrified for you," her voice broke. "I saw him take you; I didn't know if you were still alive."

Enlil pulled her in for another kiss. "We're together now," he said. "And..." he took a deep breath. "I'll never forgive myself if I don't ask. I don't know exactly how this works, Niara, but will you marry me?"

Niara's heart stopped, and she stared at Enlil in mixed shock and joy. She flung herself into his arms, kissing him again, helpless laughter pouring out of her.

Enlil responded eagerly to the kiss, his eyes bemused and slightly worried. "Is that a yes?" he asked.

Niara's spirits lifted, and she felt as if she were flying. "Yes, my dragon lover," she said, staring at Enlil in adoration. "Absolutely yes."

Enlil's face lit up like the sun, and he pulled her in for another kiss. Niara wrapped her arms around him, feeling as if the world could end right now, and she could be perfectly happy.

When they finally broke the kiss off, they still stood close to each other. "I knew I had to ask you as soon as I saw you again," Enlil whispered. "The entire time we were apart, you were all I could think about. I never want to be separated from you like that again."

Niara shuddered, and Enlil pulled her in for an embrace. "How did you escape?" she asked.

"As soon as I was awake, I shifted," he said. "Gave Sirax quite the shock, I'll tell you. He's on our side now."

Niara blinked and stared at him. "How?"

Enlil smile. "There's about ten dragons who I've convinced to join the rebellion." His eyes widened. "You haven't heard. Saemar's in an uproar. There are bloody battles going on everywhere."

"I know," Niara answered hastily, before he could elaborate. She raised one hand to touch her forehead. "I saw."

"Ah," Enlil relaxed. "I think the rebels will win. Izila was not expecting dragon turncoats."

Izila. Niara swallowed. "She...Mazda's light. Enlil, I..." she broke off. How could she explain everything that had happened to her, that the Lord and Lady had given her a mandate to slay Izila, the Great

Burner? He didn't even know that she communicated with the Lord and Lady, if he even knew who they were...

"What is it?" he asked.

She swallowed again. "I..." she paused. "Mazda's light. The Lord and Lady..." She shook her head. "They wanted me to bind Auriel again, which I failed to do. I released Mazdaanmanyu instead. He—they'd—been bound in Mount Halon. Now the Lord and Lady want me to slay Izila." She held her breath, waiting for the surge of questions.

To her surprise, Enlil only looked thoughtful. "So that's where your marks come from," He glanced down to where their hands were joined. "I knew it had to be something of the sort." He met her eyes. "Izila?"

She nodded. "I have to go to the capital, I know that, but Enlil," the words came pouring out of her, pent-up emotions that she had no idea she had been feeling. "I have no idea how to do this, or even why. I don't want to kill anyone, not even her." She closed her eyes, the specter of the men she had incinerated passing before her. "Maybe the Lord of Life and Loss can pass such an ultimate judgment, but I can't."

"Then we don't," Enlil said.

Niara stared at him, blinking, certain she had misheard what he had said. "What?" she asked.

Enlil leaned forward, his hands tightening on hers. "We don't have to kill her. Merely talk to her, come to some kind of agreement. She's the one all the dragons listen to, if we can make some kind of bargain, then all the rest will fall in line."

Despite her doubts, Niara felt hope start to build inside her. "How would we speak to her?" she asked. "Izila will never listen to me, she's the Great Burner, the one who waged war on elven civilization. And I'm a descendant of Olvae, the woman who tried to kill her, and did kill one of her consorts."

Enlil smiled. "Leave that to me." He took a step back. "Now, we need to get to the capital, don't we? Do you object to riding?"

He wasn't talking about riding the horse. Niara threw her head back and laughed, hope filling her for the first time since she'd released Mazda and Manyu. "Not at all, my love," she said. The words sounded sweet on her lips. *My love. The man I will marry.*

Niara leaned forward on Enlil's back, trying to create as little wind resistance as possible for him. His wings beat strong and steady to either side of her, buffeting the air around her. Her hands were tired from gripping the spines on his back so tightly.

We're going to need to design some kind of harness, she thought. *Or at least something that will strap me on. I would hate to fall off from here.* Somehow her fear had disappeared during the flight, but she remained aware that the ground lay a terrifying distance away.

"Almost there!" Enlil called, his voice torn away by the rush of wind.

Niara glanced down, her breath caught in wonder at the scene below her. Green fields stretched out in every direction, small pockets of rubble and buildings indicating where villages and towns had once stood. In the distance loomed the outskirts of Saemar, the walls still standing, but the city itself in ruin. Memories of Niara's visions over-layed themselves on reality. The palace itself, which would have risen up over the wall, the towers of the palace a beacon for miles around, lay in ruins, a giant hole in the center of the city the only indication of where it used to be. Around the palace she could see more ruins and rubble where the wealthiest families would have lived or had their townhouses. Oddly enough, outside the walls, or the neighborhoods closest to the walls themselves, had sustained the least damage, where the dragons had likely allowed the poor to live as normal, now serving the dragons instead of the nobility.

Something about that will have to change, Niara thought. *Even once the dragons no longer rule, something has to be changed about the way Saemar is governed. Andreas was terrible for the country. I know Auriel was probably mostly to blame, paving the way for his ascension, but the system is so vulnerable to abuse. What if we get another king like Andreas? Mazda's light, who is even going to be king?* She blinked at the thought, momentarily distracted as Enlil started his descent. *Andreas didn't have children. There's no one left of the royal line.*

She pushed the thought away. Time enough to concern herself with that once Izila was dealt with, and they had an agreement as to how Saemar would be governed. Whatever agreement they came to would have to include the dragons; it would be impossible to get around that. *No binding the dragons now Auriel is permanently free,* Niara thought. *Besides, that would bind Enlil as well, and I don't want to do that.*

As they drew closer to the ground, she could hear the sounds of battle and conflict from inside the walls. Enlil had chosen a safe spot to land, concealed between some of the buildings, yet near to the gate. As soon as they landed, his form shifted, and he stood next to her in human form.

"Safer to travel through the capital like this, I think," he said.

Niara agreed with him. The sound of conflict loomed even louder from here, shouting, screaming, and the occasional boom as something broke and collapsed. It would be far safer for them to sneak into the city as two humans, rather than as an elf and a dragon.

Humans. She put her hands to her ear, only now remembering she had lost her headscarf long ago, and without the fancy hairstyles she used to wear, there was no other way to conceal her ears.

Enlil followed her gesture. "I don't think anyone will notice," he said.

Niara grimaced. It was possible, certainly, with the confusion, but if she ran into anyone she'd used to know…

And who will that be? she scolded herself. *It's no more disruptive to be an elf than a human right now.* Besides, it wasn't like she had a choice.

She nodded and reached out, instinctively taking Enlil's hand. Enlil took it with a smile and squeezed it slightly before they turned toward the gate.

"Niara!"

The voice wrenched Niara from the present day, back to a time years ago, before the destruction of Auriel's rise. She spun to face the voice, her eyes wide.

Vinet stood between two of the ruined buildings, standing tall and proud, shrouded in a long cloak.

"Mother!" Niara didn't even bother to question her presence. She dropped Enlil's hand and ran forward, enveloping her mother in a fierce hug. Vinet returned it just as fervently.

"Mazda's light, you made it," Vinet breathed. "You're safe."

Niara pulled back, questions boiling to the surface. "Where have you been? How did you know to call me? Did you know what the plan was?"

"My inquisitive daughter," Vinet whispered. "No, I didn't know. I acted on faith alone, and it seems it was right." She smiled and looked over Niara's shoulder. "And this is your friend?" she asked. "I've seen glimpses of him, but nothing more."

Friend. Niara looked back to Enlil, who was waiting, his posture slightly awkward. *So much more than that.*

"Mother," Niara began. "This is the man I will marry, Enlil. Enlil, my mother, Lady Vinet et-Alim of Ninaeva."

Enlil gave a courtly bow. "A pleasure to meet you, Lady Vinet," he said.

"Marry?" A smile spread across Vinet's face. "Congratulations."

Niara took a deep breath, wondering how to tell her the rest, that Enlil wasn't human as he appeared, but instead a dragon, that instead of trying to kill Izila, they were here to negotiate.

"Well, isn't this a happy little family reunion," the voice made all three of them turn, and Niara's heart froze. Jumping down from the rooftop, bow in his hand, accompanied by five men in the burgundy uniform of Auriel's soldiers, was her father. Behind them stood Ralanni, the elven woman who was her father's right hand.

"I knew you would be here," Jaim said, walking toward the three of them. "I could feel you as you drew closer. I didn't expect your mother to be here, though. Such a shame. I don't think Izila will be pleased to see her."

Enlil moved to stand in front of Niara and Vinet, shielding them with his body. "Stay away from them," he said.

Jaim raised his eyebrows. "Do you really think you can stand against me, boy?" he asked. "You have no chance."

Enlil smiled, a thin, dangerous smile Niara had never seen on his face before. "Try me," he said.

Beside her, Vinet gasped. "Jaim?" she breathed.

Jaim's gaze met hers. "Vinet," he acknowledged. "I thought you'd forgotten me."

"What—" Vinet's eyes flickered to Jaim's ears. "Why—How—"

Jaim smirked. "Glad I managed to surprise you, after all these years," he said. "Unfortunately, I don't know if you'll ever know the truth. Izila has ordered you brought before her, and I don't intend to disappoint."

Enlil took a deep breath, and Niara knew he was preparing to shift into dragon form, to defend them. She placed a hand on his shoulder, her thoughts racing. "Don't," she whispered.

Enlil glanced back at her, his brow knitted in concern. "What?" he asked.

The sun brand tingled on the back of her hand, a reminder of the power she could call upon if necessary. "We wanted to speak to Izila," she said. "This way is as good as any."

Enlil still looked concerned, but he nodded. Niara squared her shoulders and stepped forward.

"Take us to Izila, the Great Burner, then, Father," she said. "We have much to discuss with her."

Jaim blinked, as if he hadn't been expecting that reaction. "No demands for an explanation?" he asked.

"I had my explanation when you sent one of your elves to kidnap me in Shan Serin,"

Niara said grimly. "Anyway, I've spoken to Taledon. Most of what you told me was a lie."

Jaim flinched as if she'd struck him. "You speak his name?" he whispered.

Niara couldn't stop herself from smiling. "At his permission," she said. "Are we going to see Izila?"

She'd put Jaim off balance. He looked over his shoulder at the five soldiers and grimaced. "Come with us, then," he said. "All three of you."

18

THE GREAT BURNER

The sounds of battle were a constant chorus as they moved through the streets of the capital. Niara walked close to Enlil and Vinet, their shoulders nearly brushing. Ahead of them strode Jaim, his bow out and an arrow knocked, ready to fire at anyone who presented a threat. The five soldiers surrounded them, swords drawn, but pointed outward instead of at the three prisoners. Ralanni held the rearguard, her bow in the same position as Jaim's.

Niara's throat closed as they came closer and closer to the center of the city, to where the ruins of the palace lay. The streets were narrow and treacherous, trees uprooted and thrown to the side, making their path dangerous to travel. Once, one of the soldiers nearly stumbled into Niara, and she had to force herself to remain calm as he glared at her, shouldering her into Enlil. She felt Enlil's tension as he reached out to steady her, and she rested a hand on his arm, willing him to stay calm, even as she told her own heart to do so.

Despite herself, she was not prepared for the scene as they turned onto another street, one that was far too familiar. Niara swallowed as she recognized the shapes of the old townhouses, and she steeled herself for the scene she knew would come. They walked a few more blocks down the street, and she caught sight of where the familiar wrought-iron fence should have been, where the house should have risen like a comforting, welcoming sanctuary from the hustle and bustle of the city. Evalynna would have been waiting just inside, and the fire would have been lit in the library, Nazir would have been waiting to comfort Vinet after a long day in a council session.

Instead of the remembered comfort, however, the house lay in a pile of rubble. Even the wrought-iron fence was twisted and warped, and the trees in the front garden were bent and broken, only one, the young ash, still somehow standing straight and tall.

Her hand tightened on Enlil's, and he squeezed back, comforting her without even knowing why. She took a deep breath. She would rebuild the townhouse, she promised herself, just as she would rebuild Ninaeva, the capital, and Saemar. She peeked at Vinet, knowing she must be just as affected by the sight as she. After all, it had been her house for far longer.

To her surprise, Vinet didn't even glance at the townhouse as they passed, her eyes instead fixed straight ahead, though not at Jaim, instead focused on some distant point. Niara reached out hesitantly to take her mother's hand, and Vinet only gave her a brief smile before her absent gaze returned.

Niara didn't know what to think about Vinet's reaction. She stared down at their joined hands, and her eyes widened as she saw a red line, a beginning of a tattoo, around her mother's wrists. It continued upward, disappearing underneath the long sleeves of the robe. Vinet had never had a tattoo before.

Nor did you. Niara didn't have to look at her left arm to know exactly where the rose and thorns lay. The Lady's mark had been gentle, at least. Unlike the Lord's, or Mazda's.

The path to the palace was still familiar to Niara, even after years away. She didn't have to think about the direction they traveled as they turned left, then right, and finally ended up on a road which led straight to the palace. She felt her breathing grow quicker as they took in the ruin in front of her. It was one thing to see it in visions. It was another to see it in reality. The carved steps had been completely destroyed along with the towers, leveling everything into a pile of rock and rubble.

Jaim sped up his pace, and the soldiers moved closer to the three, urging them faster. Niara could hear why. The sounds of battle were more intense here; just on the other side of the buildings fighting existed. They had been lucky not to encounter any skirmishes on the way.

Not lucky, Niara reminded herself. *Jaim can hear things just as well as I. He led us around.*

She was half-expecting her father to lead them straight for the ruined palace and was therefore taken aback when he instead turned quickly to the right, aiming for the edge of the ruin rather than the center. She kept her mouth shut, however, and only blinked in surprise as she saw the low door in the wall that was somehow still standing.

The garden, she realized.

Jaim stood next to the door, and the soldiers ushered the three of them against the wall, eyes warily surveying the open area around them. Niara could understand their hesitation. The sounds of battle were dangerously close, and it was only a matter of time before it spilled into the palace.

A roar echoed from above, and Niara ducked instinctively as a dragon, this one green and gray, swooped down, breathing fire into the street on the other side of the buildings. She winced as she heard the screams of agony that followed, and her eyes widened as she saw two people stumble out from around the corner, desperately slapping at the fire that burned through their clothes and hair.

Niara didn't think, she just rushed forward, hand outstretched toward them. She tore her cloak from her shoulders as she reached the first man. Holding in front of her like a shield she leapt on him, wincing against the pain as they tumbled to the ground, her elbow slamming hard into a rock. Enlil mirrored her actions with the other man.

The man beneath her stopped struggling, and Niara rolled off of him, breathing heavily. He shrugged out of her cloak and stared at her.

"Thank you," he gasped. He was battered and bruised, but his clothing was the same burgundy as the soldiers. His eyes widened as he saw her ears. "An elf?"

Niara felt her heart stop for a brief moment, then she reached out and offered her hand. "Can you stand?" she asked.

"Get back here!" The voice was a sharp command, and Niara saw the silver of a sword being pointed in her direction. She turned to glare at the soldier who'd issued the order.

Jaim stepped forward, one hand raised to call for order. "That was a dangerous action, daughter."

Niara scrambled to her feet. Out of the corner of her eye, she saw Enlil help the man he had rescued to his feet. The man wore ragged clothing and had only a knife, clearly either a rebel or someone who'd been caught up in the fight. Enlil leaned down to whisper something to the man, and he ran off into the shadows, Enlil standing to shield him until he was out of sight.

Niara scowled at her father, keeping his attention fixed on her. "Your men weren't willing to help their brothers," she said, her voice scathing. "I had to do something."

The soldiers shifted uneasily and refrained from looking at the man she'd rescued. Jaim merely shrugged.

"They are human," he said.

"We are all living."

The soldier she'd rescued got to his feet, his eyes never leaving Niara. "It's alright," he said.

Jaim waved a hand. "Back to your duties, soldier. The fight continues."

The soldier nodded once before disappearing around the corner. Niara continued to glare at her father.

"If you don't care about the humans, then why are you working for Izila?" she demanded. "All you care about is the elven people, uniting the Faithful and Steadfast. But Izila won't help you do that."

A flash of pain crossed Jaim's face before it turned into a frown. "You wouldn't understand, nor do you care to understand," he said. "You proved that after you absconded in the middle of the night with your human lover. Your blood is tainted, just like that of your mother's."

Niara couldn't help glancing at her mother, standing still and unmoving next to the door to the garden. Vinet didn't even acknowledge Jaim's words.

"If it's tainted, then I'm glad," she announced. "I would much rather be who I am than like you."

Jaim's expression darkened, and he took two quick steps forward and grabbed Niara by the arm. She instinctively jerked away, and in a second Enlil was standing next to her, and the next moment they were surrounded by the soldiers.

Jaim released her arm. "Come," he ordered. His eyes remained dark as he strode toward the door and knocked in a rapid pattern.

Niara caught Ralanni's eye as they waited for an answer. Ralanni's expression was doubtful. She took a deep breath and addressed her. "We could still unite the elven people," she said softly, trying to avoid Jaim's attention.

Ralanni lowered her eyes. "Do not speak to me," she whispered. Despite her words, her face reflected pain.

Niara bit her lip and looked at the soldiers surrounding her. Three of them kept peeking at her furtively, while the other two stared studiously at their feet.

"Why do you follow Izila?" she asked, keeping her voice low. "She doesn't care about any of you."

One of the soldiers lifted his head to meet her eyes. "We have no choice," he said. "And it's not a bad life."

"Shut up," one of the others hissed.

Niara glanced over her shoulder, where the two men had been on fire. "She doesn't care if one of you is hurt or killed, though. What kind of future is that?"

Her words had touched them, she could see. That, or perhaps her actions, saving the soldier despite technically being a prisoner.

"What choice do we have?" the first soldier to speak to her asked, his voice plaintive.

Niara managed a tight smile. "Wait and watch," she whispered. "Your choice may come sooner than you think."

The door to the garden opened, and Jaim waved impatiently. Niara strode forward, not waiting for the soldiers to usher her. Vinet and Enlil were right behind her, trailed by the five soldiers.

The garden could barely be called that anymore. There was grass, at least in certain places, but the flowers and trees were long overgrown or destroyed. As they walked through, they passed a bench so overgrown by a rose bush you couldn't sit down for fear of being pricked by thorns. It wasn't blooming, not yet, but Niara could see the buds where it would. Her left arm tingled, the rose and thorn mark of the Lady sending a shiver through her.

In the center of the garden, Jaim stopped and raised his arms high. "Izila! Great Burner! I have done as you commanded!"

Niara reached for Enlil's hand as the rush of wings from above heralded the arrival of a dragon. The sky suddenly filled with the glinting of gold, and she had to raise a hand to shield her eyes as the wind kicked up circles of dirt. She could only look up after Izila had landed, swallowing hard as she did so. She had thought Enlil large in dragon form. Izila was at least twice as large, golden scales and red eyes flashing.

"Jaimalaeran," Izila hissed the name. "Have you finally succeeded, where last you failed?"

Jaim flinched. "The last two members of Olvae's blood, as you requested, Great One." He gestured to Vinet and Niara.

Izila didn't follow his gesture. "You would give me your lover and daughter?" she asked. "How self-sacrificing of you, Jaimalaeran."

Jaim gave a short bow. "I would ask my daughter be left in my custody," he asked. "I have plans for her, plans which align with yours. Vinet Sindarilae you may do with as you wish."

Niara moved to stand closer to her mother, who still seemed barely aware of what was happening around her. Vinet's lips moved, as if she spoke silently, but no sound escaped her mouth.

"And who is the other you brought?" Izila's tone was lazy.

Jaim shrugged. "Niara's traveling companion. He is unnecessary."

"My name is Enlil," Enlil cut in before Izila could respond. "Enlil, son of Sara."

Izila's head snapped toward Enlil, and her red eyes narrowed as she examined him. "You…" her breath released in a puff of smoke.

Enlil gave her a slight bow. "We wish to negotiate, Izila."

Izila threw her head back and laughed, a loud, rumbling sound that was more threatening than inviting. "You wish to negotiate," she said. "After all you have done, Enlil son of the traitress, you wish to negotiate. You are the reason why my kingdom is in shambles, why Usumgal has abandoned us. And you wish to negotiate?"

Tension was plain in Enlil's shoulders. "We can come to some arrangement, Izila," he said. "As you said, the kingdom is in shambles. But if we work together, we can fix that, and make it a safe place for all peoples, not just dragons."

Jaim stepped forward slightly, pulling attention back toward him. "Have I delivered someone else of value to you, Izila?" he asked.

Izila's eyes dismissed Jaim as of little consequence. "Leave us, Jaimalaeran," she snapped. "Be grateful to escape with your life."

Jaim remained where he stood. "And Niara?" he asked. "My daughter?"

Izila finally returned her full attention to Jaim. "Did you really think I would allow the granddaughter of the one who killed my consort to walk out of here alive?" she hissed. "Leave, Jaim, or face my wrath."

"She's my daughter! I delivered her to you!" Jaim protested.

Niara knew what was about to happen, and she opened her mouth to scream, to try to warn her father, but no sound escaped. Izila raised a giant claw and slammed her foot down, eviscerating Jaim from throat to stomach. His eyes rolled back as he grabbed his ruptured torso before collapsing onto the ground. Niara stared at him in shock, at the pool of blood and guts growing around his body. Wailing, Ralanni fell to her knees in the thick fluids, burying her face into what was left of his chest.

"The word of a traitor is never to be trusted," Izila said, as casually as if she hadn't just killed Jaim. "Nor is the word of a child of a traitor. You shall all die." She drew back, her eyes flashing again.

"Grab my shoulders!" Enlil yelled as he stepped in front of Niara. She instinctively did so, feeling him start to change under her hand. She heard Izila's intake of breath and flinched, preparing herself for the blast of fire she knew was coming. A blast of heat came surging at them, and she huddled behind Enlil, knowing he wouldn't be enough to protect her, that he would likely die himself in shielding her.

A shout split the air, and Vinet raised both her arms above her head. A burst of light emanated from her, exploding out in a blue shield which encircled Niara, Enlil, Vinet, Ralanni, and the five soldiers, deflecting the blast of fire released by Izila away from them and toward the ruins of the palace. Niara stared at her mother in shock. Vinet had never had that much power before...*before the Exile. Mazda's light, the Exile.*

Enlil's form shifted, and Niara scrambled to find her balance, squeezing her legs around the base of his neck. She seized the spine in front of her, just in time before she felt Enlil's muscles tense for take-off.

Izila roared in anger that her attack had been frustrated and lashed out, snapping her jaws not at Enlil or Niara, but at Vinet. Niara cried out in fear, but the soldiers, slow to react initially, surrounded Vinet, dragging her out of the way of Izila's jaws and brandishing their swords at the Great Burner.

They did it. Niara barely had time to feel relief and joy before Enlil launched himself into the air and she had to cling to him with all her might. It was more awkward here than further back on his back, but she managed to cling to Enlil as they climbed ever higher and higher.

"Enlil!" The roar came from below them, but close, terrifyingly close. Niara risked a glance over her shoulder and saw Izila following them, an expression of rage on her face.

The shield. Can I replicate it? We're going to need it if Izila starts to breathe fire again. Vinet had done it, but Vinet had gone through the Exile. That had to have been what had given her the power.

Power. Her hand tingled, and she looked down at the emblazoned sun. Her sleeve had been pushed back, revealing the stag scar, as well as the rose and thorn tattoo. She closed her eyes briefly, remembering the scars she had seen on her mother's wrists, traveling up her arm. She couldn't be sure, but they had the same shape as the vine of thorns.

The Exile. Mazda's light, this has been my Exile. A rush of emotions hit her, a surge as powerful as the wind in her face. All of the fear of the Exile, all of her struggle to understand it, all of the time spent wishing she could avoid it...it had all been unnecessary. It was finished, it was over. She was an Eye of the Lady.

I'm more than that, she realized. There were three gods' marks on her skin, not just one. Her spin straightened, even as Enlil reached the top of his climb, as his muscles tensed as he prepared to dive.

"Get ready!" she heard him shout.

Behind them, she heard Izila's roar of anger, and knew it heralded another blast of fire. She closed her eyes and reached inward, envisioning the same blue shield that her mother had called protecting her and Enlil.

Enlil spun mid-air, and she had to tighten her grip on his spines as he dove straight at Izila, talons outstretched like a falcon attacking its prey. Heat streaked toward them as Izila roared again, and Niara shouted, a word incomprehensible to her own ears, and a blue shield blocked the fire, sending it to either side. Niara caught a glimpse of Izila's expression of anger just before the two dragons collided with a great thump, talons locking in a death grip. Niara held onto Enlil's back for dear life as the two dragons headed for earth in a headlong dive, spinning around and roaring at each other. From what she could tell, Enlil's smaller size was actually working to his advantage, his back talons able to reach Izila's vulnerable stomach, where her back talons kicked against the air.

Izila roared her frustration, and Niara knew another blast of fire was coming. *Oh, no you don't.* Anticipating it, she reached out a hand, clenching it into a fist. She stole the air from Izila's lungs, and all that released was a wisp of smoke, leaving Izila coughing as they spun to the ground.

Enlil took advantage of Izila's distraction to roar his own challenge. His muscles tensed, and Niara ducked, shielding her face from the blast of fire he unleashed full at Izila's head.

The roar of agony echoed, and Niara desperately wanted to clap her hands over her ears to block the sound. Instead, she tightened her grip on Enlil, knowing that if she were to let go, she would fall to certain death.

The blast of fire faded, and Izila stared blood-shot eyes at Niara. Her scales had protected her from most of the blast, but red shone underneath the gold, and the smell of burnt flesh permeated the air. Niara nearly gagged at the smell, so similar to the smell of the immolated humans at Shan Serin.

Izila's jaws shot toward Niara, and she screamed, pressing herself as close to Enlil as possible. She caught a glimpse of the ground and had to scream in terror again as she realized they were approaching dangerously close, so rapidly it would be impossible for them to land safely.

Enlil's muscles shuddered beneath her, and his wings flapped furiously. In an instant, Niara knew what he was trying to do. He was trying to twist them so Izila would land first, cushioning their fall. But Izila was so large he couldn't twist them, meaning they would land in a tangle of flesh and bones.

No. Not if I have anything to say about it. Niara closed her eyes, forcing herself to ignore the ground rushing up at them, to ignore Izila's roar as she lunged for Niara again, to ignore Enlil's shriek of pain as one of Izila's talons caught his side. She focused all her energy on forcing Izila to the side, using wind and pure power. She heard Izila shriek as they shifted, heard wings desperately flap as Izila tried to right herself, and heard Enlil's roar of triumph. She squeezed her eyes tighter, forcing Izila to remain there, for just a moment longer…

They hit the ground hard, and Niara tumbled end over end off Enlil's back before landing. She scrambled to her feet, heedless of her cuts and bruises, to see Enlil pinning Izila to the ground, roaring in triumph. Izila lay on her back, wings crushed beneath her, spitting and hissing in defiance and pain. "I'll kill you both!" she roared. "You, and all of wretched humanity!" She appeared ready to flip Enlil off of her, and Niara knew the ancient dragon still had the strength to do it.

Niara looked around frantically for some kind of weapon, anything that would allow her to fight against Izila. Two bodies lay on the ground next to her, one with a sword clutched in his hand.

She raced toward it and Izila roared in defiance, muscles straining as she fought Enlil. Enlil used all of his strength to keep her pinned, and he was only succeeding because of Izila's injury.

Enlil roared in pain as Niara's fingers closed around the sword, and she turned to see him being thrown to the side, rolling through the broken and ruined buildings while Izila struggled upright again. Izila moved until she caught sight of Niara, and a wicked grin spread across her face.

"Death take you," she said, breathing in again to spit forth fire.

Niara reached out the hand that wasn't grabbing the sword, attempting to cut off Izila's fire again as she ran forward, heedless of the stones and rubble in her path. Izila roared in thwarted frustration as her fire was wasted and, instead, snapped her jaws toward Niara. Niara screamed as she thrust the sword upward with both hands, putting all the power and magic she could find into the blow.

"Niara!" Enlil's shout echoed through the street, and Izila grunted as Enlil landed heavily on her back. Her jaws still came down, and Niara thrust her sword straight up into Izila's mouth. It went in deep, and Niara screamed again as Izila's teeth scraped her arms. She dropped the sword and backpedaled rapidly, hugging both her arms to her sides as they dripped blood.

Izila whipped her head back and forth violently, blood pouring from her mouth. The sword fell to the ground, and more blood flowed freely. Izila choked as her movements became slower and slower, and Enlil brought his jaws down, clamping around Izila's neck, cutting off her last struggles.

Niara fell to her knees as Izila finally stopped moving. Her arms were afire with pain. She saw Enlil shift back to human form before running toward her, arms outstretched. "Niara! Are you alright?"

Niara wanted to answer, but all she managed was a cry as her arms stabbed with pain. Enlil sank to his knees next to her, taking one of his arms gently in her own. "We did it, Niara," he whispered. "We did it."

Niara blinked as her vision began to gray. "I love you, Enlil," she whispered.

"Stay with me, Niara!" Enlil said in alarm. He looked up. "Help!"

Niara heard the sounds of running footsteps and worried voices, felt hands examining her arms, but she could only relax against Enlil as her world turned black.

QUEEN OF SAEMAR

et the builders to carry basic supplies to the west quarter," Niara ordered. She ran a hand through her hair, heedless of how it tousled her hair even further. "Their houses were in worst repair. Have another few begin collecting supplies here, so they're in a central location when the rest of the rebuilding starts."

"Yes, my lady," the man with a burned face in a ragged burgundy uniform nodded, rolling up a sheet of paper with his notes on it. He wore the same clothing he'd been wearing when she'd saved him. There simply weren't enough supplies to go around yet. "Is there anything else, my lady?"

Niara glanced up at the sun. It rose high in the sky, which meant she was late. *Manyu cursed meetings.* "No," she sighed. "Mazda's light, they're probably already at it." The rag-tag group of leaders from the rest of the country had gathered here in the capital, and although their intentions were good, the meetings usually ended up in shouting matches.

The soldier raised an eyebrow. "Better you than me dealing with them, my lady," he said. "And I'd rather be dealing with you than any of them. You actually get things done."

Niara couldn't help but smile. "Is Enlil already there?" she asked.

The soldier shrugged. "Wouldn't know, my lady. Last I saw he was flying."

He was meeting Xana. Niara remembered. She would see him at the meeting, then.

She stood up from her makeshift desk and exited the tent she and Enlil had set up as their headquarters. Around her, reconstruction was well underway. Groups of humans laughed and joked together as they carried stones and other supplies, joined by the occasional dwarf or elf. In one section, close to the ruined palace, a group of nephelm, industriously worked away on a building they had designated as their embassy.

An embassy to what? Niara shook her head. That was what the meeting was about, after all.

The door to the palace gardens hung open, having been smashed at some point during the battle with Izila. Niara walked through, unchallenged by the lone soldier who stood next to it, though she concealed a wince at the slight bow he made at her approach.

The garden looked much bigger now that Izila wasn't occupying everything. A table had been set up in the center, surrounded by a mishmash of chairs obviously scavenged from various houses. Several figures were already seated, arguing at the top of their lungs. Thalion sat next to Kishtar, Mar standing behind them, Thalion the only quiet person in the group. Rian sat next to Aevir, the leader of the Thorns examining her thoughtfully, and Evikan and Zeria sat next to Ren, the suspicious man glaring at everyone. Several other humans crowded around the table, each voicing their opinion at the top of their lungs. Niara stared at the crowd, trying to summon the desire to join them. Their squabbling seemed petty and pointless.

"They feel safe enough to squabble now," Vinet stepped through the door behind Niara, speaking as if she'd read her daughter's mind. "You did that for them."

Niara rolled her eyes. "Why don't you sit with them?" she demanded. "You're the one everyone might listen to."

Vinet shook her head. "I'm not the one who saved the kingdom," she said. "Besides, I have other duties to attend to." She kissed Niara's cheek before leaving, skirting the edge of the garden to stay out of view of the people at the table. Nazir would be waiting for her, somewhere in the shadows of the garden. She didn't know what her mother's duties were, but she knew nothing would convince Vinet to again take part in government.

The flap of wings echoed overhead, and she looked up, smiling in relief as she saw the flash of red. Enlil commanded all attention as he came in for a landing, followed by a second dragon, slightly larger and golden. Xana, the same dragon they had faced in Hillsdale.

Enlil ignored the attention he received as he shifted back to human form and caught sight of Niara. He walked towards her, took her hands, and kissed her. "How are you, wife?"

Niara smiled in return. That had been the first order of business, almost before they'd cleaned up from the battle. As soon as the first priest of Mazda had been found, they had been wed.

Enlil squeezed her hand. "Come on," he said. "Xana has a surprise for us."

Niara blinked as she allowed Enlil to lead her to the table. She greeted Thalion and Kishtar as they took their seats, the shouting temporarily stopped by the arrival of the dragons.

Enlil surveyed the table and nodded. "We're all here, then. Good. Xana has a guest for us."

Niara suppressed a grin at Enlil's handling of the situation. By not acknowledging that the discussion had already been occurring, he nullified anything that had come before.

Xana cleared her throat, and Niara's eyes widened as she saw the woman climbing down from Xana's back. "Cenna!" she exclaimed. She got to her feet and started forward as the woman landed on the ground, unsteady from her experience with dragon flight. She reached for Cenna's hands and clasped them in welcome. "Cenna, you're safe!" she exclaimed.

"Niara!" Cenna's face lit up with genuine joy. "Mazda's light, I wasn't sure you were. Markus said—" her face crumbled.

"Markus?" Niara whispered.

Cenna pressed her lips tight, obviously pulling herself together. "Markus is dead," she said.

"Oh, Cenna, I'm so sorry." Niara's heart sank. Although she'd known him only briefly, the man had been her cousin, and from what she'd seen, a good and honorable man.

Cenna straightened her shoulders. "Garreth, my son, is Duke of Tigri now," she said. "And it is on his behalf that I've come to negotiate."

Niara glanced over her shoulder back at the table. "I'm not sure we're ready for negotiations," she said. "They can barely decide how to rebuild anything."

Cenna sighed. "It's as bad in Tigri," she said. "Mazda's light, we need a strong leader. It's the only way we'll ever rebuild."

Niara nodded, Cenna's words an echo of what she herself had been thinking over the countless weeks of meetings. She straightened her shoulders and gestured. "Well, may I escort you to our meeting, Lady Cenna?"

Cenna dropped a small curtsy. "My pleasure, Lady Niara."

Niara felt all eyes on the two of them as they approached. "Please welcome to our table Lady Cenna Ashridge," she said, addressing the assembled. "Mother and Regent of Duke Garreth of Tigri."

She enjoyed the silence that came after she announced her words. She escorted Cenna to a seat but did not seat herself. Instead, she walked to the head of the table, placing her hands on the table and leaning forward.

"You've been arguing day and night," she snapped. "This needs to end and end now. It's Mazda's Rise, and the planting needs to begin, or we'll starve in a year's time. We need supplies brought to the capital, or the city will starve within a month. Izila didn't bother stockpiling for the humans here. Lady Rian, you say Lokrian fared well enough. Can you organize supplies to be shipped here?"

Rian met her eyes with perfect understanding. "Absolutely," she said. "I can't guarantee there'll be enough for everyone, though. We managed to continue farming, but our population is down, so not as much was produced."

Niara nodded in understanding. "Duskryn was doing well enough. Ren, I want you and a contingent of men to go to Duskryn and scout out the territory. Set up a base in the manor house. Xana, would you mind accompanying him?"

The dragon appeared surprised to be asked but inclined her slender head in agreement. "As long as Ren doesn't mind," she said.

Ren blinked, taken aback at being put on the spot. He looked at Niara, and she knew he was going to protest. "Lady Niara, I—"

Niara slammed a hand on the table. "Ren, we need to work together," she said. "Do you want your people in Venia to starve because you can't work with Xana? Any excess supplies from Duskryn need to be sent to Venia, and I want you to be the person to organize that."

Ren blinked again, his expression changing as he thought rapidly. He straightened, and Niara knew she'd found the key to convincing him. "I'll do it," he said. He glanced sideways at Xana. "As long as she lets me."

Xana smiled, somehow a seductive smile despite the line of sharp white teeth. "I might find some way to distract you."

Ren flushed, and a chuckle went around the table. Niara cleared her throat.

"Ellriheim can supply the population of Ninaeva," Thalion interjected. "Potentially the people of Dunbarrow as well. I know Hillsdale can fend for itself in terms of food, at least."

Niara nodded at her brother, grateful for his support. "We have no idea what's happening to the east," she said. "So, we need to scout out the area, find out who's in charge over there. Enlil, would you mind speaking to Sirax and getting him to organize a foray? Tell him to bring a contingent of humans not wearing Auriel's colors. We don't want to scare anyone."

"Of course," Enlil gave her a grin and an easy salute.

Niara surveyed the table. "That's the most immediate issue, that of food. The next is shelter. Reconstruction in the capital is beginning. I've ordered all raw supplies to be brought to the center, so they can be fairly distributed to the area that needs reconstructing first. Obviously, a good deal of rubble will need to be removed before any true building happens."

"What about the palace?" one of the humans, one whom Niara didn't recognize, asked. "Once we have a king, they'll need a place to live, and the palace is in shambles."

Niara stared at the man in disbelief. "You want to rebuild a palace first, before any of the homes, any of the other necessary buildings?" she demanded. "The palace will be last."

The human frowned. "And why are you giving orders?" he demanded.

"Because she's your queen," Cenna's voice was quiet, but it cut across the table, leaving silence in its wake.

Niara took a deep breath, her heart beating rapidly after Cenna's words. Beside her, she saw Enlil smile in satisfaction. *Mazda's light, was this part of his surprise?*

Cenna looked around the silent table. "I can see Saemar is over-wrought," she said. "Tigri is in similar condition, but we don't even have a strong leader left, not since my husband was killed in the uprising. My son, Duke Garreth, is only a boy of seven, hardly old enough to lead a country. So, I came here, with the full knowledge of his remaining family, to make a bargain with the monarch of Saemar." She stood and turned to Niara. "Garreth would swear fealty to you—and only you—Queen Niara of Saemar, and make Tigri a client state under Saemarian rule, provided you endow the land upon him and his heirs and perform all the traditional duties of an overlord."

Niara felt her fate, and the fate of the entire country, resting in the balance, waiting for her response. She met Enlil's eyes. If she did this, if she accepted Cenna's pronouncement, then Enlil would be her king. Had he thought about that? Could she make such a decision for him? *Yes, he trusts my decisions.*

She reached out a hand to Cenna, and beckoned Enlil to his feet with the other. "We would accept such a bargain," she said, making her voice as formal as possible. "I, Queen Niara, do accept your son's fealty, on behalf of myself, my husband, King Enlil II, and all the people of Saemar."

Murmurs rose from the table, and Enlil gave her a startled glance. She raised an eyebrow at him and tilted her head at Cenna. He needed to accept Cenna's offer as well.

"Ah," Enlil cleared his throat. "Yes. Lady Cenna Ashridge, I, King Enlil, do accept your son's fealty." He looked at Niara after he said the words, as if trying to make certain he said the words right. Niara gave him a slight smile, and he relaxed.

Cenna nodded. "Thank you, your majesties," she said.

Niara regarded the table. The human who had challenged her earlier appeared stunned, and the rest regarded her with admiration, approval, surprise, or acceptance. "You know your duties. Focus on rebuilding. If you have any problems or questions, find me or Enlil."

Niara smoothed down the fold of her skirt, still amazed Kishtar had been able to get his hands on the material. The Jyrian silk shone in waves of red and gold, shimmering like fire when she moved.

Beside her, Enlil wore a doublet of similar material and breeches of soft deerskin. His expression was slightly uncomfortable, as if he didn't quite know what he was doing, but Niara thought he had never looked more regal.

He met her eyes. "I didn't exactly intend this," he said, his expression rueful. "I didn't know humans and elves liked ceremonies such as these."

Niara shook her head and leaned forward to give him a light kiss. "You also didn't think about the fact that if I was queen, that would make you king," she teased.

Enlil shrugged, a sheepish grin on his face. "I'm not complaining." He took her hand. "Ready?"

Niara reached up to check the ties that held her hair in its proper place, braided around her head like a crown. The style exposed her ears for all to see, a situation gradually becoming more normal to her. Aside from the material, her dress expressed simplicity, bound with only an unadorned gold chain. She was ready.

She and Enlil walked hand in hand out of their tent. Two soldiers, dressed in the old uniform of the Regulars, waited with horses. Niara squeezed Enlil's hand one last time before she mounted. *I should change the uniform color. The elves and Tigri will have bad memories of it, and it will symbolize a new country, one for everyone.*

She could hear the buzz of the crowd as they rode. The guards had sectioned the tent off for them to prepare, but the city was full of people who had come to see their new king and queen. Even now, she could see figures peering out of windows and standing on roofs, talking excitedly to each other and pointing.

They rounded the corner and entered the straight avenue leading toward the ruined palace. People packed the street, standing shoulder to shoulder, pressing against the line of guards that were keeping a narrow path, barely wide enough for two horses, clear. Niara exchanged a look with Enlil and then raised a hand in a wave, drawing cheers.

She and Enlil rode slowly, side by side, to the edge of the ruined palace. A group of nobility stood there, including Thalion and Rian, as Lord of Ninaeva and Lady of Lokrian. Serana was there as well, holding tiny infant Gwyn, who had the same dark skin as her grandfather. Niara gave them a brief smile as she dismounted.

There were no stairs to mount, not like at King Andreas's coronation, but a dais had been constructed, and she and Enlil climbed on it. A stone table sat on the dais, a crown of entwined gold and silver resting on it.

Niara took a deep breath as Enlil deliberately reached for the crown and held it up for the crowd to see, drawing awed gasps as it sparkled in the sunlight. With a flick of his wrist, he separated it, suddenly holding two crowns in his hand, one a mirror image of the other. He set one back on the table, then turned to Niara. She smiled at the pride and love in his eyes as he lowered the crown onto her head.

A cheer erupted from the crowd, but the ceremony wasn't over yet. With equal deliberation, Niara picked up the second crown and raised it high before placing it on Enlil's head. He looked magnificent and regal.

Niara took his hand as they both faced the crowd. He squeezed her hand lightly, and together they began to sing their vows of king and queen, voices mingling in strong, clear tones that carried over the entire crowd, silencing everyone who listened.

Niara felt the weight of her vows even as she made them. The city was still in ruins, although construction efforts were well on their way. She had remained stubborn in her refusal to allow anyone to start reconstructing the palace until the rest of the city had begun to recover. A shelter had been built in the palace garden, where the business of governing currently happened. It would be years before Saemar resembled the country she remembered, if it ever would again.

She looked up as she finished her vows at the sight of two dragons flying through the sky. *It will never be the same,* she thought. She glanced sideways at Enlil. *And I wouldn't want it to be.*

"People of Saemar!" she raised the hand unclaimed by Enlil. "These have been difficult years. But an age of hope is now upon us, an age of new beginnings. We shall be reborn from the fire, emerging stronger than ever before!"

Enlil held up his hand to stop the cheer that began to emerge. "It will not be easy," he warned. "It will require hard work, pain, and sacrifice. But I believe in all of us. Especially if we work together, human, elf, dwarf, nephelm, and dragon." He looked at Niara, and she nodded. It was time. She moved to stand behind him, placing her hands on his shoulders.

She heard the gasps of awe, mingled with fear as Enlil's form began to ripple and change. They had tried to spread the word that Enlil was a dragon before the coronation, but there would inevitably be those who hadn't heard.

She balanced easily at the base of Enlil's neck as he grew to dragon form, stretching out his wings slightly for balance. They waited, allowing the crowd to take in the sight of them, the elven queen mounted on the dragon king's back. When Niara judged the silence had gone on long enough, she gestured to Thalion.

Thalion climbed up onto the dais, dwarfed by Enlil's shadow. "People of Saemar!" he called. "Behold your king and queen!"

The roar of approval that echoed through the street made Niara's heart pound. She raised both her hands high, her sleeves falling back to reveal her marks, now disguised by the dozens of scars from Izila's teeth. Beneath her, she heard Enlil roar his own triumph, and she smiled in exultation. Saemar was free.

ACKNOWLEDGMENTS

This might have been my favorite book of the trilogy to write. Niara and Enlil took on a life of their own, and I hope that you enjoyed the conclusion as much as I did.

I of course could not have even begun this work without the creativity of Megan, Rose, Neil, Nathan, Jonathan, and especially my husband Josh. My dear husband was not only our game master but my first editor and foremost cheerleader. He looked after our kids while I wrote and encouraged me to submit it for publication. I could not have done this without him.

The editors at Falstaff Books are wonderful and amazing, and this could not have been a polished story without them. Thanks to Melissa for the cover, Erin for the organization and editing, and John for getting everything together and accepting my work in the first place. With any luck there'll be more to come.

ABOUT THE AUTHOR

Tuppence Van de Vaarst has long been obsessed with history, writing, fantasy, the ocean, and magic. She taught herself to read at the age of three and read every single book she could get her hands on. At the age of eleven, she started creating her own stories. As she grew, her passion for stories never faded.

When she was eighteen, she decided to pursue her love of the ocean by enlisting in the United States Coast Guard. Although she decided military life did not suit her, she views it as a useful experience that she can now insert into her own writing. She has an MA in Medieval Studies and an MA in Library Science from University College Dublin. When she's not writing she's still surrounded by books as her full-time job is that of librarian.

FRIENDS OF FALSTAFF

Thank You to All our Falstaff Books Patrons, who get extra digital content each month! To be featured here and see what other great rewards we offer, go to www.patreon.com/falstaffbooks.

PATRONS

Dino Hicks
John Hooks
John Kilgallon
Larissa Lichty
Travis & Casey Schilling
Staci-Leigh Santore
Sheryl R. Hayes
Scott Norris
Samuel Montgomery-Blinn
Junkle
Vickie DeSantos
Quincy J. Allen
Allison Charlesworth

Thank You for Supporting Independent Publishing!

We believe that you should be able
to read your books, your way.
That's why this Falstaff Books
print edition includes a digital copy
at no additional cost!

Just scan the QR code with your device,
follow the directions on Prolific Works,
and enjoy!
You can also join our newsletter when prompted,
and never miss an awesome Falstaff Release!